The Nostrada
E
Christopher Cartwright

Table of Contents

Prologue

Desert of Barbary 1562 (Modern Day Sahara, Africa)

It had been nearly ten days since his master had taken him to this barbaric and hostile land. Day after day, their small group of devout followers, slaves, and pious men had followed him into the inland sea of burning sand. It was the hottest, driest and most vile place Jacob Prediox had ever seen in his eleven years on earth. Ravaged by Portuguese pirates, Arab slave traders, Muslim conquests and black-skinned natives, who would have been only too eager to take white slaves, the land was fraught with danger. Without soldiers for protection, local navigators, or any knowledge of where they might make provisions of water or food, the small party had entered the vast desert in search of an unknown miracle.

They had done so because his master, Michel de Nostradamus, had told them he had seen the outcome of their grand expedition. It had been written on the ancient scrolls of time that he and his men were to complete a great mission; the greatest of all. It was to be conducted in secret and not one of them, including his master, would live to see the fruits of their efforts. But one their efforts would save the world.

Nostradamus had told them all there was no reason to fear their great passage into an unknown land for a purpose that was far more important than any of their own lives.

And they had followed him, without fear – after all, what is there to fear when your future has already been? There is nothing that can be changed. It has already taken place. We are all merely puppets performing for the amusement of a far greater master.

On the tenth day, Jacob stopped. He was so dehydrated his tongue had become coated white and cracked. It had been nearly two days since the last of their water supply had run dry. They had reached yet another crest in the never ending giant sea of sand. He'd prayed with all his faith that on the other side would be a land so green and filled with fruit and water that it might actually be Eden. Instead, he witnessed row upon row of sandy waves, reaching all the way to the horizon. The sun was lowering and he wondered how many of the party would still be alive when it rose again.

Nostradamus stopped. "We'll make camp here for the night." The camel train halted. The camel-puller rounded the head camel, leading the group together. He stopped next to Nostradamus. "Are you sure you want to make camp, master? I'm certain the camels have a few hours more in them in – and I doubt many of the men will be alive in the morning if we don't find water."

"Quite certain," Nostradamus replied. His eyes searched the sand with recognition. "This is definitely the place."

The camel-puller looked at the rows of sand dunes. The location was badly unprotected from the violent winds known to start without warning within the Desert of Barbary. "If you don't mind me asking, master – this is the place for what?"

Nostradamus smiled. It was full of omnipotence and mystery. "This is precisely the place we make camp tonight, that's all."

Jacob looked up at his master who'd stopped next to him. His master suddenly looked down at him and asked, "Why do you look so sad, child?"

"Master," he said, trying to appear brave. "I live only to serve you, but my tongue is dry, my stomach empty, and I fear the death I am only too certain is very near. I want to be part of our great expedition. I want to help, but I also want to live. I've seen only eleven years on this earth. I would like to see more before I die."

"We all have masters. Even I do not have any more free choice over when we live or die than the lonely sand beetle that wonders the desert in search of a mate." He spoke cheerfully, but with frank honesty few could appreciate under the circumstances. "We perform for the masters of time. Unfortunately we live and die at their whim."

Jacob wanted to cry. No tears would fall from his eyes. He was simply too dehydrated. He'd been right – his master had seen their death, and refrained from telling them.

"Young Jacob. I see what you want to know. I have seen it all. I don't know why, but I have. The question is, will you go on – following me until the end, as you must, if I tell you what has been written?" Nostradamus' right eye curved mysteriously upwards. "What is going to happen?"

Jacob looked up at him and nodded. His crestfallen eyes, asking the words which he didn't have the strength to ask –
Am I going to die tonight?

Nostradamus looked warmly down at him from the comfort of his howdah, like a father to a son. "Yes. We will all die."

Jacob wanted ever so badly to curl up into a ball and cry, but instead he nodded in brave acceptance. If he was going to die, then his master should at least be proud of him in his last remaining hours.

"You are a good boy, Jacob. You have served me well." Nostradamus then looked at the sun dipping on the horizon. For a moment Jacob thought the old man was contemplating how many of his party would be alive when it next rose. Nostradamus shook his head, as though it were a silly thing to do. He'd already seen the truth – and the answer was indeed very sad. Nostradamus bent down and handed Jacob a small, golden brass medallion. "Keep this on you at all times. Your role here today is to be a witness to this event, so that one day in the future it will serve a great purpose – when the time is right."

"I'm not going to die?" Jacob asked.

"We're all going to die. You, the rest of my party – even I will not live forever. But you will survive this expedition. Your purpose here is not to die. I have brought you here merely to witness the events."

"What events?"

Nostradamus shook his head. "No. I'm afraid even some things are hidden from me. What I can tell you though, is that you must witness this event. Write down as much as you can and keep it somewhere safe for as long as you can."

"But who must I tell this to?"

"No one. You must live a long, worthwhile life, and on your deathbed give this medallion to your son, along with the story of the events that happen here, and tell him to give the story to his son. You need to ensure this tradition is continued!"

"Until when?"

Nostradamus raised his voice, as though the answer were obvious. "Until a girl is born!"

"What will happen then?"

"She will find our greatest treasure, at precisely the right time in history, when the world needs it to be discovered." Nostradamus sighed. "And if she is the right person, filled with honesty and integrity, with enough faith – she will save the world."

Jacob took the medallion which had been placed over his neck by his master. It was formed by some sort of brass, but as far as he was concerned it was more valuable than had it been made out of solid gold. He stared at the engravings. They depicted a map of an island he'd never seen or heard of. It was shaped like the number eight laying on its side. And on the obverse side were eight numbers which meant absolutely nothing to him. "Does she succeed? Will my great descendent one day save the world?"

Nostradamus shook his head. "I'm afraid the Ancient Scrolls of Time keep some secrets, even from me."

*

There was no way to tell exactly what time it was when the wind changed. At a guess, Jacob thought the half moon was placed somewhere near midnight when he first heard the howl of time, coming to rob the party of their lives. He wanted to hide and take shelter, but there was nowhere for him to do either. Besides, Nostradamus had been explicit. His purpose here was to bear witness to an event. So instead of hiding, he watched as the party was destroyed.

The sand-filled wind crept through the camp, forcing its way into everything. The startled camels fought with their ropes until they came free and scattered into the desert. Men tried to recapture the frightened animals, but their attempts were hopeless at best.

The locked box, the prized possession that Nostradamus had instructed them to move across the desert for an unknown purpose, looked as though it were going to be buried by sand. The men, devout until the end, were digging at the sand with their bare hands, trying to stop the fine brass box from sinking into the sand.

"Leave it!" Nostradamus ordered. "It belongs here – buried in the sand!"

"What about us?" one of the men asked.

"You have done your duty," Nostradamus replied. "Now, run for your lives. Take cover. Protect yourselves."

Jacob watched in horror as the makeshift prison, where their slaves were kept overnight was filling with sand. The large slaves pulled helplessly at the bound sticks which formed their night pen. Their eyes were wide with terror; their white teeth clenched in horror and shined against the profound darkness of their faces.

He couldn't tell if anyone had noticed the slaves' plight. If they had, he doubted if any cared enough to do something about it. The stars and the bright crescent moon were no longer visible. Jacob lost sight of the rest of the camp, but his eyes remained focused on the slaves as the sand burned at his exposed skin. The sand was rapidly flooding the prison – if he did nothing, the slaves would soon drown. He knew he should do something, but what could he do?

"It's time," Nostradamus said, handing him a single, leather water flask. "You must leave, now."

Jacob stood up and took the flask. It was full. He wanted to know where it had come from, but one look at his master's face told him not to ask questions when time was your enemy. "Where do I go?"

Nostradamus smiled. It was wild and crazy, like that of a madman. "Any direction you want."

"How will I live?" Jacob asked. "How will I possibly make it back to France?"

"Who said you were returning to France?" Nostradamus shook his head as though Jacob had asked a stupid question. "No time to tell the future. Just go. Keep walking until you discover it on your own."

"What about you?" Jacob asked. He wanted to know about the rest of the party who had already scattered into the desert. Jacob never heard a response. His master simply walked off and disappeared into the violent storm. He looked at the brass box. Only the very top of it remained visible. The rest was now buried forever. He didn't even know what it carried that was so valuable – or why his master had gone to such lengths to move it to this desolate place, further than any he'd known to exist, only to have it become buried in the sand where it could surely never be found again.

His eyes returned to the black slaves. Not much more than their heads were now visible above the sand. The slaves had begun fighting with each other, competing for space in the middle where their pen was highest and allowed the most breathing room. Jacob watched as their most basic animal instincts stirred – the desire to live.

He knew he must do something. But if he helped them, they would only kill him once freed. *Would they really?* He knew the answer to this – of course they would. He'd been their master and now he was vulnerable. He was just an eleven year old boy. How could he stop them, once they were released? Jacob thought about what his master had told him – *You will survive this, and you will tell the story to your son and his son, for generations to come, until a girl is born.*

Jacob grabbed a knife and climbed onto the top of the makeshift prison. He instantly wished he hadn't. A slave gripped his left ankle and tried to pull him down. Like a wounded animal, the slaves were trying to attack anyone who came near them, even the one person willing to help.

He kicked the slave's hand, hard. Jacob felt the grip on his leg tighten and so he kicked again. And again, until the hand released pressure and gave way. He then quickly moved to the middle of the prison's roof. There he stopped. Several hands reached for him, tormenting him. If he didn't free them soon, they would kill him and then die in the process. Five sticks were bound together by papyrus rope. He sliced at it. The first attempt barely cut through a strand. The second didn't go much further, but the third sliced all the way through.

The hatchway was pushed open and he was thrown off into the sand. He watched as at least twenty slaves escaped from the sand-filled prison and scattered into the desert storm. All except one of them. It was the largest slave. He was the biggest man Jacob had ever seen. The slave's blue eyes suddenly fixed on his. The slave's teeth shined perfectly white, and he howled like a banshee – and then he ran towards him.

Jacob turned to run, but he wasn't even standing by the time the slave reached him. He felt the slave's thick, leathery hands reach his shoulder to stop him. The slave quickly threw him to the ground so his back was up against the small wall of sand. It provided protection from the lethal storm, but nothing against the giant of a slave who approached him now.

Jacob quickly began reciting one of the few verses of the Bible he knew by heart – *Our father, who art in heaven…* He held a small knife out to defend himself. It was stupid and served little purpose. The slave could kill him without any effort. The slave approached slowly and snatched the knife out of his hand. He tucked it into the side of his loincloth. A moment later, the slave saw the leather water flask in the sand next to him. He snatched away the water flask as quick as he had the knife. The slave took two small sips and returned it. Jacob tried not to meet his eyes, as though he were a monster who could be avoided through ignorance. But the monster sat next to him. Jacob was horrified by the slave's blue eyes. He'd never seen a black slave with blue eyes before. They were an intense blueish gray, piercing, and stared vacantly at him, as though he were a ghost.

Jacob shivered throughout the night. In the morning the wind was still and the sand had settled into a beautiful day. The sun was rising and soon it would be too hot to travel. The slave was the first to stand. He looked up at the sun for a moment to orient himself, and then walked due south.

Jacob watched as the slave took thirty or more steps into the sea of sand. He'd survived the night as Nostradamus had predicted. The monster had let him live. The slave stopped. Turned to face him and grinned. "Well boy, are you coming with me?"

Jacob looked around at the desolate place in which God had stranded him. He had no idea where he was or where he wanted to get to. He had very little water and no food rations. If he did nothing, he was already dead. Jacob studied the slave's face. It was hardened by years of violence and hardship. But in the daylight, he no longer saw the slave's blue eyes as ghoulish – instead they gave him the impression of wisdom.

"Or would you like to die out here?" The slave asked.

Jacob smiled and slowly followed in the slave's footsteps. "I will follow you."

"Good."

"Where are we heading?" Jacob asked, finding a confidence he'd rarely felt.

The slave smiled. "To a kingdom far away – where my people have waited a long time for the return of their king."

Jacob took a deep breath, wondering what part of history had been changed by the rescue of a king and why Nostradamus had neglected to mention it. He shook the thought from his mind and followed the king in silence. By that afternoon he reached the highest sand dune he'd ever seen. It gave him vantage to see for miles in all directions.

He paused long enough to take a sip of water from his flask. His vision wandered all the way back to where he'd come from. He looked at the sand dunes, searching for some way to remember the place. There were no landmarks he could recognize. None at all. Only sand. It was impossible for him to ever find this place again, even if he wanted to tomorrow. Everything had been buried. And so it would remain – for all eternity.

Chapter One

Idehan Murzuk, Sahara Desert – Libya

It was a hundred and fifteen degrees Fahrenheit in the shade. Sand dunes, sixty feet high, reached the horizon in every direction like an ancient ocean, swallowed by the arid sands of time. Not a single piece of vegetation was visible. With the exception of her camp, there was no permanent sign of life. Nothing lived in this hostile land. A few nomadic tribes borrowed the land as they traversed it for trade, taking direct, labored routes using camel trains. She adjusted her green headdress. She was born in the desert, but had spent years away from it. They were painful years, and although important, she had spent a long time feeling lost. Instead of daunting her, the extreme heat made her feel alive. Today the temperature was particularly high – and none of the tribes would risk traveling during daylight.

She stood up from the desk where she scribbled notes on an old map, covered in recently marked gridlines. The tarpaulin shade cloth did nothing to alleviate the intense heat. She grinned curiously as she watched the strangers travel south. There were three camels. The first two had riders. Both men were covered completely in traditional desert robes worn by the local Tuareg nomads, but she could tell neither were nomads.

Their faces were mostly concealed with the indigo blue shesh – the traditional headwear worn by the nomadic men who'd roamed the Saharan desert for thousands of years. Their eyes were covered with dark sandglasses, designed for protection from the sand as much as the sun. One was considerably larger than the other, both in height and muscle. The other was of an average height with broad shoulders. The shorter one rode at the head, rigged like he was prepared for battle, while the other appeared relaxed in the saddle, possibly even asleep.

A third camel trailed behind, tied to the second. It carried a number of dive tanks. On the back of one of the tanks were the words, *Deep Sea Projects.* She smiled. *Deep Sea? There's no water big enough to swim in for a thousand miles, let alone dive, in the Sahara.* She was just about curious enough to stop the two men and ask. But they didn't stop to talk and she didn't interrupt their progress. It was a strange land with stranger rules, and if a couple of loners don't stop to talk to the first humans they see while crossing a desert, you don't go out of your way to find out why.

Dr. Zara Delacroix smiled. It was a wonderful smile. Full of wit and intelligence, it teased while at the same time betraying some hidden mischievousness. Her perfectly even, white teeth shined against her dark olive complexion. What could be seen of her black hair was so dark and lustrous it appeared blue beneath her green headdress. Her thick, dark, lashes guarded her hazel green eyes. These were her most powerful, seductive and deceptively pleasing aspect. To all who met her, she was exotic to her core – and for the past two years she'd been the greatest mystery of the Sahara.

She was an educated woman, an archeologist, with both ancient Persian and French blood in her veins. She freely roamed the massive ergs, the ocean-like sand basins, scattered throughout the Sahara, without fear. In a land rife with corruption, wars, dictatorships, tribal battles, and an environment capable of killing most people within a day, she walked unhindered in search of some great wonder – forever gaining followers.

She had been given the name of *Malikat Alssahra* – which, translated from Arabic, meant, *Queen of the Sahara*. It was a ridiculous name, and she thought as much, but the people who followed her thought it perfectly matched her beauty and ability to command those who followed, with great respect, dignity, and unwavering loyalty.

Rumors, if they could ever be trusted, said she'd come in search of something extraordinary. A book that not only told the future, but held the power to change it. She was willing to pay a king's fortune to find it and had hired an army of nomads from several different tribes to help her with her quest. Tribes who had never agreed on anything together, now pledged their allegiance to her. She now commanded over two hundred people, from a multitude of tribes and countries – and still more came to offer their allegiance and services.

At the sight of the two strangers, Adebowale stood directly in front of her. Like an overly protective guard dog, he was waiting for the opportunity to bite. He had only recently joined her party, but had taken a great interest in their quest and had self-proclaimed to be her bodyguard. He commanded forty warriors and brought a strange aura of unnatural power to her command. Many of the tribal nomads who wandered the region were superstitious, and she saw the benefit of working on this image.

Adebowale was her most ardent supporter. He followed her with the religious fervour of a zealot. In truth, his zeal frightened her. As though anyone who could believe what he was saying was truly mad. She put up with him, of course, because he brought forty warriors, who, although not quite as powerful as he, were certainly useful for both protection and digging. It was the protection that would be required if she ever found what she sought.

He played the role of her bodyguard, but in truth he was much more than that. At six foot ten he was a good head above most tall people. He was also somewhere in the vicinity of three hundred pounds of solid muscle. His skin was as dark as they come and his eyes a deep and frightening blue.

He smiled at her, revealing perfectly even, white teeth. "Good afternoon, Doctor."

"Hello, Adebowale," she replied.

"They found the brass howdah this morning," Adebowale said. He was the only one within the camp who treated her as his equal and not the savior, or the deliverer of the great prophecy. "It won't be long now before they find *It*."

She turned to him, her eyes still fixed on the strangers heading south. "Yes, I heard." Her voice was indifferent, but inside, her heart raced at the thought.

Adebowale shook his head. It was big and riddled with scars. The bristly hairs on his head were cut short and his eyes piercing with their almost hollow grayish-blue, giving him the appearance of some nightmarish and unreal fiend. Despite that, he was quite attractive, in a warrior kind of way. His English was articulate and expressive, showing his level of education was much higher than she would have guessed. There was the slightest tinge of an American accent. "You still don't believe *It* will be here?"

"No. I believe it will be here," she replied, finally turning to meet his eyes.

"Then why are you not down there, reveling in the joy? The new future is now and you and I are to be the bearers of that new knowledge."

Zara smiled. She enjoyed his unwavering belief in the prophecy, even though she didn't believe a word of it. "I just don't believe a word Nostradamus said, that's all."

"Then why have you spent your life searching for his book?" Adebowale asked. His cheeky smile betrayed his inability to accept what she was saying.

"Because others do, and because I can find it." A pert, and sheepish grin formed on her lips. "And like you, because I need the money they will pay me!"

"But you have spent two years searching this small area alone! Why waste your time searching for something you don't believe in?"

"I believe the Book of Nostradamus is buried here. That much is fact. What I don't believe is that Nostradamus had any idea what was in the future."

"How do you explain why so many of his prognostications came true?"

Zara shrugged. "Yeah, well he got lucky – and he left things pretty open to interpretation. It's no more impressive than a tarot card reading at a novelty shop."

"He got lucky with rare frequency," Adebowale persisted.

She smiled. "His prognostications were retrospectively interpreted, meaning someone somewhere was always going to be able to say he'd got it right. So. He got lucky – a lot."

Adebowale's smile turned to a hard stare. "Why are you here, Doctor?"

She smiled. "For the same reason as you, Adebowale – money."

"I came because you asked me, and because it was written in the ancient scrolls of time. Why else would our two families cross paths for almost four centuries?"

"So you keep telling me..." she replied. "Why is that again? I only met you four weeks ago, and I don't recall asking for your help – as much as I'm glad to receive it now that you're here."

Adebowale spoke slowly. His deep voice resonating as though he were preaching some verse in the Bible. "Because the prophecy said I would. And because it has been written that the lives of our two great families should be intertwined throughout the ages."

"Right," Zara said. She looked at his face; it was eager for some sort of acknowledgement on her part, which she denied him by ignoring the question. "I don't know what you think was so great about our two families? Your father was murdered when you were a child, leaving you to beg and work for your subsistence. As for my father, he was an archaeologist who wasted his life searching for something I still don't believe in, until the poor lifestyle and wages associated with life in the Sahara left him dead of a heart attack at fifty-two. Both of our mothers disappeared before we could remember them. I never had a sibling and yours are still in a country where you were exiled."

"Our families have both been great and will one day be again. As for you and me – I met you when you were still very young. You most likely looked upon me as another poor labourer and so you can't recall my face, but I have never forgotten you. Your father helped me because he believed in the prophecy, and in time so will you."

"You think my father organized your American visa because of an ancient family history?"

He nodded. A large white grin beaming ear to ear. "Spanning since Nostradamus came out here in 1562 – our two families have been interconnected in ways that no human being will ever truly know."

She laughed. "You think he did that because of the prophecy?"

"Yes. Why else would he?"

"Because he took one look at you and thought to himself he'd never seen anyone as big as you in all his life. You want to know destiny? You were born to play American football! Knowing my father, he probably got some sort of kickback from the coach where you played college football."

"I took no pleasure in it."

"I googled you, Adebowale. You made it into the NFL and your team played in the Super Bowl!" She shook her head. "And then you left it all behind to follow me for nothing."

"No. I got the education I needed if I'm ever to return to my country. Then I waited until it was time and then I came to help you."

"You think a degree is what you need to lead a rebellion?"

He shook his head. "It's what's in a man's heart that will lead his men to overthrow the usurpers. But an American education has taught me what I need to know to gain assistance from other nations to help me regain my birth right."

"You're dreaming again. Your birthright was taken from you when you were three years old. The very day your father was slaughtered. The Americans, the U.N. and the outlying countries have no interest in getting involved in another rebellion in Africa."

She had been too harsh, and instantly wished she hadn't pushed so far. She carefully watched his grayish-blue eyes for a reaction.

He paused for a moment and smiled. "You're right, nobody wants to be involved. And why should they? It's not their fight. There's nothing of value to the rest of the world from my homeland. It's entirely worthless. But soon, they will all flock to my country, and then we will see who offers me their assistance."

Still regretting her comment about his father's death and intrigued by his certainty, Zara persisted, "What makes you so certain?"

"Because I have seen the day with my own eyes."

She smiled. It was genuine. "I hope your dream comes true."

"You don't believe me, do you?"

"Not a word, Adebowale. But, I truly respect your faith and conviction. It must be nice to be so certain about something. As an archaeologist, I've spent a lot of my life following my father's old notes and making educated guesses, sometimes based on fact and other times hunches. I've second guessed a lot of things. Unlike you, I don't believe in what I've done with my life."

"Then why do you do it?"

"Because it seemed easy and it was something I could do. The money has been good, too."

Adebowale shook his head. "Zara, do you even know who's funding your dig?"

"No. But he's never argued on the exorbitant fees I send him. And he always pays in advance. That's a pretty good deal for any archeologist."

"So you may be giving away your most prized possession?"

"It's not mine." She smiled. "And I don't plan to give it away, either. For the amount HE's paying for it, I won't ever have to work again and you, my friend, can hire enough warriors to place you back on your royal throne."

"But if the book of Nostradamus doesn't do anything, why would HE keep paying you?"

"What can I say?" She laughed. "A fool and his money will soon be parted."

"Yes. Well, I've met plenty of white fools in my life."

"Talking about fools." She looked up at the two riders, their camels climbing the next sand dune far in the distance. "What do you make of them?"

"They're not Tuaregs or Boudins. That's for certain. There isn't a nomad in Africa who would be willing to cross the Sahara on a day like this."

"That's for sure." She shook her head. She'd met plenty of fools in her lifetime, too. Black and white. It didn't make a difference. They both shared that common human fault – stupidity. "But did you see the dive tanks?"

"Ah!" Adebowale lifted his hands up as though that explained it. "More treasure hunters! The Sahara seems to be breeding them currently."

"Treasure hunters?" Zara was suddenly interested.

"They'd be looking for the lost city of the Garamantes."

"The ancient people who were said to have learned to master their environment through the use of large aqueducts, moving water hundreds of miles to create their oases?"

"That's the one." Adebowale nodded. "They were desert dwellers who used an elaborate underground irrigation system, and founded prosperous Berber kingdoms or city-states in the Fezzan area of Libya, deep in the Sahara desert. They were a local power between 500 BC and 700 AD."

"I thought they never made it this far south into the Sahara?"

"They didn't." Adebowale smiled. It was a pleasant smile, which put people naturally at ease. He smiled frequently, and Zara had never witnessed him to lose his temper. His perfectly white teeth were a rare contrast to the complete darkness of his skin. His face, which was littered with scars, like trophies from the battles fought in his youth. "But legend has it they once had a most prosperous city deep in the Sahara. It drew water from an underground water basin hundreds of miles away, and for nearly a thousand years reigned supreme with an oasis to match Eden, brimming with life. Its name was, *The Golden Fortress.*"

"It was made from gold?" she asked.

"No. If it was, one of these treasure hunters would have found it by now. Instead it was apparently given such a name because of its wealth, ingenuity, and prosperity."

"What happened to it?"

He fixed his grayish-blue eyes with hers and then laughed boisterously. "Perhaps you really are nothing more than a treasure hunter, after all. The water basin dried up and *The Golden Fortress*, along with its advanced ancient civilization became extinct within a decade."

"There's a lesson in that for humanity, isn't there?" she said. "We can't keep terraforming the environment to meet our needs indefinitely. Do you think that is what Nostradamus meant by sending you here?"

"Not even slightly. First of all, Nostradamus didn't send us here – my father did, while he was still alive. And secondly, the only thing I believe Nostradamus meant for us to find was a massive reward for finding his original book. He wanted us to receive a dozen or more chests filled with so many French Livre that the gold coins would be constantly overflowing. And I think he got it all wrong – we'll be paid in U.S. dollars."

"In that respect, Doctor – I believe you and I share the same beliefs." Adebowale grinned. "Oh, and by the way, I wouldn't worry about the two treasure hunters – they'll be dead before the end of the day."

Zara was about to reply, when her thoughts were interrupted by the sound of hysteria down the pit. Several miners were coming out of it. One caught her eyes, and ran towards her. "Come quick, *Malikat Alssahra!* We've struck something hard in the sand!"

Chapter Two

Sam Reilly hated traveling by camel. Unlike the measured gait of a horse, a camel's walk seemed odd, irregular, and kind of jerky. Likened to a small ship on the ocean, a camel had the tendency to provoke seasickness in a rider who was used to being in control. Sam decided this experience was as close as he was ever going to get to feeling seasick. He never liked relying on animals. They were unpredictable and unable to be trusted not to run off at the worst possible time. He'd suggested an endurance motor cycle, like a KLR 650 or a BMW HP2 for the assignment, but the notion was quickly disregarded – the U.S. couldn't be seen to be picking sides in the local rebellion. Any assistance had to be from a distance, even when the stakes were so high.

If he and Tom were successful, people would guess at the U.S. government's involvement. But at least they would have maintained some semblance of plausible deniability. Worse still, if they weren't successful and were captured instead, they needed to be able to maintain the pretense of two American treasure hunters in search of gold in the ancient fabled city of the Garamantes. Sam gritted his teeth, as his beast dropped off another sand dune, jarring his back. He wished they'd come here on endurance bikes in search of the fabled city.

Instead of fighting it, Tom had worked out how to let himself sway with the beast, giving him the appearance of a sleeping man.

"Would it have really killed you to stop for a drink at the last camp?" Tom asked.

"You know the rules," Sam replied.

"Yeah, we were never here, which means as little contact with the locals as possible. Don't you think they already knew we were foreigners?"

"Why?" Sam asked.

"Because you ride a camel like you ride a horse." Tom shuffled gently in his seat as his camel dropped off the sand dune into a steep descent. "And for the record, you look just as uncoordinated on horseback. Besides, it's too hot to travel in the heat of the day – no real nomad would do that."

Sam laughed. "You don't like the Temperature Suit on loan from DARPA?"

"The Temperature Suit's great. I just doubt anyone would believe they were purchased locally."

"No. You might be right there. When Ike set up DARPA in '58, I doubt he was looking at setting up a clothing shop in Libya." Tom laughed. President Dwight Eisenhower had established the Defense Advanced Research Projects Agency in 1958 in response to the Soviet Union launching of Sputnik. "All the same, I think these suits would be very popular here."

"Sure. But who can afford the hundred plus thousand dollar price tag?"

Sam thought about the remarkable Temperature Suits. They were constructed using thousands of carbon fiber micro-tubes, which circulated cold or warm air in order to maintain a safe range of core temperatures by the wearer. Sam adjusted his position. There was no way they could have made such a quick journey through the heat of the day without it and time was vital if they would have any effect on the outcome of the war. And this time they needed to get it done right.

"How much time do we have?" Tom asked, as though he'd read Sam's thoughts.

"Not much. Perhaps a week at best. After that, we either commit or forget we knew anything about it."

"You know what happened the last time we provided weapons for the regime we wanted to win?" Tom asked.

"Yeah, we supported Saddam Hussein – and the rest of the world hasn't let us forget about it!"

"So, let's make sure we've got the right man this time."

"We do. I think he can make a real difference to the stability of the region. Besides, from what I've seen, Gabe Ngige makes Saddam Hussein look like one of the good guys. Ngige has outside funding giving his regime the real opportunity to expand throughout central Africa. We don't know where he's getting his backing from, but there are reports he's been hiring elite mercenaries to train his army, which is rapidly growing in size. He's purchasing modern weapons, and military vehicles, including armored cars and tanks."

"So, where do we think he's getting the funding?"

"We don't have a clue. The money's being fed through a series of proxy accounts. There's no way to see where the money originated, but one thing's for certain. This is the best financed Rebel Group the DRC has ever seen. That's what has everyone in Washington frightened – this guy isn't going to stop once he controls the DRC. His rebellion is going to spread into Angola, Zambia and Zimbabwe in the south, and the Sudan in the north."

Tom asked, "You think if he gets that far he'll stop?"

Sam said, "Hell no. Did Hitler stop when he was winning?"

"No. He kept advancing further."

"Exactly. The intelligence coming from Washington suggests this might be the most significant war to ever come out of Africa, with far reaching global repercussions."

"Do you think he's found a new diamond mine?"

"We don't know. It's not diamonds, that's for sure. We would have heard if anyone was moving that amount of stones out of the country. If Ngige was sending that many blood diamonds onto the market required to fund his rebellion, we would have known about it. The artificially set price of diamonds would have suddenly crashed. De Beers would have stopped the market."

"Okay, what about oil?"

"No. We could have traced that. Whatever it is, Washington is frightened, and it's going to drive a lot more governments into the region. There are fears Europe is going to be dragged into this war. That's why it's so important to make the change now, and add some stability into the region. We can't rule out the possibility that Ngige is gaining funding from the private sector outside of the DRC."

"You think they've discovered a new mineral mine that might be needed in manufacturing?"

"Possibly," Sam said. "Or even uranium and we don't want to think who would be financially backing them in exchange for the rights to uranium. The fact of the matter is somehow Ngige is being funded well enough to form an army capable of taking over much of Africa. If Ngige is allowed to continue his tirade of violence, crime will ravage an already war torn, poverty stricken continent. But if someone from the inside were to rise up – good conquering evil – all projections show this will create a follow-on effect, which will have the chance of making the greatest change for good on the continent in four centuries."

"That's if he chooses to challenge."

"He will."

"But will he win?"

"If we give him the support he needs."

"What if we don't find the diamonds?"

"Then the U.S. government will have no choice but to let the entire thing go. We just don't have the funding to come out publicly with this one. Besides, it's a two-way street. He needs to prove his ability to partially fund his forces, as well as prove that he has the ability to unite his people."

"Anyway, we'll reach the last oasis by tomorrow morning. It's the last place on the list. If the diamonds aren't there, the game's off."

Sam smiled, confidently. He stopped his camel and climbed down to stretch his legs. Sam brought up a real time satellite image of the last oasis. At this rate they would reach it by tomorrow. "They'll be there. And we'll find them."

Tom looked at the image over Sam's shoulder. "Hey, what's that darkened section over there?"

Sam stared at the image for a moment and shook his head. "It looks like we're not the only fools attempting to travel through the heat – that looks like a massive migration of nomads. At a guess I'd say there are nearly five hundred men heading this way."

Chapter Three

Zara briskly walked toward the sand pit. She consciously forced herself to slow down as she ducked under the large tarpaulin that protected her dig, and approached the first of a series of ladders. The scorching heat of the Saharan sun dropped by a negligible five degrees. Hand over hand, she climbed down the first of the makeshift ladders, built from wooden rungs tied together with strands of reeds. Taking them two at a time, Dr. Delacroix felt her heart race in anticipation.

Is this it?

Is the search almost over?

There was only one metal box carried by Nostradamus's party. If it belonged to him at all, it had to be what she was looking for. That is, if they had indeed found the top of a brass container. It had been two years in the making. The outcome of their discovery would either make or break her career, after she'd spent more than a decade looking for it. Her financier was willing to pay big to find it, but even he'd lost interest with the last of her series of failures. The thought had been a relief – no matter what the outcome of the find, the Book of Nostradamus had plagued her family's life for too long.

More than two hundred people of at least a dozen tribes had flocked from the all ends of the Sahara to excavate the pit with the impatient zeal of those who shared the wealth of their very own gold mine. Only, what she was mining would be far more valuable than any amount of gold.

Zara reached the final rung of the sixth ladder. She'd almost given up hope of finding the book. Her scientific mind had already concluded they were in the wrong place again. It seemed fanciful the thing would be buried any deeper in the sand. But she'd run out of places to dig – and so, with the knowledge that this was her last chance, she'd ordered her men to keep digging. Now it looked like she'd made the right decision, and it may have been discovered, finally, below nearly a mountain of sand.

She stepped off the ladder and began walking through the narrow tunnel of sand, hardened by years of compression by the weight of sixty or more feet of sand above. It was noticeably cooler this far below. She followed one of the diggers to the area they had been searching. The tunnel opened up to a wide pit hole.

At least forty people manned the bottom level of the pit like a swarm of black ants, seamlessly working with a combined goal. The men spoke animatedly in their own languages and dialects. They looked happy. They were here because she paid well, but they would have worked for her if she had not – because they were compelled by her story, in which their great land was the center of all existence. Some carefully brushed sand from the surface of the newly discovered structure, while others cleared sand from its sides, and a bucket chain hastily removed the excess sand.

Zara's presence instantly stopped all banter. Every one of her workers paused and stared at her as though she were their God. She smiled. It was this ability that had driven hundreds of tribal nomads to flock to help her with her goal. Inside, the irony seemed unfair – she had created an army of believers, for a purpose she didn't believe in, because she needed the money.

"Well done!" she praised them. Zara knelt down on her knees and ran her hand over the top of the hard surface. It glowed golden and confirmed that they had discovered a brass storage box. *But would it be the one she was looking for? And, would IT still be inside?* There was only one way to find out.

"You five!" she said, pointing towards a group of men.

"Yes, *Malikat Alssahra*?" they replied in unison.

"I want you to lift this out. Let's see what we've got."

"Yes, *Malikat Alssahra*."

Moments later, the five workers levered the large brass container using padded iron pry bars. The strain of their wiry muscles stretched over their dark skin, as the box fought to remain sealed in sand. They worked their levers in unison and on the fourth attempt the box relinquished its fight, breaking free from the sand. The once hardened sand to its side cracked and a moment later the five men pulled the heavy box free.

Zara carefully brushed the loose sand off the covering. It revealed a deep marking on the vault, an emblem that represented the chest's owner. She ran her fingers into the grooves. Smiled and carefully blew away the remaining sand again.

She took a deep sigh of relief. The emblem matched the family crest of Michel de Nostradame.

Jesus Christ! They've actually found it!

One look confirmed all her greatest hopes and fears. She placed two fingers to her lips and made a high pitched, sharp whistle, bringing every worker in the pit to a halt. "All right. I want everybody out."

The men instantly backed away from their discovery.

Zara turned to her most ardent supporter. "Adebowale!"

"Yes, Doctor?"

"I want you to use your most trusted warriors and take this to my tent. Once inside I need you to guard the door and make certain I'm not disturbed while I examine the book."

"Understood, Doctor."

Chapter Four

It took nearly two hours before the massive brass chest reached the surface and another hour to secure it inside Zara's tent. She stayed with the group, keeping her eyes on the box, making certain nothing had been tampered with before she had the chance to examine its contents.

Adebowale was the last to leave. He looked at her without saying a word. His eyes telling her he needed to know the truth as much as she did.

Zara smiled at him in understanding. "You will be the first to see it once I know what we have found."

"Thank you, Doctor." Adebowale turned to leave. "I will be right outside if you need me."

"Thank you, Adebowale."

Zara began examining the brass chest, alone. It had been secured by an intricate locking mechanism with seven ornamental dials. Words were engraved into the top section next to the seal of Nostradamus. She read the words to herself out loud –

*

Only the Chosen,
  onceived with one faith and born on the day of truth may open;
To see the future, the correct date must be selected, or poison will be the next
  ut, to run free like nine fires and flood the CODEX
*

Zara read the message again and sighed. It was a simple quatrain, the four lined prophetic verse, in which Nostradamus wrote all his visions. He wrote a hundred in a book like an almanac and named each book a century. The basic concept behind the quatrain was simple, but she knew Nostradamus worked on many levels. Piling layer upon layer of hidden meanings inside.

This one, she noted was missing the first letter of every second line. It might have been left out by accident, or worn away by years of movement, but it was most likely left out intentionally – and that meant Nostradamus wanted their absence to mean something. She nodded to herself, willing to play the game.

In its simplest form, Zara knew that the quatrain meant that only the chosen person would know the answer, and if the wrong number was inserted, a poison would destroy the book.

The rhymed quatrains of Nostradamus were written mainly in French with a bit of Italian, Greek, and Latin mingled in. He intentionally obscured the quatrains through the use of symbolism and metaphors, as well as by making changes to proper names by swapping, adding or removing letters. The obscuration was claimed to have been done to avoid his being tried as a magician, although Zara had always figured Nostradamus did so to avoid ever being caught out as a fraud and charlatan, who never had any idea what the future held.

This quatrain, she noticed, was written entirely in English with the exception of the last word, which was written in Latin and in capitals. At first glance it could have been simply to make the English word, Book, become Codex so that it rhymed with Next. Zara recalled that Nostradamus wrote in a number of languages, but for the more simple he wrote in his native French, or in the language of the intended audience. In her case, it made sense he'd use English or French. If Latin was used, the quatrain almost always had a higher, intellectual meaning. Which meant Nostradamus was trying to make another point about the word Codex.

Well that clears that up, doesn't it?

The crest of her lip formed a smile. Nostradamus had been a great admirer of Leonardo Da Vinci. One of Da Vinci's many inventions was a blood codex – a locking mechanism designed to destroy whatever valuables were stored inside if any attempt to force an opening was done by any other than the chosen person. Zara suddenly wished she'd concentrated harder during her cryptology classes when she studied for her undergraduate archeology degree.

Great!

So only the Chosen may answer this damned question!

Doesn't really help me much, does it?

Zara ran her fingers along each groove to get a sense of the entire word. Her finger stopped at the end of the final word, CODEX. She'd missed something the first time she'd read it. A slight lateral indentation was found between the letters CODE and X.

Could it be Nostradamus was talking about the tenth code?

Or the answer to the code being the number ten?

Or even the ending is ten.

The ending to what, though?

Zara thought about that for a moment. If there was an ending number, there must surely be a beginning, too. She stared at the image as a whole, trying to gain some sort of additional information. Trying to search for a higher plane of information. Anything that Nostradamus might have done to give her another hint. She brought her face right up to the image and then moved back again. Not looking at it in any particular order, simply letting her eyes relax both in and out of focus. The same technique used to see those magic images that frustrated her as a child, where the image ordinarily looked like a thousand dots randomly arranged, but if you relaxed your eyes just right, your mind could derive a unique picture as though by magic.

Zara swore loudly. She'd never been any good at those games. She picked up the image and simply read it out loud once more. There were two letters missing. The first was most likely a "C" to form the word *Conceived*. The second was possibly an "O" to form the word *Out*. It could also be a "B" or "H," – however *But* and *Hut* didn't make much sense. Now that she looked at the quatrain, the whole damn thing barely made any logical sense. The lines were strangely worded, giving it the appearance of some sort of attempt at poetry and rhymes by a school student rather than a great Seer and master of the languages.

She stopped. Grinned widely and then read only the words on the left hand side.

Only.

Conceived.

To.

Out.

Christ! It's a vertical word – OCTO! The Latin word for eight. She highlighted the letters to make sense, incorporating the slight dent in the word CODE – X, so that it looked like this:

Only the Chosen,

Conceived with one faith and born on the day of truth may open;

To see the future, the correct date must be selected, or poison will be the next
Out, to run free like nine fires and flood the CODE-X
Along the left-hand side spells the Latin word OCTO – which means eight. The final word spells codex which is book in Latin, but also Code – X, which means the number ten.
So we now know he wants the number eight and the number ten included in the code. Great, so now all I need is to work out all the other numbers…
Begins with 8
Ends in 10?
Zara ran her hands along the rest of the chest as she examined it looking for any hints or clues which would shed some light on the cryptic message. There were a series of seven latches on the left-hand side. Each with a separate pictograph formed by a protruding piece of metal to make an ornamental dial. She carefully turned the first one, and watched as it rotated on an axis containing the numbers zero to nine in modern numerals. Zara carefully returned the dial to zero where it had begun. Seven dials in total. Starting with the furthest along the right-hand side of the box was the image of a staff, followed by the heel bone, coiled rope, lotus flower, pointing finger, tadpole, and finally the astonished man. They were ancient Egyptian numerals and at a guess, by turning the dial she was increasing the number of the matching images. Each dial increased the number by a factor of ten.
For example, three staff represented three; three heel bones represented thirty; three coiled ropes represented three hundred, and so forth. But how and why, for that matter, Nostradamus would have chosen to use ancient Egyptian numerals for his blood codex was beyond her. He was known to write his more scholarly verses in Latin, his simple rhymes in French and Italian – but she'd never heard of him writing in ancient Egyptian.

She suddenly began to laugh. Shaking her head, she tried to find an explanation for the impossible. The *Rosetta Stone* wasn't found in Egypt until 1799 and Jean-Francois Champollion didn't successfully translate it until 1822. All in total, it was almost two and a half centuries after Nostradamus wrote the numbers for the intricate locking mechanism, which meant the brass chest was either a fake, had been built by someone who knew how to write in ancient Egyptian, or Nostradamus really did see the future.

Zara stared at the ancient Egyptian numbers again. She slowly ran her fingers along the locking mechanisms, and over the ornamental dials, trying to see how the chest remained secure after all these years. Whoever built the chest had been a true craftsman. In a time long before computers, when braziers were masters, the chest had been crafted so perfectly that it was impossible to see where the sections joined. Like a complex jigsaw puzzle, everything locked together on its own. She took out an electronic notepad and drew each of the seven Egyptian symbols. Zara saved the images so she could copy and paste them at her discretion. Zara tried a dozen or so combinations trying to see if any triggered some sort of higher order, gut instinct of hers.

Nothing was standing out to her. She shook her head, chiding herself for giving it so many attempts. The chance of randomly selecting the correct series of images was astronomical. She closed the application, and opened another. This one was an English to ancient Egyptian translator.

Time to take a new approach…

She began entering significant dates into the English to Ancient Egyptian translator. She tried Nostradamus's birthday, using the European style of writing dates – 14/12/15. It converted to 141215, which was represented in Ancient Egyptian by the image of one astonished man, followed by, four tadpoles, one pointing finger, two lotus flowers, one coiled rope and five heel bones. The beginning and ending numbers didn't match. She tried the day he died – 2/7/15, but had the same problem. She tried the date of the supposed expedition. Still nothing.

Zara stopped and stared at the ancient Egyptian numbers. A few minutes passed before she got another lead. The ancient Egyptians wrote numbers from right to left – meaning the number she was looking for began with ten and ended in eight, not the other way around.

Zara retried the original numbers and found they were all off somehow. She added another twenty odd numbers to the list, which might have coincided with the quatrain, but all failed to match the requirement of beginning with ten and ending with eight. Last, Zara tried one number she was certain had nothing to do with Nostradamus.

She smiled as she typed the numbers into the English to Ancient Egyptian calculator. It was stupid trying, but she decided she must anyway – if only to appease her late father. She then pressed enter and the calculator displayed an image she'd seen many times before.

No, that can't be possible.

It was an image she'd seen a thousand times before. She opened the top buttons of her shirt. Slowly and tentatively, as though frightened by what she might discover, and removed a medallion from where it hung between her small breasts. She stared at it for a moment. A family history, so incredible, and so fanciful that she was certain it was all a lie.

On one side the bronze medallion depicted an island that no longer existed – or at least didn't on any navigational map, satellite images, or maritime journal she'd ever seen. While on the other side, were a series of pictographs depicting ancient Egyptian numerals.

They included one pointing finger, followed by two coiled ropes, seven heel bones, and eight staff. Zara had often stared at it without ever really seeing what it meant. Converted to English, the pictograph represented the numbers 10.2.78.

Her own date of birth.

Chapter Five

The sound of Zara banging startled Adebowale into a sudden state of consciousness. His chest felt tight, and his heart pounded. It was an uncomfortable sensation that was becoming increasingly familiar to him. He felt like he'd just run a sprint for his life. Sweat beads littered his skin, but he felt cold inside.

He'd had another vision.

It was a mixture between a nightmare and a wonderful dream. He wasn't quite asleep, but nowhere near awake. Like a micro sleep, lasting no more than a few seconds, the dream felt like it had spanned hours of not-yet-lived memories in his mind. The visions were bombarding him with a much greater frequency these days. It was as though they were telling him the time was near. His future memories had become more frequent, vivid and intense – and no less painful than the first time he'd experienced them.

Adebowale had seen his death for as long as he could remember. It was one of the first memories of his life and it took him until he was five before he was able to make any sense of it. He didn't complain about it. After all, he was to have a good life. Not necessarily a long life, but longer than some. Besides, his life would have meaning and purpose beyond that which most men could imagine.

He could have tried to avoid his death, as so many try to do. Adebowale, if he really wanted to avoid it, could simply choose not to return to his homeland. The land that was taken from his father nearly thirty years ago when he was just three years old. He certainly didn't have any desire to return. And much less desire to be killed in response, but that's what he was going to do, and that was how he was going to die.

There was no point trying to change it. He knew the future was set firmly in the books of time, and he could no more change it than he could the past. Adebowale wondered if he could truly be so cruel as to play the part he had been given in this abhorrent prophecy. He looked at his men celebrating in the distance. They were weak, barely more than prisoners in their own kingdom, forced to work for a foreigner, but they looked happy, and he was about to watch that happiness be taken away.

Adebowale stood guard at her tent. He looked up at the clear sky. The stars glowed bright, unhindered by any cloud. That much didn't match up with his vision, but he was certain tonight was the night. He looked at the men who'd followed him. He considered if his part in the prophecy was really true. The thought frightened him, as much as he longed for it.

He grinned viciously. Yes. If the rest of the prophecy came to fruition, he would commit to play his part – as the betrayer.

Chapter Six

Zara tried to consider any possible explanation for the coincidence. The chance it was entirely random was mathematically so astronomical as to make it impossible. There were two likely explanations she figured.

10.2.78 wasn't her real date of birth. Her father had simply registered her as that so she would one day work out the image in the medallion and believe the prophecy. *Or the medallion was a fake*. Something her father had contrived to make her believe in the prophecy. There was a third possibility, but it was so unlikely she refused to even entertain the thought: *the prophecy was true, and Nostradamus could indeed see the future.*

She stared at the number again trying to see a reason her own date of birth didn't fit the equation. Zara wrote down her full date of birth on the top of her work desk. Next to it she copied the exact number found on the bronze medallion.

10.2.1978

10.2.78

She stared again. Tapping the back of her pencil on the wooden desk next to the two numbers, frustrated, as though the answer was staring right back at her and she was just being too stupid to see it.

The numbers 19 and nine were missing. Zara nearly ignored the relevance of the two missing numbers. After all, it wasn't unusual to leave out the 19 part of 1978. Everyone knows you're either born in the 1900s or 2000s. That is, everyone except Nostradamus. He wouldn't have been so careless to leave out two numbers which were ultimately required to make up the correct date of birth.

So she was wrong. Her birthday didn't match the image on the medallion and neither did it equate to the number found in the quatrain Nostradamus had left her. If Nostradamus had meant her date of birth, he would have expressly accounted for it in the quatrain.

She read the original, unadulterated message from the top of the brass chest again.

Only the Chosen,
 onceived with one faith and born on the day of truth may open;
To see the future, the correct date must be selected, or poison will be the next
 ut, to run free like nine fires and flood the CODEX

It wasn't until she read it through for a third time that she saw the numbers had been right in front of her all along. She underlined the word, one and nine from the quatrain. Nostradamus had written them on the second and fourth prophetic verse. The same two lines which had letters missing. She hit the table in glee. Her heart pounded and she wanted to scream. Nostradamus was telling her to remove the 19 from the equation. So he told her the first number would be a ten, the last number would be an eight, the number nineteen would be missing – *what about the two and the seven?*

Zara felt like it was all becoming clear to her. *Could the two represent the amount of letters missing?* The thought seemed more like she was clutching at straws. Even if it did account for the two, what about the seven?

She stepped towards the brass chest. She ran her hands over each intricately carved, ornamental ancient Egyptian dial. The astonished man. Tadpole. Pointing finger. Lotus flower. Coil of rope. Heel bone. Staff –

Sweet Jesus! There's seven dials!

10278 – The entire series of numbers had been accounted for. Her numbers. The date of her birth. Zara shook her head. *I don't believe I'm trying this.*

She carefully entered her date of birth into the blood codex and stared at the number, 10.2.78 – finding it difficult to find a reason for the impossible coincidence. She took in a deep breath and pressed the final two activation numbers. She held her breath as nothing happened.

The sound of two locked seals popping could be heard, followed by the release of liquid running through tiny tubes inside.

Zara swore. Because she'd gotten it all wrong. The poison was being released and the book of Nostradamus was about to be destroyed.

Chapter Seven

Zara looked at the solid lid, running her hands along the sealed edges and frantically searching for some means of stopping the damaging process. It was impossible. The process had begun and if Nostradamus had been such an admirer of Leonardo Da Vinci's blood codex as she was led to believe, the destruction process had now commenced.

A lifetime of work destroyed in minutes!

The sound of flowing liquid finally stopped. Zara continued to search for a way to enter the brass chest. Hoping there was at least some means of salvaging some of the remaining works of Nostradamus.

The lid suddenly became loose and no longer secured by whatever internal locking mechanism had previously held it. She slowly exhaled and removed the sealed lid. Inside were two large brass containers with a liquid inside. She quickly withdrew both of them after inverting and carefully standing each one upright on the floor beside her. A copper tube ran from the lid to the inside of a second sealed container. By setting the dials to the right place earlier, she'd moved an intricate piece of plumbing that now blocked the passage of the ink, making it impossible to send the ink into the book. After removing the two bottles of ink, she examined the locking mechanism. If she'd turned the dials in the opposite direction, the contents would have spilled inside the second chest. The released liquid changed the pressure inside the chest – releasing the hydrogen bond.

She removed the locking mechanism and poured the contents of the first container into a bucket. The air smelled acrid, and toxic. A moment later a hole in the wooden bucket formed and the strong acid continued to burn. Zara guessed sulfuric acid, but as an archeologist and not a chemical engineer, it was nothing more than a guess.

Zara sighed. Thankful she'd picked the correct combination to enter into the old chest. She returned to the remaining case. This one was much smaller, and sat in the middle of the original brass one. It was made from iron and had been wrapped with an oiled cloth to ensure it survived. She carefully removed the smaller container from the latches which held it in place. Two small holes remained where the other end of the copper pipes would have potentially spilled the strong acid inside, destroying the book she hoped to find.

She carefully unwrapped the oiled cloth and examined the sealed box. The metal looked in good condition. It was sealed so perfectly she could barely identify the slight dip where the two sides of the container came together. The box had no ornamental markings, scratches, or damages. It looked like it had been put together for this specific purpose and then locked away for the ages.

A single small placard made of wood was firmly imbedded into the top of the container to form an intricate handle. It had the simple words,

Here's the proof you're looking for.

Zara smiled again and wondered if someone was somehow playing the most intricate hoax on her. Or could Nostradamus have really had the foresight to know she needed proof of the date. She patiently removed the piece of wood and placed it in a sealed piece of plastic and put that in her side pocket. She would have the wood carbon dated when she got the book secured and in the lab. The buyer would be looking for proof before payment.

Zara turned the box over in her hands. It weighed around twenty pounds. On the opposite side, were four turning mechanisms. Each one numbered from one to nine. She thought back to her high school math class. A lesson in permutations and combinations told her the four digit code could be anything between 0000 to 9999, hence 10,000 combinations. *This is going to take a long time.* God how she hated math in school.

It will be four centuries before you open;

And by then I will be long removed from this world –

So by then you will see the year I was overcome by dropsy;

While others before you shall never know.

Zara read the second quatrain and grinned. It was the sort of thing Michel De Nostradame was known for. The type of game he played. The answer was to place the date of his death into the code. There was no way he'd know he was going to die then, unless he really did see the future – which she was certain he didn't.

She adjusted the numbers until the code read, *1566* – the year Nostradamus had died.

The latch unhinged and the damned box opened. Zara wondered for a moment whether Nostradamus, keen to perpetuate his myth after his death had committed suicide in 1566 for this specific purpose.

She carefully opened the box. Inside was a relatively small codex. She opened the first page. It was made of paper, and bound by thick leather to form rigid hand-bound, leather codices. She read the first sentence. Re-read it again and sat down and swore. Because the first page of the codex was addressed to her, and stamped with a wax seal containing today's date.

Which meant everything she believed was wrong – the prophecy was true.

Chapter Eight

Zara gently bit the top edge of her lip, a nervous habit she'd developed as a child, but almost never did anymore. She started at the beginning and read the first full page of the Book of Nostradamus. If the stories were to be believed, which she doubted, this was the life's work of the master seer.

Her mind raced, trying to formulate a scientific explanation for what she'd found. *Could it be a fake?* The carbon dating of the leather bound codex would tell her for certain. It was either made during the time range when Nostradamus lived or not. *What if someone else had left it for her?* She shook her head – impossible. She watched as the laborers tried to pry the box free from the sand. The box was fixed hard which meant it had been there for centuries, not days, weeks or months like a hoax.

When all possible logical explanations were removed, only one remained – and the very one she could't accept as truth. Nostradamus could in fact see the future. Which meant everything else might be true and the world was approaching its greatest danger.

She read the first page again.

*

Dear Zara Delacroix,

I am writing this letter first. You see the information in this book is going to take nearly my entire life to transcribe. In case I run out of time, I want you to first know the truth.

I was not the first to learn about the fate of humanity. I may be the last, if you fail to do what is necessary. Unfortunately, I don't know what that is. As a Seer, I receive a wealth of information. It has been passed down through the ages of time – but the masters keep some things from me. As you may well have guessed by now, I don't see it in chronological order.

Sometimes I can guess when something will happen because the event is close enough to my present day to allow me to make the connections.

For example, I may know someone in the vision. But most often, I know exactly what will happen, but no idea about when the event took place. You see for me, these events HAVE already happened. I have spent my life documenting the major events. All events affect the future, but it is only the major ones that have enough energy to disrupt the final outcome.

It is the final outcome of humanity that I leave with you in this book today.

I spent my life searching for a solution. I see the future as a series of events, held together by the strings of time. We can all see time, but for some reason I was always able to see the relationship between these strings. The closer the strings are together the more changes occur. The longer they are apart, the better. Massive strings can't be changed, so don't bother trying, as I have, and have always failed.

All strings have an end time. Some only decades in the future. Others last millennia, but all events lead to the same outcome – the human race will become extinct in your lifetime.

There was one event in which the strings of time are allowed to continue. Only one event that suggests the human race may continue. It is not a certainty, and I know very little about what will happen once you read this. Your timeline may even continue for millennia, although I'm rather pessimistic about extending the course of the human race by that much. I can't say what life is like or if people are happy or sad, or will ever know how close they came to extinction. I'm blinded past this point. I know very little about you, or why you were chosen – I don't even know if THEY picked you, or if you were a randomly selected anomaly in the fabric of our existence.

Do you know what event I'm talking about?

You, Zara Delacroix – finding my book.

By now you would have spent years doubting if I ever saw the future or was just a charlatan. In truth, I was both. Yes, I saw parts of the future, but in reality – I merely saw aspects, which I transcribed in this book. I had *visions every single day. Hundreds of visions. It was a most unpleasant life. I spent years trying to learn to block them out, but they simply came back stronger and more vividly. I documented these events, but I was never able to make sense of when or where the events occurred. Consequently, I learned very little about the future. There is an equation, which you will need to find to apply to this book if you are going to make any sense of it. In one of my visions, which I believe, if I'm to trust my instincts, took place many millennia in the past, an equation was formulated to determine the time of these events. It was created by an ancient civilization, lost to antiquity millennia ago.*

I don't know who they were, or where you will find their equation, but I do know you must if you're ever to decipher the truth and save humanity.

When I follow the strings of massive events, this is the largest of them all. It is the only one which has the potential to keep humanity alive – and while there is life, there is hope. So take this book, and use it as you see fit. I can't tell you what is expected of you, or why this changes the world. The answers in this book can be used for great power. You may save the world, but you might just as readily expedite its demise.

And to do that you must stay alive. I wish I could tell you everything you need to know, but I have written too much already, and your time is running out – fast!

As you read this the last of the burning Saharan sun is fading over the horizon. I will tell you the last thing I know about your future. Very soon, you must go for a long walk in the dark. You go alone to clear your mind

THEY will be after you. I believe the very last thing THEY want is for you to interrupt the future. Forget your past. All want to betray you. Watch the infinite starlight and free your mind from the trappings of your beliefs – they're about to be shattered forever.

Run now or you will die – and then humanity will have lost.

Chapter Nine

Zara felt her lips go dry and her throat sting with fear. She'd never been superstitious, but every ghost of her past generations was telling her to run. She closed the codex and locked the latch. The book weighed less than a few pounds. She placed it into a small backpack, along with a single bottle of water. The water wouldn't get her very far, but neither would trying to walk across the Saharan desert as Nostradamus had suggested, so what did it matter? She then carefully replaced the heavy brass lid onto the chest and spun the dials until they locked firmly. Confident that would give any thief at least some pause Zara breathed in the last of the warm desert air and stepped outside the tent.

The camp was alive with celebrations. Campfires burned. Zara smelled the rich aroma of Ashahi tea, the traditional drink of the Tuareg nomads during times of celebration. Made from Gunpowder Green Tea, it was mixed with sugar and mint and served by pouring from a height of over a foot into small tea glasses with a froth on top. Her eyes glanced at the sky above. It was ink black and peppered with more stars than she could count in a lifetime. She smiled. It meant there wasn't a single cloud anywhere.

Massive thunderstorm tonight, hey? Some prediction, Nostradamus!

"Adebowale," she greeted him. Her voice was a dry croak. The unique mixture of fear, elation and relief jamming her tongue to the roof of her mouth. "Any problems in the camp?"

"No, Doctor – should I be expecting any?" He asked, looking down to meet her hardened eyes.

She shook her head. "I don't think so. I'm just concerned by the enormity of the discovery. Definitely no late arrivals, an unexpected camel train filled with nomads perhaps?"

"No Doctor. Do not worry, the prophecy will be safe. What did you read that made you turn pale? I thought you said Nostradamus was nothing more than a charlatan?"

"He was!" she reaffirmed with an innocent smile. "But a very good one."

"The best Seers often were, I am told."

She looked up at the sky. It was crystal clear and filled with stars unrestrained by the ambient lights of a major city for more than a thousand miles. "What do you think the chances are of a thunderstorm tonight?"

Adebowale laughed. "Impossible. I was born in this desert. I have spent more time here than anywhere else in the world, including my homeland. I know this weather as though it was a part of me, an extension of my arms and legs, and I can tell you there's no storm coming tonight."

"Good." Zara smiled, feeling somewhat reassured. Perhaps it was a hoax after all – even if a very good one. "Look. I'm going out into the sand dunes for an hour or so to collect my thoughts. Make plans to move the book to Matan al-Sarra Air Base. I'll contact the buyer tonight and make sure he's got a plane waiting for us there. I'll need to examine it at a laboratory before I can confirm its authenticity."

"Yes, Doctor – the men will be ready, I promise."

"Good. Can you personally guard the book and make certain no one enters my tent until I return?"

Adebowale bowed his head, reverently. "As you wish, Doctor."

"I mean it, don't leave this to any of your men – it's too important."

Adebowale looked at her warmly. "Do not worry, Doctor. I will protect it with my life."

Zara turned to walk out of the camp and hoped to hell Adebowale's words wouldn't come back to haunt her.

Chapter Ten

Zara climbed the first sand dune and headed south. It was dark. She knew it was dangerous to walk far from the camp by herself, but needed to be on her own. The discovery had single handedly confirmed the basis of the theory on which she'd built her entire academic career, and at the same time, shown her how far she was from acquiring the equation. She had long argued that even if Nostradamus did in fact see the future, there was no way he could determine an accurate way of measuring the time of the events. It would be like walking into a cinema and watching a single scene. Without seeing what came before, you couldn't determine the time or date of that event.

She reached the peak of the second sand dune. Zara paused long enough to glance at the makeshift camp that had been her home for the past three months. Her final attempt at finding the book. The campfires burned brightly. She could hear the loud, boisterous laughs, of many of the men who labored for her – they sounded so happy.

Her eyes continued searching past the camp to the dark horizon. No other lights burned. The sea of sand turned into darkness. She breathed deeply – perhaps Nostradamus was lying. There was no sign that anything bad was going to happen to the camp or her people. The thought was crazy. She was on an archeological expedition. No one in their right mind really believed Nostradamus really left a book that yielded unimaginable power in the desert – did they? *Did she?* She asked herself.

Zara turned and continued down the next sand dune, all sixty feet of it. She climbed the third followed by the fourth. Breathing deeply as her feet lifted off the sinking sand as quickly and as lithely as they stepped, she slowly gained height in the massive mountain of sand. She was Queen of the Sahara and she didn't fear the walk through the desert sands.

It wasn't until the fourth sand dune she began to laugh. At the crest she looked back at the camp, now at least two miles away. The light from the camp was prominent. There was no risk of losing it altogether, but the

Saharan desert was a dangerous place. Even in the night, the extreme weather changes and sudden sand storms had lethal outcomes.

What was she thinking?

There was no way Nostradamus could see the future. He wasn't any more of a Seer than she was. The thought was impossible. There had to be a better explanation. Besides, even if he was right, and there was going to be an attack on the camp tonight – why would she walk across the desert without any food or water? The concept was absurd. She would die of exposure, thirst, and stupidity within a day or two.

She needed to get away and collect her thoughts – that's all.

Out of range of the laughter and merriment from the camp, Zara found the silence comforting. Even if this was the biggest hoax, she could be funded for years of research before she proved it. The myriad of stars reassured her that there was a purpose in everything in the universe. No matter how important. This was simply what she needed to do with her life. Zara wondered what her financial backer would say when he heard about her discovery. Would he continue funding her search? It might take years to achieve it, but the results would be worth it.

Would he believe in the Nostradamus Equation?

She thought about that for a few moments. Comforted by the silence, Zara opened the old codex. Skipped the first page letter addressed to herself by Nostradamus's own hand. She made a mental note to check the handwriting with documented letters by the master Seer.

There were three versions of Nostradamus's long-term predictions, named, *Les Prophecies*. The most complete surviving version being an omnibus edition that was published after his death in 1568. In that account there was one unrhymed and 941 rhymed quatrains, grouped into nine sets of 100 and one of 42. Each group was identified as *Centuries*.

She stared at the first real page of what Nostradamus described as the most dangerous book in the world – and swore loudly.

Centuries VII

Zara quickly read the first few quatrains. Feeling a terrible sense of wasted time. They were identical to the ones she'd read years earlier. *Centuries VII* could be purchased anywhere around the world. It was most notable of all the *Centuries* collections because unlike the rest of collections, which included one hundred individual quatrains, it contained just 42.

*

1.

The arc of the treasure deceived by Achilles,

the quadrangle known to the procreators.

The invention will be known by the Royal deed;

a corpse seen hanging in the sight of the populace.

*

2.

Opened by Mars Arles will not give war,

the soldiers will be astonished by night.

Black and white concealing indigo on land

under the false shadow you will see traitors sounded.

*

3.

After the naval victory of France,

the people of Barcelona the Saillinons and those of Marseilles;

the robber of gold, the anvil enclosed in the ball,

the people of Ptolon will be party to the fraud.

*

Zara stopped reading. It was all for nothing. She wanted to cry, but nothing would come out. The entire thing was an elaborate hoax. There was nothing powerful or special about the book she'd discovered. It was no more than a decorative version of *Les Prophecies*. She quickly skipped through the rest of the pages.

Why would my father do this to me?

How many generations of lies?

She was angry and swore profusely as she flicked the remaining pages with merciless speed, splintering the four hundred year old paper as though it were a pile of scrap. Zara stopped short of throwing the book in the sand and paused.

Because this version contained the missing quatrains of *Centuries VII*, numbered 43-100.

Chapter Eleven

Zara felt a sensation crossed between dread and euphoria. Unable to let herself believe again, she was unwilling to relinquish something she'd spent her entire life working towards. She looked up into the starlight and screamed out loud. When she was finished, Zara settled down to a reverent silence and noticed a second note for her.

It was addressed to her, handwritten and signed, *Michel De Nostradamus*. It was hastily written on the side of codex, next to quatrain number, 43.

*

As you will see, the following were much too dangerous for any one person to ever bear witness! I wrote them and then immediately removed them from Centuries VII before the damage could be done. I myself was uncertain what to make of them, but the danger in their power is obvious.

I pray upon discovering the equation, you will know what to do with them.

God speed,

Michel de Nostradamus

*

Zara sat there in silence, contemplating what she might find once she read and studied the 58 missing quatrains. Her heart pounded in her chest and her mind begged her to look immediately, but she waited. After so many years searching, she needed a moment to grasp the enormity of what she was about to see. A strange feeling of peace arrived, as though her life's purpose was somehow about to be revealed.

The sensation was fleeting, and the silence soon broken.

Destroyed with the sound of thunder cracking in the distance. Immediately followed by the stirring of a low level sand storm. It was the same type of localized meteorological event responsible for killing more people than the desert itself. Tourists who wandered from their camps to stargaze, only to become lost in a violent sand storm. Zara chided herself for not taking more precaution. It had been a good walk, a whim. And it might just end up costing her life.

Zara ducked down low and covered her face with her green headdress in an attempt to protect her eyes. She looked at her smartphone. GPS was unable to locate any satellites above the sand storm. She switched to her compass App and pointed it towards the camp before her camp completely disappeared. She then ducked down low and slowly braced herself for the long journey back – terrified of what she would find once she reached it.

Rain dumped on her from a cloud carried by the fast moving winds in a way she'd never experienced in a lifetime traveling the Sahara.

"You've got to be kidding me?" she said out loud. The rain drenched her clothing bringing with it a delicious reprieve from the desert's heat and ice cold fear into her heart.

I don't believe the prophecy's really coming true! Even as she thought it, she doubted herself, trusting a scientific answer would somehow explain it all.

The wind blew Zara onto her back. She rolled on her side and quickly got to her feet again. Dipping her head low again she focused her eyes only on the compass bearing. The storm stopped as quickly as it had begun. The dry sand fought to swallow the rain. Two more sand dunes away, she saw a bright orange glow coming from the camp. She'd never seen such an intense glow anywhere in the desert before. Her mind searched for an answer, but never found a solution. Instead, her thoughts were interrupted by the distinct sound of gunfire.

My people! They're all going to be slaughtered!

Zara ran towards the camp. She needed to get back there. Everything else that Nostradamus had written could have been faked, but no one on earth knew a storm would rage through the camp tonight. Her pulse raced. Not because of the effort of running, but because of what the storm meant. She recalled the warning Nostradamus had given her – *Free*

your mind from the trappings of your beliefs – they're about to be
shattered forever.

She crawled to the peak of the sand dune closest to her camp. Down below she saw the destruction. The large mesh of interconnected tarpaulins were missing. What remained of the bounded wooden sticks which formed the camp's skeleton was crooked or missing entirely. The dry sand had swallowed all evidence of the recent rain; the only sign of its presence being the sudden introduction of humidity in a land that rarely experiences more than a few inches of rain per year. She saw men running through the camp. They appeared to be feverishly working to bring order to the destruction. Their skin was dark and they wore green camouflaged clothing – and held AK-47s in their hands.

Zara felt her throat tighten and her chest pound. The image just confirmed the first step of the prophecy had come true, and her world would be shattered forever.

Chapter Twelve

Zara slid forward until she could get a good view of the camp. There were bodies huddled together at the northern end of the camp. They might be sleeping, or they could be dead. Either way Zara couldn't tell and even if she could, there was nothing she could do to help any of them. At least a hundred camels were penned down at the edge of the camp, their masters working hard to keep them from fleeing. Her eyes turned to focus directly on her tent. The tarpaulin had disappeared, but the brass box vault remained. Adebowale was missing, and for a fleeting moment she allowed herself to believe he'd made it out alive. She recalled his words when she left – *he would protect the book with his life* – and she doubted he survived.

She heard the shots fire and saw the sudden flashes of light bursting from the weapon's nozzle. One of the bodies she'd seen lying at the northern end of the camp had moved and one of the attackers emptied his full magazine into the remaining bodies until there were no movements left.

Who the hell are these people?

The sound made her focus on her own life again. Nostradamus had written that she'd survive, but she would have to head south. How could she possibly do that? There was over a thousand miles of sand between her and the southern edge of the Saharan desert in Chad. Even knowing where the periodic waterholes and few oases were, she could never cross the desert on foot.

Zara crawled up to the edge of the sand dune, trying to dig herself as low to the ground as possible. She watched two men enter the remains of her tent. They examined Nostradamus's brass vault. The box which had housed one of the most extraordinary relics ever made. The two spoke to one another animatedly.

"Master, Ngige!" the second man yelled into a radio. "I think we found it!"

A black SUV drove through the middle of the camp. A Range Rover Autobiographical edition. The sort of thing whose ownership was limited to royalty, the ultra-rich, and film stars. She'd never seen anyone attempt to drive one through the Sahara. From what she'd heard it was sort of a cross between a race car and an all-purpose, go-anywhere, four wheel drive. A man stepped out of the vehicle, leaving the door open and the engine running. He wore dark green camouflage seen on the other men in the camp, but there were golden crowns on each of his epaulettes.

Zara watched him approach the two men standing next to the brass chest. They both saluted him and she guessed the man with the crowns was their leader.

"We found it, Ngige!" The shorter of the two men said.

Ngige shook the man's arm. "Well done! We have found it!

So they had come for the book of Nostradamus. Zara looked at the black Range Rover. It was her only possible chance of escape, and it might as well have been on the moon for all the chance she had of reaching it. Even if she did make it, there was no telling whether or not someone else was still inside.

"Gabe Ngige! Gabe Ngige!" The men started shouting the name and firing their AK-47s into the air like madmen.

Pandemonium raged through the camp and Zara thought her odds of making it may have just risen to a percentage point above zero.

Gabe Ngige – *why does that name sound so familiar?*

Chapter Thirteen

Zara slid down the remaining edge of the sand dune while the mayhem and hysteria of success flooded through the camp. This was her only chance. Her only possibility of surviving was to roll the die and get lucky. It was a long shot, but she had to take it. She heard the distinctive rat-a-tat of at least fifty AK-47s being fired into the air. She was now out in the open, entering the camp, and committed to her attempt to steal the Range Rover. Zara focused on the vehicle and didn't bother to look at the shooters. At any moment one of those bullets would kill her, but there was nothing she could do about that – the future had already been decided.

She ran down the last section of the dune and to her own surprise reached the driver's seat and closed the door. Zara took in a deep breath, looked around, still expecting to find someone else inside. She didn't. It was empty and she was still alive. The air conditioning was set low, providing an environment of comfort she hadn't experienced in the past two years, since she moved to the Sahara. The car smelled new. The cream Napa leather seats were piped with black. The man driving was taller than her, but not by much and her body sat perfectly inside.

She threw the Range Rover into gear. Released the electric handbrake and planted her foot down hard. The supercharged engine had great acceleration. Better than turbocharged. No lag. The high-end, sports SUV took off with a lurch. There was a moment of reprieve before any of the soldiers noticed their leader wasn't in his vehicle, followed by a large amount of screaming and barking of orders. A tall soldier approached from up ahead of her. He waved his hands and shouted, "Stop there!"

The man had made a millisecond failure to act and still hadn't aimed his weapon at her. Instead he'd stepped in-between the two sand dunes in which the camp had been built – making it impossible for her to drive around him. She hit the car horn to warn him without thinking.

And it did warn him.

He picked up his AK-47 and began raking the SUV's hood. Sparks flew as the bullets ricocheted across the military grade windshield. The owner, presumably an African drug lord, had purchased the top end protection add-ons.

The soldier stared at her – his eyes vacant and his mouth open as though he wanted to scream, but no words were coming out. At the last moment his eyes went wide and realization dawned on him. He was going to die. Zara didn't lift off on the accelerator for a second. She pushed her foot harder to the floor, willing the Range Rover to somehow gain more speed.

The man went under the hood with a crippling crunch, without even a shudder or reduction in speed to the two and a half ton SUV. Zara didn't feel any remorse. Instead she felt elated to be alive and free. She'd rolled the die and scored a one in a hundred possibility, at best, of surviving – and won. Her eyes glanced at her rearview mirror. The gruesome mixture of crushed bone and flesh brought everyone out of their victory revelry. At least a dozen men had already mounted their camels, while more still fired at the Range Rover.

She steered left to climb out of the camp and avoid a direct line of sight for her attackers. The SUV responded immediately. Rack and pinion steering. Fast response. Its Desert Hawk tires eating up the sand.

More gunfire echoed through the sand valley and the rear windshield was quickly scattered with bullets, sending star-like fractures in its modified bullet resistant glass. There was only so much it could withstand. The rear windshield, pelted with hundreds of bullets broke free of its hold and fell forward onto the rear seats.

Zara ducked her head down low. At any moment she expected to feel the pain of a bullet piercing her skin at an unimaginable velocity. She wondered, with the morbid fascination of someone who'd already accepted her fate, if she'd even know she'd been hit before she died.

Instead, she felt a different sensation. The contents of her gut suddenly rose and she felt the Range Rover lose traction on the ground below. It felt like minutes, but was less than a few seconds – the powerful SUV had cleared the top of the sand dune and was now on a free fall down the opposite side.

She landed with a jolt as the soft sand on the downward side of the dune was sprayed above over the hood, sending sand scattering over the windshield. The steering wheel swung wildly. Zara fought with it, trying to keep the SUV from rolling. If one of the front wheels dug into the sand her escape was all over – the SUV would roll and even if she survived the crash, she'd never be able to escape her attackers who were swarming after her.

The steering became more responsive as the sand dune leveled out. She pushed hard on the accelerator and began up the following mound. By the time she reached the crest, Zara no longer heard bullets raking the back of the SUV. She smiled. She was reaching the outer limits of their accurate firing range. Her eyes darted to the rear-view mirror. A tail of bright orange fire raced towards her. It took a split second to recognize the tail end of the rocket.

The SUV dropped of the crest, descending steeply, and the poorly-aimed RPG flew high by several feet. She heard the roar of its rocket motor blast overhead. She sighed with relief. It would take too long for her attacker to load and fire a second one.

Zara recalled the view from her rear-view mirror. Several attackers on camels had begun their pursuit. They would never keep up with the high speed Range Rover, but they didn't have to. She looked at the dashboard for the first time since stealing the vehicle. At present usage, the SUV had 400 miles worth of fuel remaining on its long-range, dual tanks. She needed a thousand to reach the southern tip of the Sahara, deep inside Chad. She could reach any number of oases, but that wouldn't help much. She wasn't worried about dying of thirst. It was her attackers who would be the death of her.

Despite her misgivings, Zara sped south, heading deeper into the Saharan desert – where her heavy Range Rover left deep imprints in the sand for her trackers to easily follow.

Chapter Fourteen

Zara pointed the powerful SUV due south and kept driving. She was safe for now, but needed to put as much distance as she could between herself and her pursuers. One thing was certain as she watched her fuel diminish – she would no longer be driving by sunrise. The mercenaries she'd left behind at her camp would come after her. And if they ever reached her, she would die.

If she could forge a two day head-start on the men on camelback she might just lose them if she walked softly. *But where would she go?* Anyone who knew the area would also know she would have to aim for the Bilma oasis. It was the only one close enough that she might have the chance to reach before dying of dehydration. They would know that too, which meant she'd need to lose them after reaching the oasis, or better yet – bypass it entirely and find another one altogether.

Zara knew one. It was at least another eighty miles past Bilma and almost definitely out of her reach. She swore. It was unlikely she'd even reach the first oasis. At a guess she'd run out of fuel at least forty miles before it. She shook the thought from her mind. There was nothing she could do – just watch her fuel, wait, and see. Then adapt to her circumstances and see what options came up. She might get lucky and come across some nomads willing to come to her assistance.

Zara quickly found desert driving required a unique combination of speed, finesse and technical skill. It was critical that she tackled the dunes with precision. Knowing the right time to go full throttle and the right time to slow down took experience and clear judgement. Zara had neither, but she mastered the skill quickly out of necessity.

At 2a.m. Zara spotted the peak of Emi Koussi out the left-side window of the Range Rover. Standing at 11,204 feet, the ancient volcano in the Tibesti Mountains of northern Chad cast an enormous shadow over the night's horizon. It was also one of the few visible landmarks for many miles. Zara made a quick mental note of her most probable location. The region had few topographical changes with which to navigate by. She looked up towards her right. Sharing the horizon in the west were the faintest images of the Air Mountains, no more certain than a mirage. She shook her head, unwilling to believe what she was going to do next. She continued driving due south – into the Erg of Bilma.

The Erg of Bilma in the Ténéré desert region of the south central Saharan Desert was the last place she wanted to visit right now. The Erg's sand grains were supplied from the Tibesti Mountains by the Harmattan – a northeasterly trade wind which blew steadily for most of the year. The Erg of Bilma spread out southwest from the Tibesti Mountains into Chad and Niger. From there it would be another 745 miles until she was free of one of the world's deepest sandpits, and a further 400 miles until she was entirely free of the Saharan desert.

There were nearly 1100 miles of thick sand dunes between her and the southern tip of the Sahara desert inside Chad or Niger. The deeper sand dunes would further reduce her mileage and certainly weren't her first preference. Zara considered turning left, heading on towards Egypt, or even taking a wild and reckless giant U-turn to reach the Mediterranean by passing through Libya. Any of these paths would have made more sense, given the fact that she was driving further away from her freedom. Instead, she drove due south into an Erg she could never hope to cross – because that's where Nostradamus told her she would go.

At the heart of the Erg, approximately 300 miles further south, and at least 50 miles further than the Range Rover would continue to travel, was the oasis town of Bilma. A once thriving trading post, vital to the trans-Saharan trade route stretching between Central Africa and Libya, it now remained home to fewer than 2500 people. If she reached it, there might just be a chance one of those people would be willing to find a way of getting her out of the country.

All of this, of course, relied heavily on the answer to one question – could she reach it before they did?

Chapter Fifteen

It wasn't until the early hours of the morning – about seven a.m. when the engine first coughed and then misfired. The fuel gauge rested below empty. The thirsty V8 sucked on fumes. It drove for another six minutes before choking and conking out permanently.

Zara tried the starter button.

The engine turned, but nothing fired. She pushed the starter button another three times and then stopped. She couldn't will the SUV into driving across the desert without fuel. She unclipped her seatbelt and stepped out to look in the back of the vehicle for anything useful. Two large jerry cans were attached to the back of the lift gate next to the spare tire, and both were full of bullet holes and empty. She pressed the lift button and the hatch opened. Inside, there was a single half-empty gallon bottle of water. Otherwise the rest of the luggage compartment was bare.

Zara shook her head. *Where did they plan to drive to once they'd found the book of Nostradamus?* Without additional fuel, they never would have made it out of the Sahara, even if they drove north. The only alternative was that the camels carried its additional fuel. It didn't matter, however they planned to make it across the desert it wasn't going to help her.

Zara looked up at the first light. The morning's sun crept towards the horizon in the east. There was another forty or fifty miles to reach the oasis of Bilma. She cursed herself for diverting towards the east in an attempt to miss the town and reach the second oasis. Now that option was out of the question. If she was lucky, she might just survive long enough to reach the first. She grabbed the half-filled gallon bottle of water and pulled her headdress over her face again. It was going to be a long walk. She left the Range Rover and turned her back to the rising sun and began walking west towards Bilma.

By her reckoning she might reach it by dusk. If it was winter she would have made it easily. In the middle of summer her chances of survival were low. By eight a.m. the sun was high enough to burn. Zara protected her face from the harsh light reflected off the dunes in front of her with her green shesh and continued to walk. Ordinarily she'd never even attempt to walk through the thick sand dunes during the heat of the day, but she needed to keep making distance if she wanted to survive. She moved quickly, at a rate somewhere between a walk and a slow run. Her feet trod lightly, never allowing them to pause long enough to sink into the deep sand before lithely taking another step.

She prayed for a sudden dip in the barometer to send the otherwise stable Harmattan trade wind into a heavy gust, lifting the grains of sand and burying her footprints. Instead, the barometer went higher, and the Harmattan stopped completely. Without wind, the temperature soared. By one p.m. it scorched to a hundred and twenty-two degrees Fahrenheit. There was no way she could keep up the pace in that sort of heat. She found the steepest section of the rolling sand dune and sank into its side. The temperature dropped marginally, but it might just be enough for her to survive.

She forced herself to sleep until the sun dipped and the heat became tolerable. Zara took comfort in the knowledge her attackers and their camels would be forced to wait until the temperature dropped too, before continuing. By six p.m. the sun was making its way over the western horizon and she began to move again. She traveled on and off through the night. Keeping the pace of a brisk walk for an hour and then having a five minute break, she carried on through the night. By morning she was exhausted; her feet ached and her stomach was empty. No longer driven by the release of adrenaline after her immediate near death experience, the pain and weariness began setting in. Zara consciously made the effort to ignore the sensations. She still had another ten miles to go before she reached Bilma.

The sun hit the eastern horizon and quickly rose above her head. It felt hotter than the day before, if that was even possible. Zara struggled to keep pace, relying heavily on large gulps of the remaining water. She stopped rationing, and focused on keeping herself moving through the heat of the day. If she didn't reach the oasis by tonight, her attackers would catch her by tomorrow.

By two p.m. she drank the last of the water. She cursed herself for not being more frugal with her rations. She felt frustrated and confused. Had she misjudged the distance to the oasis, or worse yet – missed it completely? Even as she struggled to go on in the worst heat of the day she wondered if the oasis had lain hidden just beyond the next sand dune?

She checked her compass and stayed true to her course. Her mind was playing tricks on her. Teasing her and tormenting her that water was nearby. She wanted to build a makeshift camp to protect her from the sun's heat and wait until dusk before going again, but by then it would be too late. Instead, she forced herself to keep going. She'd never made the mistake of becoming dehydrated in a desert before – and she had crossed this particular desert more times than she could remember. Of course, normally, she waited for the right weather, rode a camel – and wasn't running for her life.

Sometime after four p.m. she began having hallucinations like conscious dreams, and she struggled to differentiate between her past and her present. She remembered things about her mother and her father that she hadn't thought about for nearly two decades, when she was still a child. At first the hallucinations frightened her, and then she welcomed them. They brought her to a place filled with peace and happiness. Zara fought to maintain focus on reality. She was conscious that if she let herself go and succumbed to the enjoyment and peace of the dreams they would be the last she ever had.

Her mind wandered to her past. To the skipped childhood spent following her father on his obsession to locate the book of Nostradamus. Even as a child she was certain the prophecy was nothing more than a foolish dream, thought up by one of her great ancestors who needed to make themselves feel more important than they were.

Zara's father was an archeologist. Only he cared little about ancient history. He was driven by an unshakeable belief in the prophecy and that together the two of them would locate the final resting place of Nostradamus's book. Unlike her father, who was close to madness with obsession and almost religious fervor, Zara had never really believed the stories.

His obsession drove her mother, Darius, to death. Darius followed Zara's father throughout his travels. On the year Zara's mother died, her strong-willed mother had decided to take Zara to Cairo after deciding it had become a ridiculous notion to have a young girl and wife wandering the desert in search of a fabled prophecy.

On that trip, the winds were particularly strong through the night. Her mother climbed out of their tent to strengthen its lines and keep it from being blown away. At the very same time, an unusually large, yellow *Leiurus Quinquestriatus*, known colloquially as a Deathstalker scorpion climbed out of its burrow to investigate the strange vibrations coming from the heavy wind.

The scorpion, having recently given birth to its own offspring, was particularly aggressive. It stung Zara's mother several times. With each sting, the scorpion injected its venom with the dangerous neurotoxins agitoxin and scyllatoxin.

Her mother died within minutes.

Zara's male guides had decided the best solution was to return her to her father. She often thought her father should have sent her away. Made her study abroad, but instead he took her in and decided it was a sign that the prophecy was fast approaching. She traveled with him throughout the Saharan desert searching for an Erg that matched a description of a story, passed on from father to son for generations. She loved that time she spent with her father, but at the same time hated herself, because she felt she had been responsible for her own mother's death. In time, she focused this guilt into anger at her father, who had become more and more focused on the prophecy. It was his obsession, and in the end – he died without ever finding the book of Nostradamus.

Zara wandered in and out of consciousness. Her mind focused hard on one fact. *The prophecy, the riches, the end of the human race – it was all bullshit!* And now she was going to die in the desert because she'd let herself become a part of it. Her mind drifted like the sand which rolled down the dune beside her.

Only it wasn't bullshit – her father had been right all along. The book of Nostradamus proved the existence of the prophecy. She had been wrong and her father had been right. And now she was going to die of thirst in the middle of the Sahara desert and she didn't even know who had attacked her camp and killed everyone who had supported her quest for the past two years – two hundred men and women who had followed her faithfully, trusting her to bring them to the glory of Nostradamus's prophecy.

At the bottom of the steep dune, sand rolled into the still water making the smallest of ripples. The palm trees formed shade and the entire place looked like some sort of utopia out of Eden. The oasis looked so real she wanted to delve into its cold water and immerse herself in its mythical and rejuvenating powers. Zara tried to lick her lips. All she tasted was the dry salt and it burned at her tongue so much it hurt. She could no longer balance and found herself freefalling down the steep sand dune. She lost track of the amount of times she rolled.

At the bottom of the sand dune she entered the cold water with a splash.

This must be it. I'm getting close. I'm starting to hallucinate – I'm really going to die.

I failed the prophecy.

Chapter Sixteen

It took Zara a few minutes to realize where she was. Her core body temperature retreated as she felt the cool water cover her to her neck. She let the cold water enter her mouth. She swished it around until her mouth and lips were soothed and then spat it out. She then carefully swallowed a small amount of water. She'd heard of men dying after stumbling upon an oasis in the middle of a great desert and drinking themselves to death.

She took a second small mouthful of the fresh water, submerged her head and then slowly reappeared. Her giant hazel eyes stared out from just above the waterline, like an alligator – waiting for its prey.

It was the first time she noticed she was not alone.

A camp had been set up at the far side of the waterhole. A small fire lit, and the rich aroma of the nomadic Tuareg people's tea brewed. Nearby three camels drank, sheltered by the five palm trees surrounding the edge of the small oasis. Her eyes scanned the area for a sign of their riders, but couldn't find any. She'd passed the edge of the Bilma oasis. Not the main one in which the town was built, but a smaller one on the outer edge of Bilma. That put her a further forty miles east than she expected. That was good, it might give her a little more time to add some distance between herself and her attackers. Her eyes searched for the nomads to whom the camels belonged.

Zara slowly stepped out of the water and quietly climbed the bank of the sand dune to retrieve her pack. She carefully opened the bag, ignoring the wooden case which housed the book of Nostradamus. Instead she unzipped an inside compartment and withdrew a small knife. It was a razor sharp butterfly knife. She slipped it into her trouser pockets and crouched down to carefully approach the camels. Her instincts telling her not to trust strangers in a desert.

"Hello," she called out. "Anyone here?"

No answer.

"I'm going to steal your camels if someone doesn't answer me."

Still no response.

Zara looked for somewhere the owners could be sleeping. There were five trees, approximately fifty square yards of water – and sand. The place was otherwise empty.

She patted the camel closest to her on its neck. "Where are your masters?"

The camel snorted and then continued drinking. The beast looked tired, and worn. Its owner had ridden him hard. There was no way she could entice such an animal to ride again today.

"You've had a rough day, haven't you?" she said, kindly. The camels were intimate to the nomadic people of the Sahara, who needed them for everything they did. It was inconceivable someone had been careless enough to lose all three. "I've had a pretty shitty day, too," she confided.

Zara quickly filled up her water canteen and began loading the camel with supplies. "I'm going to need your help," she said.

The camel backed away.

It was the first sign it had shown of being frightened.

Zara put her hands out. "Hey, it's okay. I know an even better waterhole nearby."

The camel knelt down with its front legs stretched out and its hind legs resting buried in the sand. It gave a loud snort and then rested its head on the sand beside the oasis. The beast closed its eyes, and Zara watched its breathing become slow and relaxed. There was no way she was going to be able to coax the beast into carrying her straight away. Her best bet was to give it a few hours rest and then attempt to rouse it into moving.

She patted the camel on its neck. "It's all right. Have a break. In a few hours I'll take you to an even nicer place."

Zara had focused so much on befriending the camel that her ears, normally highly attuned to the sounds of the desert, hadn't noticed the three riders and their camels descend the sand dune into the oasis behind her, until they were no more than twenty yards away.

She turned to run, and was met face to face with the rider of a fourth camel.

Chapter Seventeen

Zara felt the man's hands grip her arms before she could do anything. She took one look at the three men who were approaching. They must have tricked her. They rode camels, but had left the three camels waiting at the oasis to fool her into thinking she might have a chance to escape. She struggled for a moment to get free, but the sight of the other three riders approaching was enough to stop any further movement. She relaxed, her intelligent hazel eyes taking in the entire scene, searching for solutions where none existed. Her run was over. She'd failed. And now all was lost.

There were three men approaching plus the one who held her roughly and a total of seven camels. The oasis was filled with still water. There were no signs of other nomads. These must have been the fastest of her attackers. The rest of her enemies were probably still moving towards her, trying to survive the hostile environment of the Sahara. She grinned as she recalled how fatigued the three camels she'd examined were and wondered how many of her attackers had died in their attempt to catch up with her. If she could break free she might still outrun them in the desert. She was willing to bet her ability to survive in the desert against any of these men.

But first she still needed to free herself.

"Where's the book, darling?" the man holding her asked. His breath smelled bad, and what teeth he had left were rotten. He twisted her arms painfully behind her back.

"What book?" she replied.

The man tightened the pressure on her arms until she was forced to bite down on her lip to stop herself from screaming. "Do I need to ask again?"

"Oh, that book?" Zara replied. Her voice was casual without any indication of fear.

"I thought that'd jog your memory," the man snickered. "Well, you're not going to make me ask again, are you?"

"It's over there," she said, pointing towards the camels. "Do you like the camels I found? They looked pretty exhausted. You must have run them pretty hard to get here – I packed it in the bag with the camels."

The man ignored her. Instead spoke to his companion. "Check her camels. See if you can find it!"

Her camels? She thought about the three worn out camels she'd found, lamely drinking at the oasis. *If they're not his, then whose are they?* She remained focused, taking in her situation and concentrating on her options instead of letting fear get in the way.

There were four men against her. Each of them was armed with an AK-47. She had a flick knife in a pocket she couldn't reach. They were all bigger and stronger than she was. All four of them were deathly tired from the hard desert crossing. So was she, but she could probably outlast any one of them in the desert if the camels disappeared – but she would still be trapped.

Zara felt them bind her ankles and wrists with narrow strands of rope which cut deep into the soft tissue of her wrists.

"My men tell me you've been dubbed the Queen of Sahara because you have searched all her sandy Ergs, traveling freely without concern for harm from the harsh elements or bandits."

Zara remained silent while trying to slip her hands free from their bindings. It was impossible. The bandits had tied the rope so tight it cut into her wrists. She kept searching, calmly looking for her next move. There was always an option. She just couldn't see one.

"All that walking..." her captor said sympathetically. "...must have made you thirsty. Would you like a drink?"

Zara stared at the oasis. Although not very wide, she'd heard it was quite deep. She shook her head, realization striking her like the bite of death adder. "No. You don't want to do this. You still need me. Only I can interpret the book."

"Only you can interpret the book?" he asked.

"Yes. It tells the future, but not in a logical method. Only I can make sense out of Nostradamus's riddles."

"That's not what Adebowale said. He said you don't have a clue what to make of the damned riddles, so that makes you worthless to our master." Her captor laughed. "Ironic, isn't it? The Queen of Sahara can travel throughout all the deserts with impunity from the blistering heat, but drowns in a waterhole. Don't you think?"

"No. You're making a big mistake. You need me!"

"I don't need anyone. Least of all you."

Zara felt his boot dig into her back and a moment later she was falling face down. She took a deep breath and plummeted into the water. The water felt cool and refreshing on her tortured skin. Zara, true to her word, focused on her next priority. Somehow, she had to keep her head above water. She lifted her knees up to her chest and kicked. It propelled her forwards, but not to the surface where she needed to get.

It's working – I just need to position myself so that I move in the right direction!

She rotated her shoulders until she was facing the surface and tried to kick again. She tried a third and a fourth time without any success. The jolting spasms caused her body to move towards the surface, but never quite there. Her lungs were burning and her chest begged her to open her mouth and take a breath.

Just a few more goes, that's all I ask!

On the seventh attempt her head broke the surface. She instantly took a deep breath. The air tasted heavenly – sweet and divine. Zara opened her mouth, eager to take a second breath, but her head was already below the water again.

She quickly tried her kicking movement again. A sense of panic raced through her as she realized she was sinking. With each kick, the surface appeared further away. She'd swallowed a large amount of water, and her body had taken a naturally negative buoyancy.

Her rational mind fought for another solution. Nostradamus had told her she would survive and it was her existence that paved the way to set in motion a series of events which would prevent the inevitable extinction of the human race. She didn't remember him saying anything about drowning in the Saharan desert?

The thought made her smile. Her oxygen starved mind didn't miss the irony, despite the suffering. Her body stopped fighting. She no longer kicked or tried to reach the surface. That chance had already left. Her only option for survival was a miracle. The world above her went dark. Her ears ached from the increased pressure.

Who would have thought the oasis was so deep?

This wasn't how I was supposed to die.

I was supposed to save the world.

It was the last thought she had before losing her voluntary control over the muscles of the diaphragm. She drifted closer towards an unconscious state and her mouth opened up, giving way to an involuntary urge to take in a deep breath.

It was time to die. She'd tried her best and failed. Her mind had racked itself trying to analyze the situation, somehow make sense of it, and come up with a solution. There weren't any. She'd done the best and lost. It made her happy. It wasn't her fault. She had nothing to feel bad about.

Zara breathed in deeply.

The cold water was a relief to her burning lungs. It felt good. Tasted good. Cold and refreshing. She breathed again. Somehow, the second breath felt even better. Her body relaxed. The sense of adrenaline fueled panic finally subsided.

This must be what it's like to drown.

Who knew it would be so peaceful?

The darkness seemed to fade away. She breathed again and opened her eyes. A new light formed in front of her. A face followed the light and she wondered what she was supposed to do now – was she supposed to move into the light or run away from it? Her first instinct was to run from the light. Never enter the tunnel of death. Her rational mind argued against her philosophy. Arguing that she would be dead even if she tried to avoid the light.

She decided not to run from the light, but nor did she feel inclined to race towards it, either. Zara breathed in again and saw the face began taking shape.

It was a man's face.

And it seemed to be smiling at her.

The face was getting closer. Although she couldn't quite tell if she was moving towards it, or it was moving towards her. She could see more of it now. The face wasn't quite smiling at her. The mouth was hideously distorted.

She could hear the sound of the strange creature breathing. She wanted to breathe, herself, but something was stopping her. The face changed again and it was smiling at her. Somehow, in this dream – if that was what she was calling her in-between life and death state – she was now suddenly able to breathe again. It felt so good. She'd always assumed that in death, you could feel nothing. Instead, she felt every sensation, intensified.

She felt her hands and ankles break free from their restraints. Once again she was looking into a man's face. She'd never seen the man before. She quizzed her memory, but failed to find any recollection of him. If this was her transition to the afterlife, surely the last face she saw would have some sort of meaning, or importance to her.

She stared at him. There was little she could recognize. There wasn't even a hint of him being someone she once knew, even for a passing moment. He wore something over his face, but his eyes were visible.

They were the most intense blue she'd ever seen.

Chapter Eighteen

Zara tentatively took another slow breath in. *I'm breathing from a dive regulator?* She could feel the bubbles run across her face as she exhaled. Her eyes, now accustomed to the water, made out the shape of the man who'd saved her life. He wore a dive mask, regulator and board shorts. It gave him the appearance of a SCUBA diver at a coral reef on a paradise island. Far from the treasure hunter in one of the few waterholes deep enough to dip your head under within the Saharan desert. It didn't matter, the man would be executed once he surfaced.

Her mind raced to where she'd seen him and his companion yesterday. But where was the companion? The diver had cut her free and it felt good to be able to move her arms and legs again. He'd saved her life – for now. *But how long would her reprieve last?* When they came up for air, the men would kill all three of them. That's supposing the second diver hadn't been killed already.

Her thoughts were interrupted by something in her hand. It was cold and she hadn't placed it there. It took her a moment to realize the man next to her had put it in her hands. He motioned her to look at it. It was a rectangular piece of dark stone. Words were written on it in chalk.

YOU OKAY?

Sure, if you count discovering that all that you thought was a lie turned out to be truth, and that a man who you've never met before has just hunted you across the desert to kill you... then sure, I'm fine.

Her mind slowly caught up with her and she wrote a reply.

FINE.

FOUR MEN ABOVE WILL KILL US WHEN WE SURFACE.

MUST STAY HERE AS LONG AS POSSIBLE.

The diver nodded his head. She felt the dive slate pull away as he wrote a new message.

WAIT HERE 10 MINUTES.

He removed his dive tank, weight belt and buoyancy control device, placing all three in her hand. They had been sharing his primary and secondary regulator which ran from the same tank. She instantly found it easier to remain on the sandy floor of the waterhole. She watched as the diver took his regulator out of his mouth and smiled at her. It was a confident smile. The sort you'd expect from someone used to succeeding.

The diver then began swimming to the surface.

Zara quickly reached up and grabbed him by his ankle. The man returned to her. She wrote quickly on the dive slate he'd given her.

WHERE ARE YOU GOING?

The diver casually reached for the secondary regulator mouthpiece and took in a single breath of air as though it was something he might want to think about doing while he was on the bottom of the oasis. He picked up the dive slate, wiped off her question and wrote a reply. A moment later he handed the slate back to her and swam towards the surface.

Zara looked at the dive slate.

TO NEGOTIATE

Chapter Nineteen

Sam climbed the sand dune at the edge of the oasis. He wore board shorts, a wristwatch and held his snorkel in his hand. The soldiers, whoever they were, talked loudly in French, which narrowed their origin down to any of the north-western countries of Africa. Sam listened intently for a few minutes, thankful he'd spent three years in France as a kid.

One of the men, who wore crowns on his shoulder epaulets kept yelling about a book. Sam couldn't quite make out the name of the book or why it was so important. He watched as the men ripped apart his riding bags, and the small amount of equipment he'd brought into the desert. They found the two Uzi's stored in the camel bags and immediately emptied all thirty-two rounds from each weapon with excitement.

"Leave them!" The leader yelled. "Where's the book?"

"It's not here, sir!" one of the men said.

"It must be! Where else would she have left it?"

Sam spotted the small backpack in the sand. He also saw the footprints leading to the oasis and back around to where the woman he'd helped had most likely searched his camels. He quickly opened the bag, hoping she'd kept a weapon inside. A gun would be optimal, but even a knife would help. Instead he found a large book, bound by a leather and brass codex. It wasn't much of a step to presume this was the book the soldiers were after. There was nothing else of value to him inside.

"I don't even know if these are her camels," said one of the men wearing military camouflage clothing.

The man with the epaulets yelled a response. "Of course they're her camels."

"No. She stole the Range Rover. We picked up a single set of foot prints in the sand. She was definitely on foot."

"Which means – someone else was here, helping her? Spread out. Find them!"

Sam quickly buried the book in the sand. Whoever they were and for whatever reason they wanted the book, Sam was confident he didn't want to let them have it.

Unable to avoid the confrontation, he stepped over the sand dune, holding his dive snorkel in his hands.

Two of the soldiers spotted him immediately. They pointed their AK-47s at him and Sam prayed to hell the two had the discipline to wait for their commander to search him before they killed him.

Sam smiled. It was practiced, and meant – *I've done something really stupid, but it's okay I'll get out of it.* He spoke in his most boisterous, and confident American accent. "Hi there!"

The leader turned to face him directly.

Sam shook his head, holding the snorkel in his hand. "Boy, you guys are never going to believe how far lost I am!"

Chapter Twenty

The man with the epaulettes looked up at him. "Who the hell are you?" The man was confident as he spoke; his brown eyes scrutinizing, and his face set to the hardened image of a man familiar with interrogations. "And what are you doing here?"

"Sam Reilly," he replied, studying the stranger. Definitely the most senior of the three men he'd seen. He spoke English without an accent. His face showed several scars. At least three obviously missing teeth and those that were still in place were rotten. Unlike the other two mercenaries with him, who carried AK-47s, this one wore a sidearm. Confident in his men, the weapon had remained in its holster. Sam uncrossed his arms. "I'm searching for the hidden treasures of the ancient Garamantes."

The commander laughed. It was loud and boisterous and stopped as suddenly as it had commenced. "I am General Gabe Ngige. Did you have any luck?"

Sam took a gentle breath in as he heard the name. The coincidence was staggering. *But what was he doing in the Sahara, searching for an old book?* "I beg your pardon, what did you want to know?"

"Did you find the ancient city of gold?" General Ngige asked. "The Garamante civilization lost to centuries of greed, myth and legends."

Sam grinned. "You don't believe it exists, do you?"

"No. And I don't believe you were searching for it, Mr. Reilly." Ngige looked at the two Uzis next to the camels. "So, do you always go armed when you're looking for treasure?"

"Yeah, well you never know what sort of people you might run into in a big desert like this. Not all of them are likely to be as friendly as you."

"You know what I think?" The general crossed his arms.

"What?" Sam asked, feigning indifference while the other two men in camouflaged desert uniforms searched him for any weapons.

Ngige stared at him. His face hard and intense. "I think you're here with the girl. I think you were searching for the book of Nostradamus."

"That's what this is about?" Sam asked. "You're after an old book of lies by Michel Nostradamus? What the hell do you expect to find?"

"Answers! I expect to find answers!"

"To what?"

"To the future, of course!" General Ngige smiled cruelly. "I think it has already cleared up your future. You will give me the book now or I will do things to you that will make you wish your death could come sooner. So, tell me, where did you hide the book of Nostradamus."

Sam took stock of his situation. There were four guys. He knew who one of them was. General Ngige was probably the most dangerous person in the world right now. His recently successful coup to overthrow the democratically elected President of the Democratic Republic of Congo, lead to an unheard of rise to power. Not since Fidel Castro overthrew Fulgencio Batista in 1959 to become the new dictator of Cuba, had one man wielded so much power in such a short space of time. Whoever was backing him, must have known something the rest of the world hadn't, because one thing was certain – General Ngige was being well funded.

He gritted his teeth. That just left the other two men. Mercenaries, he guessed. Unlikely to be vigilantes, bandits or rebels – otherwise he'd already be dead. Instead, they were disciplined. Each of them had waited for an order from their commander before moving. And the commander had waited to interrogate him – find out who he was and why he was there. Two of the men were armed with AK-47s.

Only the general wore a sidearm. A Berretta M9, semiautomatic. Sam knew the weapon well. He'd been issued one as an Officer in the Corps. It took a casing containing 9×19mm Parabellum, the most common military handgun cartridge in the world. The weapon was also known for its reliability. It boasted the ability to fire 35000 rounds before having a misfire. If he lived long enough to get the chance to fire the weapon, Sam was pleased to know that the odds were it would work.

Sam smiled. "All right. I'll show you where she hid it. But I'd like a smoke first."

"No cigarette. Haven't you heard they are bad for your health?" The general laughed at his own joke.

"I guess I won't be alive long enough to worry about emphysema!" Sam joined in the laughter at his expense. "Seriously, you're going to kill me and you won't give me a smoke?"

The mercenary next to Sam looked at the general.

Ngige nodded. "Give it to him."

The soldier handed Sam a cigarette. Sam took it. "Thanks." He placed it in his mouth and smiled. "Can I trouble you for a light?"

Sam watched the soldier look at his commander for approval. The general nodded and the soldier lit the cigarette. Sam breathed in deeply. His father had offered him a fine Cuban cigar when he was just fifteen years old, after winning his first sailing regatta. The thing tasted like shit then and he never developed a liking to the stuff. He managed to finish it at the time, through several bouts of heavy coughing, but he felt good none the less. Not the taste, not the sensation, but what it represented – his father, who was always the best at every single thing he tried, had given him the cigar in acknowledgement that he'd achieved something.

Standing next to General Ngige, Sam took another puff and flicked a couple pieces of ash into the water. He looked at Ngige. "Why do you want the book so much? I was told you sent a small army to fetch it."

The general looked around, as though he were trying to make an important decision about whether or not to talk. The better sense failed and his arrogant side won. "You see, a great man came to me as a child. He said he'd seen the future. I figured the guy's some sort of loony, so I let him go."

"Go on. What did he tell you?"

Ngige smiled. It was genuine and displayed his affection for the memory. "He said I had risen to great power throughout Africa. He told me he was a builder. A kind of master architect, planning the construction of a new future – and that in it, he had seen a tremendous change. He provided me a long list of predictions for my life. Each one more staggering than the first. In a few years I was to receive an inheritance from a wealthy relative I'd never heard of. His will and last living testament would stipulate that the money be spent on an education at the University of Cape Town. There I would meet a man with somewhat severe views of the politics within the Middle East and I would find myself offering my services to a rebel force, fighting for a cause I then knew nothing about. What it teaches me is that I love to fight. And for no other reason than that, I fought in eleven other conflicts throughout Africa and the Middle East as a mercenary, until I have a reputation as one of the great fighters in the world."

"So as a kid, you were told you were going to spend your life fighting other people's wars?"

"Yeah. Which was strange because at the time I had little stomach for the conflicts in my own country. It was at this point I asked the stranger how any of this had anything to do with getting rich and starting a revolution in my own country. Do you know what he said?"

"No," Sam said.

"He said he would meet me when the country needed me the most and give me the money to fund a war. Said he'd give me all the money I needed to take over the world. One day I was going to lead a revolution that would conquer all of Africa and send ripples of fear, despair and bloody war throughout the world – and when it was all over, Africa would stand united as one nation. The greatest nation on earth!"

"What did you say?"

The general laughed. "I was ten years old living in Zaire during the seventies. I'd never been to school and the only thing I knew how to do was look after the sugarcane fields my parents owned before they were brutally murdered. I survived eight of those years living through rebellion wars. That was my future. That's what I knew. If I was lucky I might have become some child soldier to a rebel force who'd take me under their wing and protect me. I was never going to lead a revolution. Besides, I had no interest in doing so!"

"So, how much of his prophecies came true?"

"Every damned one of them. My great uncle, twice removed, died and left a fortune to education. I became involved with a man who preached that real change required violence, and for a reason I'll never know, decided I wanted to watch this violent change take place in a faraway land so that I could decide for myself if it was required. It turned out, I agreed with the violence and it agreed with me."

"Did you ever see the man again?" Sam persisted.

"The builder?" The general nodded. "Three months ago. I had heard things were getting pretty bad back home in what is now called the Democratic Republic of Congo. The President was weak, and had let the country fall into ruin. When I got there the same stranger who'd predicted all the changes in my life turned up again. Would you believe it, I swear the man hadn't aged a day! Sometimes I wonder if he wasn't the hand of God, telling me what I needed to do?"

"And what did he tell you to do?"

"He gave me a fortune in gold. Not in bullion but weird religious artifacts and things. One of the things he gave me was this solid golden skull. The thing looked hideous, but also beautiful somehow at the same time. I asked him what the hell I was supposed to do with it all... and you know what he told me?"

Sam shook his head. "What?"

"Save the world. He then told me to raise an army and overthrow the current government. Once I had done that, he said I would unite all of Africa. He was so confident and everything else he'd told me had come true, I was certain that I had been given some higher purpose by God himself. And then when I felt so powerful, you know what he tells me?" The General paused for effect. "He tells me there's a book, written by

Nostradamus. He tells me he's paid a woman to find the book and that I must destroy it."

"What's inside the book?"

The General squinted at him, and answered the question obliquely. "I asked the strange builder of the future..."

"And what did he say?"

"He said he had no idea what was written inside. Only that if it was ever read the world would be sent down a tangent. A path it was never meant to follow. It may surprise you, with your western mindset, but the alternative path of the future could be a much worse one. And so I'm destroying the book, mobilizing the largest army since World War II and uniting Africa."

Sam looked at the general and thought quick and hard to answer two questions.

How did Ngige, or his mysterious benefactor know of a future that so closely resembled the worst case scenario predicted by the greatest minds of the intelligence agencies in the U.S. and abroad?

And, what was inside the book of Nostradamus that prevented that future from coming true?

Chapter Twenty-One

"Now, I'm afraid it's time you finish that cigarette and give me the book," the General said. "The sun is coming up and it's time I get a move on."

Sam nodded and took two long, deep drags in from his cigarette. He watched as the smallest of air bubbles surfaced on the otherwise still water at the edge of the oasis. His lungs stung as he inhaled the smoke, and he had to consciously make the effort not to cough. The butt of the cigarette, fueled by the oxygen rich air, glowed, burning at an unimaginably hot temperature. He withdrew the cigarette long enough to speak.

"It's in the sand." Sam said as he watched the tiny air bubbles reach the surface of the otherwise still water at the edge of the oasis.

"Where?" General Ngige asked.

More bubbles surfaced, three feet behind the general. "I buried it about twenty yards over there," Sam said, pointing away from the oasis. About halfway up the sand dune. "You should still see the recently overturned sand where I buried it."

"Deng," Ngige said. "See if he's telling the truth."

"Yes, sir," the mercenary replied.

General Ngige looked at Sam. His mouth was set hard, but his voice soft, almost betraying a sense of loss for what he was about to do. "Where do you want it?"

Sam shrugged. "If you're giving me a choice, I'll have it on a deserted island in the Caribbean in about fifty years from now."

"Very funny, Mr. Reilly." The General shaped his fingers to make a pistol and said, "Between the eyes or the back of the head?"

"Well if you're going to be impatient, I'll take it between my eyes. You can look at me while you do it."

"General!" The mercenary at the edge of the sand dune yelled. "I've got it!"

"Well… well. I must thank you for your honesty, Mr. Reilly," General Ngige said. "I really don't like torture, although it is the only choice in certain circumstances. I am so glad that you didn't force this to be one of them."

Sam drew a deep breath in, as though it were his last. The cigarette burned right down to its butt. The mercenary next to him attached a full magazine to his AK-47.

In the distance the three men heard the second mercenary yelling something. All three turned to look, and saw the mercenary waving both hands frantically.

"What does that fool want?" the General asked.

"It appears he's trying to warn you about something," Sam said, cheerfully.

"What?" the General asked.

"This!" Tom yelled, withdrawing the sidearm from the General's holster. In the same movement he aimed the Berretta at the closest mercenary – the one pointing his AK-47 towards Sam – and pulled the trigger.

The mercenary swung his weapon around. But he was too slow. By the time he faced his attacker two Berretta 19mm parabellums struck his forehead – turning it into a pink spray in an instant. His weapon finger pulled at the trigger, emptying all 32 shells in a wide arc by the time his body hit the ground.

The General reacted with reflexes that were much faster than his age suggested. Swinging his right arm he punched Tom in the area known by boxers as the sweet spot at the side of his jaw. The inertia forces the mandible sideways potentially sending all residual energy into the brainstem with the greatest likelihood of knocking most opponents out.

Tom Bower was far from average.

He was a giant of a man. Six foot, eight inches tall. Framed in two hundred and forty pounds of muscle, hardened by a lifetime of heavy physical labor. He'd never boxed professionally, but he'd had his share of bar-fights when he was younger and he had no trouble holding his own. If there was ever a man whose jaw was built to take a beating, Tom was that man.

Sam watched the General's fist make contact with Tom's jaw. He was certain the impact hurt the General as much as it did Tom. The impact rattled Tom momentarily, but was far from enough to put him down. The General looked surprised that Tom was still standing. Ngige launched forwards for the Berretta, which was still locked in Tom's massive hand. Like a crazed banshee, he bit at Tom's hand, trying to free the weapon.

Sam ground the butt of his cigarette, burning at a temperature of eight hundred degrees Fahrenheit, deep into the General's right eye. The General screamed in agony. Instead of fighting, the General turned and ran.

Chapter Twenty-Two

Sam raced to catch the General and then dived to the ground. AK-47 shells raked the sand eight feet to his side. The second mercenary, the one who'd gone to retrieve the book of Nostradamus, no longer afraid of hitting his commander, had taken aim and was firing at them.

"You okay, Tom?" Sam asked.

"I'm good," Tom replied. "He got a lucky hook shot at me, that's all."

Sam shuffled forwards on his elbows and knees. He picked up the AK-47, which had fallen when Tom had killed the first mercenary. "Let's just hope this guy doesn't get a lucky shot off."

"You get him, and I'll get the important looking guy!" Tom said and started running towards the General.

Sam lined the crosshairs with the mercenary standing in the distance. He breathed in deeply. Forced himself to relax and breathe out slowly. Consciously slowing his heart rate in the process. Midway through exhaling he paused for an instant and pulled the trigger - releasing a burst of three bullets.

The shots went wide by several feet to the left and the mercenary dropped to the sand. The weapon hadn't been correctly calibrated. Sam gritted his teeth and searched for the mercenary again. He'd watched the now dead mercenary reload the full magazine just before Tom arrived. Sam made the mental calculation. At least ten rounds fired before the mercenary died, plus the three he'd just fired. That left him with seventeen from the original thirty round magazine.

"You got eyes on the shooter?" Tom asked.

Sam scanned the sand dune in the distance and stopped. The back of the guy's legs were just visible above the sand. Nothing to shoot at, but so long as the other guy's head stayed down, they were safe. "I've got him. He's holed up over there."

"Are there any others?"

"No. Just him and the guy who got the lucky punch."

"Okay. You take care of the shooter and I'll get the other guy!" Tom said.

"Sounds good."

Sam watched Tom come to a crouched standing position and run in the direction of where the General had fled. Tom's height, combined with his massive frame made for an awesome opponent. Sam quickly returned his glance toward his attacker.

The shooter lifted his head, unable to resist the target. Sam corrected for the inaccuracies of his weapon and squeezed the AK-47's trigger.

Sand, approximately two feet to the left of the shooter's head, turned into small clouds of dust. Sam watched as the shooter's head disappeared again. Sam gritted his teeth. He'd overcorrected.

Over the sand dune, where Tom had run, Sam heard the distinct popping sound of the Barretta being fired. He hoped the sound meant the General had been shot, but there was always a risk the General had a second weapon.

Sam adjusted his position slightly to the right, trying to get a clearer shot. Nothing. All he could see was the guy's ankle and boot. It looked like the shooter was less interested in showing his face again.

Sam swore. He could wait in the stalemate for hours. Neither of them getting a clear shot until one of them slipped up. Sam sunk into a relaxed firing position. He carefully made the adjustments to his focus. Moving approximately two feet further to the right and then settled, ready to fire.

He breathed in slowly. And then exhaled even slower. Each breath slightly adjusting the position of his weapon until he was certain of his aim. On the third breath Sam squeezed the trigger – and a spray of pink mist replaced the boot.

Sam grinned. Finally, the AK-47 was firing true.

He heard the guy yelling in his own language. It didn't matter that Sam couldn't speak a word of it. Swearing sounds the same all around the world. Sam focused in where the shooter had disappeared.

There was nothing but sand.

It meant the mercenary was well trained. Even a good soldier would be inclined to roll around in agony. It would be a reasonable mistake, and if the shooter had made it, Sam would have killed him.

But the mercenary was well trained. Disciplined. And that meant more waiting. Sam heard the rapport of three shots fired from the Berretta followed by the mechanical clicking sound of an empty chamber.

Sam had run out of time. If Tom had run out of bullets he was in trouble. He stood up and ran toward the injured mercenary. Sam's trigger finger squeezed the edge of the trigger. He was ready to fire the first shots if he had to. Without hesitation he ran up the sand dune.

The mercenary reached for his weapon. His mouth set hard, and his eyes filled with intense hatred, the injured man aimed the AK-47 right at Sam. But his reaction was too slow.

Sam fired several shots in rapid fire succession. He bent down and searched the mercenary's lifeless body. He took two full magazine as spares for his AK-47 and then called out to Tom.

"You okay, Tom?"

No answer.

Shit! Sam ran through the thick sand dune, following the deep imprints where Tom's heavy feet had trod.

He rounded the first crest and found Tom slowly walking back towards him.

"Tell me you got him!" Sam said.

"No. He was quick for a man who just lost his eye. By the time I reached the second ridge I knew I wasn't going to catch him. I emptied the

Berretta trying to get lucky and put him down, but he disappeared over that far ridge."

Sam swore. "How could you let him get away?"

Tom laughed. "What can I say, I never was a very good runner. By the way, you're welcome."

"For what?"

"I just saved your life!"

"And I appreciate it. I just wished you hadn't let him slip through our fingers in the process."

"Don't worry," Tom replied, looking at the burning sun rise above the horizon. "Without water, the desert will finish him off before nightfall. Who was he, anyway?"

"General Ngige. The rebel leader of the Democratic Republic of Congo – and the most dangerous man in Africa."

Sam and Tom turned to walk back to the oasis.

"What's he doing this far north?" Tom asked.

"Beats me. He says he came to find the book of Nostradamus."

"Why? What did he expect to read in it? His future?"

"No. He thinks he already knows his future."

"Then what did he want it for?"

"Said he needed to destroy it, to protect his future."

In the distance, on the other side of the oasis, Sam could see a figure swimming towards the surface. Above it were several bubbles. The woman whose life he'd saved, was about to surface. *Good. She might just give me the answer to a number of questions.* He glanced to the other side of the oasis and spotted a fourth man – another mercenary, carrying an AK-47, running towards her.

Chapter Twenty-Three

Zara waited as long as possible to surface from her refuge beneath the cooled water of the oasis of Bilma. The longer she remained there the more likely her attackers would leave, or be killed by the treasure hunter who'd saved her life. There was still a high probability the treasure hunter would have been killed instead.

She stared at the dive gauge through blurred eyes, unprotected by a mask. The gauge read 10 BAR or possibly 70 BAR. It was impossible to differentiate between the one and the seven the more she stared at the instrument with blurry eyes. Zara had done a dive course years ago, while on a short vacation to the Red Sea off the coast of Egypt. BAR, she recalled, was a measurement of pressure representing a standard atmosphere. Or technically slightly less than a single atmosphere at sea level. Ten BARs meant there were ten times the pressure which the air would exert on the tank if it was at sea level. Depending on the size of the dive tank, BAR represented a different value of air. For example, a 3L tank is going to hold significantly less air than a 12L tank. For each BAR of pressure in the larger of the two tanks, the diver would have four times as much air volume.

There was no way she could remember all the technical details, but Zara knew that 10 BAR meant she was dealing in minutes before the tank ran out. She slowly maneuvered herself toward the surface. Stopping her ascent at three feet from the surface, because she heard gunfire.

She remained at that depth until it became hard to draw air from the regulator. Once she could no longer breathe at all, she moved right to the edge of the oasis and surfaced. Zara allowed no more than her eyes and nose to break the surface and even then, she was right up against the shoreline. The sound of gunfire had ceased. She turned in the water and scanned the oasis. The treasure hunter's camp she'd spotted earlier had been tossed into disarray. The camels had all gone. *Did that mean the treasure hunters had left without her?* They would probably want their dive equipment back. It was more likely the beasts had been spooked by the gunfire and run off.

Her eyes stopped at the location where she'd first fallen into the oasis. Zara's gaze traced the footprints from the water, up the sand dune, to where she'd dropped the book of Nostradamus. Next to her old footprints, were a second set of deep impressions in the sand. At a guess, they were from a large man, unaccustomed to the gentle movements required in traversing deep sand. Her glance stopped about a third of the way up the first sand dune – where the book was now missing.

She felt the uneasy pervasiveness of panic. *Gone! It can't be lost now!* She wanted to scream out loud, "Give it back!" like a child at a playground who'd lost something precious. She forced herself to exert discretion. No book was worth losing her life over.

Zara carefully made a 360 degree turn. Scanning the area in multiple ninety degree arcs until she was certain the place was empty. Just when she was certain, Zara heard the cheerful voices of two men approaching. The question was, were they the treasure hunters who'd saved her life, or the rebel soldiers who'd tried to take it?

She ducked further into the water and waited. She didn't have to wait long. Two men shuffled down the steep sand dune on the opposite side of the oasis. One was tall and one average in height, and shared the solidly built frames of men accustomed to hard work for most of their lives. They both wore board shorts and looked like they were at the beach on vacation, except that the shorter one was carrying an AK-47.

Who are these people?

Zara stood up, ready to find out. Across the oasis, the diver who'd saved her life, raised his AK-47 and aimed at her. In the instant it took for her to comprehend the impossible, she tried to duck under the water to avoid the spray of bullets which raked the water and sand no more than a few feet away from her.

In an instant Zara discovered she hadn't reacted fast enough – and now might have to pay for it with her life.

Chapter Twenty-Four

Zara felt the heavy arm wrap around her neck and lock. Her captor knew just the right amount of pressure to keep her from being able to move at all while allowing her to remain conscious. She tried to reach her flick knife in her pants pocket, but couldn't reach far enough downwards. Instead, she launched both her hands at the arm, trying to free herself. It was tough like leather and thick as any bodybuilder she'd ever seen. She dug her short fingernails into the skin as hard as she could. Her captor didn't even grimace. She tried to find somewhere more vulnerable to attack. Her fingernails scratched at his face. The pressure on her throat tightened, instantly stopping her from being able to breathe.

"Do that again and I'll snap your neck," he said.

Zara made no reply.

"Now, you're gonna tell me where that book is, bitch!"

Zara tried to speak, but her captor was pressing on her neck so hard her windpipe was being crushed. She made little more than a muffled, incomprehensible sound. Her eyes fixed on the two treasure hunters on the other side of the oasis. Both were running down the sand dune towards her. She grinned. *Would they really save her life twice in one day?* She needed to buy time. Zara pointed to her neck and tried to speak again. More garbled noise came out, but nothing comprehensible.

"If I release some of the pressure are you going to talk?" he asked.

Zara nodded. She felt the pressure loosen slightly and took a deep breath in. "Yes."

"Good. Now, where did you hide the book of Nostradamus?"

"I can't remember," Zara replied. "My mind's been a little rattled by the recent events. I nearly drowned and now you're trying to choke me."

"Remember soon, or your neck will snap under my arm like a chicken bone," her captor reminded her.

Zara watched as the two men on the other side of the oasis split up. One ran clockwise around the oasis, while the other went counterclockwise. They were going to double up on her captor, preparing to target him from both sides. She quietly mumbled something incoherent. The pressure on her throat noticeably loosened again.

"I buried it in the sand."

"Where?"

"Other side of the oasis. Can't be sure where, but you'll find it eventually."

"I need you to show me exactly where you buried it."

She dipped her head, like she no longer had the strength or the will to live. Her captor pulled on her hair until her head faced him. Her captor was dark skinned. He wore a camouflaged uniform like the others who'd tried to drown her. His brown eyes were wide, and he smiled as their eyes met. He had a well-developed jawline and heavy facial features, which were disrupted by his pleasant smile. It gave him the appearance of a man who didn't want to hurt her, but would force himself to, if it was the only way to achieve his goal.

He looked really happy. She guessed the treasure hunters had somehow beaten the other three men, including his commander – *so why was he so happy?* The answer hit her hard. *He wants the money, he doesn't care about a rebellion. He thinks he's going to be rich!*

She saw the shorter of the two treasure hunters, the one with the AK-47, approach quietly. She mumbled something inaudible.

"Speak up!" her captor demanded.

Zara looked directly in his eyes. "Go to hell."

"No doubt I will. But first I intend to get rich, and so I'm gonna need that book."

The soldier looked at her eyes, as though she might betray where she hid it. She stared back at him, challenging him to look away. Abruptly his grin set hard as he noticed her eyes glance to the left. At the same time, Zara felt the pressure on her throat tighten to the point she nearly passed out. The man spun around to face the man who had rescued her.

"That's close enough. Any further and I break her tiny neck. I could do it in a heartbeat. Like pulling the wings off a beautiful butterfly."

"What do you want?" The shorter man asked without lowering his AK-47.

"I want the book."

The treasure hunter smiled confidently. It appeared honest and unpracticed. She noticed the lines of his smile formed easily, like a man who smiled often. There was more to it though. Something that said, *I can have it all in life.* Comfortable. Confident. He then shrugged. "Or, I could shoot you dead now?"

"Wouldn't work," her captor responded without taking any pressure off her windpipe.

"Why not?"

"You might hit me, or you might miss. Either way, I would have enough time to break her neck. And don't think I haven't noticed the second man to my left."

The treasure hunter appeared genuinely indifferent. "I can live with it, either way."

"Look. This situation could go really bad both ways. But if you give me the book, we'll all walk away."

"What makes this book so damned valuable?"

"The book of Nostradamus tells us the future. You know the future and you know what will happen with the stock market, lotto, you name it, the book has the answers – a man without morals could do very well with such a book. I've had a hard life, but no more. Now I want to get paid. I get the book, or the girl dies."

"I'd prefer it if you didn't do that…"

"This isn't between you and me. So fuck off!"

"But I think I can make it between the two of us. Because, although I don't know anything about Nostradamus and this stupid book everyone keeps talking about, I'm pretty certain I came across it earlier. Do you want it?"

"I've already told you, the girl dies if I don't get the book."

"Well. We can't have that now, can we?" The smaller of the two divers reached into a satchel he was carrying and withdrew a leather and brass codex.

Zara stared at it. *Damn it. Please don't give it to him!*

The soldier loosened his grip at the sight of the book. "It's good to see you've decided to play ball."

"Now what?"

"Now you hand me the book and then go about whatever it is you were doing out here."

The smaller of the two divers grinned. "Okay. Sure."

She saw the book spinning through the air. A four hundred year old document written by Michel De Nostradamus and now some idiot was throwing it through the air. It landed in the water behind her.

The pressure on her throat relaxed, as her captor tried to catch the book. In the process, she was able to lean down just enough to reach her butterfly knife. She opened the knife and in one single smooth transition, sent the blade straight between her captor's 4th and 5th intercostal space in a powerful upwards motion. The blade severed his aortic arch. It was a death sentence that would take place in a matter of seconds.

The man tried to scream, but just couldn't get the air out. She withdrew the knife, and blood spurted out through the open wound with the force of a jet engine. Zara felt the pressure around her throat go limp and the massive man fall onto her back. She rolled onto her side and the dead weight dropped into the now reddish water.

She raced towards the spot where the book had struck the water. Its heavy brass codex dragged it under the water like a stone. She dived down after it, but quickly realized she would need the dive equipment to reach it. The book had already sunk to the bottom. By the time she reached it, the book would most likely be destroyed.

Zara surfaced and walked towards the two treasure hunters. "Do you have any idea what you've done?"

The shorter of the two treasure hunters backed away as she charged at him. "Yeah, we just saved your life for a second time today."

She stopped at the bank of the oasis without saying another word. She washed the blood off the blade of her knife and carefully folded the butterfly edges in on themselves, so the blade was no longer visible.

The shorter of the treasure hunters grinned. "I'm not so certain I'd do it a third time, though."

Chapter Twenty-Five

Sam looked at her. She was extremely beautiful, and he would have considered her quite stunning if she wasn't so angry. She had a dark olive complexion. It was her natural skin tone, and not caused by months spent under the harsh rays of the sun. At a guess, Sam figured she had Egyptian ancestry, although she spoke English with a tinge of French in her accent.

She had lustrous black hair, emerald-hazel eyes, long dark lashes, and high cheek bones that gave her face a regal appearance. He'd noticed her small bud of a mouth was quick to smile after he'd questioned whether he'd go to the effort of saving her life for a third time. She held herself with poise, and a sense of authority reserved for those of noble birth or born into wealth. Those who believed in their heart, they were better than others. She wore a blue akhebay, the loose fitting robe which protected everything below the shoulders of a nomadic woman, and most commonly worn by the Tuareg people of the Saharan desert. But he was willing to bet the outcome of the rebellion in the DRC, there was no way she'd spent her life in the desert. Her dark skin was unblemished, her hands looked clean and her sandals were made by the high tech hiking clothing company, Gore-Tex.

She appeared indifferent to the copious amounts of dark red blood which stained her wet robes. It made him wonder if perhaps she wasn't so high and mighty as he'd first expected. He noticed she quickly pocketed the butterfly knife, and was now frantically searching her dead captor. Unable to locate whatever it was she was after, she shuffled to the edge of the oasis and tried to climb out.

"Are you all right?" he asked offering his hand to help her up.

She refused his gesture and stood to her feet on her own. "I'm fine. I just wished you hadn't thrown my life's work into the water."

"Don't worry, we didn't," Sam replied.

"I saw you throw the brass covered codex into the oasis," she said.

Sam shrugged. "That was a six hundred year old book filled with original maps of the region. We bought it to help find what we were looking for."

"You were looking for the ancient Golden City of the Garamantes, weren't you?"

"Yes. We've been following the maps and notes of early explorers in the region."

"And did you have any luck?"

"No. It would appear the Golden City of the Garamantes is a myth."

"I could have told you that. The Garamantes built many cities in the Sahara, but none of them this far south and none of them filled with gold." Her voice was confident and imperious. Her eyes darted between Tom and Sam. Then she spotted the backpack Sam had found earlier. It was lying on the edge of the water. She quickly pulled it out and frantically emptied it. She stood close to him, meeting him eye to eye and challenged him. "Where is it?"

"Where's what?" Sam asked.

"My book!" She walked around the oasis, moving towards the next corpse and started searching. "If you've stolen it I swear to God I'll kill you both."

"I'm sorry. Let's start again. My name's Sam Reilly, and this is Tom Bower. What's your name?"

She ignored his question and persisted, "Where did you hide it?"

In an instant Sam realized he was wrong about her. She wasn't born into nobility or wealth. Her sense of authority stemmed from a background in leadership. Although, who she lead, he had no idea.

"Do you mean, a leather bound, brass binder codex?"

Her eyes showed instant recognition. "Where is it? What have you done to it?"

Sam smiled and pointed to the sand dune further along. "It's buried in the sand."

"So you did take it!"

"No. I merely buried it for safe keeping – whatever it is. I figured anything these guys were willing to kill to get their hands on, should probably be kept from them."

She looked at where he'd buried the book and said nothing. She then walked up the next sand dune. She immediately spotted where the sand had recently been turned over and used her hands to dig the codex free.

Sam turned to face Tom, who was grinning in fascination. "Well, what do you make of that?"

"I don't think she likes you, Sam."

"No. Too bad. But from what I've seen so far, I can't say I'm too fond of her either."

They followed her, and watched as she found the leather bound book and shook off the sand. Once confident it was dry and free of any sand, she undid the latch and confirmed the pages were still there. She smiled. It wasn't quite a model's smile. Instead it was definitely something more empress-like. It portrayed her relief, but also showed that she was in command of the situation.

She latched the codex and turned to face him again. "Now. Where are the camels? We need to get out of here!"

Sam put his hands in his pockets and sighed. "Well. About that. I'm afraid one of the camels took a bullet to its head in the crossfire and the others got spooked and ran off."

She spat on the ground. "Fools! How could you let them get away?"

"I'm sorry," Sam said without hiding the sarcasm from his voice. "I was a little busy at the time – trying to save your life again!"

She ignored him and walked back towards where the camels had been. She found her green headdress and wrapped it around her head and face, leaving just enough room to see out. She picked up a large plastic water container and placed it in her carry pack, and then headed south, further into the Erg of Bilma.

"Where the hell are you going?" Sam yelled.

She turned for a moment and looked to the north. A giant sand cloud was visible several miles back. Sam thought it was either a small sand storm or a legion of rebels on camelback. "I need to get away – before the rest of his men arrive."

Sam turned to Tom who was already focusing his binoculars on the sand storm. "Tell me that's not what she thinks it is!"

Tom's jaw went rigid. "At a guess I'd say at least five hundred men on camel. Maybe five miles back. It could be closer to a thousand."

"Ah, Christ..." Sam swore and then picked up the two remaining carry bags he'd taken off the camels earlier in the day to set up camp. He and Tom quickly donned their cooling suits, wrapping their nomadic robes over the top. Sam grabbed his full water bottle and sand goggles. He checked the remaining Uzi. Its chamber was empty. There were no bullets left in its magazine and the spares were kept in the remaining pack, which had still been attached to the camels that had run into the desert. The second Uzi had been thrown into the water by one of the soldiers. Tom handed him an AK-47 he'd stolen from one of the dead men. Sam checked – the magazine was full.

"I found five spare magazines for that, too," Tom said.

"Thanks."

"So, what do you want to do?"

Sam turned to face south, where two light footprints lead deeper into the Erg of Bilma. "Now we follow the strangest woman I've met for a long time."

Chapter Twenty-Six

Adebowale heard the sound of roaring water fighting its way through the tunnel. The strength of the noise was getting louder. It was driven by the unimaginable pressures from above as the torrent charged through the narrow passages and warrens of the mine with the energy of a tsunami. Compared to the approaching onslaught, Adebowale's massive and athletic structure appeared weak and fragile. There was nowhere to run. Given a ten minute head start, the water would reach him well before he could ever escape. There was nothing for it, and yet he tried to run.

He always did.

Every time it was exactly the same. He felt the burning sensation in his legs and arms as the release of adrenaline stimulated his fight or flight response. He'd played college football in the US as a quarterback and despite his massive frame was capable of moving quickly when he wanted. He felt the tendons of his calves, designed for short bursts and sprints, propel him like a racecar. It felt good. Like maybe this time he would make it.

The pitch of the churning water increased and he imagined his death at any moment. Despite his speed, he felt like he was running through mud. With each movement his legs were being slowed as though an invisible coil was restraining them.

Ahead, the passage split into two directions. Left and right. Adebowale chose left. Somehow it felt correct. The narrow tunnel had a distinct incline to it, which meant he was gaining elevation. He'd made the right choice! The only way to outrun the water, was to rise above it.

The tunnel appeared dark ahead. The dimly lit lights that lined the shaft looked like they'd suddenly been cut off. He continued running at full speed in a way that only an athlete could and then he stopped. Directly in front of him, a large cave-in had blocked his progression.

He'd run out of places to escape! He turned and watched as the water raced toward him with lethal finality. In an instant, and like last time, Adebowale realized he'd been here before. And like every other time before that, the water struck him with such force he lost consciousness before his mind could even register the sensation of the cold water on his skin.

He woke up, struggling to breathe. His chest pounding, and his lungs stung. Sweat dripped from his blood drained skin. Adebowale looked up at the sun. The pain lasted longer than usual this time. He still felt difficulty breathing, and his tongue felt dry and cracked. His right shoulder throbbed.

He'd had another dream.

It made Adebowale feel good. For once he was glad of the visions which had cursed for as long as he could remember. It reassured him that he was going to die in a place very different to the one he was now trapped.

He tried to move his arms again, see if there was any more give than last time – before he'd passed out. The restraints had been well placed. Although the rope bound his wrists, and allowed him to move his hands, they were too far apart for him to reach with his fingers. He tried to bend his knees and adjust his position, but even they had been bound so well that he'd been forced to remain standing since his injury.

They had shot him three times in his chest. The bullets, he guessed, had pierced just above his right lung, narrowly avoiding killing him. The shots had been targeted there on purpose. It had never been his enemy's intention to let him die a quick death. Instead, he'd been left to die beneath the heat of the sun – the Sahara's most deadly weapon. If dehydration didn't kill him today or tomorrow, his wound would fester and send him into a delirium filled with the nightmares of his future.

He looked at the sun and laughed. The heat was going to be particularly bad today. A person in good health would be lucky to survive until sunset, but someone with his injuries would certainly die. He wasn't afraid. He'd seen his death and it wasn't today. The laugh became louder. The insane rant of a man who'd discovered the benefit of knowing the precise circumstance of your death was that, until that time, he was immortal.

Chapter Twenty-Seven

It took Sam nearly fifteen minutes to catch up with the woman whose life he'd just saved. He'd followed her tracks at a pace between a fast walk and a jog and then slowed to a pace just above a walk to match hers. She paid little attention to him. Tom trailed behind, like the tortoise and the hare.

Confident, slow and steady was going to be the only way to walk across the desert, Sam wondered how long she could keep up like this, knowing it would be a death sentence for her once the sun reached overhead. He and Tom still had their experimental DARPA cooling suits, but she had nothing but her robes. The town of Bilma was another forty miles south. They might actually reach it, but he doubted she would if she kept moving at such a high pace.

He said, "Hello. Let's start again. My name's Sam Reilly and my friend trailing behind is Tom Bower. What's your name?"

"Zara Delacroix." Her eyes never left the horizon. "Doctor Delacroix."

"Medical, or of Philosophy?" Sam asked.

"Philosophy. Archeology. Why do you ask?"

"Just curious." Sam smiled. "What's your story?"

She kept walking and said nothing. Her face was barely visible because of the finely wrapped green headdress. From what he could see, her jaw was hardened with determination and her eyes fixed on the horizon.

"Hey, I just saved your life!" Sam persisted.

"No you didn't!" Her eyes turned on him, without pausing in her stride. "You postponed my death by a day or so. Nothing more."

"Why? Who's coming for you?"

She remained silent, focused and intent.

"We can help defend you," Sam said, holding out the AK-47 he'd stolen from one of the dead men. "Just tell me what's going on?"

She shook her head. "I wouldn't bother wasting your energy carrying the AK-47."

"Why not?"

"If they catch up with us, we're dead. No matter what weapons we have. There's too many of them. Close to a thousand I'd guess. Maybe only five hundred will reach us in time, but that will be sufficient." She spoke good English, with a heavy French accent.

"Who are they?" Sam asked.

She shrugged. "Mercenaries, nomadic tribes, rebels from any number of Africa's discontent nations, who can say? He will have placed a massive bounty on the return of the book I'm carrying. There will be enough gold capable of making any man a master. And all of these men want to be their own master."

"Do you mean, General Ngige?" Sam asked.

She nodded. "That's the one."

"The current rebel leader who appears to have staged the most successful military coup in the DRC's history?"

"Yeah. He came over here with an army of mercenaries from throughout Africa to steal a book I've spent my life searching for. Although why he's suddenly discovered a newfound interest in archeology beats me."

He kept pace with her and said nothing.

"General Ngige was in the group of men who tried to kill me back there at the oasis. You must have killed him when you saved my life." She spoke matter-of-factly, without any tone of appreciation or hint of gratitude. "You're lucky you did. I've heard that he was probably one of the greatest military strategists of our time. He commanded loyalty from his soldiers that bordered on religious fanaticism. In exchange he looked after them well. They were well funded, well trained, and all of his men were offered land once they won the war."

"You know a lot about him?" Sam asked. "If you've been in the Saharan desert for some time searching for this book, I'm surprised you know so much about what's going on in the Democratic Republic of Congo."

"I have a large following myself." Again, she said it as a statement, not as a boast. "People have flocked from all over Africa to help me search for this book. One of them came from the Kingdom of Zaire, before it became the DRC. He lost everything in the coup during the early nineties, and has spent the last thirty years planning on returning with an army. He keeps me well informed. Believe me when I say, you're extremely lucky to have killed Ngige when you had the chance. If he was still alive, I would recommend killing yourself now before he captures you, which inevitably, he would do."

Sam sighed. "I suppose now's as good a time as any to inform you that we didn't kill General Ngige. Although I doubt he will survive through the day, let alone long enough to catch us."

"What do you mean? He never would have let us escape if you hadn't killed him!"

"Tom stole his handgun, and I burned a cigarette butt into his right eye. He ran off into the desert while we were fighting his mercenaries. By the time Tom went after him, Ngige had too much of a head start. We figured the desert would have finished him off well before sunset. He had no water with him."

"I think you underestimate General Ngige. The man could survive out here for weeks without food, water, a compass or clothing. He wasn't just given the position of leader. He was born into it. He was made the perfect soldier. He'll be alive, and he's going to be pissed as all hell. So now I'll be dead by tomorrow, and you will too."

Sam thought back to Ngige's own description of how he'd been given the position of rebel leader by a strange man who could see the future. He doubted very much the man was anything but mortal. He would die, quick as any other mortal, if a bullet was placed in his head. He figured now was the wrong time to mention that's exactly how General Ngige had been given the job of the leader of the Rebellion.

"What's so important about the book?" Sam continued.

"They think it will make them rich. It holds the key to what has happened before and what will happen in the future. Most importantly, they want it because of the prophecy."

"What prophecy?"

"In the fifteen-fifties, before Nostradamus fell into ill health, he made a journey into the Saharan desert. With a small group of chosen followers, he entered the Coast of Barbary in what now lies the coast of Libya and Egypt. The group walked into the burning desert without protection, without any knowledge of what they would find, and all because Nostradamus assured them that they were going to save the world."

"From what?"

"A warrior who would go on to conquer the world."

Sam smiled, condescendingly. "Genergal Ngige believes if he gets the book, he will be the one to conquer!"

"I guess so."

"So, did Nostradamus and his group of followers save the world?" Sam stared at her. His piercing blue eyes examining her response.

"Well, if the prophecy is true, which I'm starting to believe it may be, they made it deep into the Sahara in what is now Southern Libya. There, a large sand storm developed without warning, killing almost everyone within the group, and burying the book written by Nostradamus."

"A book of prophecies?" Sam asked. "This is all about some fabled prophecies?"

"Yes. But there's a little more to it than that. You see, there was one survivor other than Nostradamus himself. That survivor was said to one day have a son, who in turn had a son, and this process continued, until one day a daughter would be born. The birth of that daughter would signify the time was near to complete the prophecy. The daughter would discover the place where the book had been buried in the sand for nearly four hundred years, and in doing so, she would save humanity."

"And the girl was born?" Sam asked.

"I was the girl."

"This is about some stupid book written by Nostradamus?" Sam continued again.

"Yes."

"Then why not leave it for them to find and we'll get on with our lives?"

She shook her head, and made her descent down the steep gradient of a large sand dune. "I can't do that."

Sam struggled to keep his footing as she skipped lithely down the next sand dune. He lost balance and slid down to the bottom of the dune. Sam watched Tom follow his example, sliding more carefully.

Sam sped up to catch up with Zara again and continued where the conversation had left off. "Why? You need the money that badly?"

"No."

"Then what is it?" Sam asked.

"What I do with the book now is very important. It will affect the future."

"In what way?" Sam persisted.

"Don't ask. You wouldn't believe it if I told you. I didn't believe it even when my own father told me and I was just five years old. Instead I had to see it with my own eyes."

Sam grinned. He'd seen some pretty amazing phenomena in his time. "Try me."

"Okay, what I do with the book now will determine if humanity gets to continue to exist – or whether it becomes extinct."

Sam humored her. "So what are you supposed to do with the book to save humanity?"

"That's just it. I have no idea, whatsoever – and neither did Nostradamus."

Chapter Twenty-Eight

Zara stopped for a moment and took a drink of water from the flask she'd taken off the dead mercenary who'd nearly killed her at the oasis. It was midday. The sky was a pale blue and so hot it looked almost white. The sun a diffuse glare, blurring the lines of the sand dunes and the sky into one mangled wreck of heat, as though it was located everywhere. She squinted as she forced herself to look back at the horizon where they had come.

A plume of sand rose ungainly into the sky like a giant smoke stack from an old steamship. They were getting closer. She glanced at her new companion. He'd noticed it too and said nothing. His mouth was set hard with determination; his blue eyes were pensive and he looked like he'd surmised precisely what she had – their pursuers were approaching rapidly, gaining on them significantly every hour, and driven by greed.

Zara attached the lid to the flask, looked at him and said, "They're half a day's ride away, at best." She started walking again without waiting for his response.

"We'll never outrun them on foot," Sam said, putting his flask away and trying to match her pace.

"No. I'm hoping we won't have to."

"You think we're close to the camels?"

"No. I'm hoping we're getting further away."

Sam looked around at the sand in front of them. "Further away?"

"Have you seen tracks recently?" she asked.

"No. I lost sight of them coming down that deep sand dune. I assumed you were still tracking them."

"I was until I realized we'd never catch up to the camels in time. Even if we did, they looked in a poor condition, certainly unlikely to be able to carry us out."

"So you decided to make the conscious decision to change direction, hoping your pursuers would follow the heavier camel prints in the sand, instead of slowing down and noticing ours?"

She nodded and said nothing.

"Won't they see us on the horizon?"

"Might do, if we aren't quick enough."

"And are we?"

She nodded again. "They're going to need to stop and water their beasts before they continue. They'll wait in the worst heat of the day in the expectation they'll easily catch us afterwards. As for us, we'll have to keep walking through the worst of the heat. Can you do that, Mr. Reilly?" She said the last bit as a challenge.

"It looks as though we don't have much of a choice, do we Dr. Delacroix – "

"Just, Zara," she corrected him. "I think we're well beyond surnames whether we like it or not."

"Pleased to meet you, Zara." Sam smiled at her, revealing a kind face and handsome blue eyes.

"You won't be once they catch up with us, which they almost certainly will."

"Wow, aren't you full of optimism. Look, Tom and I have been in a few close scrapes over the years – we're not easily killed. We'll find a way out of this."

"This is not the ocean, Mr. Reilly. I think you'll find the Sahara is far less forgiving than any sea you've ever visited."

"How did you know who I am?" Sam asked.

"I'm an archeologist. I read your dissertation on the Mahogany Ship."

"What did you think?"

"I think the Sahara is a much larger desert than anything found in Australia, and far more dangerous than you grant it."

Chapter Twenty-Nine

Sam stopped at the crest of the next highest sand dune. He checked his compass and looked out. At least six other dunes were easily visible in the distance. A small town, barely anything more than a trading post blended with the horizon like a mirage. "How long do you think it will take to reach?"

He watched as Zara made a mental note of their location. Zara had no navigational equipment, no compass, sextant or GPS, but she spoke with the authority of someone who'd traveled the regions for so many years and intrinsically knew her precise location. "I could do it in three days. With you, it might take four. We'll have to continue at this pace. It will be a hard walk before we reach Mao. That's considering you and your friend survive the journey at all."

"Mao?" Sam looked at her face to see if he'd misunderstood her. He vaguely recalled looking at the place on a map earlier, but he and Tom had ruled Mao out as being too far south for the American agent to make the diamond transition, so they had left it. "Are you talking about the desert outcrop deep into Chad and bordering Niger?"

"Yeah." She smiled at him. "Where did you think I was heading?"

"I don't know about you, but Tom and I are heading to the township of Bilma. It's less than fifteen miles to the west of us. Once there, we should be able to pay someone to get us out."

She laughed. "Who do you think you're dealing with? Someone inside General Ngige's rebel army will have a satellite phone. By now, Nigige would have phoned his contacts in Bilma. We go there, we'll get captured for sure." She shook her head. "Much better to risk dying out here than getting captured by one of Ngige's men."

"Okay, so even if you can make the trek on foot – what is it, two hundred miles?"

"Two-fifty," she said without pausing to calculate.

"Then what?"

"Then we get the hell out of the Sahara and the whole damned African continent for that matter. I work out what the hell Nostradamus wanted me to do with his damned book or sell it and make my fortune. And you can go back to searching for whatever it really was you were looking for here. Because I'm pretty certain you know better than to go looking for the Golden City of the Garamantes this far south."

Sam said nothing and watched as Tom caught up with them. He appeared completely unfazed by the exertion of nearly six hours hard walking through the desert. As Sam expected, Tom's slow and steady method was going to allow him to win the race.

Tom looked at the two of them. "Where do you want to head?"

"We're working that out now," Sam said looking at Zara. "She wants to skip Bilma and head further south on to Mao. What do you think?"

"I think crossing a desert on foot with only a few flasks of water is insane."

"So, you think we head to Bilma?" Sam asked.

Tom shook his head. "No. Crossing the desert on foot is insane, but heading towards Bilma is suicide. There must be close to a thousand men following our trail. Anyone with that much of an army in the area must have people capable of resupplying them. With Bilma being by far the closest, I doubt we'd last the hour, before someone handed us over to the General." He grinned. "And after you burned out one of his eyes, I can't image him being very understanding when he gets you."

Sam looked back at Zara again. "Okay, Mao it is. What direction is it?"

Zara pointed and both Sam and Tom took a compass bearing with their wristwatches.

"All right, I'll meet you there," Tom said and continued his slow and steady pace down the next sand dune.

Zara followed, next to Tom, making sure no one followed in each other's footsteps, so that the trail was hard to follow if Ngige's men ever pick it up. Sam trailed last, taking one last glance over his shoulder at the sand plume, the only sign of the army gaining on them. It had moved towards the west, and for the first time since they'd left the outlying Bilma oasis, the size had shrunk – which meant their pursuers had taken the bait, and were following the camel's tracks and not theirs.

Sam grinned and caught up with Zara. "What's the population of Mao?"

"About nineteen thousand," Zara replied.

"Won't Ngige have contacts there, too?"

"Of course he does, but I doubt he'd believe we'd be stupid enough to try and cross the desert on foot."

"Without anywhere to fill up on water we'll never make it, will we?"

"I grew up in these deserts." Her hazel eyes appeared a dark green in the sunlight. They were wide and full of mystery. There was something hardened about her face that Sam couldn't quite place. It seemed at odds with her natural beauty. There was the sort of resounding confidence, and hardened resolve, of a person who'd experienced some incredible pain for so much of her life, that it had simply become a part of her. She had accepted it as a fact. It was neither good nor bad. Yet, despite that, she was still quite capable of seeing the beauty of some of the most unique experiences of life. Her hardened face was broken by a grin. He'd seen that sort of grin before in the mirror. It meant, whatever happened, she was going to beat it. "This place is full of water if you know where to look."

"And you know where to look?"

She nodded and said nothing.

"So, if we make it, and Ngige's men don't capture us in Mao – how do you propose we get out without being caught?"

"I have a friend. A good friend. He comes and goes from time to time. He owns a small plane. A Beechcraft Bonanza 36. Runs a private charter and supply service throughout the region. He'll get us out. That's if we survive long enough to reach Mao."

Chapter Thirty

They walked through the day and most of the night, pausing infrequently to drink and rest. Zara took the slightest sigh of relief when she noticed the plume of sand completely absent from the horizon when the first light of the predawn sun finally broke the next morning.

By midday it sweltered to 121 degrees Fahrenheit. She stopped to drink and stared at her two companions. They both looked tired, but nowhere near as much as they should have been. She remembered reading somewhere that Sam Reilly spent time in some sort of military specialist forces unit before turning to a unique career in both marine biology and maritime archeology. She knew very little about his friend, Tom.

Were they both still members of an elite armed force?

Or were they here as mercenaries?

She doubted it. Sam Reilly was much too rich to offer his services as a mercenary. Besides, she'd never heard of a Tuareg nomad crossing a desert on foot with such ease, which meant they were using some sort of mechanical device to assist. But how, she couldn't imagine.

She watched both men from a distance. They appeared to be chatting amongst themselves as though they were old friends out for a stroll without a care in the world. Part of Sam's desert robe had loosened and opened at the back. She saw he wore a shirt underneath. It was silver and shimmered remarkably. For a moment she wondered if it was the intense heat playing tricks on her eyes, like a mirage – before she grinned with understanding.

Got you, you bastards!

She carefully replaced the lid to her water flask and swung it's strap over her shoulder, before hurrying to catch up with both men who were now walking side by side, chatting. "All right, one of you want to tell me why you were really here?" she asked.

"What do you mean?" Sam asked.

Tom shrugged as though the conversation wasn't for him, and picked up his pace to distance himself. She watched as he continued following the same bearing they'd been on for the past twenty-four hours.

"At first I thought you and Tom were hardened, ex-soldiers, capable of super human stamina. I've never seen a westerner walk through the Sahara during the hottest times of the day, almost unaffected by the sweltering heat. Then I realized you're wearing some sort of temperature suit. I've read about them. Real expensive. Mainly used in the military. Kind of experimental, although, if you two are anything to go by, I guess they're no longer experimental."

She stared at Sam's face for a reaction, but he gave none and remained silent.

"So, what's your story?"

"What story?"

"What were you really doing in the Sahara with those dive tanks?" Her eyes fixed on his with mesmerizing scrutiny.

Sam met her gaze and to his own surprise, offered her the truth, or a very near version of it. "We were looking for about five million dollars of raw diamonds."

She asked, "Why?"

"Does anyone ever need an excuse to want to find five million dollars?"

"I mean, why do you care?" Zara asked. "I may have read a little more than the one dissertation about the Mahogany Ship. I know a little about you. Your father owns Global Shipping and you manage a strange offshoot called Deep See Projects. Until recently, most people assumed you were the typical third generation in a wealthy family."

Sam stared at her blankly, betraying little recognition.

She smiled. "The third in a wealthy generation often spends the fortune the earlier two had spent their lives accumulating. Interestingly, in recent years, you've created some wealth in your own right, made significant archeological findings, assisted several governments in complex ocean problems, and made quite a name for yourself as a bit of a trouble shooter."

Zara stared at him, waiting for a sign of acknowledgement. Either agreement that she was right, or an attempt to clear up her version of his life's history. When she didn't receive one she said, "So, you're looking for diamonds?"

He nodded his head, but remained silent.

"In the Saharan desert?" She smiled. It was practiced, and teasing, generally capable of making any man open up to her. "Not a lot of diamonds found in the Sahara, you know."

"I know, we didn't find any," Sam said.

"Are you going to tell me anything, or shall we go our own ways."

"That depends," Sam said.

"On what?"

"On how much you know about the United Sovereignty of Kongo?"

"Nothing," she lied. "Should I have?"

"They were a small group of people who wanted to overthrow the current dictatorship in the Democratic Republic of Congo. Their leader stems from a modern-day Bundu dia Kongo sect favoring the reviving of the original kingdom of Kongo through secession from Angola, the Republic of the Congo, the Democratic Republic of the Congo, and Gabon."

She projected an appearance of indifference, but her mind immediately raced to her self-professed body guard in Sahara, Adebowale. He had once told her his family, who were leaders in the Bundu dia Kongo movement had been killed when he was just a young boy, and he'd spent his entire life trying to find a means of returning. Adebowale had told her their two lives had been intertwined for centuries since his great ancestor, a Kongo king, had been saved by her great ancestor – and that one day, the great prophecy would come true, and their families would unite Africa with a success never before seen throughout history.

"So, what's new?" she asked.

"This one has the backing of the U.S. Government."

Chapter Thirty-One

She walked in silence for a while. Contemplating what Sam had told her. It seemed impossible to her, but so did a lot of other things until forty-eight hours ago.

Is it possible Nostradamus knew I would meet Sam Reilly?

She asked. "I thought you guys didn't take sides anymore in non-elected rebellions and leadership coups. Didn't you learn your lesson, after Saddam Hussein?"

Sam smiled, like he'd heard the same argument before. "We don't. Not publically, anyway. But they have a new leader, and this guy looks to be the real deal. Someone who might just have a chance of stopping the merry-go-round cycle of changing dictatorships, each one more ruthless and dangerous than his predecessor. Current Intelligence Agencies from around the world believe the current dictator is going to send Africa into one of the greatest wars the world has ever seen. In contrast, our person has the chance to bring some real long-term stability to the region. He paid a hundred million dollars in uncut diamonds in exchange for modern weapons to initiate his coup. An American agent confirmed the diamond exchange had taken place, and was just in the process of extracting the diamonds when he went missing."

"Who's the guy?" she asked.

"What guy?"

"Who's the leader of the United Sovereign of Kongo?"

"We don't really know."

She stared at him, flummoxed. "Your government offered a hundred million dollars worth of weapons to fund a coup, whose leader you don't even know?"

"We know about him. I know. It sound ridiculous."

"It is ridiculous," she said, emphatically.

"The truth is the entire movement is underground. When West Berliners talked about changing government before the wall came down in 1988 they couldn't do so openly. Instead, they had a series of communication codes, hand gestures, and signs to show what side they're on. Our agents estimate if the DRC were to have a truly democratic election today, the leader of the USK would win with an approval rating in the high eighties. What's more, we believe, he has the possibility of uniting a part of Africa that has struggled with rebel wars and famine for many years."

She shrugged as though she really didn't care what happened to the war torn nation. "And so what happened? He lost the diamonds in the desert, and the U.S. government thought to send you to find them again?"

Sam grinned. "Yeah, you'd be surprised how close you are..."

"Why go to the trouble? Why not send the dictator they want to support the weapons? It would serve the same purpose? Why the search for diamonds?"

"Because, as you said, the American government has a policy not to take sides in foreign policy. In this instance, we're merely selling weapons to a private investor."

"That sounds like a pretty weak excuse," Zara said. "So how did you end up here?"

"The leader of the USK was siphoning blood diamonds out of the DRC to fund his regime. It was a dangerous game, but he has such a devout following that he was able to take great risks. He was able to access the diamonds, but the problem came when he wanted to get them out of the region. The least guarded, and therefore safest route, ended up being through the Sahara desert."

"So what happened?"

"There was a system. One of his men would travel into the desert, stockpile the diamonds, and then return to camp. Then someone from our side, outside the region would go and retrieve the diamonds."

"So what went wrong?"

"Six months ago, the transporter from the outside – our guy – disappeared." Sam paused. "Without any means of discovering that his partner was dead, the first guy in the process, kept depositing the diamonds. Stockpiling a fortune. That was over six months ago now."

"And you think he's been throwing them into a waterhole?"

"Yes. Where else could you put them?"

"Why not bury them in the sand?"

"You've spent long enough in the desert to realize that people can always track a person in the sand. Especially one that comes out into the desert every week. No, he's come to a waterhole, dumped his diamonds inside a secure vault and then returned. That way, if questioned he could simply argue he was searching for water and returned. All waterholes are covered in footprints."

"So you're still involved in the military?"

"No." Sam laughed. "I'm done with that life. Tom and I are here, purely as treasure hunters, hired by the American government to retrieve some stolen diamonds."

"Plausible deniability, if something goes wrong?"

"Something like that."

"Any luck finding them?"

"No."

"Really?"

"Do you see me carrying a few additional bags of highly overpriced carbon?"

She looked at him and shook her head. "Where were you going to look next?"

"We weren't," Sam said, emphatically. He pulled out a map from his top pocket. It looked old. Maybe circa 1950s, but relatively little changed in the Sahara during that time. It had been recently laminated to protect it from water. Sam passed the map to her. "We've dived all of the waterholes in this region without any luck. We were going to head home tomorrow. That was before we met you, of course."

"Have you tried expanding your search grid?" she asked, unsure why she even cared whether the American government received its diamonds to fund a war she knew little about and cared even less for.

"No. We're certain it's in there."

"How can you be?"

"Because someone kept watch on our guy for the past six months leading up to his disappearance. We know exactly where he's been. We know every single waterhole he's been to."

"You've been spying on him?"

"First of all, it wasn't us. It was our employer. And secondly – of course they were spying on their own agent. You think they'd entrust a single one of their agents with a hundred million in uncut diamonds without keeping an eye on their investments?"

"Do you have a map of all the watering spots where you think he's traveled?"

Sam nodded and handed it to her.

Zara shook her head. "Can I have another look at your map?"

"Sure, but like I said, we've dived every one of them now. We must have got it wrong somehow. He must have been using a different technique."

She stared at it for a minute. "How do I know which ones you've visited and which ones you haven't?"

"For starters, we've visited them all."

"All of them?" She gently bit the bottom of her lip as she thought about the region. She'd traveled through the area many times and used every well and every waterhole at some stage, previously. "Are you certain?"

"Yes. Everyone on that map."

"And the waterholes on this map are marked with a small circle?"

Sam nodded. "A U inside the circle means underground, such as a well, and an O inside the circle means aboveground, such as an oasis."

Zara looked at the map again. "What about the ones not marked on this map?"

"There are no other waterholes in the region. This map has all of them. This is the same map as our agent."

Zara grinned. "Then you missed one."

"No. We've dived every single waterhole on this map."

Her eyes glanced at the dozen or so waterholes and then stopped. "You've missed one."

"No. We've tracked his movements through satellite imaging. These are the only places he travels through his round south to north and returned circuits which have matched up with the other seller."

She shook her head. "No. You definitely missed one. There's a secret well dug here. It's very old, deep, and covered when not in use. Rumor is that the old Berbers built it more than a thousand years ago. Few still use it. And those who know about it try to keep it a secret. But it's definitely there."

"How can you be so certain it still exists?"

"Because I used it two months ago."

She drew an asterisk on the map, approximately ten miles ahead of them. "It's right here."

She watched Sam study the map and grin. "Are we going to pass this spot, the way we're going?"

She matched his smile. "You bet we are! In less than twenty-four hours I hope to be filling my water flask at that well."

Zara looked at Sam. He looked pleased, but not surprised. Like a person accustomed to getting lucky, or making it when he was all out luck. His grin said life was one big game and he wanted to enjoy every minute of it. It was arrogant and cute at the same time. Of course she was happy to help the man who'd saved her life, twice in the past day. But there was a small part of her, albeit not a very good part of her if she were to be honest, that almost wished he would search the well and discover the diamonds weren't there – just to see the smug grin fall from his face.

A moment later she saw how that would look. Because in the distance, she heard the distinct sound of a single engine plane flying low, which meant they were either super lucky and about to be rescued, or General Ngige had a spotter plane in the air, and everything they'd achieved was about to come to nothing.

Be careful what you wish for...

Chapter Thirty-Two

The light aircraft's engine hummed in the sweeping sand-filled expanse of the Erg of Bilma. The volume increasing with every second. Sam searched the bluish-white sky behind the three of them for the first sign of the machine. He wished Tom hadn't gotten so far ahead. Not that it mattered, Tom could hear as well as he could, and would have already taken action. Sam watched as the tiny aircraft, no more than a four person, single engine plane, broke the horizon of a distant sand dune.

It was flying at approximately a thousand feet he guessed. Much too low for a charter plane in the process of ferrying passengers in-between oasis towns. That meant it was searching for something – it was looking for them.

He looked at Zara and yelled, "Hide!"

Zara slid down the crest of the sand dune. Sam followed her. Each of them shimmied their bodies side to side until they were mostly consumed by the sand. Anything to deceive the pilot and spotters. He looked directly at her. If the pilots spotted anyone it would have been him, and not her. She looked like she blended into the sand.

Her eyes were wide, but showed no fear. "Do you think this will work?"

"I doubt it."

Sam heard the constant hum of the engine reduce pitch. The pilot had seen something and was taking the aircraft down to get a better look. The aircraft sounded like it was coming in close enough to land, although Sam knew there was no way any pilot could be coaxed to put a plane down in such deep and undulating sand. He took a deep breath and buried his face in the sand – as the aircraft flew mere feet overhead of the sand dune.

He rolled to his side and saw the plane's fixed undercarriage was so low he could have almost jumped up and grabbed it. A moment later the engine increased pitch and the aircraft climbed.

"Damnit!" Sam said as he threw off his backpack and removed the AK-47 he carried slung over his shoulder.

Sam loaded the 32 round magazine into the bolt and took aim at the aircraft, which was already becoming a tiny dot in the sky. He cursed himself for not preparing to shoot earlier. It would have been an easy shot as the damned aircraft flew overhead at a few feet above his head. Now it climbed rapidly, making it nearly impossible to hit. There was no doubt they'd been spotted. No other reason for the plane to maneuver as it had.

If there was any doubt in his mind about the pilot's intentions, they were crushed when the pilot released a thick trail of smoke as he climbed. The bastard was making an arrow into the sky. The aircraft then circled and began descending in a line next to the first one.

Sam didn't wait to see what the pilot was trying to write. Either way, it was obvious he was trying to draw a target on their back so that the hoard of pursuers would find them. Sam firmly shoved the butt of the AK-47 into his shoulder. He closed his left eye and lined up the front sight block with the aircraft's windshield using his right eye.

His breathing naturally fell into a rhythm.

Inhaling slowly.

Exhaling slowly.

On the first natural respiratory pause – the moment when the diaphragm naturally relaxes and the lungs neither inhaled nor exhaled – Sam squeezed the trigger. He emptied the entire 32 round magazine at the cockpit. The shots went wide and the pilot continued to control the aircraft. It was an impossible shot and he'd missed. The aircraft angled out of its dive and headed toward Zara and him.

Did the pilot have access to a machine gun?

It seemed unlikely. Otherwise the pilot would have simply shot them when he first had the chance and claimed the prize all for himself. Sam's eyes locked onto the pilot's face. He was still too far to make out any real image, but the eyes looked focused and the aircraft was coming straight at them. His mouth, if that was even what Sam was seeing, appeared fixed in a sinister grin. Zara was already running along the sand dune and so, Sam dived down it – trying to increase the distance between the two of them.

And then he heard the staccato of shots being fired.

Chapter Thirty-Three

Sam rolled over and took a deep breath in. He looked at the aircraft now past him. It flew level and parallel to the sand dune. It's right wingtip no more than ten feet from the dune. His shoulder was sore, where he landed, but he felt all right. He touched his face and the back of his head and then looked at his hands. There was no blood. His head was okay. He then ran his hands over his torso, hips and legs. Still no blood. He stood up. His shoulder hurt, but he could move it all right. Nothing that would kill him. He shook his head. Unable to imagine how any pilot would miss a shot like that, and then it struck him exactly how a pilot could miss such a shot.

"Zara!" He ran diagonally up the sand dune toward her.

She stood to meet him. "I'm okay."

He reached her, wrapping his arms around her. It was half an embrace and a panicked desire to see where she'd been hit. He ran his hands over her shoulders and back. Then withdrew from her and looked at her face.

"Turn around," he said.

"Why?"

"I need to see if you've been shot."

"I haven't!"

He walked around her, checking her out. She looked okay.

She smiled at him. "I'm okay, Sam. But it's nice to know you care."

He grinned suddenly. No longer looking at her. He watched as the aircraft's right wingtip clipped the side of the sand dune and slid down the steep decline. Sand tore through its prop, and over the wings. It skidded until finally coming to rest four hundred feet away.

Sam said, "Tom must have fired those shots!" He then picked up his AK-47, loaded another 32 round magazine, and looked at the downed aircraft. "Come on Zara, let's go."

She said, "I hate to burst your bubble, but there's no way you're going to be able to repair it, if that's what you're thinking."

He ignored her comment and kept running.

Sam left deep footprints in the sand dune as he followed the trail the aircraft left when it skidded down the dune. The entire front end of the aircraft was buried in sand. A mangled arm of the propeller raising out from the sand, the only evidence of the engine below. The windshield was mostly buried.

He lifted the AK-47 and aimed it toward the door.

"Anyone alive in there?" he shouted.

No response.

Zara placed her hand on his shoulder. "He took a big hit when the nose ploughed into the sand. I don't think we're going to find him alive."

Sam nodded. Hoping she was right. He then spotted Tom running toward them. He waited until Tom arrived. No reason to get shot by a near-dead pilot out of impatience.

He heard Tom's heavy breathing approach. "Nice shoot, Tom."

"Thanks." Tom looked at the wrecked aircraft. "What did I miss?"

"Nothing by the looks of things. We're trying to work out whether we have a live pilot or not here. Do you want to cover me, and I'll find out what?"

Tom raised his weapon and aimed at the door. "Go for it."

Sam stepped forward and unlatched the door handle. The sand was keeping the door wedged shut. He dug away a bundle of the sand using his hands only until he could open it a little. "If you're alive in there, I want you to know, we're going to get you out of there. But I'd really appreciate not being shot in the process."

No response.

"If you know what I mean…" Sam said.

He pulled heavily on the door and it opened right up. Inside the cockpit looked intact. The electronics were lit up and the radio was still receiving some sort of static. The pilot hadn't fared so well. His legs had taken most of the energy as the front end of the aircraft slammed into the sand, sending his femurs, the long bones in his leg, into his torso. Surprisingly, his face looked untouched. His eyes were open wide staring vacantly ahead.

Sam said, "You can relax, Tom. The pilots no longer in the mood to fight."

Tom asked, "Does he need medical help?"

"I think he's past anything modern medicine can do for him."

"Do you want me to come inside?"

"No. Wait outside. I'll be out in a minute."

Sam looked past the grotesque remains of the pilot and reached for two unopened bottles of water in the compartment behind him. He glanced at the open tail spacing for any food. And found the emergency rations bag. Inside were another two bottles of water, several packets of dehydrated food, some medical supplies, and three glow sticks. He picked up the bag and climbed out of the broken wreckage.

He let the door close and then quickly opened it again, because he heard the familiar static of the aircraft's radio.

"Come in Zogbi! Come in Zogbi!"

Sam's eye's darted toward the writing on the side of the aircraft.

It read, *Zogbi's Chartered Flights.*

"Zogbi. We copy your last transmission. Three people spotted sixty miles south-east of Bilma. We're on our way. We'll have men there within five hours. Good work!"

Sam felt bile rising in his throat. His good mood had already deserted him. He turned around to face Tom and Zara. "We might have a problem."

Chapter Thirty-Four

Sam looked at Zara's face. Her usually hardened façade had been chipped. Her overtly self-centeredness had been tarnished by the prospect of getting them all killed. Her hazel-green eyes welled up, but no tears fell.

She said, "I'm sorry to get you and Tom killed."

Sam shook his head. "Not yet, you haven't."

"There's at least five hundred men charging towards us on camels. They're tired, they're thirsty and their greedy. Driven by the dream of great riches that capturing us will provide there's no way we'll outrun them all the way to Mao."

"What about the waterhole?" he asked.

"The well is covered with a steel door, which in turn is filled with sand to maintain secrecy, but the trackers will find it quick enough. Heck, someone amongst them would even know about its existence already."

"That's okay, where I'm planning on hiding, they won't follow."

She asked, "How?"

"You'll see. Just find me the well, and I'll find you a place to hide for eternity."

"That's it. I'd rather not have to die there."

Sam said, "Neither do I. Our agent spoke of an ancient place of sanctuary, hidden beneath the sea of sand, where he and his counterpart could make the regular trade of diamonds without anyone ever finding them. A place, I'm now guessing was in fact built by the Garamantes we both were lead to believe never made it this far south."

"They'll track our footprints to the well."

Sam shrugged. "Doesn't matter, they'll never find us inside."

"If they're certain we went in there, they'll dig the place out with their bare hands."

"No they won't. They'll try to circle outwards, searching for our tracks again. The entire place will be covered in footprints, and they'll keep scratching their heads over how they lost their greatest prize after getting so close."

"What if you're wrong and this is just a well like any other?" she asked.

Sam crossed his arms. "Then we'll die there."

Chapter Thirty-Five

Four hours later, they were getting close. Zara made several mental notes about their location as she descended the sand dune. They might reach the well within the hour. Her mood was developing a second wind. If they could reach it in time, and Sam Reilly was right about the smuggler's cave, she might still get out of this alive.

Distracted by her thoughts, she didn't see the desert horned viper. It was half buried in the sand with just its head sticking out. Its supra-ocular horns stood upwards like the horns of the devil. Startled, the normally relatively placid creature, began rubbing its scales together making a distinctive rasping sound.

It was the sound, more frightening than a rattlesnake, which startled Zara.

She screamed a vicious oath and jumped out of its way. She ran twenty or more feet down the sand dune before she landed on her side and rolled. When she came to a stop, she quickly stood up and looked back up the sand dune, where she could already see the snake rapidly sidewinding in the opposite direction.

Zara breathed in and gently exhaled. She'd never been particularly frightened of snakes, but nor was she very fond of an early, and painful death by poisoning. She reached for her bag and swore again. It was still twenty feet up the dune.

She quickly climbed to retrieve her bag. Picking it up, she noticed it was lighter than it should have been.

The book's missing!

Her eyes scanned the area and found the book of Nostradamus half open in the sand. She ran over and grabbed it, quickly brushing the sand off before placing it back in its casing. She then stopped, and caught her breath, because a small sheet of folded paper fell out of the codex.

Zara picked the paper up and unfolded it. Tiny holes in the paper formed in the crease, suggesting it had been that way for centuries. She glanced at the paper and shook her head. It was a carefully scribbled note written in the same hand as the other one allegedly by Nostradamus.

She began reading it...

Today you will meet a man who has traveled from someplace far away. He has been sent to this land for a very specific purpose. You must not let him complete that purpose. No matter how much you might want him to.

She finished reading the second half of the note, unable to believe what was written, and yet certain it was true.

"What are you reading?" Sam interrupted her.

She smiled. "Re-reading actually. It's another note Nostradamus left me. But like everything so far, I don't quite know what to make of it."

He asked, "Can I help?"

She folded the note, slid it inside the binding and locked the codex again. "No. This I have to do on my own."

"Okay." Sam stood up from their five minute rest stop and continued walking south.

She watched him leave. His feet sank heavily into the sand as he stepped. She knew Sam could never see the note. If he ever saw the second half of the note he would never trust her again.

How could he? She bit her lower lip. *I don't even trust myself with the new information.*

Chapter Thirty-Six

Sam ran downwards along the gradually declining sand until it leveled out. His blue eyes scanned the region, searching for a sign of the well Zara had told him about. The entire region was filled with sands which softly undulated into constant waves of perfect dunes. The sand, once eroded from the Air Mountains and Ténéré Mountains, had been carried along the plains for thousands of years.

Unable to see anything but sand, he turned to face Zara. "Where is it?" Sam asked.

Zara smiled. "Right in front of us."

"Where? I don't see anything?"

"I'll show you. See that spot over there, where the sand looks like it's been recently burned by fire?"

Sam glanced at it and nodded. It could have been a place where local nomads had recently used a fire to boil their tea. Definitely nothing explicit enough to be used as a landmark, unless you already knew exactly what you were after.

Zara walked slowly towards the darkened sand. "It used to be the site of the *Tree of Ténéré* – what was once considered the most isolated tree on the planet. An ancient *acacia raddiana*. The last remnant of trees within the region when the Erg of Bilma was still a wet-region, flowing with life. *Acacia raddiana* have been known to commonly live upwards of 650 years, but this one might have been around much longer. Until recently, it, along with the Arbre Perdu, or Lost Tree in the north were the only trees noted as landmarks on caravan routes through the Ténéré region of the Sahara Desert in a map at a scale of 1:4,000,000."

"It must have drawn from a water table somewhere below us."

Zara nodded again. "During the winter of 1938–1939, when fears of war in North Africa were becoming increasingly frequent, a well was dug near the tree to improve supply demands from Niger and Chad. Do you know what they found?"

Sam shook his head. "What?"

"The roots of the tree reached the water table at a depth of a hundred and eight feet."

"That's the well we're looking for?" he asked.

"No. That well was filled in 1941 by Mussolini's troops, in an attempt to block supplies from the south. The one we're looking for is nearby."

"What happened to the *acacia raddiana*?" Sam asked.

"The water dried up and with it, all kinds of vegetation."

Sam grinned. "No. I mean, what happened to the last tree?"

Zara sighed. "Some drunken idiot crashed his four wheel drive into it."

Sam laughed and glanced around. There was nothing but sand in every direction all the way to the horizon. "Out here?"

She nodded and stopped at the darkened sand. "Afraid so."

Sam watched as she took in her exact location in relation to the sun and turned to her left. She took small, measured steps forwards. He followed as Zara counted out sixty-five steps and stopped. Without saying a word, she began digging in the sand with her bare hands.

Sam and Tom quickly joined in. Within minutes they'd cleared the top sand and found a large iron cover. The original well probably never had a cover. Sam guessed it was a more recent addition, brought by some traveling smuggler who wanted to keep the trail blocked off to most travelers. Take away a major water supply in the desert and you exclude travel routes.

Sam and Tom pulled on the cover. It was heavy. Even between the three of them, they were having trouble shifting it. They cleared away the rest of the sand. At the base an old padlock barred the entrance.

"Christ!" Zara said. "Who padlocks the only water for hundreds of miles?"

"A new addition?" Tom asked.

She nodded. "Locking the only source of water for hundreds of miles is akin to giving someone who needs it, a death sentence. I can't even imagine who would do this."

"Someone who doesn't want it to disappear." Sam took the butt of his AK-47 and slammed it into the padlock. On the fourth try, the rusted lock gave way.

Sam helped Tom pull open the heavy, hinged, cover and all three of them stared into the well. It looked deep. A lot deeper than he was expecting. Every foot of the hundred and eight below the surface, which Zara had described of the once nearby well, possibly even more. Narrow enough they could easily use the sides push their legs off and slowly shimmy down to the water, but not too narrow to make it difficult to maneuver. Sam wondered whether they'd be able to climb back out once their feet were wet, afterwards. He decided now was the wrong time to voice his concerns.

"It's deeper than I was expecting," Sam admitted.

"It's a hundred and sixty feet deep," Zara said.

"There's a second water table?"

She looked pleased that he'd made the connection, and smiled. "Yes."

Sam removed the emergency kit he'd taken from Zogbi's wrecked plane and dropped it on the ground beside the well. His eyes glanced up at something that glistened on the horizon. He squinted against the sun as he tried to make out exactly what he saw.

"What is it?" Zara asked.

Sam sighed. "We have company."

Tom's eyes darted to the horizon. He was blessed to be born with 20:10 vision, or a visual acuity score twice as accurate at distance than the average person with 20:20 vision. "There's three riders on the ridge. No. Wait. Make it four. They've crept ahead of the rest of our pursuers. They're riding camels, pretty quick by the looks of it."

Zara studied the horizon. "They must have come from Bilma. They're riding fresh beasts."

"How long do we have?" Sam asked, turning to Zara's lifetime of experience in traveling through the region.

"An hour. Maybe less?" she replied.

Sam stared as the riders approached down the sand dune near the horizon. They had crept at least two, possibly even three miles ahead of the rest of their pursuers. They came fast. Their beasts, most likely out from Bilma were fresh and willing to be provoked into moving at speed. Four riders in total. They had come to kill everyone and capture their prize – the book of Nostradamus.

For some reason his mind turned to the four horsemen of the apocalypse: war, famine, fear and death. There was no way he could determine which one was coming, but all he saw was death. It seemed so unbelievably unfair. After all the distance they'd traveled, they were going to get caught climbing into the ancient well and their hiding spot. Behind those four riders a dust plume spilled high into the horizon. The rest of their pursuers were scattered somewhere between two and three miles behind.

Zara looked up at him as though she could read his concerns. "If you don't kill them now, they'll know for certain that we're in the well."

Tom loaded the remaining magazine into the chamber of his AK-47. "Then we'll have to make sure they don't get to see us go in."

"Okay," Sam said. "I'll check this well out. Zara, you and Tom circle back and make some additional trails in the sand for them to track. Hopefully they'll think we filled our water flasks, and kept going south, towards Lake Chad. We might still lose them, after all."

Chapter Thirty-Seven

Sam opened the emergency supply kit he'd stolen from Zogbi's downed aircraft and withdrew two green glow sticks. He pocketed the first one and then cracked the second one by bending the tube. He watched as the activator, hydrogen peroxide, flowed from its broken ampoule into the phenyl oxalate ester and fluorescent dye, where it mixed and created the chemical luminescence. The stick glowed brightly green. He tucked it into his belt and took one last glance into the distance. The four rider's had disappeared down a sand dune – he would have to be quick.

He sat down on the edge of the well and placed his left foot forward with his right leg backwards. Using a technique popular with rock climbers called stemming, he began his descent of the well. The concept was to place your hands and feet on opposite ends of the rock walls and push outwards as though trying to push through.

Maintaining as much external pressure as possible, Sam began his descent. He shuffled downwards. Shifting his weight from each side to descend and using his hands primarily for balance. Apart from the risk of a life threatening fall if he slipped, the process was quite simple and didn't require much effort compared to traditional rock climbing. He didn't stop to consider the consequences of slipping. If he didn't find a place to hide soon, Ngige's men would kill him just as quick.

Within minutes his feet reached the still water at the base of the well. He carefully lowered his left foot into the water, maintaining an increased oppositional pressure with his hands, Sam slowly dipped both legs into the water and then dropped.

His head plunged below the waterline and his feet never reached the bottom. He quickly resurfaced. It was a good sign. The water was deep. If it had been shallow his theory would have already been debunked.

He took a couple deep breaths in and out in a process known as hyper-oxygenation and then dipped his head beneath the water again. He opened his eyes in the cool water. Obviously untouched for at least a month, the water was intensely clear. Sam removed the glow stick from his belt and held it out in front of him.

The water in the well glowed green all the way to the sandy bottom.

The water gave the well the impression it wasn't very deep. A classic mistake in free-diving was to assume the water's bottom was shallower than it really was because of the water's clarity.

He swam downwards, using his arms in long sweeping strokes, while his legs kicked vigorously. The well ended somewhere around forty feet below the waterline. The solid stone brickwork used to form the internal wall of the well, continued all the way to the bottom, which appeared filled with sand.

Sam hyperventilated and then dived, face downwards toward the bottom. The water was deep, but barely an effort on his part. He worried more about Zara, but guessed he would deal with it once the time came.

If he found the lost chamber...

The old stonework stopped a couple feet from the sandy bottom. In its place were several large stones. They looked like they belonged. Most likely original pieces of stone carved off while the original construction took place.

Sam ran his hands along the larger stones. Nothing moved. They were all solid. Through the awkward haze of his unprotected eyes he found nothing that benefitted his cause. No place large enough to hide, even for a short time. He'd hoped at the very least, there would be a protected ledge where they could hide while their pursuers passed by. He expected they would send hundreds of rounds of ammunition down the barrel of the well, but he doubted many would have been interested in climbing down after them.

But instead, he found a solid circumferential stone wall that descended all the way to the ground. There weren't even any cramped ledges which he could slide under or squeeze through. He ran his hands through the sand, slowly. He didn't want to stir up the silt, but he needed to find what he was looking for. Perhaps his agent had buried what he needed?

His heart started to race. Sam's body wasn't being tested. He'd been a free-diver since he was a boy. If he was going to die here, it wasn't going to be from drowning.

What if I'm in the wrong well?

He turned slowly in the cramped space to look directly above. He was glad the well hadn't been dug any narrower or he would have struggled to turn around inside. To help, he used his right hand to hold the largest of five boulders at the bottom of the well. He pulled hard and shifted his body around to face upwards.

Happy, to have made the turn, he gripped the stone again to keep himself from surfacing immediately.

In an instant, the stone began to lift with him.

Did my hand just slip?

Sam moved the glow stick so he could see the stone. It still appeared firmly fixed in place where he'd seen it earlier. He pushed harder, but it made no difference. His lungs burned and as his dive watch showed he'd been free diving for close to two minutes. Sam shook his head, unable to explain what moved, and quickly swam to the surface.

Above the surface of the water he went through a process of blowing off the excess carbon dioxide built up during his dive, by taking slow, deep breaths. Two minutes later, he turned and dived below again.

This time he immediately dived to the large stone he thought had moved so he could examine it again. Sam was almost certain the thing had moved. He tried pushing it to the left and then to the right. Neither allowed him to shift the enormous stone even an inch. He pulled down heavily on the stone. Again, nothing moved. He shook his head, he must have been imagining things.

There was no secret vault.

And that meant it was all over. He'd gotten it wrong. Perhaps their agent had never buried the diamonds inside a well after all. Sam used the same stone to help turn himself upwards again. He would need to tell the others. It was time to make a new plan.

Maybe there was still time to kill the four closest riders and take their camels?

He pushed off the large stone to swim towards the surface. Only this time, it moved again. He hadn't imagined it. There was definitely movement as he pushed away. Sam stopped and stared at the giant stone, examining it like a surgeon preparing for an amputation. He went through the same three axis of movement which were possible and then tried the one axis that was impossible – lifting the massive stone upwards.

The stone was enormous. Nearly three feet in height, the massive stone looked like it was wedged deeply inside the wall, making it impossible to lift. He didn't expect much response as he attempted to lift the stone, but instead found it lifted freely from the ground – revealing an opening inside.

With his other hand he moved the glow stick so it shined inside. The opening was quite large once you got through the initial entrance. He tried lowering it again and then easily lifted it once more.

Sam grinned.

The damned thing is perfectly balanced on a fulcrum!

He gritted his teeth, and holding the glow stick out in front of him, quickly pulled himself through the secret opening.

Chapter Thirty-Eight

The entrance lead to a much larger tunnel. It traversed in a horizontal direction for approximately twenty feet before gradually turning upwards. The distance didn't stress him, but would be close to impossible for a non-free-diver. He hadn't even considered if there was even air on the opposite side of it.

He'd already passed the point of no return. Now, all he could do was swim into the darkness and pray that he would find a safe exit. He kicked his legs, swimming diagonally upwards until his head broke the dark surface.

The other side opened into a large clearing, like a subterranean lake. The radiant green light of his glow stick stretched at least fifty feet forwards in a forwards arc. Sam swam upwards until his head broke the surface of the water and he found himself inside a massive subterranean cavern. He took a deep breath in. The air felt cool and sweet on his throat. He felt his heart rate eased and he felt his entire body relax.

The green glow stretched to the other end of the cavern – approximately fifty to sixty feet away. The entire place looked like a half dome shaped cave above an underground lake. It would be a cold, wet, place to take refuge for a number of days while they lost their pursuers, but it would do the job. His biggest concern was that if they couldn't get out of the water they would freeze to death.

Sam turned around to orient himself and make the quick journey back to the well to get the others. In the process he noticed the tiny ripples he'd created along the surface all stopped at the same section at the middle of the lake.

He grinned. There was an island at the center of the lake.

Sam didn't stop to investigate. He'd found what they needed to hide from their pursuers and cheat death. Now he needed to quickly return for Tom and Zara. He found the opening to the original tunnel and followed it all the way to the end where the large stone blocked his progress. The light from his glow stick was fading and without it, the tunnel appeared extremely dark.

The tunnel gradually became narrower until the stone blocked his progress. Sam placed his hands firmly on the ground and tried to push down as though he were doing a push-up with the stone resting heavily on his back. It didn't take too much effort and the stone tipped backwards opening the tunnel fully.

He climbed through the opening. Inside the well once more, he turned to the light and pushed off the sandy bottom. Kicking hard, he swam to the surface. His head broke the surface and he took a deep breath of air again.

Sam placed his left foot in front and his right one behind. He used the oppositional force to step up so his torso rose above the water's surface. Using his hands for balance, he placed additional weight on the balls of his feet and pushed downward.

His left leg held, but his right one slipped and he fell back into the water. The water made the well slippery to climb. He tried again and achieved the same result. On the fourth time he used his right hand to grip a curved stone in the wall of the well and pulled himself out of the water. He slowly kicked free some of the water on his feet and then commenced climbing again. It took around four to five minutes to reach the top of the well. Sam climbed out and saw Zara staring back at him.

"I found it!" he said, looking at her. He smiled. It was gloating and came naturally. "I told you it would be here."

Zara stared at him, but said nothing. She blinked and her long dark lashes opened. In the afternoon light, her eyes appeared dark and unreadable. Behind him, Sam heard the distinctive loud click of a large magazine being slid rearward and secured into the mag well of an AK-47.

Sam didn't bother to turn around. His eyes met Zara's at once. They revealed the despondency of their fate in an instant.

She shrugged. "I'm sorry, Sam. They found us, first."

Sam took a deep breath in and exhaled slowly. He figured it was a good sign they hadn't killed him yet. He casually turned around to see all four riders aiming directly at the two of them. He raised his arms suppliantly and smiled. "I was wondering when you would finally catch up."

Chapter Thirty-Nine

Sam glanced at his own AK-47. It stood upright about five feet away, with the butt of the weapon sticking into the sand next to the well where he'd left it with the hope of protecting the weapon from the sand while he dived the well. Zara had told him, she predicted it would take at least another hour for the riders to catch up with them. Even so, he should have been better prepared. He should have been faster down the well and back up again. None of that mattered now – because he'd gotten it all wrong. It might just be the last mistake he would get to make.

His eyes darted back toward his attackers. They wore the indigo blue robes of the Tuareg nomads and all but their eyes were covered in protective cloth. One held an AK-47 pointed casually toward him, as though the rider knew it wasn't going to be needed to persuade him to hand over the book. The other three carried Sterling submachine guns. All four appeared amateurish in the way they held their weapons. More like kids who'd recently been given toys than professionals. Even so, Kony 2012 showed just how well the AK-47 had been used to kill a lot of people by child soldiers throughout Africa. At a glance, the AK-47 looked clean and well oiled, while the other three weapons were old and poorly maintained.

Sam glanced at the Sterling submachine guns.

The bolt was open, with the working parts held to the rear of the weapon. Like other open-bolt weapons, the bolt goes forward when the trigger is pulled, feeding a round from the magazine into the chamber and firing it. Like any other self-loading design without an external power supply, the action is cycled by the energy of the shot, which sends the bolt back to the rear, ejecting the empty cartridge case and preparing for the next shot. It meant that it didn't take much effort to fire and keep firing.

He noticed the bolts had helical grooves cut into the surface. The purpose being to remove dirt and fouling from the inside of the receiver to increase reliability in the Sahara where sand was abundant. Without exception, each groove appeared blocked with sand and the riders were ignorant or too lazy to dismantle and clean it. The weapons hadn't been stripped and oiled in a very long time. If he got lucky, in a firefight, at least one of the weapons would probably jam and misfire – but three working weapons against none was still a very uneven fight.

Sam looked at his attackers. His hands remained in the air in supplication. "All right, now what?"

The rider with the AK-47 dismounted her camel. She spoke with the authority of one used to being obeyed. "Now, you hand over the book of Nostradamus."

"What book?"

She smiled at him. "Cute. But I'm afraid I don't have a lot of time. You may not have noticed but we have an army following, and they're not going to be quite as nice when they get here. Your friend has already told me she stole the book and you hid it for her down the well."

Sam forced himself to smile. "So, if you know where it is, why don't you go get it yourself?

"Because I have no intention of climbing down that well," she said. "Instead, I'm counting on your kindness."

"Kindness! You think General Ngige is going to show a great kindness to the people of the DRC?"

The woman in command laughed. "You still think General Ngige's in control here, don't you?"

Sam asked, "He isn't?"

"No."

Sam was genuinely surprised by the new information. "From what I've heard, he's the head of the rebellion?"

"That's because the world looks at the puppet and rarely at the puppet master."

"Someone else is pulling the strings?"

"Yes."

"Who?"

"Someone who's interested in starting the largest war to ever effect Africa and doesn't wish to be found. Someone who wants the book of Nostradamus destroyed before the future becomes irreparable."

"I'm afraid I can't help you," Sam said.

"Mr. Reilly, I don't think you understand what's at stake here. You are exposing the future to the greatest danger it's ever seen."

The use of his name shocked him. Up until that point, Sam had assumed the riders were nomads who had chosen to get rich fast off a bounty. They were hunting Zara Delacroix, but shouldn't have had any idea who he was. "Who are you?"

"My name's not important. I'm not important. I'm a Tuareg nomad. A wanderer and a nobody. I perform unique tasks throughout the harsh land of the Sahara. Today I am merely a messenger. And I'm here to tell you it's time to change sides. The US government backed the wrong person and the future won't tolerate it."

Zara stared at her without saying a word.

"The future won't tolerate it?" Sam asked. "I didn't realize the future wanted anything."

"That's one of the many things you've recently gotten wrong. The future is set. It knows what should happen. Not what is easy, but what is necessary. My master knows what it wants. Nostradamus knew what it wanted and was too weak to obey its will. He chose to challenge the future and instead was killed by it."

"The future killed Nostradamus?" Sam asked. "I thought he died in his bed after suffering with gout and poor mobility for years?"

"After making his journey into the unmapped and dangerous Sahara to bury his book, Nostradamus spent many months subsisting on shellfish along the North African coast until he was picked up by a European slave ship."

Sam stared at her, unable to follow her train of thought. "And so?"

"Shellfish are rich in purines."

"I'm sorry, I'm still not following you."

"Purines break down into uric acid, which form into crystals that deposit in the joints and cause pain and inflammation."

"And you think the future did this to stop Nostradamus from challenging its path?"

"No. Nostradamus had already made his attempt to change what will and must occur."

"So, why poison him then?"

"The future was punishing him."

She's talking as though the future is a living, breathing, evil thing. "Okay, let me get this straight. Nostradamus thought he'd found a way to beat the future, so he wrote a book and buried it in the Saharan desert where no one could possibly find it until Dr. Delacroix arrived."

His captor nodded and said nothing.

"So, what's inside the book of Nostradamus?" Sam asked.

No one answered.

"What doesn't the future want changed?" he persisted.

His captor turned to face Zara. "Do you want to tell him what you discovered inside the book of Nostradamus?"

Zara shook her head. "No. I can't!"

Their captor lowered the AK-47 at Zara. "You can and you must!"

"I haven't worked it out yet. I don't know!"

"Yes you do. You just refuse to accept it! Now, tell him!"

Zara looked at the weapons pointing at them and then back at him. Her jaw was set firm and her eyes piercing as though she'd come to a decision with terrible consequences. "I'm sorry."

"Then I'll tell him!" Their captor said. "The future will –" her words stopped as a multitude of bullets tore through her chest.

Zara was the first to recover. She ducked down and threw a handful of sand in the eyes of the other three assailants. Sam tackled the one closest to him, who pulled at the trigger sending a barrage of bullets into the air in a wide arc.

Next to him, the second nomad fought with the Sterling's bolt which had jammed. While Sam struggled to get control of the nomad he'd tackled, the third assailant aimed directly at him. The man took three steps toward him and shoved the barrel of his submachine gun hard against him.

Sam felt the pressure on his temple. The man was making certain he didn't miss and get the other guy. His confidence meant that Zara was already dead. He gritted his teeth, as though his will alone could somehow stave off his death.

A moment later he heard the trigger click and the shot fire.

You really do get to hear the sound of the shot that kills you? A split second later, Sam felt the pressure of the submachine gun's barrel ease away from his temple. He turned his head slightly and saw a fine mist of red where his attacker fell.

Sam turned his vision toward the sandy crest in the opposite direction. There, nestled high up on the sand dune behind them, Tom was standing up, having taken the man out a moment before he was able to fire.

At the same time Zara kneed the remaining nomad in his groin. He dropped the Sterling submachine gun with the jammed bolt. The weapon dropped to the ground. It landed on the hard edge of the well. The force dislodged the bolt and the Sterling emptied all thirty-four rounds aimlessly.

Sam dropped into the dune. The sharp whine of bullets flying past him making him hug the ground desperately. When the Sterling finally stopped firing Sam stood up. It had killed the two remaining attackers. He quickly ran over to the woman who had been in charge. She'd been struck in the chest and was bleeding hard. There was nothing he could do to prolong her life.

Sam said, "Please. I need to know. What is this all about?"

She turned to face him. Blood draining from her mouth with every breath. Sam sat her up and rested her back against his knee. She coughed and some more frothing blood expelled from her mouth. She tried to talk, but the words wouldn't come out.

"What is it?" Sam asked, desperately. "What do you need me to do?"

"Protect the future!"

Chapter Forty

Sam watched as the stranger who'd been his captor just minutes beforehand gave up the will to breathe. She coughed a few more times as her body vainly attempted to expel the blood from her lungs and then stopped completely. Sam didn't bother to check for a pulse. Without an immediate surgical facility and team of cardiothoracic surgeons, her injuries were unsustainable. She would be dead soon and there was nothing he could do to rouse her enough to answer the question he so desperately needed to know.

Zara brushed away a couple of flies from her face, already drawn by the smell of death. "Well, that worked well. I was beginning to worry Tom had lost interest in the plan – it took him so long to shoot."

Sam said, "I wish he had."

Zara bent down to take a Sterling submachine gun from one of the deceased and search for spare magazines. "What the hell does that mean?"

Sam grabbed the newer AK-47 and three additional full magazines. "It means I want to know what was really inside the book of Nostradamus."

"I told you, I don't know what was inside the book. It's filled with riddles. So far, my time's been spent a little preoccupied since I found the damned book, trying to keep myself alive. As I told you, the letter that Nostradamus addressed to me, described his visions of the future as a series of strings of significance. Watershed moments that changed everything. Big changes. These have carried on through the ages. With each possible event, he's seen the subsequent strings for both futures. But for my generation all human strings cease to exist."

"Which means?"

"The human race will become extinct in my life time."

Sam pointed to the now dead woman next to him. "That woman told me you knew exactly what was inside the book of Nostradamus. She said I'm on the wrong side and I need to protect the future. What did she mean?"

Zara avoided his gaze, turning instead to watch Tom run down the steep sand dune toward them. "I don't know. I promise I have no idea."

"That's crap!" Sam grabbed her by her shoulder to stop her from walking away from him. "She was quite explicit. She said to you, do you want to tell him, or shall I?"

"She was mistaken. I've barely had time to flick through the damned book. It's full of riddles that will take years to fully decipher, if anyone ever does!"

Sam said, "But you paused. You stopped. I saw your face. You were torn."

She swore and looked away. "You wouldn't believe me if I told you."

"Try me." Sam looked at her. Her hazel-green eyes were intense with passion and intelligence, but there was something else there, too. Something he hadn't seen before – *was she ashamed?* "For what possible reason would Nostradamus have traveled all the way into the Saharan desert simply to bury and hide his most prized possession – the book which had given him all his power?"

"Do you know how Nostradamus predicted the future?" she asked.

"I always guessed he just made it up, got lucky, and became the King's best friend."

"No. He was a true Seer."

"Really? As a scientist, you can't possibly expect me to believe this."

She ignored his complaint. "The way he did it wasn't magical. It was pure science. You see he could follow the outcome of each significant incident, which would lead to another and another, until the final outcome for an event would occur. Meaning at the end of several hundred events, he could predict the outcome of a certain event today."

"The butterfly effect?"

"No. It's not quite as simple as the movies like to make it out to be."

"You think the movies failed to do adequate research into the science of predicting the future?"

She ignored his sarcasm. "The way it works is like this. Picture yourself driving along a straight, long, flat road in the desert with nothing around to hit. There's a series of forks in the road but you keep the steering wheel pointed dead ahead. Now imagine a motorcycle or a smaller car bumps into you. You might be forced to drift off the road, but so long as you remain driving, you can simply steer it back on course."

"You're saying the future is pre-ordained and no matter what little bumps go along the way, the future will re-direct itself."

"Exactly."

"Then what are we doing trying to change it?"

"Because if you're driving that car down the long, straight road and a truck collides with you – the car will become permanently destroyed. Creating with it a brand new path. You see, make a big enough challenge to the future, and it won't like it, but it might just be persuaded to change."

"What event?"

"He didn't say. Simply the ending of the world."

"How?"

"Didn't say."

"Okay, so why didn't he just change things in his time to create the change needed. Why go walking through the desert?"

"Because the future's already pre-ordained. Destined by some higher divinity. He didn't believe in the butterfly effect – he tried it multiple times. He could change small things, but the things which really mattered, simply fought back until the destiny of man returned to its original path. He looked, trust me he looked. But all lines lead to the same catastrophic event, which lead to the demise of humanity."

Sam said, "Fuck with the future and it fucks with you?"

"No," she shook her head. "Nothing quite so sinister. Simply that new events will occur and those will eventually trigger the same outcome."

"Well that's just great. So, now we know that the future's been ordained, and there's nothing we can do to affect it – what's the point of living?"

"Exactly."

"When is this catastrophe supposed to occur?"

"Now."

"Now when?"

"This year, to be exact."

"So, if he knew we were all going to simply vanish... why go to the trouble of burying his stupid book?"

"Because out of the billions of lines of futures that he investigated, just one provided him with an unclear future."

"He can't see everything?"

"Everything except the outcome of one event. All he knew was that if that one event occurred, everything afterwards became foggy."

"As in, the world ended?"

"No, as though a new line had been created with no known future."

"It was a long shot, but he took it."

"What was the image of the event that changed everything?"

"Me."

"You?"

"I found his book."

Sam studied her eyes. They were magnificent and at the same time truly deceptive. A true interrogator from the dangerous years of the Second

World War couldn't have broken her mind. "There's something else, isn't there?"

"Yes."

"But you're not going to tell me."

"I can't. I'm sorry. You're just going to have to trust me on this. If Nostradamus went to all this trouble, and dramatically shortened his own life, so that he could change the future – you must have faith that I'm working on the right side of this event."

"I find it hard to believe anyone is on the right side of this."

Tom stepped in between the two of them. "What's going on?"

"Nice shooting," Zara said.

"Thanks, Tom. Nice shot." Sam smiled.

Tom asked, "What's going on?"

"Zara was just explaining why she has to keep the biggest secret in the world from us to protect the future."

Tom nodded, without any sign of understanding. His eyes were focused on a plume of sand converging in the distance. "They're close. I suggest we finish this discussion hidden deep inside the well."

Chapter Forty-One

Zara watched Sam and Tom strip their robes and boots. Beneath they wore a thin, silvery undergarment that looked like a three-quarter-length wetsuit and shimmered as they moved. They looked like something out of a bad science fiction movie from the seventies, but she guessed the DARPA funded, thermal suits, were there for their function, not their looks.

She removed her own loose fitting robes, headdress and sandals. She placed them in a plastic bag. It would be impossible to climb or swim while wearing them. Underneath, she wore a cotton turquoise tank-top and matching boyshort underwear. She tied her long dark hair in a bun. Two years traipsing through the desert on expedition had left her lithe and athletic. At the same time, her Persian and French blood had made her naturally exotic.

Tom, she noted, had dutifully turned around. While, Sam, on the other hand grinned and then quickly turned around.

She said, "Don't even think about saying anything, Sam."

Sam ignored her. Instead, he broke the remaining two glow sticks. The chemicals inside swirled and mixed, sending out a green phosphorescence. He handed one to her.

Sam said, "We have two glow sticks. I'll carry one and you carry the other. You follow my light, and Tom will follow yours. We don't need to go too far. Follow my light and you'll get through the tunnel safely. Got it?"

"Sure."

Zara watched as Sam climbed down the well. He'd previously described in painstaking detail exactly how to climb down using her hands and feet to provide opposing forces between the stone walls of the well. She watched as the four camels disappeared over the sand dune to the south. If they were lucky, their pursuers would assume they had killed the four riders, stolen their camels and were riding south. If their pursuers didn't take the bait, they would have to pray like hell that Sam's hidden smuggler's cave was every bit as good as he said it was.

Zara edged her way into the narrow well. There was nothing difficult about it. Nothing new, either. Her father used to send her down similar wells when she was a kid to fetch water. Not that she was going to let Sam Reilly know it. She climbed down quickly with Tom following several feet above her. She watched Sam drop into the water and then followed him in. There wasn't much room on the water's surface with her and Sam preparing to dive. Perched several feet above Tom rested with both his legs forward and his back against the stone wall as though he was waiting for lunch.

Sam looked at her. "You know the plan?"

Zara kicked her legs and kept her head above water. "I've got it."

"Give me about ten seconds after I dive and then follow me down."

She nodded. "I said, I've got it."

Zara watched the soft, lime green turn to a dark green like seaweed, as Sam disappeared deep below. She felt herself involuntarily wanting to hyperventilate as she saw how deep the well went. Not because she was afraid she couldn't make it. Despite growing up in the Sahara, she actually quite enjoyed swimming and was reasonably good at it. Whenever her father stayed somewhere long enough with a waterhole she would often dive down and see how far she could travel underwater, pretending she was searching for sunken treasure. Swimming she could do, but confined spaces scared the hell out of her – but there was no way she was going to be telling Mr. Reilly that.

Zara took two more deep breaths in and out. She looked up and saw Tom looking like he was hanging around on school camp.

"I'll be right behind you," he said.

Zara nodded and then dipped head first into the water. She opened her eyes. The cold water stung at them and her entire world looked like a tunnel filled with a hazy green glow. She swam downwards and covered her own glow stick. Her eyes began to adjust to the water and she was able to distinguish the light at the bottom of the well from her own.

Sam looked up at her. She could now see him clearly in the light. He didn't look that far away. Zara kicked her feet and swam downward, but it seemed to be taking a long time to reach the bottom. She opened her jaw and tried to equalize the pressure in her ears, which was building up and making her head feel like it was going to implode.

She watched as Sam moved a giant stone, which teetered at the bottom of the well and then disappeared inside a secret opening. A moment later the stone returned to its original position, but between the stone and the sand was Sam's glow stick. She reached the secret passage and immediately moved the stone as Sam had explained to her earlier.

The opening wasn't very big, and she wondered how Sam had slid through so quickly. She felt her heart race as she slid inside. It felt small and she instantly felt a panic attack coming on. The sort she used to have as a child after she'd become stuck inside a mine shaft she and her father were exploring. She had never forgotten the feeling. The walls felt like they had moved and were closing in on her. Squishing all sides of body until she could no longer expand her chest enough to breath.

Suddenly her chest felt tight and she wanted to breathe. She couldn't move forward and there was no point trying to go back. She had to make it through. Ordinarily, she would have forced herself to breathe slowly and calm herself.

But I can't breathe, can I?

I'm more than forty feet beneath water and a hundred and sixty feet underground!

Rationally, she knew she had to make it through the tunnel to escape. There were no other choices. A rational person would make it through. If Sam Reilly could do it, so could she. Heck, if Tom Bower, the giant of a man, was going to get through after her, she must be able to make it. Even so, the walls simply closed in on her.

She started to fight them by wriggling her torso and pulling and scratching the walls with her hands. It wasn't helping. All it did was make the walls close in. She was certain she'd wedged her chest between the two walls and could now feel the entire weight of all forty feet of water above her, crushing her lungs.

But the pain was too much. She wanted to open her mouth and scream!

Instead, she felt something push on her feet from behind her. She slid further forward and her right hand struck something. Another human being's hand. It gripped hers and she squeezed it back, hard. A moment later, the hand pulled her through until the tunnel opened to a large submerged void.

The sudden relief was quickly squashed as the glowing light shined off the surface of the cavern. It was large and sloped in a generally upward direction, but there was no sign of air. Logic suggested that if she had dived forty or fifty feet downward, she must ascend that much again to find the surface again.

It was her worst nightmare. She'd survived her momentary feeling of claustrophobic sheer terror, only to discover herself trapped in an underwater subterranean water shelf. Before she could truly take in her new environment, she felt someone pull her hands and throw her forward through the shallow tunnel.

Her head finally broke the surface. She gasped. Her hands and legs felt numb. The world was dark. She'd dropped her glow stick in the struggle to reach the surface. She breathed deeply. The cold air soothed her. She'd entered a massive subterranean void. There was no natural sound, but her rapid breathing echoed throughout the cavern.

Where am I?

"Are you there, Sam?"

She heard the echo of her own voice, but no other response.

There's no way I made it and Sam didn't?

"Tom? You around?"

Again, there was no response.

Zara considered the possibilities. There was a high chance that she was the only one to make it through. Perhaps Sam had passed out in the process of trying to rescue her? Or possibly he'd gone back to help pull Tom through the secret passage? Either way, she'd been on the surface long enough to allow her breathing to settle into a normal pace. And that meant Sam and Tom had both been underwater for a long time.

Too long to survive?

Her nightmare never seemed to end. The thought of being stuck in the dark void, with no light and no chance of retracing her route out again told her rational mind there was only one outcome for her – she would die here.

Zara waited a couple minutes and then shouted for anyone who could hear her. She waited another thirty seconds and tried again. Somehow, her words sounded even more distant and crippling as they were the only ones to return.

She forced herself to take in a slow deep breath before exhaling even slower in an attempt to settle her mind. One thing was certain, no one could survive five or more minutes beneath the water without SCUBA equipment. Which meant only one thing. She was all alone, in a dark world – a sarcophagus of her own making.

Sam had said at the center of the lake a small island existed.

Once there, she might at least climb out of the water and get dry. Even if Sam and Tom never returned, she could rest, collect her thoughts and plan for the future.

She swam into the darkness. Slow, careful and quiet strokes. If she didn't make much noise, it stood to reason, that she would hear if anyone came for her. After about five minutes her hand struck something, hard. It was like a stone wall. She ran her hand along it and then reached the top. The surface was flat.

Zara carefully pulled herself out of the water and onto the subterranean island. She laid down, closed her eyes and relaxed. It was the first success she'd had since entering the well. Nostradamus had told her she was going to have a difficult time escaping, but she would survive. Right now, she had no idea how she was going to make that prediction come true.

But she was still alive! She grinned and relaxed. *Rest first and then work out how I'm going to live long enough to find the Nostradamus Equation.*

Chapter Forty-Two

Sam took in a deep breath as he surfaced. It wasn't quite a gasp, but the distance seemed further in the dark. The place seemed smaller. There was no way of knowing for sure without light, but he knew it was. The way a termite instinctively knew the precise amount of wood to eat so that a house doesn't lose its structure and collapse, Sam knew the air pocket he'd come up inside was smaller than one before it.

In the process of helping Zara reach the surface he'd dropped his glow stick and had swum back toward the secret tunnel to make sure Tom could find his way. Tom had grabbed his leg and then followed his movement toward the surface.

Next to him, he heard Tom surface and take a casual breath, as though he'd been out for a morning dive at the beach.

"You okay, Tom?" he asked.

"I'm all good. How's Zara doing after getting stuck?"

"I have no idea. She's not here."

"Christ!" Tom said, "You let her drown?"

"I don't think so. I took her to the surface. I know her head broached the surface. I even heard her take in a deep breath. She seemed all right. I didn't wait to see though. It was dark, I'd dropped the glow stick and was worried about you."

"Zara!" Tom yelled. "Are you here?"

The echo ricocheted quickly as though they were in a small cavern. Almost no delay between the sound going out and returning again. There was no response other than Tom's voice and the two of them didn't wait for one. Instead the two of them swam around the room in opposite directions.

"We're in a large dome," Sam said. "If you keep your left hand on the wall, and I keep my right one on the wall we'll meet somewhere back in the middle."

"Got it!" Tom said.

Sam quickly swam around the dark room, cursing his mistake of losing the glow stick. He should have carried the only remaining one, but he didn't want to carelessly use it when it was the only spare light they'd have down there. His right hand dragged along the smooth wall.

He didn't yell out again. Instead he listened. Waiting for the sound of breathing or any evidence that Zara was still alive. It was a large subterranean lake, and might take some time to reach the other side.

Sam moved quickly.

His right hand felt like it had changed by a ninety degree angle. It might have been less. Perhaps only forty-five, but he was definitely no longer following the circular wall he'd expected. He swam several feet down the tunnel and then stopped. There was a light draft coming from the tunnel. The air tasted fresh, and moved. Unlike when he'd dived earlier into the subterranean lake, where the air was perfectly still, this tunnel had a definite draft. The revelation hit him like a cannon.

We're in a different cavern!

Sam turned and placed his left hand on the wall so he was now facing back out the way he came in. "Tom, you still there?"

"I'm still here. The wall stopped being round. Where are you?"

"I'm down a tunnel. Wait there, and I'll come to you, so we don't get lost. We'll need to find our way back to the main cavern where I left Zara."

Sam started swimming back the way he came.

Tom said, "She's going to be pissed as all hell at you, buddy. That girl was already terrified and now we've left her in a dark void."

"She'll forgive us, when we return. So long as we do return."

Sam blinked a couple times, trying to adjust his eyes to the darkness. They were more than a hundred and sixty feet below the ground. It was impossible for light to reach them. But ahead of him, he spotted the first sign of light he'd seen since surfacing. It looked blue and shimmered. His eyes couldn't quite make out what it was. He swam faster and then collided head first into Tom.

Both men swore.

"You all right?" Sam asked.

"I'm all right, what about you?"

"I'm good."

"What are you grinning like an idiot for, Sam?"

"It will hit you in a second."

Tom swore. "Christ! I can see your face! It's blue and kind of creepier than I remember it, but at least I can see."

"It's our DARPA thermal suits," Sam said, already swimming back toward where they had come from. "Their chemicals are changing the color from grey to fluorescent blue as they attempt to mitigate against the cold water."

"So all we have to do to be able to see is stay cold?"

"Yeah, something like that."

"What if we increase the desired temperature parameters?"

Sam adjusted small temperature gauge on his right upper arm. "You're right. It will drain the power quicker, but we should be able use it on short bursts if we want to greatly increase the lumens."

Tom checked his own power module. "At current rate of consumption, my suite has approximately three days to go."

"Then let's not waste the energy."

As Sam swam across the small cavern he looked up at their new environment. It was another dome, like the one he'd found earlier. Only instead of being massive, this one was no more than ten or so feet in diameter. The ceiling was a perfectly formed a dome.

Tom looked at the ceiling above. "What do you think, Sam?"

"I'm doubting any smuggler went to the trouble to build anything this advanced. Which means this must have been built by the ancient Garamantes."

"You mean, we stumbled across the Golden City? The same fictional one we used as an alibi for why we were carrying dive tanks into the Sahara?"

"It looks like it."

"I wonder. Do you think the other stories about it being a golden city are true?" Tom asked.

"I'm more interested in whether or not their subterranean aqueducts really did travel hundreds of miles between cities."

Chapter Forty-Three

Zara rolled over onto her side. Something had changed in her environment. They say, when you lose one of your senses, the other senses become more responsive in order to pick up the slack. In this case, she didn't even know what had changed. Only that something had changed. Her eyes had become adjusted to existing in complete darkness, but now, somewhere in the distance, the darkness turned slightly blue.

She sat bolt upright and then stood up. On the far side of the lake she could definitely see something. It wasn't much. A blue haze beneath the water. Not bright enough to see what it was, but at least confirmation she was not alone. She stared at it, willing it to grow. And the light did grow. A second light followed behind. Both objects were moving quickly beneath the water.

There was just enough light to make out the island she was standing on. She spotted the water-tight backpack that Sam had brought down earlier, which carried her robes, and emergency provisions. Next to the backpack were three small bags of stones.

Instinctively, she bent down and picked up the largest one she could find and prepared to throw it at whatever enemy was now approaching. The thing looked like two vile blue monsters. She wondered if they could be some sort of fish that had evolved to live underneath the well, in perfect darkness. Her heart raced and she picked up a second stone to hurl.

The first monster broke the surface with a gasp, followed by the second one. They were both on the far side of the cavern. They turned and faced her directly.

"Zara! Thank goodness, you're all right."

Zara recognized the confident voice of Sam. She squeezed the cold stone in her hand and was tempted to pummel it at him, anyway.

She said, "Where did you two go? I thought you were both dead!"

"Sorry. I dropped the glow stick when I went back for Tom. When we surfaced we were in a different cavern and without light, so we had no idea we weren't where we were supposed to be."

Tom popped his head out of the water, a few feet next to Sam. He looked calm and there was no evidence he'd been holding his breath. Tom looked directly at her and smiled comfortingly. "You okay, Zara?"

"Fine," she said.

Zara watched as the two men quickly swam towards the island and climbed out. They looked like giant blue, glowing, fish. The sort of unique deep sea creatures which had evolved to live in just such a place as this. Their thermal suits no longer silvery, but glistening in blue.

"I see you found out how to make your own light?" she said.

"Yeah, that was good luck," Sam said opening the backpack to dry himself with his robe. "I never noticed and certainly never expected to need the thermal suit to produce light. They won't last too long. The power will run out. So we're on clock, if you know what I mean?"

"For what?" Zara asked.

"To find a way out, of course!" Sam stopped. His eyes darting towards the cold stone she still gripped in her right hand. "What's the story with the stone? You look like you want to use it to smash someone's head in?"

Zara said, "Don't tempt me! You left me alone. I thought I was going to die here, in this cold, dark, place."

Sam said, "I said I'm sorry."

Tom grinned. "Sorry to interrupt. You two can fight about who hates each other more later. Can I ask where you found that stone?"

"Over there," Zara pointed to three small bags made from gazelle hides.

Sam smiled. He walked up to the first one and loosened the drawstring. Inside there were enough diamonds to fund a revolution. "They don't look like much more than dirty rocks to me?"

"Do you know anything about diamonds?" she asked.

"I know they're the most artificially overinflated commodity in existence, but apart from that, no."

"Those dirty so called rocks are worth enough to fund a dozen military coups."

Chapter Forty-Four

Sam turned the temperature on his thermal suit up to its maximum setting. At the same time Tom switched his off completely to conserve energy. They were going to need the batteries to work as long as possible. Sam's body shimmered with the deep blue glow as it quickly heated up to an uncomfortable temperature inside. The light glowed and permeated every corner of the subterranean cavern. All three of them looked up in awe. They were standing directly beneath the oculus of a massive dome.

Sam grinned as his eyes followed the contours of the enormous dome downward until he was looking at Zara. "This place remind you of anything?"

Zara's hazel-green eyes stared up in fascination. The edge of her lips curled upwards and she bit her lower lip and then screamed, "The Roman Pantheon!"

Sam nodded. "Which means?"

"The Romans conquered this far south?"

Sam shook his head. "No. Quite the opposite in fact."

Zara didn't bother hiding her skepticism. "You think the Garamantes conquered Rome?"

"Not conquered. But certainly heavily influenced the development of Roman architecture."

"That's absurd. The Roman Empire was miles ahead of the rest of the world at the time. In the arts, sciences, and engineering. There was no comparison. And to consider their development was challenged by an ancient tribe of nomadic people is laughable."

"And yet, true."

She smiled. "Christ! You're serious! Why?"

Sam tilted his head to the side until a grin matched his slant. "Oh, I have my reasons."

Zara shook her head. "No. There's never been any evidence to suggest the Garamantes ever traveled this far south. Besides, this dome is too complex for them to construct. If anything, I'd have to guess these are older than we're thinking. I think the ancient Romans built them before the Sahara dried up and turned to sand."

Sam grinned. "No. I can prove it right here, right now that the Romans didn't build this dome. I'm going to prove it to you, if you'll listen!"

"What do you think, Tom?" Zara smiled at Tom, who had already cozied up to one of the bags of stones and stretched out comfortably. "Was this dome built by Romans or Garamantes?"

Tom fluffed the bag of stones, as he would a pillow and turned away. "I honestly don't care one iota who built them. All I know is that we've been running on adrenaline for nearly forty-eight hours just trying to keep alive, and before that Sam and I had spent nearly a week in the desert. Now I'm just glad the dome exists and I can rest up while the two of you plot some new means of our demise."

Zara turned her palms outwards and looked at Sam. "He's not even a little curious?"

"Not particularly," Sam suggested. "He's more of a practical kind of guy."

"So, you don't think this was an elaborate smuggler's den?" she joked.

"Do you know any smugglers who could compete with the Roman architects of the day?"

"So you do think it was built by the Romans!"

"No. I think it was built using similar technology as the Romans. It's been long agreed that the Garamantes and the Romans shared similar architectural and engineering designs for their aqueducts."

"Yes. And I thought it was largely agreed that the Garamantes learned their trade from the Romans. If anything, I think the presence of this dome here means the Garamantes were using Roman engineers to build it. Maybe they were trading with them for the intellectual property?"

"I think if you stare at the ceiling long enough you'll see why this wasn't built by the Romans. Certainly not between the 500BC and 700AD when the Garamantes were supposed to have lived."

He watched her eyes study the large dome. She started with the base of one of the four large pendentives. These were the triangular segments of a sphere, which were tapered to points at the bottom and spread at the top to establish the continuous circular or elliptical base needed for the dome. Her eyes studied the skirting between the bases where the water met the dome walls, and then moved upwards along the stone walls, which were still mostly covered with a mixture of limestone, like cement. Her eyes stopped at the giant hole in the ceiling directly above them. Possibly even sixty or more feet high. The opening looked like a tiny opening to the stars. Sam knew the size was an optical illusion and the opening could have been quite wide.

Zara stopped. Her eyes met his. "Okay. I'm an archeologist, not an architect. Tell me why this wasn't built by the Romans?"

"You were so close," Sam said. "The Roman influence is undeniable, but the Roman's never could have constructed this during any period BC."

"But the Garamantes were around up until the 700AD!"

"True, but work like this would have taken at least a hundred years to construct and they would have only constructed it if they still had plenty of water to look after it."

She asked, "So?"

Sam said, "The Romans didn't develop pendentives until the 6th-century. It was first used in the construction of the Eastern Roman Church, Hagia Sophia at Constantinople!"

Zara glanced at the massive pendentives again. "Whoever built here, knew how to use pendentives a lot earlier than the 6th century."

"Exactly."

Zara asked, "What are you suggesting happened?"

Sam said, "I'm suggesting this place was built by the Garamantes and that they were much more advanced than history has lead us to believe."

"There's been a long standing debate about the similarities of the aqueducts built by the Garamantes and the Romans. Some have argued the Garamantes stole their ideas from the Romans, but some have questioned, whether or not it was the Romans who had learned from the Garamantes?"

"That's great, but even for an archeologist, I'm currently more interested in how we're going to escape. We just need to stay down here long enough for our pursuers to pass by and then we can surface."

Sam shook his head. "You know that's not possible."

"Why not?"

"Even if we waited a week, which is the minimum we'd need to wait to escape, we'd still be stuck in the desert. By that time, we'd have gone a week on these tiny rations we took from the downed plane. We'll be malnourished, starving, and in no shape to cross a desert on foot. Then, if we make it to Chad, or Bilma, there'll be too many people there looking for us."

"So, have you got a better plan?"

"Well, as a matter of fact, I do."

Chapter Forty-Five

Sam said, "The oculus was used by the Romans, one of the finest examples being that in the dome of the Pantheon. Open to the weather, it allows rain to enter and fall to the floor, where it is carried away through drains. Though the opening looks small, it actually has a diameter of 27 feet allowing it to light the building just as the sun lights the earth. The rain also keeps the building cool during the hot summer months."

Zara dawdled, unsure where he was going.

"The Romans, however, failed to discover a proper handling of the pendentive—the device essential to placing a dome over a square compartment—that was finally achieved by the Byzantine builders of Hagia Sophia at Constantinople around AD 532–37. The pendentives, which are triangular segments of a sphere, taper to points at the bottom and spread at the top to establish the continuous circular or elliptical base needed for the dome. In masonry the pendentives thus receive the weight of the dome, concentrating it at the four corners where it can be received by the piers beneath. Prior to the pendentive's development, the device of corbeling or the use of the squinch in the corners of a room had been employed. The first attempts at pendentives were made by the Romans, but full achievement of the form was reached only by the Byzantines in Hagia Sophia at Constantinople. Pendentives were commonly used in Renaissance and baroque churches, with a drum often inserted between the dome and pendentives."

"You've already told all this to me!" Zara said. "What I want to know is how you suggest we escape?"

Sam continued, as though Zara had said nothing. "If we can accept the Garamantes had the technology to build a pendentive, we can also accept the hypothesis that they used an elaborate underground irrigation system, and founded prosperous Berber kingdoms or city-states in the Fezzan area of Libya and Chad, in the Sahara desert."

"You think they built irrigation tunnels between their other cities?"

Sam nodded. "Known ruins include numerous tombs, forts, and cemeteries. The Garamantes constructed a network of underground tunnels and shafts to mine the fossil water from beneath the limestone layer under the desert sand. The dating of these foggara is disputed, they appear between 200 BC to 200 AD but continued to be in use until at least the 7th century and perhaps later. The network allowed agriculture to flourish, but used a system of slave labor to keep it maintained."

"What are you going to do? Find these foggoras and walk out of here?"

"Yeah, something like that."

Sam turned off his thermal suit. The power slowly shut down and the light faded. In the darkness Tom snored. Sam gently pushed his back with his boot. Tom rolled on his side and stopped snoring. The cavern became silent as it was dark.

"What now?" Zara asked.

"Now we rest."

"After that?"

"We're going to go find a way out of this mess."

Sam listened to her shuffle on the ground, as though she were uncomfortable and trying hard to find a position to sleep.

She asked, "What about the people you work for?"

Sam smiled at the naiveté. "Will they come for us?"

"Yes."

"They could risk serious international relations if they were seen coming in weapons blazing to retrieve two American treasure hunters."

"But will they come?" she persisted.

Sam said, "You bet your ass, they would. The people I work with would turn the world on its axis to save our lives. They'd come in guns blazing until they found us, if..."

"What?"

"If only they had any idea we were missing. I carried a GPS tracker, but it's on one of the camels we lost. As far as my people know, I'm wandering around aimlessly across the Sahara – which means we're on our own."

Zara made no reply. Instead she sat, rigid, in the dark. Pensive. Sam rolled over. Happy to leave the conversation alone for the night. To a small degree, he still felt a certain level of guilt that he hadn't planned his mission better. If he could have communicated with his team on board the *Maria Helena* they would all be out of this mess by now.

The ground was hard and uncomfortable. Sam had slept in worse places over the years, but his mind struggled to switch off. After about five minutes the silence was broken.

Zara asked, "What do you think happened to your agent?"

Sam paused. "Who?"

"The diamond smuggler."

Sam didn't wait to think about it. "He would have been executed."

"How do you know he was killed?"

"Because he didn't show up at the rendezvous point in Morocco."

"So you think General Ngige's men got to him?"

"I'm certain of it. Satellite images showed his forces in pursuit the day before we lost contact with him."

"So maybe they captured him and he's still alive?"

"No. General Ngige doesn't take prisoners unless they're valuable. And the General didn't make any requests, so we know he didn't keep our man alive. Simple as that."

She asked, "What was he like?"

Surprised by the question, Sam thought about it for a moment. Zara didn't strike him as being a sentimental kind of woman. There was no reason he could see that she would be interested in an American agent. "I don't know. I never met the man. I got out of the military years ago."

She laughed. "That's right. You're here, strictly as a treasure hunter."

"Right," Sam confirmed.

"What do you know about him?"

"Nothing." Sam thought about it for a moment. "Not much. He held dual citizenship with the U.S. and Egypt. His brother still lives and works in the region. His father was a desert dweller. A Saharan nomad, who'd survived by trading throughout a series of sandy outcrops. We know nothing about his mother. She probably died when he was very little."

"What was his name?" She spoke the words softly. There was a little tenderness that he hadn't heard in her voice before.

"Mikhail. I don't know his last name. He had an excellent reputation in the region."

She made a sound. It was barely audible. But in an instant, it told him all he needed to know – and why she was so interested in the man.

Sam said, "You knew him?"

He felt Zara throw her arms around his neck and hold tight. Wet tears rolled onto his neck.

She said, "Yes he was my lover."

Chapter Forty-Six

Mikhail stood up to stretch. There was a slight bend in his spine, but it was as close to freedom as he would receive during his stay at the Lake Tumba Lithium Mine. He'd lost count of how many days he'd been there. None of it mattered to him. Inside the mine life and death came around every other day. If he wanted to live, he would have to beat everyone around him. He'd lost a lot of weight. If he lost any more strength he might not make it. Few people lasted in the mine very long. Those who did had to make friends fast, or beat some very powerful enemies.

Dikembe was one such friend Mikhail had made. He was the largest man Mikhail had ever met. He had to be almost seven foot tall and solid. Rations were served to those who pulled the most amount of lithium brine out from under the mountain. Dikembe, who was the largest, had been pulling massive amounts of the liquid brine for many years. He was given whatever rations he required.

In order to keep control of his slaves, General Ngige provided the same amount of food and water to the men of the mine every twenty-four hours. The prisoner count fluctuated somewhere between five hundred and a thousand men. It didn't matter if this number increased or decreased, the same amount of rations would be provided, so long as the prisoners carried the required amount of lithium brine to the surface.

All lived below the cold sunken earth, in a labyrinth of mine shafts, tunnels, and excavation sites. There were eighty-four individual levels. Mines involved shafts which were vertical and tunnels which were horizontal. It had a series of mine shafts driven along opposing arms, so that there would be plenty of additional ways to reach the surface if a cave-in occurred along any one tunnel or shaft.

The Lake Tumba Lithium Mine had existed for nearly four decades as a gold mine. When the gold veins ran out, or were no longer profitable the mine was sold multiple times until it failed to find a bidder.

Once there, it sat dormant until General Ngige discovered a new purpose for it. A working mine has always been useful as a prison. It served as a deterrent and for the purpose of producing gold. Only, now it served an additional benefit of providing the highest yielding stores of lithium brine in any mine in the world – which made it one of the most valuable pieces of soil anywhere in the world.

If the legends were to be considered true, General Ngige and Dikembe both had an intricate knowledge of the mine, after being forced to work it nearly twenty years ago as children. Both men vowed to change the world they lived. Dikembe prayed to make it a better place, while Ngige wanted nothing but revenge.

Mikhail watched Dikembe finish his bowl of food. Rice, mixed with fish. He ate like an animal. Quick, without leaving a scrap of food and ravenous.

Mikhail said, "Now what?"

Dikembe stood up. His hunched shoulders, striking the tunnel's ceiling. "Now we rest so we can perform tomorrow."

Mikhail had heard the argument many times before. The man had the patience of Gandhi. "What about the plan?"

"When the time is ready."

"And when will that be?" Mikhail looked at some of the other men who laid on the floor, no longer able to support their failed bodies. "Your men already have the weapons they were promised. When will we attack?"

"When the time is right and all is ready."

If the guy wasn't twice his size, Mikhail seriously considered hitting him. "Can't you see? Dikembe, your men are dying around you. Their once strong and healthy lives, withering away to greet death, for nothing!"

Dikembe walked away, descending further into the mine, silently.

"You owe them a better death?" Mikhail stopped him, by reaching the giant's massive shoulder with his hand. "And you owe me a better explanation, after all I have done for your cause."

Dikembe looked at him. His gray-blue eyes somehow ghoulish in the poor light. "You don't know a thing about this mine, do you?"

"No. But I know I don't intend on dying here for no purpose at all, while a coward waits for his own oblivion."

The giant stopped. He turned around abruptly. For a second Mikhail thought the giant was going to kill him with his bare hands. Instead the man looked to the ground below. With his massive finger, he drew a series of horizontal and vertical lines. There were four separate mines, each one extending miles upon miles in a series of tunnels, spanning every direction. The four mines were all joined by a rectangular tunnel that formed at level ten. And above that, three tunnels traverse in an ascending direction, until all three joined together and finally reached the surface.

Dikembe said, "This is the Lake Tumba Lithium Mine. There are eighty-four levels. As you know, throughout a twenty-four hour cycle we need to extract a total of ten tones of lithium from inside this maze. That includes both the metal separated from other elements in igneous minerals and the lithium salts extracted from water and brine pools."

Mikhail nodded and said nothing. Dikembe wasn't telling him anything he didn't already know.

Dikembe drew a line across the top levels of the mine. "At night time, Ngige's men lock gates at this section, keeping us trapped below level ten."

"Yes, but give me enough time and I'll break through those grates."

Dikembe ignored his request. Instead he drew the three main tunnels that led to the single tunnel that extended all the way to the surface. He then met Mikhail's eyes. "Do you know what's directly above these three tunnels?"

"No."

"Lake Tumba and nearly three hundred million gallons of water."

Mikhail nodded. If anyone tried to tunnel out, they would have no way of knowing when or where they would reach the bottom of the lake. Even if they didn't try to escape, General Ngige must have ordered dynamite to be drilled into the ceiling of one of those tunnels. At the first sign of a revolt, the dynamite would be blasted and all of them would drown below.

"There must be something we can do?" Mikhail said. "Maybe we could somehow build our own barrier. Or find another tunnel out?"

Dikembe nodded. "It will be hard. The work needs to be undertaken after lithium has been extracted for the day. And it needs to be done so quietly. Using a chisel only, to carve a fault in the tunnel's roof. And it needs to be completely invisible by the time the first guards enter the tunnel in the morning."

"But it must be possible!"

"It's possible. Of that I'm certain." Dikembe spoke with the slow, deep and almost reverent voice of a spiritual leader. A man born to lead men to greatness. "It's taken nearly a year. But the work will be complete by the end of the week."

Chapter Forty-Seven – Malta

Nestled on the eastern side of Malta's Grand Harbor, the *Maria Helena* casually swung a hundred and eighty degrees on her anchor, as the peak tide turned. The outward appearance suggested she was once little more than an icebreaker, more recently retrofitted to meet the demands of her wealthy owner who wished to play mariner at all ends of the globe. A large helipad stood out on the aft deck, and several weather and navigational instruments were visible above the four story high bridge. Otherwise, the ship was relatively barren. It had a reinforced steel hull with sharp, angular lines, making her exceptionally stable at sea.

Along her hull were the words, *Deep Sea Projects*.

Inside, she contained some of the most advanced marine and submarine equipment available. To manage this equipment and support the range of deep sea projects around the globe, was a unique team of highly intelligent people, all specialists in their respective fields. After three weeks at harbor, most of these experts had passed the point of enjoying their reprieve and were now finding they were thoroughly bored.

The eastern wall of Malta's Grand Harbor turned gold as the setting sun struck it. Sitting alone at a workstation inside the bridge, Elise pulled up the GPS tracking chart. Stared at it for a few moments and then checked the previous forty-eight hours to confirm her concerns.

She gently bit the top corner of her lip. Sighed and then called out. "Matthew, get your ass in here."

"What have you got?" Matthew, the ship's skipper, replied as he climbed the steel steps up from the deck below.

She didn't wait until Matthew was on the bridge to explain. "This is the GPS tracking beacon Sam's been using. Either he's completely lost focus and direction, walking around aimlessly, or his sat phone is on his camel and he's lost his camel."

Matthew smiled reassuringly. "I wouldn't worry, too much – Sam hates riding. I wouldn't be surprised if he didn't do something stupid like get rid of his camel because he couldn't handle the damned thing."

Elise asked, "He hates riding camels?"

Matthew nodded. "Horses, camels, donkeys. We've tried him on all of them over the years. Can't relax you see. Hates to lose control. He'll be fine. He'd have to do something pretty stupid to run into trouble in the middle of nowhere."

"That's what I'm afraid of."

"And that's what Tom's doing there – making sure he keeps Sam in check."

Elise brought up the image of the last waterhole where the camels had taken a direct route three days ago. "We know someone was guiding the camels at this point. The lines are too direct to be accidental. Afterwards, they seem to go around in circles before repeatedly returning to the same oasis."

"Where's the oasis?"

"It's called mini Bilma Oasis. Somewhere in Niger, bordering with Chad."

"Okay, can you get me current satellite imaging?" he asked.

"I'm already on it. The computer's currently communicating with the satellites overhead. I'll have an image for you any second now."

Three separate images appeared on her screen. Each taken from a separate satellite and representing a single snapshot of the location. Elise clicked on the first one. The image blurred for a moment while the resolution finished pixilating.

The image became instantly clear. Elise stared at it for a few seconds and then her eyes met Matthew's. His hazel eyes had the kind of steely resolve of a man with decades of command under his belt. The sort of person who knew when it was his job to make decisions that might cost the company a fortune for nothing, or worse still, the lives of his people.

Matthew depressed the microphone for the internal speaker system. "All right, team. Vacation's over. I want everyone on the bridge right now."

Chapter Forty-Eight

Elise waited until the last person from the crew entered the room before she spoke. She looked around the room. Veyron, their engineer, Genevieve their chef and general jack-of-all-trades, and Matthew, their skipper. All professionals. Every one of them the best in their respective fields. Disciplined. Tenacious. Exacting individuals capable of achieving anything they set their minds to. Elise smiled as she recalled how she'd come to be part of such a team.

She was by far the youngest person in the room. Most people guessed she was in her mid-twenties. Elise didn't know her exact age. She'd been orphaned at birth and years later had been picked up by a random IQ and cryptic reasoning test the CIA had run through all schools and public child centers. Her results had been off the charts and the CIA had taken her in and raised her as their own. Their very own weapon to beat the next generation of computer hackers. She instantly related to computers and evolved with them at a time when the internet was slowly being introduced to homes around the world. One day she decided she didn't want to work for the CIA anymore and simply wrote herself a new identity. That's how she came to be working for Sam Reilly on board the *Maria Helena.*

And now Sam Reilly and Tom Bower were in serious trouble.

Despite her age, people listened when she spoke. "Three days ago we lost track of Sam and Tom. Somewhere deep in the Saharan desert. The last time we had photographic surveillance of both men they were about two hundred miles south of Libya, bordering Niger and Chad at an oasis, enjoying an afternoon swim."

Elise opened the first of the images on the overhead projector. It showed the small jellybean shaped oasis in the middle of a sea of sand dunes. There were five palm trees. Next to the water on the northern side, were several pieces of rubbish and debris. She enhanced that section of the image and the bodies of two people were clearly visible. They wore the jungle camouflage uniform of any number of rebel forces found much further south in the Sudan, Congo, Nigeria, the Central African Republic, or even the Democratic Republic of Congo.

No one spoke.

Elise clicked to further enhance the image of a third deceased person on the southern side of the oasis. "This is where my day really turned bad!"

The dead man was lying on his back and his uniform, despite being quite reddened had an emblem of a snake holding an AK-47. It was almost cartoonish, if it wasn't so serious. It was the sign of the African United Conquerors. And if they were that far north it meant only one thing. They knew about Sam Reilly and were coming to stop him.

"Ah, shit!" Veyron was the first to recognize the significance. "When do we leave to go get them?"

Elise looked at Matthew. "Do you think the Secretary of Defense would authorize help from the USS Mississippi? It's currently stationed in the Mediterranean Sea."

"Are you kidding me?" Matthew shook his head. "With a covert operation like this, she'd have to sacrifice her agent. Even if she was the one to recruit Sam as her personal problem solver."

"We have to go after Tom and Sam," Genevieve said. "Their own government can't – so if they're in trouble, we need to be their solution."

Elise said, "There's one other thing I haven't mentioned. A massive hoard of General Ngige's men is out there in the desert. They've been slowly heading south through the Erg of Bilma. The good news is that while they're on the move, they don't yet have Sam and Tom. The bad news is we don't have a clue why the General would risk moving so many of his soldiers this far away from the Democratic Republic of Congo. But we have to assume he had a damned good reason. The most likely, being that he knows about Sam Reilly coming for the diamonds."

Genevieve nodded. She'd heard every word and none of it made a difference to her. "Okay. Matthew, take us in as close as you can to the Libyan coast without getting us killed. I'll pilot the Sikorsky. We'll mount two Browning machine guns in case we get into any trouble. Veyron and Elise, you'll arm the machine guns and we'll go in and get our boys back."

No one had a better idea.

Elise smiled. This is why she loved her family. These people would shift the world to help each other. There was no discussion about whether the U.S. government would approve of their rescue attempt. Heck, even flying a heavily armed helicopter over Libyan airspace was likely to have them shot down and start a war, but the team could get around that. She would have to hack into the Libyan Civil Aviation Authority and write a special permit for approval to fly within the airspace. Perhaps she could associate the helicopter to one of the oil companies inside Libya. They would be screwed if someone actually looked at their helicopter and its armaments, but it would be enough to stop the Libyan Airforce from shooting them out of the sky within the first few minutes of entering Libyan airspace.

It could be done.

Matthew stood up. He was by far the most conservative on board the ship. Everyone looked at him. He was the only one who might consider objecting. Certainly the most likely to find legitimate reasons to object. And there were many.

His face was focused and his eyes determined. "Okay. Remember our boys are stuck in a desert with a hoard of madmen after them. Let's get a move on!"

Chapter Forty-Nine

Desert City Bilma – Niger

The Sikorsky flew a total distance of 815 miles from the coast of Libya directly through to the desert town of Bilma on the north eastern border of Niger. The flight had taken five hours and almost completely depleted their long range fuel tanks. The Erg of Bilma was one of the largest sandpits in the world and seemingly one of the most hostile environments to match. The prevailing wind gusted from the northeast, known as the Harmattan, which pummeled sand at a speed in excess of 70 knots for nine months of the year. The giant, rolling sand dunes were the hottest, driest and most inhospitable regions of the Sahara. The town reported an annual rainfall of less than one inch and the nearest known wells in the region were hundreds of miles away.

Genevieve banked the chopper to the right and ran along the Kaouar Cliffs. Their 328 foot high face appeared white against the surrounding sand and provided her first visual navigation aid since entering the large Erg. About three minutes later, she spotted a glimpse of the town. Once upon a time it was a thriving metropolis, where travelers using the Great Saharan caravan routes from Azalai to Agadez could stop and make provisions for their journey. The Kaouar oases were still famous for salt and date production, and are still the only place of provisioning along the route of the great Bornu to Fezzan caravan trail. Up until the 19th century, this route was the main point of contact between the African Sahel and the Mediterranean civilizations. Its current population was under 1600 and its people survived solely on date cultivation and salt production through evaporation ponds.

She looked down at the oasis town below. A small city of adobe buildings lined the plains, where the Kaouar escarpment in the north protected it from the constant northeastern winds. To the east of the city, large saline pans were dug into the side of the town. Genevieve instantly thought the place looked like it belonged in the set of an early Star Wars movie rather than somewhere people actually lived.

Genevieve glanced at Veyron. "You're certain we can find reliable aviation fuel here?"

Veyron nodded. "Certain. I talked to a guy this morning who says he flies a twin-engine Beech G36 Bonanza throughout the region. Says he mostly transports mail and fresh goods that can't be produced in the town. Sometimes takes individual passengers, but not often. He says there's an airstrip at Bilma and it has good quality aviation fuel. Uses it every week."

"You've got to be kidding me?"

Veyron smiled. "Says there's a guy there who robs him blind, but what's he supposed to do? He has to refuel his plane somewhere in the Sahara. And there aren't a lot of suppliers you can trust."

Genevieve lowered the collective, which reduced their altitude and started their descent. "All right I'm going to land next to the runway. Anywhere in particular I need to put us down?"

"Anywhere will do," Veyron said. "Our contact guy will drive out to refuel us."

Genevieve hovered just above the ground and then lowered the collectively fully to the ground, placing the skids firm in the sand. The rotor blades whined to an idle. She ran her eyes along a cluster of instruments. Confident everything was in working order, she flicked the power switch to off and shut down the engines.

Elise unclipped her seatbelt and stared up at the muddy and higgledy-piggledy town. "Why would anyone want to live out here?"

Genevieve laughed. "I don't think many people planned it. They were born into it and never quite worked out a way of escaping."

Elise slid the helicopter door open and was the first to climb out. Veyron followed and Genevieve was the last out. She watched the rotor blades whine to a stop before carefully walking around the aircraft, checking for any damage taken during the long flight. If they needed to get out in a hurry, she wanted to make certain their ride was sound.

She noticed Elise attempting to tie her tesirnest, a traditional piece of cloth worn by Tuareg women over a light dress. She intricately ran the indigo blue robe around her body, finishing with it carefully wrapping around her head, while leaving her face open. Tuareg people, Genevieve recalled, were the only Islamic culture in the world where the men wore the veils inside town and the women wore headdresses with their faces exposed. Both Tuareg men and women traditionally wore indigo-blue robes. The dye used in coloring the cloth would leak over time and become absorbed in the wearer's skin, giving a slight bluish tinge to their faces. Due to this the nomadic desert people acquired the name of the Blue Desert People, which had persisted for centuries until present day.

Genevieve checked the rotor tail for any chips, oil leaks, sand, or damage caused during the flight. She ran her hand, lovingly, along the helicopter's tail and back to the opening where Elise finished tying the last of her cloth across her shoulders by applying a special knot.

Tuareg women were also recognized for their seniority in the social structure of society, with men being beneath the females in the order of the family household. Women were allowed to divorce their men and were unconditionally entitled to their household savings, while men were not allowed to divorce.

Elise turned to face her. "What do you think?"

The deep blue robe, delicately left open to expose her face and the dark blue make-up applied to her face accentuated the deep purple of Elise's eyes. If it were possible, the image made Elise even more stunning than she ordinarily appeared.

Genevieve smiled. "I think if I had any inclination of being gay, I'd ask you to marry me."

"Thanks." An awkward upward crease formed at the corner of Elise's lips. "I think. I'm more interested in whether or not you think we'll pass as Tuareg nomads?"

"Hell no. I think they'll take one look at you and wonder which empress has arrived."

Elise closed her eyes. She looked like she was imagining an empress coming to town. She nodded and said, "That will do, so long as they give us the information we need."

"About that. How do you think we go about this? You think a couple of Tuareg women can just walk up to a public place in Bilma and someone will tell us where Sam and Tom ended up?"

Standing outside the helicopter Elise placed a metallic briefcase on the floor of the Sikorsky. She typed in a code and the weapons case opened. Inside was an Israeli Uzi, a Glock 19, and two German made grenades. "Yeah, I think we can do something like that."

Elise removed the Uzi and stripped it. She then checked the firing mechanism and reassembled it before starting again with the Glock. She was quick. Always had been. It was part of her inner psyche. She had a naturally sharp, systematic and analytical mind, and completed the entire process in under a minute.

Genevieve watched as Elise glanced over to see how far she had gotten with her weapons. It was a challenge. It made her smile. For Elise it was still a game. One she played well, and for a newcomer had developed an expert proficiency in a relatively short space of time.

But Genevieve had spent her life with weapons. For her, it wasn't a game. It was a part of life. Genevieve blinked without saying a word. She had already stripped her weapons and reassembled them in nearly half that time. Then again, she had done little else than work with military hardware for a lifetime before joining the *Maria Helena.*

Chapter Fifty

Elise slipped the Uzi into a holder built into her robes. The Glock, she nestled into an ankle strap on her right leg and attached two grenades to a weapons belt beneath her robe. If General Ngige's army of rebels were still searching the city, the last thing she wanted to do was get caught in a firefight under equipped.

She watched as Genevieve finished tying her tesirnest. She'd brought a similar array of weapons with one addition – a razor sharp, 13 inch hunting knife. At a glance, the blade was Damascus steel. Elise wasn't an expert in knives, but recognized the hardened metal from its distinctive patterns of banding and mottling, reminiscent of flowing water. Such blades were reputed to be tough, resistant to shattering and capable of being honed to a sharp, and resilient edge, popular among hunters. The handle was made of Karelian birch, turned a well-worn brown color. At the base of the blade was a single word, written in Russian.

"What's the blade say?" Elise asked

Genevieve grinned. "Some secrets I'd rather keep."

"Sure." She pulled her robe over her shoulder to conceal the Uzi. "All right. Shall we go bring our boys home?"

Genevieve nodded and said nothing.

They left Veyron to mind the helicopter and test the quality of the fuel before he purchased any. Elise and Genevieve entered the squat town through its first opening. It looked less like a gate and more like a crack in the poorly constructed wall. There were no other openings visible along the southern side of the town. The air was hot to breathe. The mercury was well above a hundred and ten Fahrenheit and a strong smell of goat manure mixed with squalor wafted from inside. Elise heard some children playing in the distance, and the sound of the moldings of salt-cones being cracked at the saline pans. She analyzed every sound she heard and then relaxed. There were no sounds of large groups of men yelling, or weapons firing, as expected if General Ngige's army was present.

She took a deep breath and stepped inside.

The temperature dropped immediately. At least twenty degrees at a guess. The opening lead to a small semi-covered adobe, which was a mud-piled array of buildings, leading to more of the same structures. Three goats were tied to an iron ring protruding from the clay wall. The animals made no reaction as they entered.

They breached deep into the desert city through a series of narrow laneways, corridors, and tunnels. Further inside was a swathe of mud homes. Nothing quite as ordered as mudbrick, but simply mud piled upon mud to make up the primitive protection provided by an adobe. There were no doors for privacy. Only openings, where the mud had either collapsed or been left intentionally free.

It was quiet. Outside there were the sounds of children playing and men working, but in here the only ones she heard came from the few goats. They walked approximately three hundred feet inside the township without speaking.

Maintaining a northern direction, they followed a pathway toward the heart of the township. It wasn't quite a road or an alleyway. Most of it was covered in some way or the other. But it was definitely a main pathway from the south to the north of the city, which meandered its way in a disordered approach through a multitude of mud houses that were interlaced throughout. Elise started to feel like she was walking down an old western town, where a shootout was inevitable and the townsfolk had all gone inside to avoid the fight.

Elise glanced at Genevieve. "Does it seem a little too quiet around here?"

"No. I think everyone's outside working." Genevieve spoke loudly and then whispered. "They're following us."

Elise felt her heart race as adrenaline engaged her fight or flight response. Her eyes darted between each opening and her ears strained to hear her attackers. It disconcerted her to know that Genevieve had already picked up they were being pursued, but she still couldn't hear or see anything to suggest so. There was nothing but a feeling. A sense like you were being watched. She let it go and picked up her pace, following the warren of low clay buildings which meandered through the salt plains in a random and disordered way. Up ahead there was an opening in the roof where the town shifted upward and an old saline pan had previously been excavated by hand.

That was the goal. From there they might be able to defend themselves against whoever was following. Also, the opening on the side of the hill would allow Veyron to witness a firefight if it came to that. Not that he could do much to help.

"There," Genevieve whispered.

Elise scanned the series of openings in the building on the right of them. There were eyes staring out at them. They were brown and focused.

Elise asked, "You got a plan how you want to do this, Gen?"

Genevieve smiled. "No. I'm here with you. I kind of figured you'd thought this thing through."

"That was silly of you."

"All the same, what do you want to do?"

Elise sighed. "Get to the end of this main drag until we're up against the wall and then we confront them."

"That's a stupid plan. That wall looks more like a place to stand for a firing squad and there's no exit route available."

"You got a better idea?"

"No."

"Then I guess we'll stick with mine."

Elise stopped at the solid wall and turned around. Her eyes scanned the area in front. No one had faced them yet, but she could see all the eyes staring at her. She breathed in and reached for her weapon, but felt

Genevieve's hand on her shoulder. Genevieve didn't say a word, but her eyes told her enough – they said, there's too many to win this if it comes to a firefight, so keep your weapon hidden for as long as you can.

Elise raised her hands. "You can all come out now."

Nothing happened. She changed to French, the only other language she knew. "You can come out now."

Genevieve followed and whispered. "This is your idea of a plan?"

"I'm still waiting for a better one."

They waited and nothing happened.

Only silence.

And then a crowd of more than a hundred people approached.

Chapter Fifty-One

Elise watched as the crowd approached slowly. There was no yelling. No war cries. They all stared at her face as though they were possessed. They moved toward her, taking a single step at a time, in perfect harmony. There were men, women and children amongst the crowd. The children were at the front of the crowd, followed by the women and then the men. No one held a weapon. Individually, the mob were no match for their Uzis, but their bullets would run out long before everyone was dead.

Despite its extreme poverty, the town of Bilma experienced little to no crime. Why would it? Poor people have nothing to steal. The families lived in a commune, sharing a common roof and water supply with the rest of the inhabitants of the town.

The adults stopped.

But the children continued in utter silence.

Elise left her Uzi holstered and greeted them all with the palms of her hands held out open. "Hello. My name's Elise and this is Genevieve. And we need your help."

The children slowed their progress, if that was even possible. They took one, simultaneous step, every tenth second. Their eyes fixated on Elise and completely ignoring Genevieve.

Genevieve said, "This is pretty weird."

Elise smiled and removed her headdress to show her face. "Hey, at least they're not pointing guns in our face."

The children stopped.

A moment later the children's mouths opened wide and identical to each other. The women behind stood up as though they were about to guard something precious, while the men locked arms and formed a semi-circle around the entire group, trapping her and Genevieve against the wall.

Elise said, "Okay. Now this is getting weird."

Genevieve replied, "You think?"

A strange and powerful sound erupted from the still mouths of the children. Their eyes, wide and possessed, fixated on Elise. The eerie noise continued for at least two minutes. Never changing volume or pitch. It was sharp, and poignant, and beautiful at the same time. The sound, although terrifying given its situation, would have been worthy of the Monteverdi Choir.

When it stopped, the kids advanced toward them.

Elise glanced at Genevieve. "Don't kill anyone."

Genevieve smiled back. "I'll do my best, but if they start with the singing again, I might have to reach for the Uzi."

Elise watched as the children pulled at Genevieve with surprising strength, driving her to the back of the crowd. Once there, the women made her stand with them.

"Back the fuck off!" Genevieve swore.

But the women ignored her. They didn't hurt her. Instead they simply grabbed her every time she tried to move and forced her to stand still.

Elise breathed in deeply and then slowly exhaled. She forced herself to relax and held the palms of her hands outward. The children reached for her hands. Their touch was gentle. Each child taking it in their turn to make contact and then swap with another child.

Their eyes told her everything she needed to know. They weren't dilated and fixated because they wanted to hurt her, they children were mesmerized by something about her. They wanted to reach out and touch her fingertips, as they would their God.

But she wasn't anybody's God.

In the middle of the crowd, where the women were still trying to force Genevieve to stand still, Elise saw something that made her heart skip a beat.

No, Genevieve, can't you see these people don't mean us any harm?

Genevieve was once a deadly assassin. No one knew it as a fact, but everyone on board the *Maria Helena* had long suspected she'd left a violent past behind her. Watching her now, Elise knew it for a certainty.

She moved like an assassin. A single, agile movement. The outcome of which, found Genevieve with her right arm hooked around one of the women's throat and her Damascus bladed knife resting at the point of the woman's carotid artery. "All right everyone. I said, back the fuck off!"

But nobody moved.

Elise watched as the entire crowd remained fixated on her alone. Even the woman now held prisoner, hadn't taken her eyes away from her.

Elise leaned forward and then stood up, taking a solid stance. In the process her sunglasses dropped to the mud floor. "Enough. Stop this!"

A loud gasp resonated from the crowd in unison. Instantly afterwards, every person bowed before her. Elise watched as the only two people in the crowd who were now not on the floor bowing, was Genevieve and her captive. The captive fought against the sharp, Damascus steel, until Genevieve relinquished the fight and allowed her to bow.

Chapter Fifty-Two

Elise allowed the silence to carry on for thirty seconds, before she put an end to it. She smiled kindly. If at that moment any of her audience had any doubt that she was a Goddess it was suddenly removed when her sunglasses fell and they saw her purple eyes.

She said, "Who is in charge here?"

No response.

"Who speaks for your community?" she persisted.

A man at the back of the crowd removed his veil. "I do."

Elise smiled, kindly. "What is your name?"

"Nayram." The short man returned her smile and bowed. "And you must be Elise. *The savior.*"

"I'm Elise, but it's the first time I've been called *the savior.*"

"It might be the first time, but I promise you, it won't be the last."

"How do you know who I am?"

"Because I grew up here. My father was born here, and so was his grandfather." Nayram spoke as though everything he'd said justified it.

Elise said, "Thank you, everyone, for your warm welcome, but now I must speak with Mr. Nayram privately."

Every person in the vicinity dissipated immediately. People returned to their daily tasks. Children played games at the edge of the town. Women picked dates from the trees which littered the oasis, and men set about cracking saline pots once more.

Elise watched Nayram look at Genevieve and then back at her. His eyes darting between the two and a worried crest formed between his brows. "Do you want me to get rid of her?"

"No. She can stay."

He seemed uncertain about her decision, but nodded anyway.

"Thanks," Genevieve said, in English.

Elise asked, "Do you know why I came here today?"

He smiled and spoke with a certainty she hadn't seen in him before. "Why of course, you are here to repair the future."

Elise laughed. "Okay, now I know you have me confused with someone else. Do you know how I fix the future? It sounds unlikely. I didn't even know it was broken."

"It's broken. That's for certain. Strange times have sent us down the wrong string." He smiled cheerfully. "That is why you are here. To repair the event and keep the future where she belongs."

"Sure," Elise nodded with uncertainty. "We're looking for two friends of ours. A big tall guy and one around average height. Both built like Sherman Tanks. Americans. Treasure hunters. Look uncomfortable as all hell on a pair of camels. They went missing a couple days ago. I don't suppose you know anything about them?"

He shook his head. "I am afraid I know nothing about your friends. Where were they when you lost them?"

"North of here. Two days ago they were filling up on water in the mini-oasis of Bilma. That must be about sixty miles north-east of here?"

"Seventy."

"They were heading south, so we assumed they passed through Bilma. Any chance they would have skipped Bilma and headed on to Mao?"

"No. Everyone stops here on their way through." He shook his head. "But there was a raid on a dig a few hundred miles north of here."

She asked, "An archeological dig?"

"Yes. A large archeological excavation site. There's a camp to the northeast. They were looking for a sacred book. Many of our men went there for work. Three days ago it was attacked by a large group of warriors, carrying many weapons. AK-47s, big guns, an armored car. A lot of people died, you might want to look there. Your friends, if they were there, most likely were killed."

Elise nodded. "I understand."

"Is there anything else we can do for you?" he asked.

"We were told you could provide fuel for our helicopter?"

"Yes, of course. Right away, we'll send the truck out to refuel your helicopter. My friends will provide you with refreshments and water for your journey."

"Thank you."

Nayram guided the two of them through the ancient desert city. Stopping briefly while three women gave them a small bowl of dried fruits and a flask of water. Elise and Genevieve thanked the women and gladly accepted the food as they walked.

Genevieve looked at her blankly, unable to follow the fast conversation in French. "What did you learn?"

"Not much. Nothing good. A camp was attacked north-east of here. He thinks our friends might have been caught up in the gunfight."

Genevieve shrugged. "That sounds like something Sam and Tom might do, left alone without you or me to show them the error of their ways. What about you?"

Elise asked, "What about me?"

Genevieve smiled. "You're not going to pretend we didn't just witness these people turn you into their deity, are we?"

"It has to do with my eyes. I have naturally purple eyes."

"Really? I always assumed those were contact lenses?"

"No. Purple's my real color. I wear contacts only when I want to fool people."

"Okay, so they don't like purple?"

"There's an ancient Egyptian legend about a bright light shooting across the horizon. It was the hand of God. Every person the light came into contact with became permanently scarred with bright purple eyes. They became immortal and highly intelligent. There was a group of travelers who witnessed the event. They were called the *Six Hundred*. They traveled the lands, living free and powerful lives. But most of them eventually got bored. Gods don't like to remain friends with mere mortals. So most left. But legend has it, a few still roam the desert. Those are the throwbacks. The ones heaven and hell weren't willing to see. Those were the fiends to be frightened of. They were hunted to extinction by the living until only the purest remained."

"So what's the truth?" Genevieve looked like she hadn't bought a word that she'd said.

Elise grinned and stared at her. "What's written on your blade?"

Genevieve paused and unsheathed her weapon. Despite its age, the blade shined like it had only been forged today. Her eyes stared at the blade and the word, but Elise could tell she wasn't really looking at it. Instead, her mind was recalling something from a long time ago. From a world she'd fought hard to leave behind.

Genevieve looked up. Her eyes meeting Elise's firm gaze. "Solntsevo."

"What does it mean?"

"It's a place."

Elise asked, "In Russia?"

Genevieve nodded. "In the district of Kursk Oblast."

Elise grinned in response, but remained silent. She'd been given a unique privilege in learning about Genevieve's past. The crew of the *Maria Helena* had given up running a tipping bet on where she'd come from and what she used to do before joining. Instead, they simply accepted her as a wraith – a person with no past.

"What's so important about Solntsevo?"

"It's where my father was born. He was a prominent local businessman there. Very successful. Equally dangerous and mean when he had to be. In his business, that was always. We had a falling out, many years ago. I ran away and made sure he'd never find me again. My father wasn't the sort of man you challenged and got to live. I leave the name here because I never want to forget where I came from – and what I have to lose."

Elise listened in silence. Acknowledging that Genevieve didn't have to explain it all. They all had a past somewhere. Some not very pleasant or as honorable as their present.

Genevieve looked at her and smiled. Acutely aware she didn't have to go on, but at the same time wanting to. "It's where I left a previous life behind in a place where no-one gets a second chance. Every time I kill with this blade, I want to remember the world I left behind, so that I make sure never to return, despite the urge." Genevieve sheathed the blade and turned to face her. "So, what's the story about your eyes?"

"There's nothing quite so secretive. Fact is, I have no idea. I've always had purple eyes. They call it *Alexandria's Genesis*, but most doctors still debate if the condition is real or not. It's not a rare form of albinism, as most people would have guessed. I don't have any trouble seeing in the bright sunlight. I never got to meet my parents, so I don't know where they came from." She laughed. "And if I'm immortal, I have a long time to find out."

"Okay, then how did you know about the legend?"

"There's several different versions of them scattered throughout the internet. Mostly completely false, but several refer to the Six Hundred who were turned immortal in ancient Egypt. As we've all seen before, the most compelling legends have just the tiniest bit of truth to them."

"At least enough truth to scare the hell out of the natives here."

"We're not afraid of you," Nayram said, in perfect English. "We worship you for what you will one day do for our people."

"You called me *the savior*, but you don't have a clue what I save your people from. What makes you so certain I'm the one you're looking for?

218

What makes all of your people so certain? I could have been anyone. I was wearing sunglasses until the very end. Already, the children had gathered."

"The children were testing you."

"How?"

Nayram said, "We all knew you were one of them – the *Six Hundred*. But we couldn't be sure whether you'd been refused by heaven or hell. The children's shrieks would have forced an evil God to attack. But you stood there and graced them with your kind smile."

"But why me? What made me stand out, so that your entire town should take note?"

"There's a painting I'd like you to see. It's on the way out. Come, I will show it to you. It's been here a very long time. Everyone knows about the image."

"What's the painting of?"

"It depicts two women approaching from the air, upon a beast with wings that spun faster than the eyes could see. They came here, searching for something. We provide them with refreshments, and they leave us, so that one of the women may go on to become *the savior*. That woman had the purple eyes of the *Six Hundred*, so you see, you are her."

"I don't see," Elise said. "Your people must have surely seen helicopters before?"

"Yes. But this painting was done in 1562 by an old man who had taken refuge from the worst sand storm in the history of Bilma. He said his name was Nostradamus, and that this woman here, would save the future from a catastrophic event."

Nayram stopped and they looked at the image painted on the stone wall. It depicted two women climbing out of a helicopter. One was barely visible beneath her indigo robes – she wore a darkened shadow over her robe, like a halo of evil, while the other one glowed like pure goodness. The good woman had her tesirnest tied in such a way that it exposed her face. It was beautiful. With obvious Eurasian ancestry, the face was a blend of cultures. Silky dark hair, high cheek bones, and exotic purple eyes that were rich in intelligence and kindness. The sort of facial features and artistic hyperbole, created by an ancient people to depict a fictional Goddess of unimaginable beauty.

Genevieve was the first to gasp – because the woman in the painting was identical to Elise. Below the painting was a series of numbers carved into the stone. Chiseled out of the soft stone by hand nearly four hundred years ago, the numbers showed today's date. "If you're *the savior* with the white halo, what does that make me?"

Elise studied the darkened haze that shadowed the image of Genevieve. It could have been anyone, but everything else about the painting suggested it was her and Genevieve arriving from the helicopter. It was hard not to be frightened of the image Nostradamus had painted of her friend.

"*The savior's* friend and one hell of a protector when one needs it and right now, I think the future needs all the help it can get." Elise smiled. It was reassuring, without being patronizing. "All right, we've seen enough. If the future is so certain I need to save lives, I don't see any reason why I shouldn't start with saving Sam and Tom."

Chapter Fifty-Three

Adebowale heard the roaring sound of water fighting its way through the tunnel toward him. Driven by millions upon millions of pounds of pressure from above, the torrent charged through the narrow passages and warrens with the energy of a tsunami. Compared to the approaching onslaught, Adebowale's massive and athletic structure appeared weak and fragile. There was nowhere to run. Even though he was given a ten minute head start, the water would reach him well before he could ever escape. There was nothing for it, and yet he tried to run.

He always did.

Every time it was exactly the same. He felt the burning sensation in his legs and arms as the release of adrenaline stimulated his fight or flight response. He'd played college football in the US as a quarterback and despite his massive frame was capable of moving quickly when he wanted to. He felt as the tendons of his calves, designed for short bursts and sprints, propelled him like a racecar. It felt good. Like maybe this time he would make it.

The pitch of the churning water increased and he imagined his death at any moment. Despite his speed, he felt he was running through mud. With each movement, his legs were being slowed as though an invisible coil was restraining them.

Ahead, the passage split into two directions. Left and right. Adebowale chose left. Somehow it felt correct. The narrow tunnel had a distinct incline to it, which meant he was gaining elevation. He'd made the right choice! The only way to outrun the water, was to rise above it.

The tunnel appeared dark ahead. The dim lights which lined the passageway looked like they'd suddenly been cut off. He continued running at full speed in a way that only an athlete could and then he stopped. Directly in front of him, a large cave-in had blocked his progression.

He'd run out of places to escape! He turned and watched as the water raced towards him with lethal finality. In an instant, and like last time, Adebowale realized he'd been here before. And like every other time the water struck him with such force, he lost consciousness before his mind could even register the sensation of the cold water on his skin.

He woke up, struggling to breathe. His chest pounding, and his lungs stung. Sweat dripped from his blood-drained skin. Adebowale looked up at the sun. The pain lasted longer than usual this time. He still was having difficulty breathing and his tongue felt dry and cracked. His right shoulder throbbed. Something's not right. The water should have killed him. There was no reason for him to have pain in his left shoulder.

Adebowale gasped.

He'd had another dream. He consciously forced himself to take in a deep breath and open his eyes. Everything was still dark. It could have been night time, but he felt the heat burning at his skin. No. It wasn't night time. His vision had become severely blurred.

Something wanted to take him away from this world. He turned his palms outward in supplication. The death he feared for so many years he now longed to receive.

He felt vibrations through the post he'd been tied to. Adebowale opened his eyes. The light was improving, but only just. The sun was opening again, as though it had been eclipsed by something. And that something was moving toward him.

The vibrations turned into a sound he recognized. The blades of a large helicopter thumped overhead and the light returned, as the aircraft banked to its left.

Chapter Fifty-Four

Elise sat in the front passenger seat of the Sikorsky's cockpit as Genevieve banked the helicopter for a better view of the ruined camp. It looked like more than a couple hundred laborers had been employed to work the excavation site. The tents, belongings and equipment were all burnt. Their embers had died days earlier.

It wasn't until their second pass that Elise noticed them.

They had been dumped into a large opening in the sand, presumably where the main excavation site had been until recently. The entire ground below appeared to be moving. A sea of black ebbed backwards and then crept forward eerily as though driven by the monotony of the ocean's tide. It took Elise a few seconds to realize what she was looking at. Her eyes and mind unable to accept the facts.

The men had been dumped inside the main dig and burned, along with their simple possessions. Their bodies had been exposed to intense heat and molded to the sand to form a mangled composition of blackened glass and human remains. Above this, flies, driven by the horrific smell, had nested. From the cockpit of the Sikorsky, high above, it gave the appearance of a moving, living, blackened sea. The type that formed on a stormy night.

Genevieve swung the helicopter around, intentionally, leaving the mass of death. They'd seen enough. There was nothing but nightmares to be gained by looking upon it any further. An atrocity had occurred here. But there was nothing they could do for them now.

At the northern end of the camp three men had been bound to wooden posts. Their arms had been stretched outward as though they had been crucified in the extreme heat. Elise stared as they went past. It looked like they had been tortured before being executed by firing squad. Their faces were permanently fixed in a contorted vision of abject horror and unimaginable pain.

One of the faces still looked like it was screaming in perpetual horror. The helicopter banked around the terrible vision and Elise was about to tell Genevieve to keep going to the waterhole – their problem wasn't about a local tribal war. But then the face appeared to follow her, haunting her to find the truth about whatever great atrocity had occurred.

Only it didn't just appear to be moving. It had followed her. "Jesus Christ! That man's alive."

"You sure?" Genevieve asked.

"Certain," Elise confirmed. "Take us around for another look to make sure we don't have any other living company and then put us on the ground."

"You really want to get involved?" Genevieve said, ruthlessly pointing out their mission wasn't for humanitarian needs.

"Are you suggesting we leave that man to die?"

"I'm suggesting he'll be dead pretty soon regardless of what we do for him. According to your friends in Bilma this raid happened three days ago. No way could someone have survived strung out in the sun without water for that long."

"He might know what happened to Sam and Tom."

"There's no way he's going to be conscious enough to tell us."

"Even so, I want to try. If he's too far gone, I'll give him some morphine and we'll put him out of his misery."

Veyron gripped the firing mount of the Browning heavy machine gun at the open starboard-side door as Genevieve landed. Genevieve kept the engines running and looked at Elise.

"You've got five minutes," Genevieve said. "After that, I'll shoot him myself."

Chapter Fifty-Five

The Sikorsky landed approximately thirty feet away from the three men tied to pikes. Elise was certain one of them was still alive, but now that she was on the ground, she couldn't see any obvious sign of life from any of them. Veyron brought the mounted Browning heavy machine gun around to cover her. Elise climbed out of the Sikorsky, keeping her head down as blades above continued to whir at speed in case they needed to leave in a hurry. Her right finger gently paused on the trigger of her Uzi as she scanned the area. Her eyes darted from the excavation site with the burial ground, to the remains of the burned tarpaulin canopies and back to the three men tied to pikes.

Even three days old, the acrid smell of charred bodies wafted through the air. She involuntarily felt bile rising in her throat. Death was never more pervasive than when it was sensed by your nose. Ahead of her, the sound of an incomprehensible amount of flies competed with the noise of the rotating helicopter blades.

Elise fought the urge to vomit. Her self-preservation instincts kicked in, telling her to run. Not to wait for an ambush. So she ran to meet the man who appeared alive from the air. At her far right, he was the largest of the three men by nearly a foot in height and fifty pounds of muscle. The first two men were clearly dead. Maggots had already formed in their head and chest bullet wounds.

The third person, the one whom she'd thought she saw move from the air, appeared almost just as lifeless. He was tied by his neck to the vertical spike, while his wrists were bound at the ends of the horizontal beam. It looked like a makeshift and cheap version of a crucifixion had taken place, before he'd been shot. His breathing, if he still breathed at all, was shallow and barely evident. He had three large bullet wounds to the left-side of his chest. On his forehead, a single bullet hole was visible. She stepped up close to the man. There was no exit wound. Sometimes a stray bullet will lose velocity, so that it only has enough power to enter, but not enough to exit the human flesh. Even so, there's only one place a bullet to the head can travel, and the brain isn't very forgiving. A fly crawled out of the open wound and the man's face didn't flinch.

Elise felt the bile rising in her stomach again. This time, she couldn't control the involuntary response and vomited. She pulled her hair out of her face, and turned around. She'd seen enough. If this man was alive, he wouldn't be for long. Her eyes followed the smell of burned bodies around the camp. She was all alone. Everyone was dead. She wasn't going to find another living person down here. Elise looked back at the helicopter and began walking in that direction.

"Water!" a deep voice, no louder than a whisper, spoke.

She turned to face a dead man. More ghoul than alive, his open grayish-blue eyes stared vacantly at her without seeing. Flies still crawled out of the grotesque wounds in his chest. The man was going to be dead soon. There was clearly nothing she could do for him.

Had he really spoken?

"Please!" the man begged.

Elise stared at the man's face. He looked straight through her as though he were blind. There was nothing she could do to save his life. But she couldn't leave him to suffer as he was, either. She gripped her Uzi and raised it up toward the man's face. It might be the most humane thing she could do for him.

Elise, the savior – she recalled the words Nayram had said to her, and lowered her weapon.

"I'm sorry," she said. "I have morphine. Would you like me to give you some? You must know I can't save you, but I can take away your pain."

He made no response.

Instead his head slumped downwards, as though he'd given up the will to fight off death any longer. She lowered her weapon. *Perhaps all he wanted was to hear someone tell him it was okay to die?* He took several slow, deep breaths. Known as Cheyne-Stokes, they were often the last breaths a person takes before they die.

Elise wanted to leave, but somehow felt as though she owed it to the man to watch him die. He breathed in deep and then slowly exhaled. She watched as this continued for several breaths. Each one, she expected to be his last. On the ninth, he lifted his head. His ghoulish eyes opened again. And this time they looked at her with recognition.

He smiled, revealing a full set of white teeth that appeared at odds with his scarred face and warrior's body. "I don't need morphine."

"What do you need?" She hurried by his side and offered him some water from her bottle.

"I've been waiting." His voice was deep, calm, and almost hypnotic.

"For what?"

His entire body went rigid. Every muscle contracted individually as though a current of electricity had been discharged through his entire body. When it stopped he lifted his head up and stared at her. "I've been waiting for you, Elise."

"You have?"

"Yes. The United Sovereign of Kongo has been waiting for your help."

"You know about the USK?"

"My name is Adebowale, but you know may know me as *Mtu Wa Watu Moja*."

Elise translated his name from its ancient Swahili origins. "*Man of the One People*." They were the only words she knew in the language, and only because she had spent the past three months trying to find out as much as she could about the man. "You're the leader of the USK?"

Chapter Fifty-Six

Elise cut the ropes from his wrists and throat. Free from the confines of the pike, the man staggered forward and fell to the ground. His muscles, wasted from days of dehydration and stagnation were no longer capable of holding his massive frame.

She reached out to help and he pushed her away. "No. Don't. I'm three times your size, I'll crush you. Let me fall."

Elise eased him toward the ground.

He rolled on to his side. He tried to straighten himself up using his arms, but they merely pushed vainly into the sand. He smiled and looked at her. "More water, please."

She handed her bottle to him. "You're an American?"

He took a drink and shook his head. "No. My family came from Zaire, which is now known as the Democratic Republic of Congo. As you know, there is very little about the country that is democratically elected. My family was once a proud people – kings throughout the Congo. When I was just a boy, a rebel leader cut my father down with a machete like he was a dog and took over the country. Fortunately, he, along with several other rebels has died in the years since then – but still the pain festers in my wounds."

"You want revenge?" Elise said.

"No. The man responsible for my father's death was killed when I was just a boy, by a childish rebel who thought he could topple another king. The cycle has continued many times, and still my country suffers. I dream of uniting my country in such a way as to leave everlasting stability and growth in a once proud region, which has suffered greatly since Portugal colonized it in the 16th century."

"Okay, so how did you end up living in America?"

He stared vacantly in silence. Either he didn't hear her, or didn't want to answer.

"Were you a refugee?"

"No." Adebowale shook his head. "On the night of my father's death, my mother sent me away. I ran, further than I could have ever believed. I stole a boat and rode the Zaire River north. When I could no longer travel the river I got out and traveled north by foot. I eventually found work laboring for a man in Egypt. He was an archeologist traveling the Sahara in search of an old relic. A book written by Nostradamus, which held visions of the future of humanity. At the time he didn't speak to us much, instead he told us where to dig and we dug. When I was sixteen years old, and after four years of constant laboring and good eating had put another hundred pounds of muscles on my body, he stopped me and asked if I'd ever played American football. I shook my head, thinking he was mad. When would I have had time to play a game I'd never heard of? He then told me he could arrange for American schooling if I wanted to play some game."

"So you went to America to play football?"

"No. I went to America to get an education, so that one day I might rise up and bring order and stability to my people who so desperately long for peace."

She smiled kindly. "How long did you play football?"

He closed his eyes while he thought about it, and then opened them again. "Six years. I made it pretty far, I suppose. It was a means to an end. I got the education I needed and then returned to Africa to commence my process of change."

"Why did you go to Libya, if your fight was in the DRC?"

"To help the daughter of the man to whom I owe so much – and to instigate the start of a great prophecy."

"And what prophecy is that?" she asked.

He sat up, as though possessed by a demon. His grayish-blue eyes pierced her soul as he spoke with his deep voice – the voice of someone long since dead, a corpse performing a civic service. "The very same prophecy that brought you to Africa! I'm talking about the very same prophecy that has lead the greatest interest and gathering of nations in history."

"Go on," she said.

He blinked. "The reason Sam Reilly came to Sahara. To place the USK into power before the greatest world war commences over a rare natural resource."

Chapter Fifty-Seven

Elise heard heavy footsteps behind her. She looked up and saw Veyron carrying the Browning heavy machine gun. He must have unclipped the weapon from its helicopter mounting. Sweat poured off his face. He was breathing hard.

"Time to go," Veyron said. "We've got company."

"Who?"

"A group of nomads. About a mile south of here. They're armed. Genevieve spotted them on the radar coming over one of the sand dunes."

"All right," Elise said. "We need to get this man to the helicopter."

Veyron bent down to feel Adebowale's pulse. The man's eyes were closed and he was no longer able to be woken. It was as though he'd used the last of his energy staying alive to this point. "He won't live long."

"Yes he will."

"Where are we going to take him? There are no hospitals nearby and he won't live long without surgery."

Elise looked at Veyron. Her jaw fixed with determination and her purple eyes imploring him to help. "We'll get him to the *Maria Helena* and I'll take the bullets out myself."

"You've got to be kidding me!"

Genevieve ran over. "What the hell's taking so long? We've got to go!"

Veyron looked at her. "Elise is adamant we need to take him with us."

Elise met Genevieve's harsh gaze. "I'll explain when we're in the air. Right now we need to get him on board. He's important."

"To what?"

"Everything."

Genevieve swore. "Ah, Christ! You're serious, aren't you?"

Elise nodded without saying a word.

Veyron handed the heavy machine gun to Elise and then bent down to lift Adebowale using an old fireman's lift. Displaying remarkable strength he was able to lift the enormous man. Elise followed them back to the Sikorsky.

Veyron laid Adebowale on his back in the middle section of the helicopter. Elise closed the side door and Genevieve got them back in the air. Elise quickly inserted an intravenous cannula into the large vein at the bend of his arm, known as the cubital fossa. Genevieve increased their altitude and banked to the right to avoid the incoming group of armed nomads. Elise primed an IV line with saline, attached it to the cannula and opened it up to full. The liquid would help counteract the man's severe dehydration and might just save his kidneys from irreparable damage, but he would need blood products to survive – and someone was going to have to remove the bullets from his head and torso.

Genevieve looked over her shoulder, back at her. "You want to tell me what this is all about, Elise?"

"We need to save this guy's life."

"He looks like he's going to die to me," Genevieve said.

"He won't."

"What makes you so sure?"

"I don't know what to tell you, Genevieve. It was as though he knew exactly why we'd come to the Sahara. And that he was at the center of everything Sam and Tom were doing in the Sahara."

"That's impossible. We're nowhere near the DRC. Nothing we've done or said, would give him the indication that's why we're here."

Elise smiled. "And yet he knew."

"Even if he didn't," Genevieve said. "The coincidence alone is quite creepy."

"So, where are we taking him?"

"Back to the *Maria Helena*."

"Why not a hospital?"

Elise shrugged. "He says he needs our help."

Genevieve said, "He'll die without a doctor."

"He says I can remove the bullet and he will live."

Genevieve shrugged. "It's his life. I'm still not very happy about it, though."

"Why?"

"I don't really care whether he lives or not. I'm far more interested in finding Sam and Tom."

"There's something else. He says he needs to speak to Sam Reilly immediately."

"So do I. Did you tell him it doesn't matter what they were talking about before he arrived, right now he's lost in the Sahara somewhere."

"I know. I already told him."

"What did he say?"

"He said the three of them are still alive and will find their own way back to the *Maria Helena* by the time he regains consciousness."

Veyron looked up from what he was doing in the back of the helicopter for the first time. "Who's the third person?"

"He didn't say."

Genevieve glanced back at the man lying on the helicopter's stretcher. His breathing was erratic. Veyron had told her his pulse was barely palpable.

She shook her head. "I don't know, Elise. I think you're trusting heavily in a corpse."

"He said you wouldn't believe a word he said."

"Then what did he think I'd do?"

"He said you'd take him back to the *Maria Helena* where Sam and Tom would make you into a believer."

Chapter Fifty-Eight

Zara opened her eyes. She was surrounded by darkness. The complete oblivion that can send a sane person mad. The sort of pitch black that only the blind may recognize. She breathed in deeply. The air was cool. Possibly even cold. She felt the fine hairs on her arms stand up on their ends. In a dome shaped cavern, a hundred and sixty feet below the surface of the Sahara she sat upright. Her body rigid. Listening to the silence, like a child frightened in the night. Zara turned her head suddenly. She'd heard something. It sounded like the slightest ripple of water lapping on the side of their tiny island. Her eyes focused on the sound, but saw nothing.

She breathed silently.

There was always a possibility her pursuers had found their way inside the dome. It was unlikely. Not impossible. She exhaled slowly as a faint light began to manifest beneath the water. Not quite bright enough to see clearly, it looked like a single dot bouncing around underwater. It was like an after-image in the corner of her eye – there, but not there at the same time.

Her eyes focused in on the light. As it grew, recognition dawned on her. The light was turning blue. It was on the side furthest from where they had entered the dome and was slowly approaching the surface.

Zara grinned as she watched Sam Reilly surface. Along the outer wall of the dome he carefully ran his hands along the ancient brickwork. Ignorant that she was watching, he worked his way around the dome. After shaking his head, he dipped under the water and disappeared from sight for a few moments before surfacing at the other end of the room.

At the opposite end of the dome lake he continued to study the ancient walls. She thought he was about to dive again, when he swung around and faced her. This time he noticed her. Their eyes met and he beamed like a child playing at the beach.

Zara asked, "What are you doing?"

Sam said, "I'm looking for a way out."

She laughed. "We know the way out. It's through that trapdoor you discovered and it goes to the surface where about five hundred or so men, eager to find a life of great riches, await to kill us."

"That's certainly one of the options," Sam agreed. "But there's two problems. One. Like you said, a few hundred soldiers are out there hunting us. And two, the longer we wait down here the more likely we are to starve before we get the chance to cross the desert."

"You're a hundred and sixty feet down a well beneath the Saharan desert! Where do you think you might go?" She looked at him like he was a fool. "I'm not sure if you've noticed, but the land above us was filled with sand for hundreds of miles in all directions. That means there's no way to the surface for hundreds of miles. Even if you do find the Garamante Fogaaras, there's no reason the ancient subterranean irrigation tunnels should still be intact, and even less reason to believe there's any way to reach the surface at the other end of the tunnels."

Sam nodded, as though he'd already concluded pretty much the same as her. "Even so, I think I'll have a look around." Sam shrugged indifferently. He inspected the wall nearest to him. Zara thought he looked like a kid casually collecting sea shells at the beach. He spoke to himself, not to her. "These walls were built a long time ago. It's hard to build anything that lasts this long."

"What makes you think there is another way out?"

"The water here is fresh. If you watch the water, it has a not so slow movement in that direction." He pointed to the wall ahead. "Logic suggests there's a large subterranean water table moving along here – and that water must come out somewhere."

"Two faults with your theory," Zara smiled condescendingly. "First. There aren't any waterholes around here for at least seventy miles. Second. You've already searched all the other waterholes within a hundred mile radius. And thirdly, even if the water did take us somewhere we could get out, we would drown in the process, because – in case you didn't notice it, the water is moving underground, which means we won't be able to breath in the process!"

Sam smiled, nonplussed. "Even so, I think I'll have a swim. Kill the time if nothing else."

Zara stood up to argue the point, but she felt a gentle hand on her wrist, stopping her. Zara looked down and saw Tom.

"Let him be. This is his sort of thing. Let him get it out of his system." Without saying anything else, Tom laid backwards and made himself comfortable, quickly drifting toward sleep. "After all that walking, I'm glad to have time to relax. Sleep when you can…"

"Even if you're right and this ancient water table travels for a hundred miles there's no place to reach the surface again."

"No known place, you mean?" Sam corrected her and then dived below the water again.

She watched as he disappeared for a considerably longer time. Thirty seconds stretched to a minute. Followed by two. She looked at Tom who appeared indifferent. Not just unafraid. More like a bored child, waiting to go home.

"Tom, I think your friend might have just drowned."

"Sam? Nah, he's a pretty good swimmer." Tom smiled. "When he's not talking, he has breath to last for hours."

Nearly a minute later she got up and kicked Tom. "Hey, I'm pretty certain Sam's just drowned. Are you going to do something?"

Tom sat up, stretched, as though he'd been in a deep sleep and walked to the edge of the water. It was moving relatively slowly on the surface, but she'd heard of these things having powerful undertows, capable of sucking a man downwards to his death.

"He does seem to be holding his breath longer than I would have expected," Tom said and then sat down again.

"That's it!" she yelled.

Tom nodded. "If that current's strong enough to drown Sam, there's nothing I can do to overcome it." He stared at the dark water. "Too bad, too. I liked that guy."

She shook her head in disbelief.

A moment later Sam resurfaced and took a couple deep breaths.

Zara said, "My God, Sam! I thought you'd just gotten yourself killed."

He shook his head. "No. But I think I just found our way out. It's a very narrow tunnel Tom and I accidentally came across earlier. It will be hard to get through, but if we can reach the other side, it might just take us somewhere."

Chapter Fifty-Nine

Zara backed away from the edge of the island and said, "Oh no! Not me... no way!"

Sam swam along the surface toward her. "Why? Do you prefer the idea of waiting here and taking your chances on General Ngige's men who are guarding the well, and even as we speak, working out how to get to us?"

"Unlike you, I'm terrified of confined spaces. Anything narrow and underwater, I'm just not going to be happy. I think I'd rather take my chance against Ngige's men or waiting long enough to starve in the Saharan desert."

"Yeah, I hate confined spaces too. But I really don't have an alternative, and neither do you."

Sam dipped his head and disappeared under the water again, as though he didn't want to argue the point.

She looked at Tom. "Really? I thought he was supposed to be some world-leading cave diver?"

"He is. Always hated it though. His mother gave him the stupid notion that one must try to overcome their fears, and he's spent his life doing just that. It's a bit extreme, I'll admit. I think secretly he's grown to love the subterranean environments."

Zara asked, "What about you?"

Tom shrugged. "What about me?"

"You don't look much like a diver? What do you weigh – two hundred pounds?"

"Two fifty."

"So, how did you get into cave diving? It can't be a natural choice for a man of your size."

Tom laughed. "I don't get claustrophobia. Never have. Instead, cave diving came naturally to me."

"Really?" Zara was surprised. First, to hear that Sam Reilly hated caves, and second to hear that Tom Bower, a giant, had always felt at home inside them. "How so?"

Tom smiled. He didn't appear embarrassed. More like a gentle soul and a big kid whose heart never changed since he was a child with his first real dreams for the future. "I've been getting stuck in things since I was little. Always too big for everything. In that way, cave diving's always made me feel right at home."

Sam resurfaced at the side of the island. "I've been thinking and I've made a decision."

"About what?" she asked.

"I thought Tom and I would check out the tunnel I found. If there's any chance it's going to go somewhere we'll come back and get you."

"Great. And in the meantime, what do I do?"

"It will be dark. You may as well have a rest."

Zara had seen the domed cavern in the dark. She didn't like it. One of the few things more frightening than swimming through another narrow underwater tunnel was the thought of waiting here to see if Sam and Tom were ever going to come back, or if they were going to drown and leave her to die trapped in the dark.

She bit her lower lip and then smiled. "On second thoughts, how about I come with you now?"

Chapter Sixty

Sam retraced his trip back to the smaller of the two domes, where he and Tom had erroneously surfaced when they had first arrived. Sam led the way as he slowly swam along the surface of the narrow tunnel where he and Tom had nearly become lost while searching for Zara. He quickly found the narrow tunnel. In this tunnel there were a few inches of air above the water level, so they could breathe while swimming. Zara swam in the middle of the group, with Tom following. They took it in turns to use the one watertight bag as a flotation device, with each of them, *using it for a brief break from the strenuous swimming.*

They traveled along the tunnel, following a constant and almost imperceptible flow of water. Because the tunnel was perfectly rectangular with no identifying changes in the shape or texture of its walls, it was difficult to judge how fast they were moving. Tom and Sam stopped on occasion to test their ability to swim against the current if later required. They would mark the stone walls of the tunnel with chalk and then swim for a minute. Afterwards, they would stop and measure the distance. Each time they stopped to do this, Sam was surprised by the strength of the current and also encouraged by it. That amount of water can't move unless it has somewhere to go, and of course, although it was not obvious because of the uniformity of the tunnel, the current was speeding them along its length.

After three hours in the water they saw the first change in the tunnel, and it wasn't a good one. The water height moved up the wall of the tunnel, which meant there was less distance between the water and the ceiling – less room to breathe.

Zara caught up with Sam and tapped him on the shoulder. She asked, "Do you have plan?"

Sam gave a cursory glance at the ceiling, now only about half a foot above his head. He said, "To deal with our diminishing room to breathe?"

She nodded.

He said, "Not really. I was kind of just hoping it would resolve itself."

"That's it?" She cursed and mumbled something under her breath about never trusting a man like Sam Reilly. "That's the best you've got?"

"If it makes you feel better, I have a gut feeling our problem will self-resolve soon. This won't last long. The Garamantes who built these tunnels were highly exacting people. They didn't simply decide to change the height of the tunnel. I think it's more likely there's been a cave-in somewhere further along, and it's caused a backflow of water here, or increased the depth below us. Either way, once we pass it, we should be fine."

She asked, "Can we pass it?"

"That's the big if. I'm reasonably confident we'll be all right."

Two minutes later Sam placed his hand on the ceiling and stopped their progression. Zara floated into him and stopped.

She asked, "What is it?"

Sam said, "I don't know. This might be the end of the line. Wait here and I'll go ahead and see if we can get past it. If that suits you?"

"Go," she said. "I'll just hang out here."

As Tom caught up, he reached up and touched the ceiling, coming to a stop. "Do you want me to go ahead and see what we have?"

"Nah. We already agreed I'll go ahead and check," Sam said. "Wait here and look after Zara. I'll have a quick look and see if it's possible. If I don't come back, you know the deal?"

"I won't come looking for you. I'll get Zara back, we'll wait as long as we can and then climb back up the well and escape across the desert."

"Be sure you do. You know I would if the roles were reversed, right?"

"I doubt that very much," Tom said. "But I'm better at following orders, so be careful. You know I prefer it down here in the cool water than trekking across the scorching desert."

Sam nodded. "I'll do my best."

He then dipped his head below the narrow ceiling and disappeared.

Chapter Sixty-One

Sam drifted along the tunnel, with no more than an inch or two of air between the water and the ceiling. He kept his eyes opened while floating on his back. The blue glow from his DARPA thermal suit reflected off the ceiling back down at him, as though it were a mirror. Occasionally, every twenty or so feet, a gap would form where the glow would be absorbed by an area of darkness. These areas, he soon discovered, occurred when the ceiling had collapsed leaving a small opening.

He floated into the first large one he found. It formed where three stones, each no larger than a soda can, had fallen from the roof. Not big enough to surface his entire head, but good enough for him to place his mouth inside and breath the air trapped above.

The air was not stale and foul, but felt cool, and delicious on his throat.

Sam waited there for ten or so seconds as he caught his breath, not wanting to wait any longer in case he drew the last of the air out. He dipped again and floated well below the roof line. It was at least another forty or fifty feet before he found another opening.

This one was much larger, and capable of supporting his entire body. It looked clear to him that a large pocket of the tunnel had collapsed. He surfaced and took a couple deep breaths. His eyes scanned the area. The opening appeared to go to another level. The light of his suit shined upwards approximately twenty feet until it reached another, thoroughly damaged ceiling. Bits of limestone and sand intermingled through a gaping hole where the ceiling of a second tunnel passed through the cave-in.

Sam waited until his eyes adjusted to his new environment and then grinned. There was definitely a second tunnel, about ten feet above. *Two tunnels are better than one – especially when the second one is high and dry.* He tried to grip the remaining stone walls and climb. The rocks he put his weight on fell apart in his hands. He tried another grip, followed by a third. Each one broke in his hands, sending more stones tumbling down.

He stared at the second tunnel. It was clearly visible now that he'd identified it. He shook his head and cursed to himself. *Ten feet, I can't reach a meager ten feet?*

Sam dropped back into the water and continued to swim down the flooded tunnel. He didn't get very far. A second large cave-in blocked his progression any further down the tunnel. The water sped past him, as its pressure became confined to two small cracks in the limestone wall. Neither was big enough for even Zara to slip through. Definitely too small for him to make it.

Sam performed a swimmer's tumble-turn against the pile of stone rubble which blocked his progress through the original tunnel, and started swimming hard against the current. He surfaced at the large opening to catch his breath and then swam all the way back to where he'd left Tom and Zara. It was a much harder swim going back against the current.

Surfacing, he took several deep breaths. Tom held onto the side of his right arm to stop him from floating down the current, and waited.

Zara asked, "Any luck?"

Sam said, "Maybe."

She looked at him like he was a fool. "What does maybe mean? We can either get through or we can't. Which one is it?"

Sam's eyes narrowed. "I don't know yet. It's a maybe. But I'm willing to give it a try."

Tom asked, "What have we got?"

"There's a cave-in approximately eighty feet ahead. The current is still getting past, through two small cracks in the limestone. Real small cracks. Even Zara wouldn't fit through, which means it's not going to be an option for either of us. About twenty feet back from there, there's an opening in the ceiling where another cave-in occurred. Above it I can see a second tunnel. High and dry. It looks like a good option. But we've got a problem..."

Zara frowned. It said, don't we always? "What's the problem?"

Sam said, "The tunnel's ten feet above, and the walls are too unstable to climb."

Tom said, "Okay, but surely we can get past that. I mean, between the three of us, we can build some sort of human chain or something and remove the obstacle of ten feet?"

"I think you'll find we need a human pyramid," Zara corrected him.

Tom shrugged. "Either way, it must be possible?"

Chapter Sixty-Two

Ten minutes later all three of them surfaced inside the large opening where Sam had found the second tunnel. The opening was just wide enough for all three of them to fit inside. Sam watched as Tom and Zara glanced around, judging their quandary.

Zara was the first to see it. "We have a problem."

Sam said, "Yeah, it took me a while to work it out too. But there has to be another way."

Tom said, "What's the problem? I could almost reach the second tunnel myself. If I had something to stand on."

Everyone was silent for a moment.

Tom's smile disappeared. "There's nothing for me to stand on, is there?"

"Afraid not," Sam said. "Which means, we can't make a human pyramid because the person at the bottom will just sink lower in the water until we're all underwater."

Zara said, "There must be a way!"

Tom nodded. "All we need is for a couple of these stones to hold and I can reach the second tunnel."

Sam watched as Tom tried the first stone he could reach. It fell away the same as the other ones Sam had tried. He then tried to use oppositional force between the two sides of the cave-in to climb upwards, but the opening was too wide for that to be of any use.

After the fourth fall, Tom stopped and looked at Zara. "You want to have a try. You're a lot lighter than we are?"

"Sure."

Zara reached for a much lower stone and gripped it. Lithe and agile, like a cat, she managed to use the hold to reach a second one. She spread the weight between both holds, leaning forward as she climbed to distribute the pressures evenly. Two feet from the top, a third stone held her weight. She paused there, as she studied the climb. She needed to jump to reach the top. It wasn't an easy jump, but it wasn't impossible, either.

She bent her arms and legs, slowly increasing the tension in her muscles ready to jump. Sam watched her muscles contract with the explosive force of an elite athlete. It was an easy jump for her – until the two stones she was pushing off, broke under the intense pressure.

Zara fell backwards into the water.

Sam grabbed her shoulder and helped her to surface inside the opening again. He watched her catch her breath. "You did well. Better than Tom or I."

"But not good enough." She shook her head.

Tom said, "You can try again. You'll make it. Just give it time."

They gave it time, but despite their best efforts, they were no closer to reaching the second tunnel an hour later.

Zara cursed the opening. "After all that we've done to get here, we're going to fail because of ten lousy feet!"

Sam said, "It's not over yet."

"What do you mean?" She looked like she wanted to hit him and his confidence. "Of course it is. We've found the only way out. And it's impossible to access. The water's too low to ever reach the top of that wall."

Sam persisted. "Even so, there will be a way. It might just take some time, that's all."

Zara's mouth was set hard. Her face, normally vivid with expression, showed nothing but the despondence of impossibility. "How? It's not like you can raise the height of the water."

Sam grinned suddenly. "Maybe we can?"

Chapter Sixty-Three

Both men took a dozen or more deep breaths in and out. By hyperventilating they were reducing their carbon dioxide levels and turning their blood slightly alkaline. The benefit of which, was to offset the inevitable acidity that would be caused when they held their breaths for a prolonged period during the free-dive and reduce their urge to breath.

Sam caught Tom's eye and nodded. It was time. He dipped his head under the water and back into the submerged tunnel. He quickly swam down the current until he reached the cave-in, approximately eighty feet ahead.

He glanced at the two small cracks in the limestone where water still flowed. One was shaped like the jagged opening to the mouth of a large fish or a small shark, while the other was larger and more rectangular. Sam placed his hand well above the opening and studied the shapes, mentally trying to picture a way to block their flow. He felt his arm pull toward the smaller of the two openings. The large channel of water flowing from the entire tunnel was being forced through the two small openings, causing an increase in speed and force of the current, much like a jet engine.

Sam moved away from the opening. Tom nodded and swam toward a pile of rocks lying on the base of the tunnel. Together they moved a series of smaller rocks until they were able to block the smaller of the two cracks. Instantly the strength of the current increased on the larger opening. They both then swam back to the opening in the ceiling where Zara waited.

Zara looked at them both. "What do you think, is it possible?"

Sam felt his chest burn as he breathed hard. He turned to Tom, as though to say, well, is it possible?

Tom looked at both of them with a non-committal smile. "It all depends."

"On what?" she asked.

Tom said, "On whether or not we can find a suitable rock, large enough to block the remaining gap. Even then, it's going to be a matter of time before the water punches another way through. If it made it once, it will do so again."

It was nearly five minutes before they were ready to free-dive again. Repeating the same process of hyperventilation, Sam entered the water and returned to the cave-in. There were several large stones. Some would be impossible to move, while others were definitely too small. They chose the first one which looked approximately right. It was like a kite with a wide base and a narrow point.

Together Sam and Tom rolled the medium sized stone twenty feet until it was near the remaining crack in the limestone wall. Sam stood the stone up, so that it's wider base was to the ground, and then carefully shimmied it on either end of its base until the stone stood directly in front of the opening. It was as much as they needed to do. The powerful current drew the stone in like a piece of flotsam reaching a storm drain.

It plugged the hole and the water stopped moving. Sam reached down to the ground and picked up a handful of small rocks and sand. He scattered the debris over the kite-shaped stone and was pleased to see none of the smaller stones were drawn into anything.

Sam watched for a moment and then returned to the opening where Zara waited for them.

Zara met his gaze and asked, "Did it work?"

In-between breaths, Sam said, "Looks like it."

"Now what?" she asked.

Sam pulled off a small rock from the edge of the cave-in and marked it just above the waterline. "Now we wait and see if the water rises."

Chapter Sixty-Four

It took a total of four hours for the water to rise high enough for them to be able to climb up onto the tunnel above the cave-in. Sam looked in both directions along the tunnel. Opposite the side he'd climbed, the tunnel appeared to have been completely damaged by the cave-in. That left only one direction to go, south.

They traveled quickly, intermittently alternating between a jog and a run. Sam felt good. The stories he'd heard about the ancient irrigation tunnels suggested some of them ran between cities and for hundreds of miles. This tunnel might very well travel all the way to Chad.

After about two hours, he stopped – because a second cave-in meant there was no way this tunnel was ever going to take them anywhere.

Zara swore loudly. "Tell me we can move this rubble!"

Sam ran his hands along the heavy boulders that barred their way. "It might be possible, but it's going to take a long time, and a lot of luck."

Tom was faster to reach the inevitable conclusion. "Neither of which we have right now. The water's still flooding this area. If we turn around now, we might just be able to unblock the plug. But if we wait, we'll never even reach the cave-in we entered here by. The water will start to flow down this tunnel like a flashflood, and there will be no way out."

"All right," Zara said. "I have no interest in drowning beneath the Sahara or anywhere else. Let's return to the subterranean island, and then make a try crossing the desert into Chad."

With all three in agreement, they raced back to the original cave-in. As they approached, water flowed to greet them. It was no more than five or six inches in height, but already it made it difficult to walk up the tunnel.

Tom, with his longer legs, pulled ahead of Sam and Zara. Sam lifted his legs as best he could as he ran, trying to keep up. It was the same technique used by Ironmen trying to reduce their drag, while racing through the surf. Despite his effort, Tom disappeared ahead of them.

Nearly thirty minutes later, Sam reached the cave-in through which they had entered the tunnel. It now looked like a lake instead of a gaping hole in the tunnel. Sam started to hyperventilate in preparation of the long free-dive. But before he dropped into the water, Tom surfaced.

Sam asked, "Did you reach it?"

"The plug's gone, and the water's draining freely again." Tom looked around at the water still flowing down the tunnel. "It might take a while for all this water to dissipate, and longer still before we can swim back to the subterranean island."

It took eight hours for the water to return to its normal height in the lower tunnel, where they were able to then swim against the current. It took a further four hours to reach the subterranean island. Sam pulled himself up onto the island, and then he and Tom lifted Zara out of the water. Every muscle in his body ached.

Zara said, "Well that's it. We'll have to wait as long as our food rations last, and then make an attempt at crossing the desert, into Chad."

Sam shook his head. "I haven't given up finding a way out of here, yet."

"Really?" she asked. "You're going to look for a third irrigation tunnel?"

"Why not?" Sam asked. "If there were two, there might as well be three. We only need one to lead to the surface a long distance away from here."

"What do you want to do, Tom?" Zara asked. "Do you want to make another attempt to find a third tunnel out of here?"

Tom shrugged, as though he honestly hadn't yet given the idea any thought. "Right now, I'm going to dry off and rest."

She turned to Sam, again. "When will you make a second attempt?"

"Not for a while. I'll need a day to rest and recuperate."

She asked, "You want to go to sleep?"

"Not yet." Sam took out his desert robes and used them to dry himself. "Tell me about Nostradamus. If that con artist worked out how to royally screw me from four hundred years ago, I want to know how and why."

Zara looked at him. Her eyes were intense with passion and intelligence. "What do you want to know?"

Sam grinned. "Everything."

Chapter Sixty-Five

Sam smiled as he listened to a not so brief history of Michel De Nostradamus. Zara spoke with the alacrity and knowledge of a person who'd dedicated her life to a certain pursuit of understanding, and had now been given free rein to impart that information to an eager and willing audience of one. In the light blue haze of his DARPA thermal suit, her gaze appeared intense. Next to him, Tom, true to his word, had already dried himself, switched his own thermal suit off to conserve battery life, and was sound asleep. Zara said, "Michel De Nostradamus began writing his prophecies as a series of elaborate puzzles, ranging in varying levels of intellectual difficulties. Historians believe he made a fortune by appealing to people of all ages and intelligence by providing riddles inside riddles in his strange rhymes known as quatrains. He quickly found a following of people who struggled for days upon days for hints and clues about the true meanings of his strange quatrains."

"So he was a charlatan," Sam said. "Albeit, a very entertaining one?"

"No. I believe now he did see the future, but in an attempt to avoid being identified as a heretic and burned to death by the Inquisition, Nostradamus wrote in a series of codes. He removed names, or changed them so much that even the main subjects of the truth could not be interfered with."

"So he made stuff up?" he persisted.

Zara smiled. She'd heard the arguments before. She'd even made many of them. "Names were changed, dates were changed, words rewritten. By the late 1550s *Les Prophecies* was one of the most widely distributed and read books in the world. They were written in no chronological order, and in many parts appeared more gibberish than anything of real logic and substance. I now wonder if he had another reason, altogether, for why he wrote in such a confusing way."

Sam asked, "Such as?"

"What if Nostradamus could only receive small parts of his vision. Like tiny clips of a film of the future. What if he wrote them in the order that he viewed them?"

Sam asked, "You think he really did see the future?"

"Yes. I do now. And if that is the case, then Nostradamus was telling the truth all this time and he could really see the future. Logic suggests that math, if applied correctly, may be able to rearrange the order of the prophecies until they form a clear and chronological description of that future."

Sam interrupted. "Okay, let's start a bit earlier. How did Nostradamus come to have these visions in the first place?"

She asked, "You want to hear it all?"

Sam nodded.

Zara began at the beginning. "Michel de Nostradame was born in the south of France in Saint-Remy-de-Provence. He was one of nine children to Reyniere de St-Remy, and her husband Jaume de Nostradame, a well-to-do grain dealer and part-time notary of Jewish dissent. Nostradame's grandfather, Guy Gassonet, had converted to Catholicism a half century earlier and changed the family name to Nostradame, in part to avoid persecution during the Inquisition." She paused for a moment. "A little too much information?"

Sam smiled, patiently. "No. I'm keen to discover what it was about Nostradamus that led us to arrive at our current veneration of a fortune teller."

Her white teeth shined in the blue light with enthusiasm as she spoke. "Little is known of his childhood, but evidence indicates he was very intelligent as he quickly advanced through school. Early in his life, he was tutored by his maternal grandfather, Jean de St. Remy, who saw great intellect and potential in his grandson. During this time, young Nostradame was taught the rudiments of Latin, Greek, Hebrew, and mathematics. It is believed that his grandfather also introduced him to the ancient rights of Jewish tradition and the celestial science of astrology, giving Nostradame his first exposure to the idea of the heavens and how they drive human destiny."

Sam studied her face. "Go on."

"At the age of fourteen, Nostradame entered the University of Avignon to study medicine. He was forced to leave after only one year due to an outbreak of the bubonic plague. According to his own account, he traveled throughout the countryside during this time, researching herbal remedies and working as an apothecary. In 1522 he entered the University of Montpelier to complete his doctorate in medicine. He sometimes expressed dissension with the teachings of the Catholic priests, who dismissed his notions of astrology. There are some reports that university officials discovered his previous experience as an apothecary and found this to be reason enough to expel him from school. Evidently the school took a dim view of anyone who was involved in what was considered a manual trade. However, most accounts state he was not expelled and received license to practice medicine in 1525. At this time he Latinized his name—as was the custom of many medieval academics— from Nostradame to Nostradamus. From there, life became difficult for Michel."

Sam said, "The Great Plague took hold of Europe, before igniting the Renaissance."

"Exactly. Nostradamus was probably the most renowned Plague Doctor. He recommended his patients to drink only boiled water, to sleep in clean beds and to leave infected towns as soon as it was possible. Over the next several years, Nostradamus traveled throughout France and Italy, treating victims of the plague. There was no known remedy at the time; most doctors relied on potions made of mercury, the practice of bloodletting, and dressing patients in garlic-soaked robes. Nostradamus had developed some very progressive methods for dealing with the plague. He didn't bleed his patients, instead practicing effective hygiene and encouraging the removal of the infected corpses from city streets. He became known for creating a *Rose Pill*, an herbal lozenge made of roseships, rich in Vitamin C that provided some relief for patients with mild cases of the plague. His cure rate was impressive, though much can be attributed to keeping his patients clean, administering low-fat diets, and providing plenty of fresh air. In time, Nostradamus found himself somewhat of a local celebrity for his treatments and received financial support from many of the citizens of Provence. 1n 1531, he was invited to work with a leading scholar of the time, Jules-Cesar Scaliger in Agen, in southwestern France. There he married and in the next few years, had two children. In 1534, his wife and children died—presumably of the plague—while he was traveling on a medical mission to Italy. Not being able to save his wife and children caused him to fall out of favor in the community and with his patron, Scaliger."

"Not a very good Seer if he couldn't save his wife and kids," Sam said.

Zara nodded. "In 1538, an offhanded remark about a religious statue resulted in charges of heresy against Nostradamus. When ordered to appear before the Inquisition, he wisely chose to leave Provence to travel for several years throughout Italy, Greece and Turkey. During his travels to the ancient mystery schools, it is believed that Nostradamus experienced a psychic awakening."

"How?"

"He used to spend hours staring into a bowl filled with water and herbs until he had trance-like visions." Zara continued. "Feeling he'd stayed away long enough to be safe from the Inquisition, Nostradamus returned to France to resume his practice of treating plague victims. In 1547, he settled in his home-town of Salon-de-Provence and married a rich widow named Anne Ponsarde. Together they had six children – three boys and three girls. Nostradamus also published two books on medical science by this time. One was a translation of Galen, the Roman physician, and a second book, *Les Traite des Fardemens*, was a medical cookbook for treating the plague and the preparation of cosmetics."

"He sounded more like a man of science than a writer of creative fiction." Sam focused on her face and asked, "How did he come to write puzzles?"

"Within a few years of his settling into Salon, Nostradamus began moving away from medicine and more toward the occult. It is said that he would spend hours in his study at night meditating in front of a bowl filled with water and herbs. The meditation would bring on a trance and visions. It is believed the visions were the basis of his predictions for the future. In 1550, Nostradamus wrote his first almanac of astrological information and predictions of the coming year. Almanacs were very popular at the time, as they provided useful information for farmers and merchants and contained entertaining bits of local folklore and predictions of the coming year. Nostradamus began writing about his visions and incorporating them into his first almanac. The publication received a great response and served to spread his name all across France, which encouraged Nostradamus to write more."

Sam asked, "But at this stage there was no hint that he actually believed in the visions?"

She said, "No. The book was printed during a period of great popularity for Nostradamus, due to his use of poetry to predict each coming year's expectations. Those poems were astrologically based, and constructed of either four or six lines, with each yearly publication typically totaling twelve to fourteen verses, roughly corresponding to each month of the coming year. The poems were akin to brain teasers, riddles or puzzles, with much play on words and metaphor, forcing the reader to figure out the "hidden" meaning. Because most people readily understood the intent, with his sense of witty sarcasm embraced by his readers, the almanacs were enjoyed by all."

"Go on."

"That popularity created a demand for such entertainment."

Sam said, "He found an income source that could provide for his large family that paid better than being a Plague Doctor."

She nodded. "Seemingly in response, Nostradamus had initially published *The Prophecies* with a total of 353 verses, all four-lined poems with an ABAB rhyme scheme. He did that in May 1555, dividing that number of predictions into four *Chapters*, as divisions of 100 prophecies headed as *Centuries*. Of course, he still left out forty-seven quatrains."

"But *The Prophecies* included a lot more than 353 verses?"

"True. Prior to the 1557 Second Edition, King Henry II had approved an additional 291 quatrains be added to the book, bringing the total to 642, presented in seven *Centuries*. *Century Four*, which originally only contained 53 quatrains, had filled out to a hundred; but the new *Century Seven* ended with only 42 verses. Heads were still being scratched over the first edition's riddles."

"No one could work them out?" Sam grinned. "He took his puzzles to their next level."

Zara smiled. "The problem was that no one could solve *any* of these new riddles. While delight in the almanacs was still high, people were reading this new book and thinking Nostradamus was losing his grasp on what the people enjoyed. Some might have thought he had gone mad. Therefore, his request for the approval of 300 final quatrains, bringing the total *Centuries* to *Ten*, with *Century Seven* still only having 42 quatrains, was in effect denied, pending an explanation as to what it all meant."

"So what did it all mean?"

"Nostradamus claimed to base his published predictions on judicial astrology—the art of forecasting future events by calculation of the locations and motions of the planets and stellar bodies in relationship to the earth. His sources include passages from classical historians like Plutarch as well as medieval chroniclers from whom he seems to have borrowed liberally. In fact, many scholars believe he paraphrased ancient end-of-the-world prophecies from the Bible and then through astrological readings of the past, projected these events into the future. There's also evidence not everyone was enamored with Nostradamus' predictions. He was criticized by professional astrologers of the day for incompetence and assuming that comparative horoscopy, the comparison of future planetary configurations with those accompanying known past events, could predict the future."

Zara said, "The unique and substantial events described by the individual quatrains appeared to be in a jumbled mess of non-chronological order. Jumping forwards and backwards through history, the quatrains described a combination of some events that had already been and many which were still to come. He intentionally obscured the quatrains through the use of symbolism and metaphor, as well as by making changes to proper names by swapping, adding or removing letters. The obscuration is claimed to have been done to avoid his being tried as a magician."

Sam asked, "So what made *The Prophecies* a success?"

Zara said, "You see, the writings of Nostradamus were enjoyed by many people of all levels of society in Sixteenth Century Europe. The more noble his public admirers the more people wanted to read his predictions. His most notable admirers were the Royal Family of France. He was invited to the Paris court of Henry II and his wife, Catharine de Medici. The Medicis were known for their pan-European political ambitions, and the queen hoped that Nostradamus could give her guidance regarding her seven children. Ostensibly, Nostradamus also arrived in Paris in August of 1556 to explain Quatrain 35 of *Century One*, assumed to refer to King Henry II."

Zara carefully flicked through the first few pages of *Century One,* before handing the book to him. "This is quatrain 35 of *Century One.* Probably the most notable and influential of all of Nostradamus's predictions."

Sam carefully read the quatrain out loud.

*

The young lion will overcome the older one

On the field of combat in single battle

He will pierce his eyes through a golden cage

Two wounds made one, then he dies a cruel death.

*

Sam shrugged. "So what did it mean?"

"Nostradamus told the king that he should avoid any ceremonial jousting during his 41st year, which the regent's own astrologer had also asserted. Nostradamus spent the next few years ensconced in the luxury of the royal court, but received word that Catholic authorities were again becoming suspicious of his soothsaying and were about to investigate him. He returned to his hometown of Salon and his wife and children.

Finishing volumes VIII through X, he also began work on two additional volumes of Centuries, which were unfinished at the time of his death. On June 28, 1559, in his 41st year, Henry II was injured in a jousting tournament celebrating two marriages in his family. With thousands watching, his opponent's lance pierced the King's golden visor, entered his head behind the eye, both blinding him and penetrating deep into his brain. He held onto life for ten agonizing days."

Sam said, "Tough break."

"Already a celebrated persona in France, Nostradamus became a figure inspiring both awe and fright among the populace. His other prophecies regarding France's royal line were consulted and most seem to predict only death and tragedy. Henry's surviving widow, now Queen Regent Catharine de Medici, visited him in Salon during her royal tour of 1564, and he again told her, as he had when he drew up their astrology charts, that all four of her sons would become kings. Yet all the children came to equally dismal ends: one son became king of Poland, but was murdered by a priest; another died before carrying out a plot to kill another brother; two died young as well; the three daughters also met tragic fates. The family's House of Valois died out with the burial of Queen Margot."

"And what became of Nostradamus?"

"He died in 1566. He had long suffered from gout and naturally predicted his own end, although sources say he was off by a year. Many translations of his Centuries and treatises on their significance appeared in the generations following his death, and remain popular to the present day. Interpreters claim Nostradamus predicted Adolf Hitler's rise to power as well as the explosion of the U.S. space shuttle Challenger in 1986. Biographies of the seer have also appeared periodically. For two centuries the Vatican issued the *Index*, or a list of forbidden books, and *Centuries* was always on it."

"So that was the end of Nostradamus?"

She nodded. "In the centuries since his death, people have credited him with accurately predicting other pivotal events in history, from the French Revolution to the rise of Adolf Hitler to the terrorist attacks of September

11, 2001. According to Nostradamus, the world is slated to end in the year 3797. The question is, will the human race still be part of it?"

"And there's been nothing more since Nostradamus died?"

Zara smiled. "Until now. When nearly four hundred years later, I dug up his book, and was told I alone can prevent the extinction of the human race."

Chapter Sixty-Six

Sam waited in silence. Smiled and said, "All right."

Zara asked, "All right, what?"

"How do you think he worked it out?"

"Worked what out?"

"Everything he got right so far," Sam said. "Originally I assumed he made predictions up, kept them vague, then manipulate the result later, so that it would be reported that he'd predicted the event. Like a psychic, fortune teller, or a spiritual healer."

"But then?"

"Some of his quatrains were too close to the truth. Even to be manipulated by retrospective analysis. I've started to wonder if some of his most useful predictions, as far as career advancements, were too coincidental to occur naturally. So what happened? Did he plan and execute some of the events he described in his quatrains? Was he like a modern day magician using clever tricks, such as sleight of hand, distraction, and setting up fake scenarios to improve the veracity of his storytelling?"

"You think he faked killing King Henry II?"

Sam shook his head. "Maybe he was having an affair with his wife?"

"You're disturbed. He would have been the one to end up dead if he engaged in some sort of royal affair."

"Maybe he got under Henry's skin?" Sam looked at her and smiled. "You know. Planted the seed of doubt. Told him that he would die from a jousting accident. Encouraged him to change his helmets until they became cumbersome, and eventually, provided him with his own seed of self-fulfilling doubt that inevitably got him killed?"

Zara laughed. "I doubt it."

"So what do you think it really was?"

"He was a true Seer."

"Really? As a scientist you can't possibly expect me to believe this."

She ignored his complaint. "The way he did it wasn't magical. It was pure science. You see he could follow the outcome of each significant incident, which would lead to another and another, until the final outcome for an event would occur. Meaning at the end of several hundred years, he could predict the outcome of a certain event today."

"The butterfly effect?"

"No."

"What then?"

"Compared to our ability to think in advance, Nostradamus was a chess master. He was incredibly intelligent in that way, or he simply had a natural gift for extrapolation. He could see out each line of events, all the way to the end. And each one led to the same disastrous event on earth."

"The extinction of the human race?"

She nodded, but remained silent.

Sam asked, "How?"

Zara shrugged. "He didn't say."

"Okay, so why didn't he just change things in his time to create the difference needed. Why go walking through the desert, seeking an elaborate plan that spanned centuries and utilized a complex prophecy?"

She took in a breath and sighed, like she knew what she was going to say was crazy. "Because the future's already preordained. Destined by some higher divinity. It wasn't that Nostradamus didn't believe in the butterfly effect, he knew it didn't work – he'd tried it multiple times without success. He could change small things, but the things which really mattered, simply fought back until the destiny of man returned to its original path. He looked, trust me he looked. But all the alternative lines led to the same catastrophic event which in turn led to the demise of humanity."

He said, "Fuck with the future and it fucks with you?"

She smiled and shook her head. "No, nothing quite so vulgar or sinister. Simply that new events will occur and those will eventually lead to triggers that cause same outcome to be achieved."

"Well that's just great. So, now we know that the future's been ordained, and there's nothing we can do to affect it – what's the point of living?"

"Exactly."

"When is this catastrophe supposed to occur?"

"Now."

"Now when?"

"This year, to be exact."

Sam's eyes narrowed. "So, if he knew we were all going to simply vanish… why go to the trouble of burying his stupid book?"

"Because out of the billions of lines of futures that he investigated, just one provided him with an unclear future."

"He can't see everything?"

"Everything except the outcome of one event. All he knew was that if that one event occurred, everything afterwards became foggy."

"As in, the world ended?"

"No, as though a new line had been created with no known future. The only line in which the world *didn't* end!"

"It was a long shot, but he took it."

Sam asked, "What was the image of the event that changed everything?"

Zara said, "Me."

"You?"

"I found his book."

Sam looked her in the eye, trying to gauge some sort of understanding. "And what does he expect you to do with this book?"

She shrugged. "He doesn't know."

"Because of the cinema fragments thing?"

"Probably. He didn't say. As I explained before, Nostradamus doesn't see all of the future. Only tiny scenes. Somehow he knows the scene in which I find the book changes the future. We're at a turning point. A watershed moment, where life can go either way."

"What's inside the book?"

"The fifty-eight quatrains that are missing for Century VII."

"Could you work out anything with those?"

"Not much. I'll need a lot more time to work it out. At a glance, I doubt there will be much there that I can do to change the future."

"Let me guess, it's all a bunch of riddles and poorly written gibberish?"

She cringed. "Sort of."

"Did he tell you anything useful at all?"

"He said I needed to find an equation he's never seen, but knows exists."

"What sort of equation?"

"I've nicknamed it the Nostradamus Equation, but he didn't write it. In fact, he spent a lot of his life trying to find it, and he's certain I already knew what it was and where to find it, when he wrote to me in his book."

"But what does it do?"

"Nostradamus only ever saw parts of the future. Like you just said, like tiny scenes from a movie. He documented thousands of these visions over the course of his lifetime, but had no more idea than you or me when these events would occur."

"And so the equation could be applied to his visions?"

"Yes. The equation could be aligned precisely with his *Century* predictions."

Sam asked, "Find the equation and you can see precisely when these events are going to occur?"

She said, "Exactly."

"But you can't change them?"

"Nostradamus believes they're almost impossible to change. But when he follows the strings of time, he sees one continue. And that one is me. After I find the book of Nostradamus and apply the equation to it."

"Right. But you have no idea where the Nostradamus Equation is?"

"Not a clue," she confirmed.

"Yet, Nostradamus was certain you had already found it?" Sam said. "Or at least knew where it could be located?"

"Yes. He wrote it as though it were fact."

"You said before that your father had told you about this prophecy since you were a little girl. Did he tell you anything else? Anything that could be used to find the equation?"

"No."

Sam asked, "Nothing at all."

"No." She then smiled and remained silent for a moment. "I was given this stupid medallion."

Sam looked at it. His fingers tracing the delicate inscriptions. "Could this be a map?"

"That's ridiculous. You think Nostradamus left my great, great, I don't know how many grandfathers a map so that I could one day work out the equation needed to complete his book of the future?"

"No. You're right – it's ridiculous. Then again, it's no more ridiculous than the fact that four hundred years ago he wrote you a letter and signed it with the date you found it?"

"My father thought it was a map."

Sam examined the brass medallion under his blue light. On one side were ancient Egyptian hieroglyphics. He turned it over. On the obverse side was the image of an island. It made the shape of a figure eight on its side. In mathematics, the shape meant *infinity*.

"Have you been to this island?"

"No."

Sam asked, "Why not?"

Zara breathed in and then sighed. "Because it doesn't exist. At least not on any map I can get my hands on."

Chapter Sixty-Seven

Sam handed the medallion back to Zara after staring at it for a number of minutes. If the island existed, he had people on board the *Maria Helena* who would find it. At least that was one lead. Not much, but better than nothing. And until recently, they had nothing.

Tom approached. He carried one of the bags made from gazelle hides that contained the rough diamonds used to purchase weapons by the United Sovereign of Kongo. The bag had been opened since Sam had left it with the other two on the island. He smiled. "You're not going to believe what I just found."

Sam grinned. "I think the people we're working for are going to want those diamonds back?"

"Not the diamonds. We both know those are intrinsically worthless. What I have will change something."

"What did you find?"

Tom removed a small piece of paper. Nothing fancy. Just a piece of scrap paper, with the hastily written scrawl of a person unaccustomed to handwriting. "A note. Addressed to Mikhail."

At the mention of Mikhail, Zara eyes widened, but she remained silent.

Sam took the piece of paper. "It's important?"

"Just read it," Tom said.

Sam nodded and started reading.

*

Dear Mikhail,

It was never about diamonds. General Ngige has discovered the largest lithium stores in the world. It's being mined by an army of prisoners. Our estimates suggest at least five thousand prisoners are currently being forced to work deep inside. We are happy with the weapons, but won't fight until our brothers are freed from the lithium mine. They have set it up so they can drown all of them if there's a rebellion. Instead of acting as an incendiary, it has had the opposite effect. The news has spread amongst our supporters, many of whom have loved ones inside the mine, and now they want to calm the rebellion until the prisoners are freed.

I wish there was another way. Our movement doesn't have anything more to trade. Even so, we ask for your assistance. The mine is below Lake Tumba. Now that you understand what this is all about, I hope you can see the extreme ramifications. General Ngige is being well funded by someone in Europe. Lithium is about to be the most valuable element on earth – and that means the Democratic Republic of Congo is about to become the most valuable piece of land. If you do nothing, you must understand that the world will be drawn into an everlasting land battle that will make oil appear inconsequential.

We need to find a way to free them before we can rebel.

Do that and the USK will take care of everything. Isolate us now, and the entire world will share our pain.

*

Sam stopped reading the note. It was left unsigned.

"That's where they're getting their funding from!" Sam said, looking up. "And that's why General Ngige is winning. He's being backed financially by someone else. The money is going to weapons and men. The free people of the DRC could never compete."

Tom said, "The question is who's funding them?"

Sam shrugged. "Who indeed?"

Zara said, "It could be the Saudis. You can't build an electric car without lithium batteries. They would certainly have the motive and the means to fund the rebellion."

"Alternatively, it could be any number of countries currently looking at building their own electric cars," Sam said. "While we're looking that way, there's no reason you shouldn't discuss the possibility companies already building electric cars are involved," Tom said.

Zara asked, "Such as?"

"Tesla's the first to come to mind. But Mercedes, BMW, Lexus all have their own electric and hybrid versions. They all have investments into the billions of dollars in electric cars."

"And all of those investments are worthless if they can't find enough lithium to power them."

"Did you know there's only one lithium mine in North America?

"That's a hell of a motive to sponsor a warlord."

"Someone needs to know. This changes everything. If the intelligence analysts back at home were able to process this information, I think the U.S. Department of Defense would be interested in doing a lot more than selling the USK ten million dollars worth of military hardware."

Zara looked at him. "You think this could be precisely the watershed moment Nostradamus was predicting?"

Sam nodded. He still hadn't bought everything she'd said about Nostradamus, but neither was he keen to overlook the greatest prediction the master seer had ever made concerning the future of the human race – especially when it coincided with their present circumstances. "Okay, I agree with you, but to do that we're going to need to find a way out."

"We might not have much time," Tom said. "And I can't see us finding another way out of here."

Sam said, "I think I've made a decision about that."

"What?" Tom and Zara asked in unison.

Sam powered down his DARPA suit to conserve energy. "We rest tonight and tomorrow morning we climb back up the well."

"We'd never survive. It's too soon. There will still be hundreds of Ngige's mercenaries searching for us."

"Sure," Sam agreed. "But maybe we don't need to kill all of them. Maybe we kill a few and take their satellite phone?"

"We could take them, one at a time by the well. Once we have a phone we'll contact the *Maria Helena* and get retrieved."

Zara said, "It sounds like an impossible plan."

"That's because it is," Sam said. "But I don't have another one – and we're running out of time."

He closed his eyes in the darkness and forced himself to rest. He would need to if he was to think clearly tomorrow.

In the complete darkness, Sam had no idea how long he'd slept. It was a deep sleep. He'd had a dream. It was vivid. One of those dreams in which you wake up and still wonder what was real and what was imagined.

He was crossing a desert in the night, navigating by the stars. Only he'd lost his way. Something terrible had happened to the celestial sky, and instead of an infinite myriad of stars and constellations, he saw nothing but the dark canvas of space. He was on a journey, searching for something important. He couldn't quite remember what it was he was looking for, but he knew it was the most valuable and important quest he'd ever made. He was about to give up all hope of finding it – whatever it was.

He'd stopped walking, fearful of finding himself even more lost as the time went by. He wanted to cry. He felt so close and at the same time distant from whatever it was he was searching for. He tilted his head and looked straight up.

Above him a tiny dot erupted into a fireball in the pitch black canvass. The light glowed brighter until he was no longer able to look at it without hurting his eyes.

Sam opened his eyes. The massive dome structure was so bright he could see the entire place. Startled, he glanced at Tom and Zara. Both were still on lying on the island next to him. It took a moment for Sam to realize the significance.

If everyone's asleep, who turned on the lights?

Sam's eyes followed the arch of the dome to its crest. At the very top of the dome, a massive oculus, maybe thirty feet in diameter, no longer displayed only darkness. Instead, it now erupted in sunlight, which reflected throughout the subterranean cavern.

Zara opened her eyes. "What the hell is that?"

Sam grinned. "I believe that's the way out you said would be impossible to find."

Chapter Sixty-Eight

The light traveled down through the oculus and onto the island. From there, it ricocheted around the dome, with increasing intensity, before sending a return light back through the original opening. Sam stared at the oculus. The light penetrating downwards appeared to be rectangular, but by the time it reflected off the water surrounding the island, the light appeared in the shape of a triangle. It surprised him, because the island clearly formed the shape of a perfect circle, positioned precisely below the oculus. The light lasted no more than fifteen minutes and then disappeared, leaving them in total darkness.

Sam increased the temperature on his DARPA thermal suit, and the darkness slowly turned to a stable blue glow. He looked at Zara and smiled, "See, I told you we'd find a way out."

She returned his smile. "What way out? You haven't got us out of here yet!"

"The light. That was sunlight. Where it can get in, we can get out."

She laughed. "That's the stupidest thing I've heard you say. The light could have just as easily come through an ancient pipe, no larger than a coin in diameter. The light will get in but nothing will get out."

"That's a possibility," Sam conceded. "But I have another idea."

Tom looked at him. The edge of his lip curving upwards, not quite in a grin, but definitely as a statement – *this ought to be good*! "Go on, Sam. Let's hear it."

Sam opened his mouth to speak. Paused and then grinned as though he'd suddenly been delivered a revelation. "It's the light. You see, the light that reflected upwards did so in the shape of a triangle."

Silence.

Zara asked, "What exactly is it about the triangular light that intrigues you, Sam?"

"The light that descended through the oculus was in the shape of a rectangle, but when it reflected off the waters surrounding the island, it did so in the shape of a triangle."

Tom asked, "But the island is a perfect circle?"

"Well spotted, Mr. Bower!" Sam said. "I have a theory the island is not an island at all. Instead, I believe it floats. Or that is to say, it once did, when the water levels were much higher than they are today."

"The island floats?" Zara asked.

"Used to," Sam corrected her. "Probably still does if the water level ever rises high enough again."

Tom smiled. "You think this was a giant water holding tank. Like the heart of the Garamante's last major water stores. It was protected and monitored. The light shines through the opening, down to the island. If the water is low, it shows a triangle, if it is high it shows a rectangle, if it's full, it shows a circle."

"Exactly," Sam said. "Maybe this was the lowest point in the Garamante Empire. As water flows downward, all irrigation tunnels fed through to this chamber here. The masters of the day must have known they were using enormous amounts of fossil water to irrigate their arid lands. They must have been terrified it would one day disappear. So they built this chamber and every so often, would shine light through a tunnel to get a reading of the water's depth."

Zara asked, "Why not simply walk down and measure it?"

Sam shook his head. "Not that simple. This place could be hundreds of miles from the main city. It would take days or weeks to send someone to test the water levels. Instead, they were grand engineers and built a system of reflective stones to shine sunlight into their holding tank."

No one made a comment.

Sam smiled. "So what do you think?"

Zara smiled. "I think you have a fantastic imagination, but even if you were right, it doesn't help us get out of here."

"Why not?" Sam asked.

"Because that oculus must be eighty feet above us, and there's no way to reach it."

Sam glanced at the base of the dome, where the triangular-shaped pendentives met the water. "I had an idea about that too."

"What?" she asked.

Sam smiled. "Have you ever been to Florence?"

Chapter Sixty-Nine

Sam spoke slowly. His eyes stared vacantly at the massive dome, but his mind wandered as though he was reliving a time nearly twenty years earlier when his father had taken him to visit the Italian city of Florence.

Sam said, "It's been many years since I last visited the great city, but one view still remains from my trip. One vision, so fantastic that I found its impression permanently embedded somewhere in the part of my brain that permanently stores valuable information." He grinned. "Among the contour of spires and domes one regal structure dominates the city's skyline."

Zara smiled. "Florence Cathedral."

Sam nodded. "The construction of Il Duomo di Firenze, as it is known to the locals, started in 1296 in the Gothic style with the design by Arnolfo di Cambio. But it wasn't completed until 1436 because until that time, no one could decide how to build such an enormous masonry dome without its weight causing the structure to collapse during the building process. Do you know who worked it out?"

She nodded. Her eyes were wide. "Filippo Brunelleschi, a Master Goldsmith."

Tom sat down. Disappointment showing across his face that he was being forced to hear another history lesson before being able to escape.

Sam continued. "The building of such a masonry dome would have posed many technical problems. Brunelleschi looked to the great dome of the Pantheon in Rome for solutions. The dome of the Pantheon was formed by a single shell of concrete, the formula for which had long since been forgotten. Soil filled with silver coins had held the Pantheon dome aloft while its concrete set. This could not be the solution in the case of a dome this size, and massive shoring would put the church out of use. For the height and breadth of the dome, starting 171 feet above the floor and spanning 144 feet, there was not enough timber in Tuscany to build the scaffolding and forms. Either of you like to hazard a guess how Brunelleschi overcame this problem?"

"He used a double shell, made of sandstone and marble," Tom said.

Sam glanced at him and nodded. A slightly wry smile forming on his lips. Sometimes his friend did listen to history. "Brunelleschi's dome would consist of two concentric shells, an inner one visible from within the cathedral nested inside a wider, taller external dome. To counteract hoop stress, he would bind the walls with tension rings of stone, iron, and wood, like hoops on a barrel. He built the first 46 feet in stone, after which he continued with lighter materials, such as spugna and brick. He also managed to do so, without the use of conventional, ground-based scaffolding."

Zara interrupted. "This is a great history lesson, but I don't see how any of this is going to help us reach the top of the oculus?"

Sam smiled. "Look at the size of this dome. It's not quite as big as Il Duomo di Firenze, but only by a dozen or so feet. That means the engineers and craftsmen who built this extraordinary structure must have overcome similar obstacles during construction."

Zara asked. "You think this is a Duomo?"

Sam smiled. "I'm certain it is."

"Again, how will any of this help us?" she asked.

Sam smiled again. "Because you have to picture this place without any water at all. What's on the other side of the interior dome of the Duomo?"

Her eyes hardened. "The cloistered vault!"

Chapter Seventy

Zara watched Sam slip into the cool water. Her face was a mix of anticipation and someone preparing for disappointment. She saw Sam swim gently along the surface to the edge of the dome, where the pendentive met the water. The large muscles in his back formed sharp angles with each stroke. He moved along the surface in a counterclockwise direction.

Tom dipped into the water on the opposite side of the island. Dropping like a pin and then surfacing moments later. He turned to face Sam. "I'll bet you a beer I'll find the entrance first."

Sam smiled. "You're on!"

Zara laughed. They were such typical boys. It was like watching children at the beach looking for hidden treasure. Only in this case, the treasure was real, the pirates were real, death was real, and the outcomes possibly resulting in the life and death of the human race.

And still, they looked like they were having fun.

Sam and Tom disappeared below the surface. The light in the dome faded quickly as the blue haze from their DARPA suits became buried in the water. Within a minute, the dome had turned to a deep gray, and eventually into total darkness. She stared at the water. Or more accurately, where she believed the water should have been, waiting for the light to return. She didn't wear a wristwatch and had no means of measuring the time, but it seemed to stretch.

When she was certain more than a few minutes had passed, she sat down. Zara felt the gallop of her heart, as the claustrophobia snuck in. She breathed in deeply, trying to resist the terror that was struggling to overcome her.

She forced herself to smile. *Faking it is half the battle.* She knew they hadn't drowned. Not yet and not both of them. They had probably found something. An underwater ledge or another cavern. Anything to let them breathe for a while and continue to explore.

She stood up again, finding she was becoming angry with both men. If they have found something, why not come up and let her know? Why make her wait, and suffer – in total darkness?

Around what seemed like ten minutes later, but might have been much less, Zara spotted the tiniest of blue dots in the water below. She smiled as she watched it slowly surface, bringing with it, the familiar blue glow.

A moment later, the island lit up with the strange, blue light.

Zara turned around. The island was just about glowing. *What the hell?* She glanced at the water where the blue light was still approaching. The second light was coming from somewhere entirely different. She looked up and smiled. Leaning on the edge of the oculus, eighty plus feet above, she saw Sam Reilly's face.

She squinted her eyes to make out the shape. Even at that distance, the man appeared to have an arrogant smirk of self-confidence. "Morning, Zara. I told you I'd get to the top of the dome! How about you come join me, the view's fantastic!"

"Looking forward to it!" she shouted back.

She smiled and a moment later Tom surfaced. His face cheerful as he quickly boasted, "I won. I found it first!"

I'm stuck in some subterranean hell hole with two children!

Zara asked, "You found a way out?"

"No. I found a way to the top of the dome. Of course, Sam couldn't stand to be beaten so he asked for a double or nothing bet that he could reach the top of the dome before me. I don't know if I'd go quite that far, yet, but I did find a way to the top of the dome." Tom smiled. "Have you been waiting long?"

She shook her head and smiled at his concern. "Now what?"

"Now if you follow me, I'll take you to the top of the dome, and we hope like hell the ancient tunnel leads somewhere worth going."

Chapter Seventy-One

Zara dived downward into the depths of the subterranean lake. She followed the blue light where Tom swam in front of her. It reminded her of a ghoulish apparition as the pressure built up in her ears. She tried to swallow and move her jaw, anything to relieve some of the pressure in her middle ear. The pressure changed and she was able to descend without any further pain.

The entrance was thirty or maybe even forty feet below the surface of the water. It was an arched door, which led to a narrow staircase. Apart from being submerged, the opening appeared no different than any of the thousands of mediaeval arches and stone stairs found throughout Europe. She followed Tom who swam quickly through the arch and into the stairwell.

You'll have to swim quickly once you're inside or you'll never reach it! She recalled Tom's words to her before diving.

Zara reached the top of the archway and pulled herself through. She'd reached the deepest point of the dive. Now all she had to do was live long enough to reach the surface. Inside, the series of identical stairs fit snugly between the inner and outer dome within a space no wider than two feet. The stairs ascended steeply in a clockwise direction.

She swam through and began the dangerous journey, alternating between kicking off with her feet and pulling herself upwards by drawing on the stairs, in a similar manner to an astronaut maneuvering around the Space Station.

Her head throbbed. Oxygen starvation was starting to affect her brain. She focused on the blue light ahead. No longer able to discern any visible image of Tom, her mind imagined it really was a ghost leading her toward something.

But was it where she wanted to go?

Was it a good spirit, or evil?

Her mind struggled to comprehend what she was trying to achieve. The space was dark with solid masonry walls on either side as she ascended in a continuous curve. It was impossible to know how far she climbed. She imagined the stairway wrapping all the way around the inner dome until it made a full circuit, possibly even multiple laps. She settled into a rhythm and soon the discomfort in her chest and blurriness in her mind all ceased to matter. She was moving, ascending, and that all had to mean something good, right?

A moment later, the fear returned – she'd lost sight of the blue spectral.

Zara panicked. There was nothing else for it. She'd reached the limits of her ability to hold her breath. She squirmed to make sense of anything, but now the one thing she could remember – the fact that she needed to follow the blue light – had been taken from her.

She continued heading in a clockwise direction. Constantly ascending in an identical curve, but soon she no longer had the ability to move her arms or legs. She no longer worried about whether or not she could hold her breath. None of those problems mattered anymore.

Zara felt herself sink onto the edge of the stone stairs. The last thing she remembered was the warmth. Everything felt so warm, and good, and safe. Dying wasn't so bad. The darkness had been pulled up around her like the safety of a warm blanket. It consumed all her senses and left her feeling nothing.

Chapter Seventy-Two

Sam looked at Tom as he squeezed by inside the narrow stairway, where the water met the dry section. He looked at Tom's hardened expression as he breathed deeply. "You okay, Tom?"

Tom nodded but said nothing.

Sam waded into the submerged steps of the stairs. "Where's Zara?"

"She was behind me a moment ago."

Sam swore and then dipped his head beneath the water, diving head-first downward. He followed the descending stairs in their counter-clockwise direction. He could hear the sudden throb of his own panicked heart sending blood pounding in the back of his ears. He descended for approximately twenty seconds before he saw her.

Christ! She's dead!

He didn't wait to check her vital signs. He grabbed Zara by her shoulders and pulled her backwards, and clockwise up the stairway. Sam moved with the speed afforded by his adrenaline, but it was much slower than when he swam down on his own. It felt like it had taken forever by the time his foot stepped on the dry stone and he pulled her out of the water.

Her body appeared lifeless. She wasn't breathing. Her normally dark skin appeared pale and waxy. Sam placed her on her side and with her head downwards inside the narrow stairway so her head was draining.

Her mouth was open and the water gushed out.

Sam watched as it continued to drain. One of the hardest things to do in an emergency is nothing. Sometimes you have to wait. No reason to try and help her breathe if her lungs are still full of water. It might have only taken seconds. Then again, it might have been minutes. Sam had no way to tell. All he knew was the water must have filled her lungs completely.

She must have taken a deep breath in while she was still under? Sam thought, morbidly. It would have been a conscious decision. An acceptance of her death.

Tom took one glance at her. His mouth set hard. "Does she have a pulse?"

Sam placed two fingers on Zara's neck, next to her windpipe. He waited for a moment. "She's got a pulse. It's bounding, but it's there!"

A moment later, the water stopped draining.

Zara coughed multiple times and stopped. And then started breathing on her own. Her eyes were still shut and she looked like she was sleeping. There was no way to immediately know how much damage had been done to her brain.

Tom asked, "Now what do we do?"

Sam breathed in and then sighed. "Nothing. Now we wait."

Chapter Seventy-Three

The warmth and euphoric dreams were over. In their place, nightmares filled her mind. There was a burning sensation in her chest. It felt like she'd swallowed fire and no matter how much she exhaled, the flame remained. She coughed a few more times and felt her lungs struggle to expand. It felt like they were being held by a big piece of elastic, which prevented them from fully opening. She felt something change. The gooey and fiery liquid drained from her mouth. When there was no more to exhale, she tried to inhale.

Nothing happened. The muscles of her diaphragm had lost interest. She tried again. Nothing.

Am I already dead?

The elastic over her chest snapped and now she was finally allowed to inhale. The air felt icy cold, and sweet on her burnt lungs. She coughed twice more. It seemed to take longer than she thought was normal to take a second breath. It was like her diaphragm was still debating what it wanted to do. She breathed again. And again. By the fifth time, the process seemed more natural. Definitely far from normal. Her muscles of respiration were no longer working on autonomic reflexes. Instead, she was having to consciously coerce them into keeping her alive. But at least now, she seemed to have some control over the process.

No. Not dead.

Zara tried to move her arms. Nothing happened. She tried to speak. She wanted to speak. And wanted to say that everything was all right. Whatever happened. Whatever went wrong. It was okay now. She was okay.

She couldn't remember what she'd been trying to do, or what went wrong. But somehow, it all felt okay. There was a picture of an island. The surrounding shallow waters were turquoise. The island was shaped like a perfect figure eight, lying on its side. One side of the island was completely flat, while at the center of the other side, a small mountain of sand rose a hundred or more feet into the air.

That's right! She thought. *I was on my way to an island.*

It seemed incredibly important to her all of a sudden that she reach the island. That it held the answers to every question that was so important to her. Although, at the present, she had no idea what she wanted to ask. Heck, if she was honest, she didn't even know the name of the island, or how it was going to answer her questions.

Two voices were arguing.

One said, "We should have planned the ascent better." It was terse. Like a reprimand.

"What could we have done?" the second one asked.

"I don't know, prepared her better? She'd have had a different outcome. Now we don't know what's going to happen. You were in such a rush. You just told me to bring her up. And said she'd be all right."

"And she will be all right," the second voice replied. It was abrupt and full of authority.

"How can you be so certain?"

The voice paused. Like its owner was struggling to even consider answering in such a way. It sighed. The voice, succumbing to reveal the truth, even though it didn't want to. "Because Nostradamus didn't mention anything about her drowning!"

Nostradamus. She repeated the name, silently in her mind. *What does he have to do with her future?*

She opened her eyes. They weren't quite in focus. Everything around her appeared blue. She was lying on a series of stone steps. They were hurting her back. The steps were narrow and on each side was a masonry wall.

Two men started asking her questions. She didn't hear any of them. They both glowed with a blue haze, like a spectral or ghostly apparition. She would have been frightened if it wasn't for the fact that both men appeared excited, like her arrival was the best news they'd received all day. They looked kind. Concerned. And supportive.

She opened her mouth to speak. Her voice was soft, not yet capable of producing any great resonance. Her eyes, deep-set and intense, stared wide.

"What is it?" the first voice asked.

"Go on. We couldn't hear you," the second said.

Zara grinned. "I know exactly where we have to go!"

Chapter Seventy-Four

Zara felt a man lean in and help her to sit. There was barely any room and no way that either of the men could have sat next to her. Both of her shoulders rested on opposite sides of the masonry walls, which formed the vault of her captivity. She felt one of the men rest his hands on her back to stop her from falling over.

"How do you feel?"

"I've had better days." She looked at the man who spoke, and recognized him. His voice was familiar, but it took her a moment to remember his name. "Sam Reilly."

"At your service, Ma'am."

She asked, "Where's Tom?"

"I'm up here, Zara. There's no room for the three of us."

She nodded. The place felt cramped and confining as it was. "What happened?"

Sam said, "You were following Tom into the vaulted stairway, between the subterranean Duomo. It was a long swim, and you ran out of air. You almost made it. About twenty feet off, you must have lost consciousness. We dragged you up to the dry stairs and laid you with your head down, gallons of water drained from your lungs."

"I followed you into a submerged, subterranean and narrow stairwell, vaulted between two masonry domes?"

"Afraid so," he confirmed.

She smiled. "That doesn't really sound like something I'd willingly do."

"It wasn't. We were kind of stuck. We're in the process of finding a way out. Do you remember what we were doing here?"

Zara thought about it for a moment. "The Nostradamus Equation."

"That's right, you kicked over a real hornets nest, and an army of General Ngige's men are topside in the Saharan desert searching for you. You said you knew where we have to go. Do you still remember?"

"Yes. But I can't for the life of me recall what it means."

"Where?"

"A place called Infinity Island." She glanced up at Sam. "Does that make any sense to you?"

He nodded. "You had a medallion. Something your father gave to you. He said it would make sense and be important to you one day. There's an island depicted on one side of it. The island is shaped like a lemniscate, the mathematical symbol for infinity."

"Then we'd better go find that island. I had a lot of dreams while I was out. Most of them nightmares, but some were all right. One I am certain was real."

"What was it?"

"I don't know. But I woke up with the one thought fixed in my mind – we need to reach Infinity Island if we want it to be okay."

"Okay," Sam said. "Can you walk?"

She asked, "Can you carry me up this narrow stairway?"

He shook his head.

Zara smiled. "Then I guess I'd better start walking."

"Take your time."

Zara carefully stood up. She felt a slight rush of blood to her head, like she was going to pass out. She paused. Took in a deep breath and then slowly exhaled until the feeling passed. She took a step forward and felt Sam take her hand for support.

She squeezed it, and then let go. "I'm okay."

It took nearly forty minutes to reach the top of the Duomo. The stone stairs continued in a clockwise direction around the inner dome, gradually gaining height. The spacing between the internal and external dome curved inward the higher she went, meaning that as she approached the oculus she needed to lean toward the inner dome to continue. She lost track of how many times she must have traveled around the circumference of the massive dome before she crept into the main opening where the oculus opened to the cavern below.

The narrow stairway continued as a tunnel around the oculus, before looping back on itself and returning down the way they'd come. A separate tunnel turned to the left and allowed them to climb up to the top of the second dome. She followed Sam through the upward tunnel. The stone stairs now appeared more like a ladder, as the gradient increased to a near vertical position.

She climbed through and glanced around. They were now inside a horizontal tunnel, similar in size and shape to the one they'd found earlier, which had been blocked by a cave-in and flooded. In one direction, it traveled such a long way that she couldn't see where the tunnel ended. In the opposite direction she saw a polished piece of brass on the edge of the ceiling. It was angled at forty-five degrees so that if she shined a flashlight on it, the light would reflect down the open oculus.

Zara asked, "Do you know how far this tunnel goes?"

Sam shook his head. "No. But I think it's time we find out."

Chapter Seventy-Five

Sam led the party down the tunnel. It continued for about a mile in a perfectly straight line before reaching a second tunnel, which ran perpendicular to theirs. Water ran down the tunnel. It was shallow and moved quickly. A crude dugout canoe floated in the middle of the aqueduct. A solid piece of stone, the length of the tunnel prohibited the boat from being carried away, down the tunnel. The term boat was used loosely. It was formed out of the trunk of a single acacia tree. The inside of which, had been carved out to make a small boat. It was similar to the hollow-log canoes of peoples all over the world. It was long enough to fit four or five people and the width was almost exactly equal to that of the aqueduct.

He recalled that Zara had told him the *acacia raddiana* was once prolific within the Sahara, and survived upwards of five hundred years. The hard wood must have been capable of surviving years in the water, but even so, it was impossible to imagine that such a structure would have survived since the time of the Garamantes, as much as fourteen hundred years ago.

Sam looked at Tom and asked, "What do you make of that?"

"Looks like an emergency boat," Tom said. "Like the ancient Garamantes left it there so that a scout could quickly climb in and return to the main city."

Zara stared at the boat. "I don't know, but can you imagine any way for them to even bring their boats back up the tunnels after traveling down the aqueduct?"

"No," Sam said. "Come to think of it. How did they bring the boat back up here?"

Zara said, "Maybe it's because they were never built to go all the way to the bottom?"

Tom said, "Or perhaps it was an emergency trip?"

"A what?" she asked.

"An emergency boat trip. Think for instance, the ancient Garamantes posted scouts throughout the desert. One notices an advancing Roman army. He would be able to descend down the well, get on a boat and race back to their main citadel to warn of the impending battle."

Sam said, "If that's true, then where the hell is this citadel we're apparently going to?"

Zara put her hand on the boat. The wood was dry and rigid. "It still floats."

Sam nodded. "None of this makes sense to me. If the Garamantes died out in the sixth century, this boat would have rotted away to dust by now. Which means the boat was either of a much better construction than anything our shipwrights could construct today, or the boat's a lot younger than we imagine."

Zara asked, "You think someone else has been down here more recently than the sixth century?"

Sam said, "Either this boat was brought down by someone in the past hundred years, such as a smuggler, or..."

"What?" Tom asked.

"Or, the Garamantes are still alive!"

Tom shrugged, as though he didn't care, either way. "The boat floats. The water runs in that direction. Let's take it!"

Zara glanced at Sam. "Is that wise?"

Sam sat in the front section of the boat. It took his weight easily, and appeared sturdy in the water. He smiled. "Probably not. But I can't see a better way of getting to the end of this aqueduct, so we may as well try."

He waited until Zara and Tom climbed aboard. The boat appeared stable with all three of them aboard. Sam turned around. "Are we all ready?"

Zara swallowed hard. "Ready as we're ever going to be."

Tom nodded. He was grinning like a kid at a theme park.

"All right, let's go."

Sam removed the stone block and the boat, free from its confines, leaped forward eagerly. The shallow water ran quickly, even though the angle of the tunnel appeared closer to horizontal than descending.

The weak glow from their DARPA suits barely allowed them to see what was ahead. They ran for nearly a hundred feet before the water began to speed up, even faster. It was like they were approaching a waterfall.

Tom grinned. "You get the feeling we're approaching the fun part of the ride?"

Zara gripped the sides of the boat until her knuckles shined white. "Yeah, it's great. Just like Disneyland, with the added benefit of not knowing whether or not you're about to drown or just crash onto the rocks at the bottom."

Sam said, "The Garamantes were obviously very good engineers. Do you really think they would have built a boat here to service the aqueduct if the tunnels were impassable?"

No one heard his words. Instead, the roar of the rapids ahead drowned out all sounds. Sam looked at the darkness ahead. The aqueduct looked like it was about to collide with a solid wall of stone. A reflective brass mirror, like the one seen at the top of the Duomo shined back at him.

He made a vicious oath and the boat dipped and dropped down a steep decline. The boat rushed downwards, falling thirty or more feet, before the slope balanced out and the boat shot out the bottom.

Chapter Seventy-Six

The water settled to a more natural flow and Sam turned to face his companions.

Tom's eyes were wide and his mouth open. He said, "Who wants to help me pull the boat back up and do that again?"

"Not me," Zara said. "If we ever make it out of this damned place alive, I never want to see either of you again."

Sam shrugged. "Some people are never appreciative."

The flow of the water settled into a comfortable meander.

Zara said, "Everything we know about the Garamantes suggest their success was based on their subterranean water-extraction system, a network of tunnels known as foggaras in Berber. It not only allowed their part of the Sahara to bloom again, it also triggered a political and social process that led to population expansion, urbanism, and conquest. But in order to retain and extend their newfound prosperity, they needed above all to maintain and expand the water-extraction tunnel systems – and that necessitated the acquisition of many slaves."

Sam smiled. "Luckily for the Garamantes, but less so for their neighbors, the Garamantian population growth gave the new Saharan power a demographic and military advantage over other peoples in Saharan and sub-Saharan Africa, enabling them to expand their territory, conquer other peoples, and acquire vast numbers of slaves."

"Thanks to their aggressive mentality and the slaves and water it produced, the Garamantes lived in planned towns and lived well." Zara said, "Archeological digs, have shown they feasted on locally grown grapes, figs, sorghum, barley, and wheat, as well as imported luxuries such as wine and olive oil." Zara looked at the perfectly formed tunnel, still working as intended nearly a thousand years after the demise of the Garamantes. "The combination of their slave-acquisition activities and their mastery of foggara irrigation technology enabled the Garamantes to enjoy a standard of living far superior to that of any other ancient Saharan society. Without slaves, they would not have had a kingdom, let alone even a whiff of the good life. They would have survived in conditions of relative poverty, as most desert dwellers have done before and since."

Sam said, "In the end, depletion of easily mined fossil water sounded the death knell of the Garamantian kingdom. After extracting at least 30 billion gallons of water over some 600 years, the Garamantes discovered that the water was literally running out. To deal with the problem, they would have needed to add more man-made underground tributaries to existing tunnels and dig additional deeper, much longer water-extraction tunnels. For that, they would have needed vastly more slaves than they had. The water difficulties must have led to food shortages, population reductions, and political instability. Conquering more territories and pulling in more slaves was therefore simply not militarily feasible. The magic equation between population and military and economic power on the one hand and slave-acquisition capability and water extraction on the other no longer balanced."

Zara said, "The desert kingdom declined and fractured into small chiefdoms and was absorbed into the emerging Islamic world. Like its more famous Roman neighbor, the once-great Saharan kingdom became, little by little, simply a thing of myth and memory."

"Only their irrigation tunnels have remained."

They continued along their strange journey in silence for the next two days. Intermittently taking turns to rest and sleep. In an attempt to conserve the few hours of battery power remaining to each DARPA suit, both Sam and Tom switched their machines off. For the time being, there was nothing they could do to adjust the direction of their movement, so they may as well do so in the dark, only occasionally powering up to check on their surroundings.

Sam drifted in that strange place, somewhere between conscious and unconscious. Comfortable and uncomfortable. He was close to sleep when the boat stopped its forward movement. There wasn't much of a change. It must have been gradually slowing down.

"Everyone all right?" he asked.

Tom said, "Yeah, you?"

"I'm fine."

"Where are we?" Zara asked.

Sam switched on his DARPA suit and the area glowed with the now familiar blue haze. He glanced in front of the boat. The tunnel appeared unchanged, but the shallow water was now missing. Behind, the water looked like it was flowing softly.

Sam turned to face Zara and Tom. "There must be a crack in the tunnel, where the water's now flowing into a lower tunnel."

Tom nodded. "I guess it's time to walk."

Zara asked, "Do you think this is going to get us anywhere? We might just be going deeper into the ancient irrigation tunnels!"

"We don't know," Sam said. "But there's no way we're going to swim all that way back to where we started, so all we can do is keep going forward.

Zara nodded in silent protest.

They walked along the dry aqueduct. A line, approximately three feet up along the bottom half of the tunnel, showed where the water once sat. Above it was approximately another four feet in height. If it was much lower, Tom would have struck his head on the ceiling.

It was about an hour before they took a break. There wasn't any change in the tunnel. The ancient Garamantes, if nothing else, knew how to build a perfectly symmetrical tunnel for hundreds of miles. The air was cool, and a slight draft flowed past them, in the same direction as they were heading. The breeze was new and refreshing, and it gave them the impetus to keep going with a renewed vigor.

They continued again, walking faster. Ten minutes later, something changed. Sam hurried fifty feet ahead. The height of the tunnel lowered until it was obvious that all of them would need to bend to get through. It continued like that for about fifteen feet and then opened into a giant, vaulted room. The dry aqueduct ran through the center of the room like the rail platform of an old city, where a ghost train no longer delivered water to the entrance of a great city.

Chapter Seventy-Seven – The Golden City

Sam stared at the massive dome above. It made the Roman Pantheon look like a toy. It had a diameter of at least a hundred feet. The dry irrigation channel split straight down the middle of the room, before continuing on through a dark tunnel on the opposite end. Inside the massive structure were the remains of an amphitheater. It was formed out of limestone steps, and stretched at least eighty feet into the air in a semi-circle. On the same side there were at least twenty buildings, all in a classical style as if Greek or Roman temples. On the opposite side of the channel another thirty similar buildings of various sizes. At least a hundred and eighty feet above, a giant oculus that showed no light reminded him that he was still buried deep underground.

Zara asked, "Where are we, Sam?"

Sam said, "At a guess, I'd say we're in the fabled Golden City of the Kingdom of the Sands – the treasure of the Garamante Empire."

"That's great," Tom said. "But where's the gold?"

"There was never really any gold! The term represented the wealth of knowledge found inside. This was where the great ones came to discuss the future. Think of a place filled with the great people of their time. Their versions of people like, Michelangelo, Plato, Da Vinci, and Einstein. This was a place for the greats to go. And Nostradamus! That was why it was called the Golden City!" Sam stepped toward the amphitheater. "What do you think this place was used for?"

"It was a meeting place." Zara spoke confidently. For a person who two days ago had shattered any belief that the Garamantes had ever made it this far south, inside the Sahara, she now possessed an extraordinary knowledge about the ancient civilization. "A symbol of their technological might. Think Rome in its heyday. Florence. Hell, it could be an older version of Washington D.C. when you look at it. Perhaps this is where their leaders came to debate important matters before government."

Tom laughed. "I would have loved to hear their views on climate change."

Zara smiled. "From what we know about the Garamantes, they didn't care about their environment. Instead they utilized heavy slave labor to acquire water for irrigation and crop development. They made their environment what they needed it to be to survive. When the water ran out, they became extinct."

"Sound familiar?" Sam asked.

She turned to face him. "What?"

"You said Nostradamus told you the human race was about to become extinct and now you're telling me these people became extinct due to climate change?"

She shook her head. "No. The climate didn't change. The Garamantians drew their water from ancient tables of fossil water, accumulated over approximately forty million years. It was only a matter of time before the water tables were exhausted and their civilization's need exceeded their ability to produce water."

"Yeah – what I said. An economy based on technological changes that in turn changed the climate in an unsustainable way. Ecology 101. They failed – and we are following their example."

"Talking about tunnels. There's a bunch of them heading off this way," Tom said. "I'm going to check it out. We still need to find a way to the surface."

Sam nodded. They would need to split up and work quickly to find a way to the surface – if such a way still existed. He gazed around the vast chamber. It could have fit a football field inside. The place looked like the main meeting place on a bad Sci-Fi set. A city buried inside an asteroid or a moon. There were broken, and misshaped rooms throughout. Little remained to suggest the purpose of such rooms, but he imagined a thriving market place. Fresh food stalls, exotic food from places far away, brothels, carpenters, engineers, people who practiced medicine, they would have all been there.

He stopped walking. Grinned. "This place wasn't just a meeting place. This was their city. This was grand central station! Look. What if the reason archeologists have only discovered primitive villages on the surface was because those were the stragglers or even another race altogether. What if the Garamantians didn't just build a three thousand mile network of irrigation channels – what if they built three thousand miles of networked transport?"

Zara tilted her head to the left; her mind exploring the possibilities. "It would be much easier to send food, water, and people by boat beneath the harsh desert than above."

Sam nodded as he imagined a world where food and other supplies were transported along the ancient irrigation channels, along with fresh water. He walked through the small buildings – structures that once housed the city's elite. They were simple by modern day standards of luxury, but at the time, would have been the height of decadence. Like the Romans, the Garamantians appeared to serve themselves the best.

He said, "What if these people and the remains of the old Berber civilization located on the surface were the same?"

"But you just said you thought they were different?"

"What if they were once the same civilization, but as the water dried up things started to change."

Zara asked, "What sort of changes?"

Sam said, "The same sort which always take place when food becomes scarce – the rich get richer and the poor get poorer."

"They abandoned their slaves, and general population, so their thinkers and movers could continue to live in decadence. While one part of their society died off nearly fourteen hundred years ago, the other one thrived for another thousand years!"

Tom stepped into the room. Even in the dull blue light, his face appeared flushed. He was breathing hard as though he'd been running. His brown eyes were wide and filled with adrenaline.

"What is it?" Sam asked.

Tom paused. Swallowed hard. "I've found something. I think you're both going to want to see."

Zara turned to face him. "What did you find?"

"There's a room here you're both going to want to see, right now!"

"Sure, what is it? What did you see?" Zara persisted.

Tom looked at her. Shook his head, and said, "I believe it's a message, for you."

Chapter Seventy-Eight

The entrance to the strange room stood out among the rest of the building structures beneath the dome for two reasons. The first one surprised Zara immensely, and the second sent chills down her spine.

First, unlike every other structure they'd seen, this one had a door. It was made of solid brass, with intricate images of horse drawn chariots, etched into the metal. None of the other structures had doors, and she had seen no other sign of brass displayed throughout the dome. Secondly, and more disturbingly, were the words written on the door. She stared at them, willing them to spell another word or different name. There was nothing she could do about it though. The truth was uncompromising.

The words spelled, *Zara Delacroix*.

She tried to push the door open. It was heavy. The large hinges fought against the centuries without movement. Sam and Tom put all their weight into it and finally, the door creaked open.

Inside was a discreet and unremarkable room, not too dissimilar to those they'd already seen, except that it had a sarcophagus in the center of the room. The walls were carved out of solid limestone, like the rest of the buildings. Nothing was written on the walls. A pedestal could be seen, stepped inside a small alcove. Water dripped from an opening in the ceiling and filled the pedestal. A hole in the floor, worn out through the ages, captured the overflow, and then drained into a hidden opening below. Otherwise, the room was empty.

Zara's eyes returned to the sarcophagus. It was the centerpiece of the room and if someone wanted her to find something, she guessed it was most likely going to be inside. Zara walked around the sarcophagus. It was most likely the final resting place of one of the great kings of the sand. She stopped on the other side.

Her mouth opened to speak, but words didn't come out.

"What is it?" Sam asked, his eyes glancing at the ancient script.

Zara met his gaze. "I don't know yet. There's something about this that I recognize."

"I thought you'd never studied anything to do with the Garamantes?"

"I didn't." She bit her lower lip. "This is all written in the language of modern Berber."

"That's great," Tom interrupted. "But if we don't work out how to get out of here soon, we're going to be sharing their tomb with them."

"This might be important," she said.

"So is staying alive," Tom said, cheerfully.

"Wait. I can read this."

"Well. Don't keep us in suspense. What does it say?" Sam said.

She swallowed hard. "Our problem just got a whole lot worse."

Chapter Seventy-Nine

Zara felt her entire world spin. She imagined it would have been a similar experience to the early navigators in the world who believed the world was flat, suddenly discovering it was spherical. Worse still, it might even be more like then discovering the world used satellites high up in the orbit of the earth to send messages, allowing computers to triangulate their exact position on earth using a GPS. Everything she believed had just turned in on itself.

Sam asked, "What's changed, Zara?"

"Everything!"

"What?" Tom said.

"This place was visited by Nostradamus in 1557." Zara waited for the thought to sink in.

Sam and Tom stared at her, silently.

She continued. "After the massive sand storm, which killed all of his party except for my great ancestor, Nostradamus must have entered one of the Garamante irrigation tunnels and made his way to this ancient city."

Sam asked, "Why? What did he come here to do?"

Zara paused. "He came to bury the very last Garamante. A king without a people. And he came so that I could know what he'd learned."

"What did Nostradamus learn?" Sam looked at her. "Didn't he leave everything you needed to know in his book?"

"No. After he'd left his book buried in the sands of the Sahara, Nostradamus had changed the future. Consequently, his next visions had changed as a consequence."

Tom asked, "What did he write?"

"It's a story, of times to come."

Sam asked, "What does it say?"

"It's about the fall of man. About a great civilization. The Garamante Empire. About their successes, and their losses. About their riches and their greed. About their greatness and their fallibility. At the end of the story, it says that man is no better than the locusts who multiply into destructive plagues. If the human race is to survive, we must do so in smaller numbers. There is only so much the land will stretch and bend to meet our demands – and when that is all done, our time on earth shall end like so many other animals before us."

"Wow," Sam said. "Seems pretty much on the mark of what Nostradamus was saying."

"Sure." Tom shook his head. "Pity it didn't really tell us what to do about it."

"Sure it did."

Tom smiled. "It did?"

"Yeah," Zara said. "Didn't that letter to Mikhail say it wasn't about a new diamond mine? It was about lithium. World War Three was going to be fought over lithium – and the world's largest stores were in the Democratic Republic of Congo."

"Yeah," Sam confirmed. "What are you suggesting, by backing our guy in there the human race is going to stop procreating?"

"No. I'm suggesting Nostradamus meant us to let them fight a war." Zara said. "I'm serious. Maybe Nostradamus knew I would run into you and stop you from supporting the good guys."

Sam shook his head. "Or maybe he wanted us to support the United Sovereign of Kongo so that the lithium could be mined and the world could live more economically."

"For how long, though?"

"Until it's no longer sustainable."

"But when will that be? When will there be too many human beings on this planet? Do you know at the turn of the eighteenth century what the best estimate of the total population of the planet was?"

"I don't know, a billion?" Tom asked.

"A little above two hundred million," Sam said. He spoke with the certainty of a man who knew the statistic and was as concerned as anyone should be. "It took us nearly fifty thousand years from the beginning of agriculture to reach two hundred million and it's taken us only the two hundred years since to take that number up above seven billion. The United Nations currently predicts the population to reach eighteen billion by the end of this century alone. I know. It's not scare tactics. It's science."

Zara sighed. "No, that statistic's wrong."

Sam shrugged. "It's a prediction by the United Nations. It's a ball park figure."

"According to Nostradamus, the population is going to reach thirty billion before the century is out. Do you know what the final population is going to be in the year 2100?"

Sam and Tom both shook their heads.

Sam looked at her. "The woman Tom killed before we entered the well – she said you knew something terrible. You denied it at the time, but I thought I saw your eyes look away. It was subtle. For a second I doubted it. But now that I see it again, I know where I've seen that look. It's the distinct image of a person trying to hide the painful truth. You were hiding something, weren't you?"

She nodded.

"I see that same look in your face now," Sam said. "What are you trying to hide?"

"I found a second note addressed to me in the book of Nostradamus. The first one was explicit. Nostradamus said it was the first thing he wrote before he started his entire works. The second wasn't even attached to the codex. Instead, he scribbled it on a piece of paper with a simple note. An addendum."

Sam asked, "What did it say?"

Zara said, "I had a choice. He'd never seen it before. But now he knew that I had a choice to make. He couldn't tell me what to do, because he hadn't seen anything in my future."

"What was the choice?"

"He said that I could do nothing and the human race would become extinct when my bloodline ceased in three hundred years."

"What alternative did he give you?"

She remained silent. Her eyes avoiding his and staring at the sarcophagus.

"Go on. You've gone this far now."

"He said I may attempt to change the future."

"And?"

"And if I'm successful the human race will continue far into the future."

"But?"

"If I fail that population number changes at the end of this century. Any child born today will have a high chance of being alive to see this date. We're not talking about hundreds of years in the future. We're talking about the end of this generation."

"All right," Sam said. "I'm interested. What does Nostradamus predict the population to be on the first of January 2101?"

She looked at him. Her jaw rigid and her eyes intense. "Zero – the human race would be extinct."

"Okay. So you have a choice. You can do nothing and the human race will survive another three hundred years. That's not so bad. Or you can take a chance and potentially kill everyone at the end of this generation."

"Those were the choices."

"You mean, those are the choices," Sam corrected her.

"No. Were. Past tense. This is a new note. Nostradamus obviously had another vision since he'd left the book of Nostradamus buried in the Saharan desert."

"Why? What's changed?"

"Here he says that when my daughter turns eighty-two – the human population on earth will reach zero."

Sam did the math. "For that to be true, you'd need to be pregnant right now?"

She took in a slow, deep breath. Closed her eyes and exhaled. "I'm two months pregnant. My lover doesn't even know. Heck. I only guessed when I read Nostradamus's note. I didn't believe it. But things are changing. I haven't seen a doctor yet, but I can tell you for certain, with the knowledge of a mother – I'm pregnant and I want my child to live."

Chapter Eighty

Zara held her breath. She waited for a response from either Sam or Tom. She'd betrayed their trust. But how could she have told them any earlier? She had gambled the lives of every living person on the planet, because she thought it was better to have the possibility of extending the time-line for the human race and in doing so, had jeopardized two hundred years of it.

"All right," Sam said. "Let me get this straight. Are you saying the future has already changed?"

Zara nodded. "Yes. Like I've said before, Nostradamus can't see everything. He has visions and these visions are like scenes in a movie or chapters in a book. They are very clear and provide lots of information about a specific event, but not necessarily the time and date of the event. In this circumstance, the original data that Nostradamus was working on has changed. As it is set now, he believes I'm on course to destroy humanity."

Sam nodded vacantly, and started looking around the room. She wasn't sure if he'd heard what she had to say, and was ignoring her completely, or whether he was now simply focused on something entirely different. Either way, he looked like he was miles away, and uninterested in her confession. She turned to Tom, instead. "Are you all right?"

"Yeah. Call me selfish, but I'm still more concerned with getting out of here and surviving to my next birthday than the predicted life-expectancy of the human race after the next century. I think I'll go have another look around outside. See if there's a way to reach the surface."

Zara nodded as he left. She then turned to watch Sam study the empty walls, the sides of the sarcophagus, the doors, everything. Despite the catastrophic news he'd just received, Sam's face displayed his normal level of insouciance, which she simultaneously admired and despised. He smiled, like he was hearing the score of a game of social lawn bowls.

Zara asked, "Did you hear a word I said?"

Sam smiled. "I'm not sure. I think so. I definitely might have. I'm sorry, I got distracted. Where did you finish?"

"Where did you get to?"

"You inadvertently sped up the extinction of the human race." Sam continued to slide his hand along a small crevice between two sections of the empty wall. His face appeared intrigued and curious, without a hint of concern. "Did I miss anything important, after that?"

"No. That's about the gist of it."

Sam smiled. "Good. Well that's settled then."

Zara followed him, suddenly aware that he was neither perturbed, nor interested in the news that Nostradamus had left her. She glanced at his face. "What are you looking for?"

"Answers."

"To what?"

"The next clue," Sam said, shaking his head, as though it were obvious. "The next step. Think about it. If Nostradamus went to the trouble of doing all this to save the human race from extinction, why would he stop now and write a message informing you that you'd failed and now the entire dark future was going to occur two hundred years earlier?"

She asked, "So what are you saying?"

Sam said, "I believe Nostradamus is still trying to help you find the one thing he never had. The only aid that could possibly allow you to correctly change the future."

"The Nostradamus Equation!"

"Exactly." He then stopped at the pedestal. "Ah, and here it is."

"Here what is?" she asked.

311

"The next clue."

Zara stared at the pedestal. It looked out of place in the holy room where the last survivor of the Kingdom of Sands had been laid to rest by Nostradamus himself.

She suddenly grinned. There was another note. It was written in the same scrawl she'd recognized as coming from the hand of Nostradamus.

Searching for answers?

Place the key into the pedestal and learn the truth.

"What do you think?" she asked. "Is this another note by Nostradamus?"

"I think you're clutching at straws. It's an old circular pedestal with a remarkably similar shape to your medallion, but nothing more."

"So you think I shouldn't bother?"

"No. You may as well try. I'm just saying, don't expect anything to happen."

Zara nodded. She carefully withdrew the brass medallion beneath her tank-top and placed it in the water. A single drop of water fell on to it from above, but nothing happened. The truth, it would appear, was avoiding her.

"What did you think would happen?" Sam said.

"I don't know. Anything. Something. Not nothing."

Zara reached towards the medallion to remove it from the water and then stopped – because the water began to change color and fizz violently.

Chapter Eighty-One

Zara watched for a minute, mesmerized by the suspense. She was going to know the truth. Nostradamus had been right. He knew everything. He knew she would end up inside this ancient city. Everything would be revealed to her. All she had to do was wait.

It was the acrid smell and caustic smoke that awoke her to her mistake. The pedestal wasn't designed for her medallion. It was designed as a means of torture, or punishment to see who was truly fit and ordained to be king. A test of strength and will.

And now the acid was burning her only hope to find the truth!

Zara quickly pulled on the back of the chain and ran toward the old Garamante baths, which held slowly flowing water. She washed her medallion. The brass appeared to have weathered its misuse, but tiny weaknesses in the metal work had begun to show as the acid continued to eat its way through. There was nothing she could do to counteract the damage as the acid found every tiny fault from the original metallic design. By the time the acid had dissipated she was staring at a medallion with many holes through it. Small, but large enough to allow light to pass.

Sam said, "Okay, Zara. Whatever it is, we're not going to find it here. We need to get out of here, before we starve and become too weak to escape."

She nodded. It was the truth, but still she couldn't understand what Nostradamus had wanted her to see by entering the room.

Tom entered the room again. "I think I've found a way to the surface."

Sam nodded and turned to Zara. "We have to go."

"I know. But one day, we'll come back and find the truth."

Tom led them to another room. It had a series of steps carved into the limestone to form a basic ladder. The room was narrow like a chute and ascended more than a hundred feet above. Every twenty or so feet, the steps crossed over and changed sides with a small landing area in-between. The result was that the maximum distance they could potentially fall never exceeded about twenty feet.

Tom climbed first. She followed and Sam climbed last. It was strenuous and after a few days of relative inactivity, little rest, and no food, her legs burned as she climbed. On the top of the eighth section, after ascending a total of a hundred and sixty feet, they stopped at a dead end.

This landing area was slightly larger than the others, but not big by any stretch. All three of them could stand without falling down the opening where the ladder stood, but there wasn't enough room for them to do much more than that. Above them was solid limestone where she'd expected a hatchway or an opening to the surface.

"Now what?" she asked.

Sam studied the walls, running his fingers across any gaps. "Beats me."

"There'll be an opening," Tom said. He spoke confidently as he searched the empty ceiling. "No reason to go to the effort of building such a place without having it lead to an exit."

Zara crossed her arms. "Maybe it was filled in when the Garamante elite separated from their lesser, surface dwelling relatives?"

Sam said, "Or maybe they left a door handle?"

All three of them stared at the single stone that appeared out of place. It was dark, where the rest of them were cream colored. A small pictograph showed a small funnel leading through an opening, with sand running through. Zara put her right hand on the stone and pressed until it moved inwards.

Nothing happened.

Sam and Tom both looked at her. Their faces said, let me have a try. They even moved toward her, as though they would fix it. They never reached the stone. Instead, a thunderous roar above changed their minds.

"Find something to hold on to!" Sam shouted. His voice barely audible above the rumble coming from the ceiling.

Zara's eyes darted toward the stone she'd just pressed. It had slid several inches inwards. A slight groove at the lip of the block below it gave her something solid to hold. She moved as close to the wall as possible and stared up at the ceiling above.

A long crack split the limestone above. It started small, and rapidly progressed with the spider-web pattern of a fracture of a stone striking a window. It was a simple conclusion to what happened next. Zara closed her eyes and hoped for the best.

A thunderclap shook their platform as the ceiling collapsed, driven by the weight above. A moment later thousands of tons of sand fell through the opening. It ran past them, through the ladder system, burying the ancient Garamante Kingdom of the Sands.

The entire deluge lasted no more than a minute. When it was over she opened her eyes. No light filtered in. A small amount of sand drifted down from above. She adjusted her eyes and spotted something in the darkness. Speckles of light wafted toward her attention. It took a moment to determine what she was looking at.

Zara grinned as she recognized the vision – *The infinite starlight above the Sahara*.

"You first, Zara!" Sam said.

"Well done!" Tom said.

Zara reached up through the opening in the limestone ceiling and felt nothing but sand. She looked at Tom. "Can you give me a boost up here?"

"Sure."

She placed her right foot into Tom's hands and stepped up into the opening. It was enough to reach half a foot inside the open space. There were no more ladders above. The opening led to a sandy sinkhole.

Zara pulled herself through the opening and then using her hands and legs, clambered up the steep incline of sand until she reached the surface.

The Harmattan, the predominant north-easterly wind, blew at a steady twenty knots. It would fill the sinkhole with sand by morning, burying with it all evidence of the ancient city of the Garamante people.

She stared out in all directions, where the stars met the horizons. The desert surrounded them in every direction. She blinked, took in a deep breath. Relaxed and slowly exhaled. She opened her eyes and grinned like a child on Christmas morning. Intermingled with the stars on the horizon were the interspersed lights of Mao – one of Chad's most northern cities.

Chapter Eighty-Two

The sky was filled with gray. It was the predawn somber and final vestige of peace before the scorching heat overwhelmed the land, as the sun came over the horizon and burned the Sahara once more. They all walked through the night, reaching the northern desert city at dawn. Sam and Tom followed Zara to the airstrip. In their own way, each one of them felt a gentle sigh of relief as they arrived and found the Beechcraft Bonanza 36 was where Zara had told them it would be.

Sam was the first to clamber inside. He glanced at the small cockpit and wondered what it would take to coax the little aircraft to fly without its ignition key. Tom might have been able to get it started given enough time, but the sun was already climbing the horizon and it wouldn't be long before someone would take notice.

Zara noticed his concern. "Don't worry. He'll be here. Flies every morning at first light."

"And you're certain we can trust him?" Sam shuffled further into the cargo compartment where he and Tom were nearly out of sight.

"Relax." She smiled reassuringly. "I know this guy. He's everyone's friend in the Sahara."

"You don't have a lot of friends in the region currently. Hasn't it occurred to you that a lot of his friends are also your enemies?"

"No."

"It hasn't?"

She smiled. "No. I'm certain many of his clients would pay dearly if he were to turn us over with the book."

"But still you trust him?" Sam asked.

"Yes."

"Why?" Sam persisted.

"Shush! Someone's coming!" she said.

Sam covered his head with the blue tarpaulin. He listened as the door to the cockpit opened. A moment later the pilot began flicking switches. The background light lit up the avionics with a soft red glow. He heard the grind of the engine turning over. It took three goes and then fired. The engine was warmed up, and then taken through to its maximum revolutions per minute, kept there for two minutes and then reduced to idle.

The pilot released the handbrake and taxied toward the end of the sandy runway. Sam gripped the side of the aircraft as he was battered around as the Beechcraft made its way along the dilapidated airstrip.

At the end of the runway, the pilot pressed the brakes hard. Sam watched as the pilot flicked through a series of local maps, making a show to really plan his route. Sam reached for a knife and shuffled forward. There's no reason a pilot who runs the same route everyday should be checking his maps.

The pilot placed his hand on something low where the maps had been. Sam gripped the hilt of his knife, but Zara shuffled forward first. The pilot fumbled with something inside, while his eyes darted around the cargo hold.

Zara pushed his arm down. "That won't be necessary."

The pilot paused and then turned to embrace her. "Christ, Zara! Do you know how many people are looking for you right now?"

"A few, I'd guess."

"General Ngige's placed a hundred thousand dollar price tag on your life." His eyes met Sam's, and returned to hers. "Who the hell have you brought?"

"Khalid, this is Sam and Tom. They've been helping me out for the past couple days."

"Sam Reilly and Tom Bower?"

"Yeah, pleased to meet you," Sam said, shuffling forward and offering his hand. His eyes drifted to the end of the cargo hold, where Tom now stretched his legs. "I don't think my friend here is moving anytime soon."

Khalid took it and shook firmly. Their eyes met as the pilot studied him, judging him, somehow. It was clear he knew and trusted Zara, but two new strangers might be stretching their friendship. "There's a woman looking for you. Eurasian. Purple eyes. Sound familiar?"

Sam nodded. "A concerned relative."

Khalid nodded. "She left the current location of the *Maria Helena*. Promised to charter this aircraft at three times the daily rate, if I find you."

"Bargain."

"I told her my services would cost at least four."

"Still a bargain."

"General Ngige's offering $100,000 for Zara and her book. Very tempting." He looked fondly at Zara and smiled. "But Zara and I, we go back a long way. I love this woman as much as I love my sister. So, I guess it's your lucky day. And lucky for you, Zara, that I still love my sister!"

Chapter Eighty-Three

Six hours later, the Bonanza landed at the Tripoli International Airport, in Libya. Its wheels rolled along the scarred runway with a series of bumps before rolling to a stop. The International Airport had been closed since it had been badly damaged in 2014 during the Second Libyan Civil War. The Beechcraft was small enough and slow enough that the Libyan Airforce ignored their landing in an unauthorized airport. Next to where their aircraft had stopped, a Sikorsky Nighthawk stood with its rotary blades still turning.

Sam shook the pilot's hand. "Thank you, Khalid."

The pilot shook his head. "Don't thank me. I did it for Zara. Now make sure you get her out of the country before someone decides the money is worth more than her life."

Sam nodded. "We'll look after her."

Veyron approached the cockpit and handed the pilot a neat bundle of hundred dollar bills in US currency. Khalid took the money, nodded and then pushed the engines of his little plane to their maximum, sending the Beechcraft rolling along the runway, and back into the air.

Thirty seconds later, Sam, Tom, Zara and Veryon were all sitting inside the Sikorsky and they, too were back in the air. It was a short flight. In less than twenty minutes, they landed on the helipad at the aft section of the *Maria Helena.*

Sam slid open the side door of the Sikorsky and climbed out. Tom was next out, followed by Zara. Veyron opened the navigator's side door and came around to the undercover section directly behind the *Maria Helena's* main pilot house.

Veyron shook Sam's hand. "Welcome back. We were starting to think you'd found the diamonds and decided to run away with them."

"We found the diamonds. Would have happily run away with them, if it wasn't for coming across this young lady, who it appears half the people in the Sahara are interested in killing." Sam turned to Zara, "This is Veyron. He's our chief engineer. Veyron, this is Zara Delacroix. A renowned archeologist in the region."

Veyron shook her hand. "Pleased to meet you, Ma'am."

She nodded. "Thanks for getting us out of Libya."

The loud whine of the Sikorsky's engines finally ceased, and the blades became silent as they slowly settled, and stopped turning. Sam watched as Genevieve climbed out of the cockpit. She wore an expression which said *I don't give a fuck what anyone thinks, right now.* Her hair, so dark brown it was nearly black, was cut short and neatly tied back, giving her the appearance of an elf. Probably the most deadly elf on the planet. She had deep blue eyes, full of intelligence, and long eyelashes. She wore no makeup whatsoever. Never did. Her naturally tan complexion appeared to be the result of hours working under the sun, rather than genetic heritage.

Sam smiled, as she walked straight up to Tom and threw her arms around his neck. She kissed him passionately on his lips. It lasted about thirty seconds, and then she broke the entanglement, and walked away, having said nothing.

Sam smiled at her as she went past. "Thanks for coming and getting us, Genevieve."

Genevieve met his eyes, ignored his comment and said, "Not a word, Sam. I don't want to hear a word."

He turned to make a comment to Veyron, but the man quickly turned to run through a series of safety checks on the Sikorsky.

Elise stepped onto the deck. "So, you made it."

Sam smiled. "We made it. I hear you came looking for us. Thank you."

"Forget about it. I was mostly indifferent. I figured you got yourself into the problem, you could get yourself out of it. But Genevieve was pretty keen to come get the two you, and equally keen to kill anyone who got in her way."

"Yes, well, I guess we now know why she was so emphatic." He turned to Zara, "This is Zara Delacroix. She's the reason we were late."

Elise looked at Zara, studying her like she would a fine painting. She smiled, reassuringly. "So, you survived. What about the book? Are you still in possession of it?"

Zara nodded. "Yes."

"Good."

Sam asked, "How do you know about Zara and the book?"

Elise's smile was mischievous and tormenting at the same time, without revealing anything about what she knew. "We have a visitor, Sam. You're going to want to meet him, right away. We found him at a Libyan archeological camp. He says he's heavily involved in the United Sovereign of Kongo and he needs your help. Oh, and bring the girl, she's going to want to hear what he has to say, too."

Chapter Eighty-Four

Adebowale sat up when he saw his visitors enter. His wounds were healing well despite it only being two days since Elise and Genevieve found him in the camp and managed to remove the bullets in his abdomen. They didn't bother trying to find the one imbedded in his head. Elise had informed him that he would die in a matter of months if it wasn't properly operated on by a neurosurgeon. He'd refused to lose the time it would take to travel to a mainland hospital and then perform the risky procedure. Besides, what did it matter to him? He already knew how he was going to die, and it wasn't from an infection in the brain, that's for certain.

He smiled and offered his hand. "Sam Reilly. It is nice to meet you."

Sam gripped his hand, warmly. "Adebowale. It's good to meet you, too. I have to tell you, my position in Sahara was purely as a treasure hunter, trying to locate some lost diamonds, and I'm not authorized to negotiate any deals on behalf my government."

"That's fine. I don't need the help of your government to do what must be done. What I need, is your help."

"My help?"

"I will explain soon." Adebowale glanced at Zara, who was standing quietly beside Sam. "Why Doctor, I don't think I've ever seen you so lost for words."

She blushed. "I'm sorry, Adebowale. I thought you were dead, as the result of my own failure. I just heard you started the USK movement. I heard you were beaten pretty badly by General Ngige's men, and left for dead. Are you feeling any better?"

He smiled kindly. A big, full smile of a naturally born leader. "There is nothing that time won't heal. Tell me, do you still have the book?"

"Yes."

"Good. Keep it. The time will come, soon, when you will need it to find the answers. Without it, all will be lost. You are a very intelligent woman, Doctor, I think you will work out what it means in time."

"In time for what?"

"To save the human race from extinction, of course."

She paused. Her eyes wide, and her mouth slightly open. She held her tongue between her teeth and then grinned. "How could you possibly know that?"

"Because General Ngige is terrified of the book. He believes that the book of Nostradamus is the only thing stopping him from ruling the world."

Zara asked, "What does he think will happen if the book is destroyed and he's allowed to rule the world?"

"He told me the human race will cease to exist in three hundred years."

Zara stared at him. "And that doesn't bother him?"

"No. He told me, why would it matter, he would be long dead by then."

Sam sat down beside him. "What do you need me to do?"

Adebowale opened up a computer tablet. He typed a series of GPS coordinates and pressed enter. The computer quickly ran through a series of search programs, until it identified the location, and magnified it using current satellite images. The image showed a lake in the northern region of the Democratic Republic of Congo. He passed the tablet to Sam.

Sam took it, glanced at it, and asked, "How could this end humanity?"

"A mine runs under this lake. It once provided large amounts of gold to the world, but was abandoned decades ago, as it became no longer economically viable. Recent geological surveys, however, reveal mammoth lithium stores inside that mine. They're big. Very big. Nearing fifty times the amount of currently known lithium around the globe."

"You think this will cause a third world war?"

Adebowale nodded.

Sam asked, "Over lithium? Are you kidding me?"

Adebowale stared at him. His eyes fixed. "Do you realize how valuable lithium's about to become?"

"I don't know. Judging by your look, I guess very. Other than batteries, and crazy people, what is it used for?"

"Just that. Do you know what batteries are currently in big demand?"

Sam said, "Electric Vehicle batteries."

Adebowale nodded. "Current predictions suggest nearly twenty-five percent of all cars sold within the next decade will be entirely electric. That's good news for the planet, but how do you think they're going to make that many lithium ion batteries?"

"I didn't know lithium was so rare?"

"It wasn't. Not in the quantities we once used it for. But now we're talking about changing the game entirely. Do you know how many lithium mines there are in all of North America?"

"Ten or Twenty?" Sam took a wild guess.

"One."

"You're kidding me!"

"Don't look so shocked. Ethiopia, Venezuela, Germany and Australia currently have the highest lithium reserves. The total of all of which is insufficient to meet the expected demand of the next decade."

"And now we can add the Democratic Republic of Congo to the list – with potentially fifty times the lithium reserves of the rest of the planet."

"Which is going to make it the most valuable piece of soil on earth."

"And it's currently being run by some despot. If we let him succeed, any number of countries are going to want to make deals with him. And if he doesn't deal, there will be war. It needs to be protected."

"But we'll never be able to do that with General Ngige in power."

Sam said, "You have the weapons. You have the support of nearly eighty percent of your people. Why haven't you started the counter rebellion?"

Adebowale closed his eyes as though he was thinking. When he opened them he spoke with the slow confidence of a man born to lead. His deep voice resonating with divine patience and logic. "The time to overthrow the corrupt rebellion is almost here. A rebellion takes time and patience. You need to wait until the situation has boiled to breaking point, and the people are ready to fight."

"Are the people ready?"

"Yes."

"Then why hasn't the USK attacked?"

"Because they are waiting?"

"For what?"

Adebowale sighed. He looked like he was in physical pain. "Nearly five thousand of their brethren to be released."

"From where?"

"As general Ngige ran through the cities of the DRC, wreaking havoc, he took prisoners. Those prisoners are now being forced to work in the largest lithium mine the world has ever seen."

"So. Rebel then. Free your people and lead them to victory!"

"It's not that simple."

"Why not?"

"The mine is buried beneath Lake Tumba."

Sam asked, "Which means if you attack?"

Adebowale said, "General Ngige will detonate a bomb in a tunnel below the lake – drowning at least five thousand of my kinsmen."

"So how could it be achieved?"

"I have a plan." Adebowale smiled. It looked unnaturally kind coming from such a brutal face. "But I'm afraid I'm going to need your help, once more."

Chapter Eighty-Five

Sam climbed four sets of stairs and entered the bridge. Matthew sat at his navigation table, studying a series of charts for the West Coast of Africa.

Matthew glanced up. "Welcome back, Sam."

Sam said, "Thanks. Have you seen Elise around?"

"She's in her computer room, down below."

"Okay, thanks."

Sam ran down the series of stairs until he reached Elise's computer room. The door was slightly ajar and he knocked on it, before entering a moment later. She was sitting at a desk with four computer screens simultaneously connected, and she typed a steady staccato of data into the keyboard.

He asked, "What are you doing?"

Elise smiled at him. "I'm searching for all known information on the Lake Tumba mine."

"Good." He took a seat opposite to her. "Did the Secretary of Defense approve of the plan?"

"No. She wouldn't hear of it."

"So why are we looking at the maps of the Lake Tumba mine?"

Elise grinned. It was halfway between innocent and diabolical. "I realized, we're just going to have to adjust the plan. Same premise as before, but much less people involved. Complete deniability for the U.S. Department of Defense. Just you, Tom and Genevieve. You follow his plan to free the prisoners from the mine, and he says the rebellion will start."

Sam nodded. He could work with those conditions. He stood up to leave, and stopped. He heard the distinct sound of a small diesel turning over, followed by the subsequent sound of the anchor links running through the bow roller and into the chain locker. He'd heard the anchor raised thousands of times and couldn't possibly confuse the sound with any other. He shook his head. He'd spoken to Matthew less than ten minutes ago and was told they'd remain where they were for the next week while they planned their siege of the DRC Lithium Mine.

Matthew stepped into the room. "Change of plans."

Sam stood up. His jaw suddenly tense and fixed. "What's happened?"

"The Libyan government decided we've over-stayed our welcome. We're being moved on."

Chapter Eighty-Six

Sam found Zara Delacroix in the mission room, carefully reading each of the individual fifty-eight additional quatrains in the book of Nostradamus.

He asked, "Any luck?"

Zara said, "None whatsoever. Like in 1552 when *The Prophecies* were first published, none of these make any sense. They're all gibberish. Even the puzzles I understand, still don't make any sense."

"That's too bad. Keep at it, you're bright, you'll work it out. Are you sure we can't convince you to come with us?" Sam asked. "It's a noble cause, and Adebowale seems convinced that your two paths are meant to intertwine in this pivotal moment in history."

She shook her head. "It's his war, not mine."

Sam asked, "Where will you go?"

"Paris. There will always be a job waiting for me at the Louvre. Matthew said you're heading to Malta. If I can hitch a ride with you, I'll catch a commercial flight from there to Paris."

"That's really what you want?"

She nodded. "That's what I want."

"What about the Nostradamus equation?"

"I'm going to try and forget about Nostradamus and his damned predictions. He told me he only saw the visions in fleeting time glimpses, and had no idea how I was supposed to stop the extinction of humanity. Maybe you were right, maybe he really was nothing but a charlatan? Either way, it doesn't matter." She pulled out her medallion and stared at the island she'd nicknamed Infinity because of its shape similar to the mathematical symbol for infinity. "I asked Elise and Matthew to search various databases of known islands, and this one doesn't exist anywhere.

And neither does the Nostradamus equation. So, I'm out. Maybe Nostradamus got this one wrong, this time."

"And Mikhail?"

"What about him? You said yourself he's dead. No point me dying for the memory of a temporary lover."

"All right. You've made up your mind. Tom and I have a meeting with someone in Malta. We're leaving now, if you want to join us. I know you don't have anything to pack."

"Okay, great." Zara nodded. "Sam."

"Yes?"

"In case I didn't get around to it before... Thank you." She smiled at him. "For saving my life, getting me through the ancient irrigation fogarras, everything. I really appreciate it."

Sam paused in the doorway, and grinned back. "You're welcome."

He turned and left up towards the Sikorsky. Tom had already powered up the Sikorsky and run through its series of safety checks. Sam slid open the side door and Zara climbed in, placing her bag with her computer and the book of Nostradamus on the chair next to her. Sam closed the door and climbed into the navigator's side of the cockpit.

Sam fitted his headset and turned to Tom. "How are we looking?"

Tom said, "Fueled up. Engine's warm. Oil pressure's good. We're good to go."

"Good. Let's head off then."

Tom said, "Hang on a second."

Genevieve opened the door next to Tom. He looked at her, and said, "Everything all right?"

She didn't answer. Instead she kissed Tom passionately on the lips. It lasted for about thirty seconds and then she pulled away. "Stay safe, and don't let Sam lead you into trouble."

Sam smirked and turned away.

Genevieve saw his expression and said, "Don't say it."

"What?" Sam asked, grinning.

"I said, don't."

Sam nodded his head. Genevieve was an intensely private woman. He'd never even heard of her showing her affections in public, let alone in front of the rest of the crew before. He caught Tom's gaze. One glance and he knew to keep his mouth shut. It was one thing for Genevieve to kiss Tom when he arrived on board the *Maria Helena* after she thought he was dead, but another thing entirely to do so under normal conditions. It made appear normal, instead of her usual hardened self.

Genevieve closed the cockpit door and walked away.

Tom smiled. "I guess, now we're good to go."

Chapter Eighty-Seven

Zara was the first to see the tiny speck of an island appear. It was wedged somewhere between the horizon and the infinite turquoise waters of the Mediterranean Sea. The first of the three Maltese islands which made up the tiny Mediterranean outcrop. Once there she would board a commercial flight to Paris and Sam Reilly would disappear from her life.

The Sikorsky's rotor blades made a droning whoop, whoop sound which echoed in her head as they flew toward it. She took in a deep breath, slowly. Her hazel-green eyes stared vacantly at the island, while her mind drifted pensively into her past. A prophecy that had extended into her great ancestry. A life spent searching for a book she only now believed in. The discovery of the book of Nostradamus. The missing 58 quatrains. It had been a wild ride. The culmination of it all, leading to someone she'd never heard of wanting her dead.

General Nige was the weapon of that person's desire. But she still had no idea who wanted the book bad enough to kill her for it. She would need to donate the book to the Louvre of course. It would be the only way to protect herself. They would make copies, and a digital database that could be studied at universities around the world. It was the only way to remove its intense value.

She'd met a lot of interesting people along the way. None more so than Sam Reilly. He was a hero of a different sort. All the normal characteristics were there. He was tough, handsome, and righteous. His piercing blue eyes betrayed his intelligence but also his kindness, simultaneously. His confident grin made him appear youthful and mischievous. He was focused, but settled, in any circumstance. Knowledgeable, but quick to listen and learn from those who knew more than he did. From what she saw, he served his country, but that patriotism extended beyond the borders of American soil. He served his fellow man, and acted for the goodness of the human race, which he often expressed his most fervent belief in – despite the many signs of discord throughout the world.

Despite growing up inside a privileged world of wealth, politicians, and diplomats, he didn't have a conceited bone in his body. He was rich enough to never work again, yet he chose to serve. He worked for fun, because he enjoyed it, and because a certain job needed doing, and he was uniquely capable of doing it. He believed in duty and what is right, above self-gratification and one's own desires. Even though he looked contented to wonder the desert as a nomad, subsisting on local cuisine, she imagined he would look just as much at home, rubbing shoulders at a cocktail party with world leaders and billionaires.

She could have definitely loved a man like that. She breathed out slowly again.

In another life.

And in another time.

Because right now, she had a job to do. She'd followed Nostradamus as far as she could. Now she had to explore the future for herself. See what it had planned for her. By deciding to continue searching for the Nostradamus Equation, she was willingly risking the lives of future generations. She would risk sending the entire human race into extinction at the turn of the twenty second century, for the very remote possibility that she could change the future. A future where the human race becomes extinct in three hundred years.

She still didn't know why she had done it. What had made her take such a tremendous gamble? It wasn't even hers to make – it was not *her* risk. Zara thought about that for a moment. She knew the answer, deep down, although she struggled to admit it to herself.

Because Nostradamus had told her she would succeed…

And because she couldn't live in a world where her unborn daughter was the last generation of the human race!

The helicopter banked hard to the right and straightened out on a direct northerly course. She felt her stomach lurch at the sudden change in pressure and at the same time, bile rose uncomfortably in her throat. Her eyes glanced at Tom, who appeared confident at the helicopter's controls. Next to him, Sam was plotting a new course into the GPS.

Zara leaned forward. "Malta's back that way. Where are you heading?"

Sam shook his head, apologetically. "There's been a change of plans."

"Why? What's going on?"

"We just took a mayday call. There's been a large submarine earthquake in the waters south of Sicily. A seismograph located at Portopalo Di Capo Passero on the southern tip of Sicily recorded a reading of 8.2 on the Richter scale. Its epicenter is estimated at approximately thirty miles due south of the coast of Sicily. The water there is shallow. There's going to be a massive tsunami. The Sikorsky has a large carrying capacity, and long range fuel tanks. We've been requested to help look for any survivors along the coast."

She nodded. "How close are we?"

"We'll be there within the hour. We can't rescue anyone from its initial battery of waves, but we might help some people who get swept out to sea afterwards. The *Maria Helena* has already turned to make its way there, too."

Zara asked, "Will those living on the Sicilian coast survive?"

Sam said, "It depends. If their early tsunami warning system is good, people will have time to evacuate. The greatest enemy is complacency. Tsunamis rarely look dangerous as they approach. It's only once they strike the coast that their potentially devastating force is realized."

She nodded, but said nothing.

Had the future just challenged her decision to abandon Nostradamus's warning, and continue to search for the Nostradamus Equation?

Chapter Eighty-Eight

The southern coastal town of Pozzallo, in the Sicilian Provence of Ragusa, had once been a strategic landing point for trade relations with Spain, stretching back to the Renaissance. These days, its primary resource, like so many other coastal towns, was tourism. People came from all over the world to visit its pristine stretches of shallow beaches and calm waters.

Standing on an old stone fortification named the Pandolfo Palace, a tourist smiled. He had traveled to many places, but this one held the unique distinction of actually being precisely as beautiful as the travel magazines had boasted. It was shaping up to be the perfect summer day. The sun was directly above. He stared out at the tranquil turquoise water.

The tsunami crept toward the low lying shores of Southern Sicily at a speed of four hundred and eighty miles per hour. The crest of the wave stood at barely one and a half feet. It provided the tourist with no reason to doubt his safety. A glance by those on the beach would assume the Mediterranean Sea was behaving normally today, with shallow waves, and no violent crests. Lulled, the tourist, tempted by the pristine waters of the Med, decided to take a swim.

Employed by a high-end European car company, he had recently negotiated a deal worth a cool billion Euros to source lithium for their upcoming Electric Vehicles. The deal meant that the company he worked for wouldn't have to compete for lithium, and would be able to concentrate on the technology instead. It had also made him very rich. He was being paid with stock-options. If it worked, as he knew it would, he would be a very rich man in the next few years.

Feeling content with that thought, he stepped into the warm water until he was waist deep. He closed his eyes and then floated on his back. The warmth of the sun reached every inch of his body, while his back remained a perfect temperature. Not hot. Not cold. If there was ever such a thing as heaven on earth, this must have been it.

The tourist placed his feet firmly on the sand. The water was up to a little less than his waist. He stared at the beach. Something had happened. Everyone was running toward something. He barely noticed the water receding. People screamed. There must have been an accident.

I hope no one has been seriously hurt...

The water receded further and he was now standing in wet sand, while the water retreated further. Somewhere in the back of his mind, it confused him. He would have turned and looked behind him under normal circumstances, out of curiosity, more than concern. But now, his attention was set, focusing on the unknown drama unfolding on the beach.

He heard the roar of a thousand motorboats at full throttle and turned to glance over his shoulder. There were no motor boats. At least none that he could see. Instead, a wall of water, at least ten feet high, raged toward him.

Where did that come from?

The tourist stood still. He didn't run. Instead he watched as his death came hurling toward him at nearly five hundred miles an hour. A split second later, the monster struck him – and his world disappeared.

Chapter Eighty-Nine

Sam looked out at the open expanse of dark blue water. Even at full speed, it was going to take at least an hour to reach the Sicilian coastline. Inside the Sikorsky, all three of them were silent. Waiting for a report from the Sicilian coast. When the report came, it informed them that a ten foot tsunami struck the coast, but casualties were relatively low.

Each of them glanced at one another in silence. They each wore the same expression – *did we just change history?*

Sam said, "How long, Tom?"

He grinned. "You tell me. You're navigating."

"No. I mean, how long have you and Genevieve been an item?"

"You don't think I'd be stupid enough to kiss and tell when it comes to Geneveive, do you?"

"Come on, it's me?"

"And it's Genevieve. You know the woman was an assassin or something? You've seen her. It's like she was a hostage breaker. An interrogator who was strongly opposed to the Geneva Convention's rights for Prisoners of War. I wouldn't last two minutes when we returned and she'd know exactly how much I told you."

"What if I told you something?"

"Like what?"

"Like..."

Tom swore. "Holy shit, she was an interrogator! Hell no. I'm not telling you anything until she tells you first."

"Okay, forget about how long. What I want to know is where do you want it to go from here?"

"After Billie left I waited. I really thought she'd find what she was after and come back for me. As time's gone by, I realized that was never going to happen. But then I waited, because how does anyone compare to Billie?"

"How, indeed?"

"Then things happened with Genevieve and me ..."

"And?"

"It was an accident. A lot of fun. Nothing more. Followed by another accident. Pretty soon, we were both looking forward to our accidents and for the first time in a year I'd forgotten about how much I missed Billie."

"Wow. You can pick them, can't you?"

"What's that supposed to mean?"

"First you fall in love with Billie, who, let's face it, is beautiful but rough as they get. Now you look like you're in pretty deep with Gen, who – did I mention, killed her last boyfriend?"

Tom looked sideways from the pilot's seat and met his gaze. "Christ are you kidding me!"

"Yeah, gotcha." Sam patted him on the shoulder. "You know I have nothing but admiration for Genevieve. She is a truly wonderful woman."

"Thanks. Hey, we're coming up on the epicenter of the earthquake."

Sam studied the map for a moment. "Are you certain?"

"Yeah. Certain. Check out the GPS coordinates. We're coming right up on it. Why?"

Sam looked at an island below. It was shaped like an oddly formed eight on its side. More like the symbol for infinity or a lemniscate. "That island isn't on the map."

Tom banked the helicopter to the right and circled the island. It was still dripping wet. Seaweed, algae, and fish lined the solid sandstone planes, while the single mountain held a massive lobster. "Is it just me, or does it look to you as though that island was just born?"

"No. It looks to me like the island was born a long time ago – the tectonic shift has only just now returned it to the surface of the sea."

"Never seen that before."

Zara leaned in toward the cockpit again. "Can you get low enough to drop me on that island?"

Sam smiled for the first time in the past hour. "Yes. I'm sure we can get low enough to step off. I'll join you."

Tom met his eyes. "Are you kidding? Aren't you worried about secondary tsunamis?"

"No," Sam said. "If this is the epicenter, the tsunamis will be heading outward from here. This place is one of the safest coastlines around."

Tom continued to circle the island without reducing his altitude. "Why the hell would you want to explore it right now anyway?"

"Because that island is identical to the one Nostradamus told Zara to find – which means the future either intentionally brought us here, or tried its best to keep us from landing. Either way, I want to know what's on that island."

Chapter Ninety

Sam watched the helicopter take off. He felt a little guilt about not continuing with Tom on their original mission to search for survivors along the Sicilian coast. His steadfast pragmatism overcame the sensation. This entire thing apparently had to do with some sort of divine plan; a future only Nostradamus had seen. If this island held the key to the Nostradamus equation, then he had to find it.

The helicopter banked north and the droning sound of its rotor blades quickly disappeared. Sam secured his backpack and looked at Zara.

She asked, "Do you have a plan?"

He nodded. "Yeah. Now we find the Nostradamus equation."

Zara laughed. "Yeah, good plan!"

Sam stared at the island. Tom had left them on the western side of the island. The one that was mostly flat, while the opposite end had a small mountain in the middle. The entire island was a little less than a mile, end to end. Maybe a quarter of a mile wide. Two perfectly circular islands, standing side by side, with a joining partition of sandstone approximately ten feet in length, making both circles form into a single island.

The ground was mostly covered with white sand. Despite coming from the ocean bed, thirty feet below, there was limited seaweed or other signs of plant life. The occasional fish could be seen dying where it lay stranded. Crustaceans, disoriented by the strange turn of events, left their homes and wandered idly in search of the ocean. There was a strong smell of sea life in the air. It wasn't yet offensive, because the island hadn't been out of the water long enough for the sea creatures to die and start to decompose, but in a day or two they were going to need a mask just to breathe on this island.

They walked in a broad counterclockwise circle around the western circumference of the island. The edge of the island was nearly ten feet out of the water and was formed by hardened sand. Sam guessed it would be hard to climb up again if he fell over the side. The vertical sand banks that marked the edge of the island had already started to break away and fall into the water below. Sam felt the future was already hurrying him along, as the ocean began the tedious process of reclaiming the island.

A large chunk of hardened sand fell into the water below. Sam stepped backwards, making a mental note not to get so close to the edge again. "I won't get that close again."

Zara asked, "Do you think it's all sand?"

"The island?"

"Yeah."

Sam stared at the white sand that formed the western circle. It looked like a postcard of a deserted island. "No. The edge might be hardened sand, but sandcastles don't survive in the ocean. This place must have the geology of hardened stone at its core."

Once they reached the other end they cut right through the middle of the island and stopped where thousands of polished black stones were layered on top of each other to form a connective tissue between the two circles of the island. Each stone was identical in shape and color. They looked out of place between the sandy circular islands. More like someone had meticulously layered each one precisely where it now sat.

Sam squatted down and picked up one of the stones. It was small enough to fit in the palm of his hand, but heavy like a dumbbell, which meant it was most likely solid all the way through. The stone had been polished so perfectly he could see his own reflection.

"It's obsidian," Sam said.

Zara picked up another stone to examine it. "Obsidian doesn't belong anywhere near here."

"It doesn't?"

"No. Obsidian is a naturally occurring volcanic glass. It's formed when lava, extruding from a volcano, cools rapidly with minimal crystal growth.

Most often found in obsidian lava flows, where the chemical composition of silica is extremely high, making the molten liquid extremely viscous."

"Come again?" Sam grinned at her erudite explanation.

"It means the liquid moves slowly because it's thick and gluey, making it difficult for crystals to form. The end outcome of this process is that obsidian is hard and brittle. It fractures in sharp edges popular throughout the stone age for cutting and piercing."

"Okay. So what makes you so certain it doesn't belong here?"

"Because I've studied ancient Egyptians extensively, and they went to great lengths to find obsidian for weapons and tools. They had to trade for it because the only two places in the Mediterranean where the stone was found was in Turkey and Italy. And in both cases, they weren't found on the coast."

"Which means?"

Zara placed her tongue between her teeth, and then smiled. "These stones were intentionally moved here."

Chapter Ninety-One

Unable to find any purpose or meaning to the stones, Sam walked across the obsidian bridge and onto the eastern side of the island. He and Zara followed the coast in a clockwise direction. Like the western circle, the bank was formed with hardened sand. That sand was now slowly being eroded by the constant lapping of the Mediterranean Sea.

They circled the eastern coast by one thirty in the afternoon. The coast appeared almost identical to the western side of the island. It formed a perfect circle that matched the exact diameter of its western sibling. With the exception of a few misplaced and sorry-looking sea creatures, the ground was barren. Its white sand made the perfect tourist's picture of a deserted island.

Where the eastern side changed from its western sibling, was in the center of the island. Unlike its counterpart, which was completely flat, this side had a small mountain at its center. They cut into the center with a northerly track until they reached the base of the mountain.

"You see anything?" he asked.

Zara looked upwards for a few moments before answering. "I see a deserted island and a small mountain."

"Seem strange to you?"

"Everything here seems strange to me," she said. "Was there anything in particular you were referring to?" Her response was curt, and just shy of pugnacious.

He glanced at her. "You do know I'm here to help you right?"

"Sorry. I'm just pissed off, because I feel like this entire thing is one big game that Nostradamus is playing with me. Nothing makes scientific sense. If he's just playing a game, I resent it. And if he *wasn't* playing a game, and his visions were correct, then that means the future is going to do all it can to stop me from finding the Nostradamus Equation."

Sam turned his glance to the mountain. "It's okay. I don't understand it any better than you do. Do you want to know what I see?"

"Sure. Go ahead."

"The mountain appears entirely made up of hardened sand."

Sam leaned against the base of the steep mountain and pressed his fingers deep into the sand. The mountain resisted for a moment and then gave way to the pressure exerted by his fingers. It was hardened sand. But sand none the less. He looked at her face. She looked intrigued. But there was something else in her face, too. She appeared to be enjoying herself, like this was the real reason she followed her father's footsteps into archeology.

He asked, "Have you ever heard of a sandcastle surviving once the sea swallowed it?"

Zara tried to push her hand through the hardened sand. "I know a lot about sand, actually. I grew up in the Sahara. It doesn't behave like this underneath the sea. Maybe the tectonic shift which caused the submarine earthquake pushed the seabed up like this?"

"I don't think so. This sand looks like it's been in this shape for years. The lines of the mountain are too rigid for it to be the result of a tectonic shift."

"So what do you think it is?" Zara asked.

"I don't know. Maybe it was some sort of man-made structure many years ago. Built with sandstone, the layers of its structure have crumbled and turned back into sand."

"That's unlikely, but possible." Her eyes glanced upwards. "There's only one way to find out. Shall we climb it?"

Sam nodded and started to climb. The gradient was steep, but not impossible. Every ten or so feet the mountain formed a slight ledge to rest on. The distance between the ledges appeared unnaturally identical. The hard sand allowed perfect hand and foot grips. He would kick his feet into the sand until it formed a small foothold and then dig his fingers in above. Once at the top of each section, he stopped and rested on the ledge.

The hardest part of the whole process was making the hand and foot holds in the first place. Zara followed him by using the same hand and foot holds. After each section they would swap and the other person would build the next series of holds before reaching the following ledge.

By the time they reached the fifth ledge, where the wet and hardened sand was beginning to dry, it became easier to make a hand and foothold. At the same time, it became harder to maintain. On a number of attempts, Sam, who was following, found the holds were starting to break away. The only solution was for each person to build their own holds as they climbed.

He stopped on the sixth ledge. It was two thirds of the way up the mountain. Sam turned to face the western island below. He watched the water and the island's sandy bank collide. A large chasm, possibly twenty to thirty feet long, split into the island. Water rushed through the opening, prying it wider.

Sam started to climb quickly. "Come on, we need to hurry up."

Zara looked at him. A wry smile forming as she easily matched his pace. "Why, what's changed?"

"Look at the bank of the island. What do you see?"

"Hardened sand."

"Right. And what does hardened sand do as it comes into contact with waves, albeit small ones."

"It breaks apart."

"So what's happening?" Sam continued.

"The ocean's reclaiming the island."

"That's right and it's doing so quickly. The island has a short life-expectancy." Sam stared at her. His blue eyes, piercing. "And that means we have days, possibly a week at most, to find the Nostradamus Equation."

Chapter Ninety-Two

The top of the mountain was a small, flattened outcrop of sand in a circular shape. No more than five feet in diameter. Sam ran his fingers through the softening sand trying to find something, although what he expected to find he really didn't know. He stared as his fingers ran through the sand, revealing nothing but more sand.

He stood up and looked at their surroundings. He had an excellent view of both sides of the island, which formed a perfect lemniscate. The white sand beneath the surrounding shallow waters appeared a soft green color. Both sides of the island were the identical circumference. To the south he could just make out the pale haze of an island on the horizon. He recalled reading once that on a good day you could see Italy from Malta. He turned in the other direction and saw the haze of the Sicilian coast line.

It gave him a sudden pang of guilt. He'd traded his original mission to save the lives of people who needed help, so that he could find something that didn't exist. He hoped to hell the tsunami wasn't anywhere near as bad as they were expecting.

Sam moved to the western edge of the mountain top and looked down. Approximately a third of the way up, water had pooled on the ledge of the mountain. It appeared roughly rectangular and only about four feet in length. He stared at it for a moment and then grinned.

"What if we were wrong?" Sam asked.

Zara shuffled to the edge of the mountain peak to see what he was looking at. "About what?"

"About Infinity Island."

"Okay. So what did we get wrong?" she said. "I don't know a lot we've gotten right, so far."

"We only assumed Nostradamus saw it as a vision of a current place. What if this island was once above sea level? What if Nostradamus knew what it once was, and that you would stumble upon it today?"

"Do you mean it was once inhabited thousands of years ago?"

"Yes."

"The island looks pretty barren to me. There's no sign of civilization."

"That's because the entire island is covered in sand. What if an ancient civilization once lived inside this mountain? What if it's the remains of a city?"

"I haven't seen any evidence of any civilization."

"See that rectangular lake?" he asked, pointing toward the lake he'd seen a third of the way up the mountain.

She nodded, following his direction. "Yeah, what about it?"

"I don't think that was always a lake and I don't think this mountain was always a mountain."

"What do you think it is?" she asked.

"Have a better look at it. Take away a couple thousand years of sea life, what do you see? Have you seen that shape somewhere else?"

She gasped as she squinted her eyes and started to see it too. "It's a pyramid!"

"Exactly. And where have you seen that sort of lake in a pyramid?"

"I don't know about South American pyramids, but I've never seen a lake in any Egyptian pyramid before."

"No. But this isn't a lake is it? It's an opening now filled with water."

"It's an entrance!"

"Have you ever visited the Pyramids of Giza?"

"I've been an archeologist in Africa for my entire adult life. Before that, my father was an archeologist in Africa. What do you think?"

Sam ignored her sarcasm. "The anatomy of the ancient pyramids of Egyptian kings often include a queen's chamber and king's Chamber. With the queen's down below and the king's above. The queen's will be flooded, but I'm hoping a pocket of air may have become trapped inside the king's chamber."

"What difference does it make if the chamber's been flooded?" she asked. "What do you expect to find there?"

"The Nostradamus Equation, of course."

Zara smiled. Her hazel-green eyes, full of intelligence, acutely challenged the notion. Her smile, wide with anticipation and mischief suggested she was willing to play along until she was convinced otherwise. "Okay, I'm not saying I buy your theory at all, but for a moment, let's say I do. What do you suggest we do about it? It's not like we can get inside. The whole thing's been flooded."

Sam grinned. "Well. For that at least, I might have a solution."

Chapter Ninety-Three

It was just before nightfall when the Sikorsky returned to the island. Sam had spoken to Tom earlier in the day and had learned that the tsunami had been much weaker than expected and the southern coast of Sicily fared well. So far, the death of only one tourist had been reported. A man who had been in the water at the time and simply didn't understand that the small wave approaching had the force to kill him. Otherwise, the Sicilian coast had fared extremely well.

The *Maria Helena* was still out there searching debris for any survivors who'd found themselves washed out to sea. With night approaching Tom had refueled and picked up the equipment Sam needed.

Sam heard the whine of the engine change pitch as Tom shut it down. He nodded in acknowledgement of Tom, and didn't wait for the blades to stop spinning before sliding open the side door and retrieving the equipment he needed and laid it out along the sand. Time wasn't on their side. The island was rapidly being reclaimed by the sea, so he needed to work quickly.

There were three boxes filled with diving equipment. Buoyancy Control Devices, dive masks, regulators, fins and dive computers. He and Tom had their own equipment. The third container was filled with equipment borrowed from Elise, with the exception of the neoprene wetsuit, which would have been too small for her. Instead, it was a dark blue wetsuit. Not one of his usual dive suits. It looked old, but barely used. He'd seen it somewhere previously. Elise must have pulled it out of the older storage lockers.

Zara picked up the wetsuit. "I'm going to get changed. If either of you turns around while I do so, you'll curse saving my life in the first place."

"Yes ma'am," both men replied, dutifully.

Facing away from Zara, Sam attached his dive tank to his BCD and dive computer. He then opened the tank fully, and rotated the nozzle half a click back to reduce the likelihood of the O-ring seizing. He removed his polo neck shirt and cargo shorts. Leaving his underwear on, he donned his 3/16 inch, neoprene full length wetsuit. It was probably a little warm for the local water temperatures, but he guessed the deep chambers of the pyramid was going to be a little cooler than the surrounding waters.

Tom reached for his wetsuit and started to get changed. He laughed as he looked at the mountain of hardened sand. "Trust you to find a hidden temple."

"Thanks for bringing the gear," Sam said.

"No. Thank you for bringing me along."

Zara stepped lithely across the sand toward them. She looked up and said, "All right, you can turn around now, boys."

Sam glanced up at her. "Hey, it fits you!"

The neoprene hugged the athletic curvature of her body in a flattering way. She was tall. An inch off six foot and her figure perfectly matched her height. Suddenly he recognized the dive suit. It was the same one Aliana, his ex-girlfriend had used when she came diving in the Caribbean. The sight of it gave his heart a momentary pause. Until that moment, he hadn't realized how similar the two women were. Both extremely intelligent, career driven experts in their chosen fields. Both the same height and athletic frame. Aliana was blonde with blue eyes and attractive in the typical fashion magazine type of way; whereas Zara had dark hair with hazel-green eyes and olive skin, giving her an exotic, and sexy appeal.

Zara smiled at him as she set up her dive equipment. "What is it?"

"Nothing. You just remind me of someone, that's all."

"Well, are you going to stand there, or shall we find some answers before this island disappears?"

And Zara's a much harder woman than Aliana ever was. Sam smiled. "Let's go find the Nostradamus Equation."

Chapter Ninety-Four

Sam stood at the entrance to the small rectangular lake. The edges of the opening were rock solid. Either sandstone or sand mixed with some sort of cement. Either way, it confirmed his original theory that the opening was man-made and led to some sort of structure. The water appeared dark, giving no indication how deep the tunnel stretched.

He switched on his flashlight. "You sure you want to come with us?"

Zara bit her bottom lip. "No. I'm not sure. I hate everything about this."

"Do you want to wait here?" He asked, in honesty.

"Yes. But there's no way I'm going to let you have all the fun. If this thing really leads to an ancient Egyptian chamber, and the Nostradamus Equation, there's no way in hell I'm going to let you two explore it without me."

"All right. Good for you. Challenge your fears. If you get stuck, remember, I'll be right in front of you and Tom's going to be behind you. Don't try to turn around. The tunnel looks too narrow for that. Your dive tank will get stuck in the walls. We're on push to talk wireless communications. If you need help, let us know. There'll be somewhere to turn around at the end of this."

"And if there isn't?" she asked.

"If we hit a dead end, I'll remove my dive tank and turn around. Once I'm facing in the right direction, I'll help you with yours. Don't worry. I've dived something like this once or twice before. Just stay calm. We have plenty of air supply." Sam looked at her. Fear radiated from her eyes. "You still want to come?"

She grinned. "You bet."

Sam entered the water first. He adjusted his buoyancy and slowly descended to ten feet. He was followed by Zara in the middle and Tom keeping an eye on things from the back. The rectangular lake descended in a diagonal downward direction. His computer gauge told him the passageway ran at a forty degree slope. He was playing his flashlight beam close and then far all the way down the descending tunnel, but so far he couldn't see where it ended. The walls appeared carved out of solid stone, as though someone long ago had spent years chiseling downward to make the tunnel. He placed his dive knife on the ceiling section and pushed hard. The knife didn't advance. He breathed softly, feeling more confident the structure was solid, and only the exterior section had crumbled into sand.

Approximately eighty feet down he noticed a second tunnel, split in an upwards direction above. The upward tunnel was the exact same gradient, but in an opposite direction. Sam took a piece of red chalk and made a large circle at the entrance to the new tunnel. Then, inside, he wrote the number one.

"Are we going up first?" Zara asked, over the radio.

Sam shook his head and continued his descent. "No. I want to start at the deepest chamber and then work our way up. I can better manage our nitrogen levels that way."

"Diving 101," she said.

"Yeah, something like that."

At a depth of a hundred and eighty feet the diagonal passage opened into a large, empty chamber. Sam shined his flashlight along the walls. There was nothing. A completely vacant room, which probably took the better part of a decade to carve out. He wondered what purpose it once had.

Sam turned around to face the surface, in one quick motion. "Okay, let's start our ascent."

When he reached the opening in the roof-line that ran in the opposite diagonal direction he turned and began following the new passage. This one maintained the same forty degree angle as the original one, but instead of heading downward, this one slanted up. Sixty feet along, a second passage opened. This one ran horizontal.

Sam took out his red chalk and drew another circle. This time he placed the number two inside. "This place starting to feel like something to you, Zara?"

"Yeah. I feel like we're on a tour of a miniature version of the Pyramid of Giza."

Sam flashed his light ahead, but he still couldn't make out the end of the passage. "If that's the case, we must be heading to the queen's chamber."

Tom joined the conversation. "The question is, are they going to hide the Nostradamus Equation in the king or queen's chamber?"

"My guess, it will be in the king's," Sam said.

"Odd. My guess would have been the queen's," replied Zara.

The passageway opened into a small chamber. It was completely vacant with the with the exception of a single, sealed sarcophagus at its center. There were no writings and only a few Egyptian pictographs.

Zara swam next to him and stopped. "This is the queen's chambers."

"Do you see any reference here to Nostradamus?" Sam asked.

She shook her head. "No. It's a silent prayer for her soul. Nothing more."

"What about the future?" Tom interjected.

She checked the other sides of the sarcophagus. "No. Nothing."

Sam asked, "Any sign Nostradamus has been here?"

Zara said, "No. And there shouldn't be any, either. Remember, Nostradamus spent much of his life trying to locate the equation. He knew it was there, and knew I would find it, but he would never set eyes on it in real life."

Sam turned around. "Okay, let's double back and continue our ascent. We can always come back here later if we don't find anything in the king's chamber."

He reached the diagonal passage, turned and continued his ascent. Twenty feet up and the water ceased. Sam climbed a series of steps until he was standing in a dry passage. He removed his facemask and took a slow breath in through his nose. The air smelled stale, but breathable.

"Are you safe to do that?" Zara asked.

"Sure. This is an air pocket, left over from when the Mediterranean flooded."

"It was 3.5 million years ago, when the Atlantic Ocean breached the mountain range joining Europe and Africa, flooding the Mediterranean basin and turning it into a Sea."

Sam shrugged. "Okay, I don't know how they built this pyramid under the water, but I'm with you, there's no way it was 3.5 million years ago. And it doesn't matter. What does matter, is that somewhere along the line, the pyramid flooded and air became trapped in the upper chambers. It's stale, but should be breathable."

Tom interrupted the debate. "Zara, perhaps you and I should keep our masks on for a few minutes. We'll see if Sam shows any signs of hypoxia or poisoning. If he's okay in five, we'll know it's safe for us to remove our masks."

"Suit yourself," Sam said and he continued to climb the stairs.

At the end of the ascending passage the tunnel leveled out again and then opened into a large chamber. Presumably the king's chamber, but there was no sarcophagus. Instead an ornamental pedestal stood at the center. He looked up. The ceiling was a large, rounded dome. The surface of which was covered with both writings and numbers.

Zara removed her dive mask and regulator. "The writings are a mixture of pictographs, hieroglyphs and symbols. It looks like an ancient divergence of Egyptian pictography, but I can't make sense of any of it. I've never seen a written language anything like it, have you?"

Sam grinned. "I've seen it before."

"Really?" Her eyes opened wide. "I studied ancient linguistics for five years and never came across anything like it."

Sam met her eyes. His jaw set hard as he swallowed. "We call them the Master Builders and they've been around a very long time."

Chapter Ninety-Five

Sam stared at the ceiling trying to make sense out of what appeared mostly as ancient gibberish. Although the domed ceiling was full of writing, none of the words were grouped together. Instead, it appeared as though a child had scribbled all over it at random. The more likely alternative was that the individual words meant something by themselves.

Zara asked, "What does it say?"

Sam said, "I don't know. It can take hours to decipher a single word in the ancient language. I'll need my notepad computer. It has all known shapes and images. We'll have to retrieve it before I can make much sense out of any of it."

He lowered his eyes and examined the rest of the room in silence. The king's chamber had no sarcophagus. *Perhaps the king was still alive before the pyramid had been flooded*? Instead, a single pedestal stood at the center. On its top a small piece of glass or transparent stone stood glistening. It appeared ornamental and yet valuable, like an orb. It stuck out of the pedestal, with some sort of metallic material, like brass only more golden, blocked the surrounding sides and directed the light, reminding him of a microscope lens. Sam shined his torch at it. The light scattered throughout the small chamber like a prism.

At the top of the brass-like sidings, where the clear orb stood proudly were a series of markings, dividing the circle into fifty-eight equal portions. The first one was numbered with the Roman symbol for 43 and the very last one was 100.

Zara said, "At least we know we're in the right place."

Sam met her gaze, his eyes wide. "What makes you so certain?"

"The book of Nostradamus held the final fifty-eight quatrains. This device is somehow making reference to it. The question is, how do we use it?"

Sam tried to rotate the pedestal. The device didn't move. He tried harder, but it may as well have been bolted to the stone flooring. Studying the markings in the brass, he tried to move the brass itself without any more success. He then moved along to the lower section of the pedestal where a series of pictographs surrounded a single, beveled dial of brass, shaped like a spear.

Tom was the first to recognize the image. "That's a looking glass!"

"A what?" Zara asked.

Sam stepped closer to the pedestal and looked directly at the flawless orb. It was currently opaque, but he hoped to change that. "Tom found the first of the looking glasses in a pyramid nearly 500 feet below the Gulf of Mexico. The stone orb is harder than diamond and nearly two hundred times more translucent, meaning light and sound can travel through it much further and faster than any other known material on earth."

Zara followed him and examined the stone. "Okay, so what's its purpose?"

"To see other parts of the world," Sam said. "Think of an ancient version of Facetime or Skype, before the internet."

She smiled, without trying to hide her skepticism. "That's great. So, where are we looking?"

Sam rotated the dial shaped like a warrior's spear, waited, and then grinned like he'd just won the final hand of cards. "Here."

She placed her eye up to the orb as though she were looking through the lens of a microscope. The opacity of the orb had dissipated, giving way to very clear picture. "It's quite dark, but looks like there's another chamber below us?"

"You're right, but it's not below us."

"It's not?"

"No. The chamber you're looking at is mostly from a completely different pyramid, possibly hundreds or even thousands of miles away."

"I don't believe you," she said. "It's not possible."

"It is and what's more, I'll prove it to you."

Sam bent forward until his eye was almost resting on the orb. He then carefully rotated the dial until he heard the strange contraption clicked solidly into place. He stared at the image. It looked like somewhere deep in the ocean. The chamber glowed with fluorescence as though someone held a powerful ultraviolet black light. Under normal conditions, UV radiation is invisible to the human eye, but illuminating certain materials with UV radiation causes the emission of visible light, causing these substances to glow with various colors. There were rich purples, greens and blues that all glowed in the chamber giving it the impression of being filled with brilliant gem stones.

Zara smiled as she looked through the orb. "Okay, that one's pretty. But I'm still not convinced we're looking at somewhere hundreds of miles away."

Sam rotated the dial again and the image changed to another darkened and empty chamber. The walls were made of blocks of limestone.

Sam asked, "Convinced?"

"No. These are all still pictures. This device might simply be an ancient version of a kaleidoscope?"

Sam took in a deep breath, and rotated the dial once more. The next vision depicted a top down view of a large chamber. It was almost identical to the king's chamber they were standing in, but with two exceptions. One, the room was at least ten times larger. And two, there were people working inside. Constructing something.

"Tell me what you see here, and then let me know how they managed such a depiction with a kaleidoscope."

Zara placed her eye right up to it and swore.

She said, "They're tribal people. Quite dark skinned. Their faces are painted blue. They're almost completely naked, with the exception of some kind of loincloth. Both women and men are bare breasted. And all of them are working vigorously to finish building the chamber."

"Their faces are blue?" Sam asked. "Like the Tuareg nomads whose faces are tainted with dye that turns them blue?"

"Similar, but these people look very different than any Tuareg I've ever met. Their facial features aren't at all like that. Angular, with strong jawlines. They could be a distant relative perhaps, but I doubt it. They're taller, too. The women are maybe six foot while the men are closer to six foot, four."

"What else do you see?"

"They all look focused. Almost mesmerized by their desire to perform their task. They're working hard and constantly. No one is whipping them. There's no one guiding them. But like a group of ants, they are all simply taking part in completing their individual tasks so that the main project is completed."

"They're working as a collective!" Sam said. "No one is giving or taking orders. They are all simply doing what they have been programed to do. They are working robotically as one."

Zara looked through the glass and back at him. "Do you think they're slaves?"

"It's possible. The Master Builders have been known to use slaves before. They are also known to be perceived as Gods, and by standards of two or three thousand years ago, they certainly would have appeared as Gods by their ability to build things. I've never even considered the fact they might still be alive, and trying to rebuild another pyramid."

"So you think this is a live image, not an ancient record?"

"We've encountered these looking glass devices before, and they always seem to be giving us views from far away, not long ago," replied Sam.

Zara smiled. "A new person's just entered the room. This one's not like the others. Her genetic heritage is clearly different from the others."

"In what way?" he asked. "Does she look to be leading them? Perhaps she's one of the Masters?"

"No. She's a worker just like the others. Her face is mesmerized by what she is doing, as though she is performing the work of the Gods. But she is slightly shorter than the other women, her complexion is much lighter than theirs, but not Caucasian either. She looks possibly Eurasian. While all of the men and women there look muscular, she appears more lithe and athletic. A different sort of bone structure. She's wearing tan cargo shorts and a white tank top. She has a small tattoo of a pyramid above her right shoulder. Very pretty."

"What, are you trying to set me up on a date?"

"No. Just giving you the facts."

Sam smiled, patiently. "All right, can I see her?"

Zara moved out of the way for him. "Sure."

He looked through the orb. The looking glass showed more than fifty people working in the large room. Some were men and others were women, but the entire group appeared homogenous. Every one of them appeared captivated by their work.

Not captivated, hypnotized.

"The pretty one's gone," Sam said.

"I thought you weren't interested in a date?" she teased.

"I'm not. I was hoping I could work out where she'd come from. Then we might be able to find out where this temple is. Something here must have answers to the Nostradamus equation. If not I can't see why Nostradamus sent us here."

"He didn't send us here. He saw a version of the future where I was here and I discovered the Nostradamus Equation."

"Great." Sam backed away from the device, making way for Tom. "You found the first looking glass in the submarine pyramid. That one had views of a number of different temples and ancient structures. Have you recognized anything about this one that we might use to determine where it is or why we were meant to find it?"

Tom shrugged. "I'll see if I recognize anything, but ancient temples and pictography really isn't my area of expertise."

Zara said, "Try it. Anything at all that stands out."

Sam watched as Tom placed his eye right up against the looking glass as though it were a telescope. He stared through it for a couple minutes. His eyes darting from left to right and then stopped. His eyes now fixed on one specific detail. His pupils dilated. The rise and fall of his chest increased in frequency, as though he'd seen something that terrified him.

Zara placed her hand on Tom's shoulder. There was nothing sexual about it. A simple, nurturing gesture. "What did you see, Tom? Did that woman come back into view?"

"What is it, Tom?" Sam asked.

Tom stepped back from the looking glass. His eyes staring vacantly past both of them. There were beads of sweat forming on his forehead and blood had drained from his skin.

"Christ!" Zara was the first to work it out. "You recognize her, don't you?"

"Yes." Tom wrapped his arms around Zara, like a child. "Her name is Dr. Billie Swan – and not so long ago, I came very close to marrying her."

Chapter Ninety-Six

The sound of blood gurgling filled Tom's ears, as his heart raced. The sight of Billie had triggered a primal response, and a sudden release of adrenaline. He felt bile rising as his stomach churned; unsure whether he wanted to be sick or open his bowels. Slight tremors engulfed his normally still and hardened hands.

He looked at Sam. "That's not Billie. She wanted to find the Master Builders, not be enslaved by them. They've done something to her and we need to help her."

"Of course we do." Sam's mouth was slightly open, and his eyes uncomprehending. "I just don't know where to start. That place could be anywhere."

Tom stepped away from the orb. "What the hell have they done to her?"

Zara said, "She looks drugged."

Tom asked, "How could she have let herself be drugged?"

"Maybe she isn't?" Sam suggested. "Perhaps she's pretending. You know she's spent her entire adult life and a great portion of her childhood searching for the Master Builders. She was convinced that some still remained, and watched over us like Gods."

Tom said, "We have to go after her!"

Zara asked, "What about the Nostradamus Equation?"

Tom swore. "Fuck the Nostradamus Equation. I'm out. All I want to do is to find her."

"We need to find the equation, it's more important than anything else," Zara said. "I understand she means a lot to you – all of you, but you have to understand, if we don't find the Nostradamus Equation, none of it will matter."

Tom pounded the side of the pedestal with his open hand. "You can stay here and try and find the Nostradamus Equation. I'm leaving."

Sam asked, "Where? You have no idea where to look! That temple could be anywhere on the planet!"

Tom's jaw was set hard. His brown eyes violently determined as he said, "No. But we know someone who does."

Sam looked at him. Swallowed. "You're right. I think it's time we visit the Vatican City."

"And then I'm going to kill him!" Tom said, his voice full of vehemence.

"No, Tom. I believe you actually might, and then we'll be no better off than we are now. So I have a suggestion. Why don't you remain here and keep watching the looking glass, maybe you can work out how they're controlling Billie. I'll take Zara with me. We'll reach the Vatican before close of business and bring HIM back here for answers."

Tom shook his head. His instincts and duty were the only things keeping him grounded at all. "Okay."

"Are you willing to come with me to the Vatican?" Sam looked at Zara. "I'll explain why on the way."

"Sure," she said. Her eyes distant.

"What's wrong?"

"Nothing."

"What is it?" Sam persisted. "You look worried about something."

"It's nothing."

"Say it."

She shook her head, dismissively.

Sam said, "Just say it!"

Zara swallowed. "Did the future just try to lead us away from the Nostradamus Equation?"

Chapter Ninety-Seven – The Vatican City

The white taxi, an electric Nissan Leaf, drove silently past Castel Sant'Angelo. It continued along Via Di Porta Angelica and stopped illegally on the side of Viale Vaticano. The 39 foot high defensive stone wall stood concealing the Vatican City on the opposite side of the road. Behind it, St. Peter's Basilica protruded high into the skyline.

It was the world's smallest independent nation-state. Covering 109 acres within a 2-mile border, and possessed another 160 acres of holdings in remote locations around the world. Along with the centuries-old buildings and gardens, the Vatican maintained its own banking and telephone systems, post office, pharmacy, newspaper, and radio and television stations, web sites and satellite feeds. Its 600 citizens included the Gendarmerie Corps, who were the Vatican's civil police officers and also members of the Swiss Guard, a security detail charged with protecting the Pope since 1506 – who, in spite of their silly-looking uniforms, were as well-trained and dedicated as a Seal Team.

Sam gave the taxi driver forty Euros and stepped out without waiting for the change. The pungent and ubiquitous aroma of coffee and cigarette smoke wafted through his nostrils. Dust from the ancient ruins of what could arguably be one of the greatest civilizations to have ever lived, drifted from the central ruins.

Zara followed him and looked up at the entrance. A long line of tourists, queuing to visit the sacred city, stretched several hundred feet before disappearing inside the arched entrance to the Vatican Museum.

She bit her lower lip. "We could be here for hours!"

"No we won't." Sam started walking directly for the arched entrance. "Come with me and don't stop until the Swiss Guards arrest you."

"That's your plan?"

"Yep."

She asked, "You're certain this guy's going to be interested in talking?"

Sam said, "Certain."

"How do you know about this person?"

"He used the alias of Testimonium Architectus."

"Witness to the builders?" she sounded incredulous.

Sam nodded. "Three months ago we followed an ancient celestial map to the Falkland Islands. There we dived the inside of a blowhole and discovered a hidden room made entirely of obsidian. Constellations of stars glowed on the walls, depicting the night sky from different angles of the planet. Beneath the obsidian vault, we found a hidden tunnel. We followed it and at the very end we found an open book."

She grinned slightly. Like she knew she was being intentionally pulled into the story. "What was inside the book?"

"A series of entries spanning more than two thousand years. Each one a significant event in the lives of the Master Builders. The most recent entry being made only weeks earlier. So, instead of taking the book, we decided to watch the obsidian vault."

"For what?"

"For someone bearing witness to the Master Builders, and providing us with a link. Six weeks went by and our decision to wait and watch paid off as another entry was made. In that entry a single note was placed – *The Book of Nostradamus has been found.*"

She nodded but said nothing.

Sam continued. "At the time we thought little of it. The witness was followed, all the way back to the Vatican. I figured I'd go and introduce myself and see what I could find out, but then I got distracted because an agent went missing in the Sahara." He shook his head and smiled. "In retrospect, I might have been better off coming here first."

She smiled at him. "You may have been, but I would have been killed."

He shrugged. "There is always that possibility."

"But will he listen to you?"

"He won't want to. My guess is the Swiss Guards will try to blow us off."

"And if they do?"

"Then we mention the Nostradamus Equation has been found."

Sam reached the main entrance to the Vatican Museum, cutting through the crowds as though he and Zara belonged inside. The trick was not to hesitate for a moment. Only a fool or a person who was meant to be there, would push through a crowd who'd been waiting hours to enter.

He stepped beneath the large entrance arch. Above were statues depicting the two great artists who spent so much of their lives adding to the richness of the Vatican. On the left was the genius of the Renaissance, Michelangelo, represented with the sculptor's mallet in his hand. On the right, the young painter Raphael, with his palette and brush.

Zara glanced at the two great artists. "Amazing what those two achieved in their time on earth."

Sam nodded, without listening. He was still trying to plan his next series of responses if the Swiss Guards weren't interested in his story. Or worse, still – if he was wrong about the Witness to the Master Builders.

He stepped inside and through the metal detectors, monitored by two Vatican police officers. In their blue uniforms, the Gendarmes wore a Glock 17 on their side holsters as they waved tourists through.

Sam and Zara pushed forward, through the swathes of tourists. Passing the Atrium of the Corazze on the left, and crossing the Atrium with its Four Gates, they entered the Courtyard of the Pigna. Sam recalled learning that the courtyard was built to connect the Palace of the Innocent with the Sistine Chapel. There were three levels, joined by elegant stairways and flanked by galleries characterized by pilasters surmounted by broad arches. Both the paving and the galleries were slightly angled towards the Sistine Chapel, so that from the papal apartments the courtyard looked even bigger than it actually was.

He turned to the left and stepped through the second archway into a quiet courtyard. Zara glanced at him, her face showing her unconscious disappointment to go all this way and skip the Sistine Chapel. At the end of the courtyard two Pontifical Swiss Guards protected a wooden doorway. At a guess, that doorway led to the real Vatican City. The non-tourist city, where the smallest city state in the world performed the sometimes mundane and everyday tasks of running the state. They wore the traditional dress uniform of blue, red, orange and yellow with a distinctly renaissance appearance.

Bodyguards to the Pope, the Pontifical Swiss Guards were maintained by the Holy See and responsible for the safety of the Pope, including the security of the Apostolic Palace. Both men were equipped with traditional halberds, as well as modern firearms. Since the assassination attempt on Pope John Paul II in 1981, a much stronger emphasis had been placed on the guard's non-ceremonial roles, and had seen enhanced training in unarmed combat and small arms. Recruits to the guards must be unmarried Swiss Catholic males between 19 and 30 years of age who have completed basic training with the Swiss Armed Forces. They served as the de facto military of Vatican City. Established in 1506 under Pope Julius II, the Pontifical Swiss Guard is among the oldest military units in continuous operation.

Sam smiled at both men. "I'm sorry to interrupt. My name is Sam Reilly, and I need to speak with Mr. Testimonium Architectus."

Both men shot glances at each other, which suggested they'd been placed in an unexpected and dangerous situation. Sam sighed in relief. If they'd never heard of the name they would have told him so and dismissed him. Their hesitation was nothing but confirmation the man was inside. Each of the guards appeared uncomfortable. One lowered his right hand, possibly in preparation of retrieving his pistol.

Sam stood his ground. Speaking with the authority of a man used to leading, he said, "Very urgent business, gentlemen. The sands of time are quite literally being washed away."

The two guards made a quiet, and rapid exchange of words in their own language. One then disappeared behind an archway at the end of the room, while the second stepped forward. "Please wait here while we talk to our superiors."

Sam smiled, warmly. "Thank you."

A moment later, a second guard arrived and took the place of the one who had disappeared. A total of six minutes went by before the original guard returned with a different man.

He wore a robe of dark blue. His brown hair was thick and cut short. His blue eyes were intense, like he carried the weight of the world on his shoulders, but his smile was warm and kindly. He could have been a high ranking member of the clergy, but his age quickly made Sam doubt it. The man might have been in his mid-forties, but no older. Years of a sedentary and learned lifestyle had turned his once muscular physique into adipose. Underneath which, strength and speed appeared to have remained. He held his posture well, like a boxer. Despite the maximum age limit being set as 30 years, his belt bore the yellow, red, and orange insignia of the Pontifical Swiss Guard.

Sam swallowed, hard.

His problems had just evolved into something far more dangerous.

The stranger inserted an iron key into the heavy wooden door and unbolted the latch. "Mr. Reilly, you and Dr. Delacroix are to come through immediately. I've been expecting you for some time, now, and I don't like waiting."

Chapter Ninety-Eight

Sam and Zara followed the man. He moved with a surprising speed for his rotund stature. He led them down the stairs and across a cobbled courtyard. They turned down an alley that merged into a larger one. At the far side of which nestled a stone building that housed both a supermarket, and a small post office. Past it, the Tower of Nicholas V stood as a rich symbol of the Bank of the Vatican.

The man didn't introduce himself or speak to either of them until he passed the Gate of St. Anna and entered the barracks of the Swiss Guard. Once there, they entered the hallway and stopped at the fourth door on the left, labeled in Latin – *Swiss Guard. Minister for the Future.*

The stranger opened the door, his eyes meeting Zara's. The curve of his outer lip dipped, slightly. "Dr. Delacroix, I must beg your patience and ask you to please wait out here while I speak to Mr. Reilly, alone."

Zara nodded her head and waited as Sam followed the man inside.

The stranger closed the door and said, "Have a seat, Mr. Reilly."

Sam took a seat, and grinned. He'd never been on a non-tourist tour of the Vatican before. "I'm sorry. You're the *Witness to the Master Builders?*"

"Among other things, yes. That is one of my many tasks." The man offered his hand. "My real name is John Wallis

Sam took it. "Pleased to meet you."

"I only wish it were under different circumstances." Wallis looked around the room, as though uncomfortable about how to broach the next subject. "Good God, Mr. Reilly! Dr. Delacroix has survived!"

"Yes. You sound almost displeased, by the revelation?"

"More distressed than you could know."

"Why?"

"The Master Builders are going to be most concerned!"

"Why?"

"Because they had planned her death for nearly four hundred years, and now you've just ruined it. I have half a notion to invite her inside and kill her myself, but from what I hear, the damage has already been done, and now all we can do is go forward – with whatever it was Nostradamus was trying to achieve."

Sam stared at him. A new revelation unfolding. "You were the buyer! You were the one who paid her to find the book of Nostradamus!"

"Yes, of course."

Sam paused, trying to make sense of the new revelation. "If you knew that Zara, finding the book of Nostradamus would send the world into chaos, why did you pay for her to find it in the first place?"

"Because she was always going to find it. Nostradamus had already foreseen that. That much was fact. We figured so long as it was going to happen, we were going to be better off paying for it to happen. That way we could at least make arrangements as the event unfolded."

"Why didn't you just kill her when she was a child?" Sam suggested.

"It's not as simple as that. Nostradamus had already seen the event. That much was already determined. She was going to find his damned book, and she was going to try to change the future. But she was going to make mistakes, and in doing so, she was going to decrease the life-span of the human race."

Sam nodded. He'd heard the argument from her own lips, previously. "So what went wrong? How did you let her escape with the book?"

"The future intervened. Luck would have it that she wasn't in the camp when our men attacked. She escaped, and with her, she carried the book of Nostradamus with all its danger."

Sam laughed. He was enjoying himself, despite the incredible revelations. "Nostradamus told her to run."

John remained silent. His eyes fixed on Sam's face, as though he was trying to decide if Sam was lying. "Nostradamus predicted this?"

"Yes. Why, does that surprise you?" Sam smiled, glad to have made a visible effect on his new opponent. "Apparently he was very good, I keep being told, although I still struggle to believe a word people say about his predictions."

"My predecessor told me that Nostradamus once believed it was impossible to change the future."

"If that's the case, then why does it matter that Dr. Delacroix found the book, or for that matter, that she survived?"

"Because Nostradamus was wrong. It's part of Church Dogma – free will. If the future is set, then how can man have free will? But we know by the Word of God that man *does* have free will, so the future must be malleable, yes? The fact that Zara has survived this long is proof that the future can be changed. You see, it's not that it can't be changed, it's merely a case of being difficult to change. Big changes are impossible on their own. You need to set up a new series of events, joined together like strings, to have effect on big events."

"Zara explained it, as though we're driving a small car and we want to knock a big truck off the road. We can't do it on our own, but if we hit a bigger car, followed by a mini-van, followed by a small truck, eventually, we'll send that big truck off the road."

"Yes. A very simplistic explanation, but it will suffice for now."

Sam asked, "Why is Dr. Delacroix so important?"

"You mean, what does she do?"

"Yes."

"She will have a gradual effect on the future. She will change the course of a rebellion, and in doing so, stop a major war in the African continent that will inevitably spill out across the globe."

"But we've put systems in place to stop the war before it's begun!" Sam said.

"And they will work!"

"What's so wrong about that? So we saved humanity?"

"No. You sped up its demise." John sighed. "Humanity was on a path to cease in three hundred years – instead, it will now cease to exist by the end of this century! Thank you Mr. Reilly."

"Why?"

"There was supposed to be a World War III. It was going to be disastrous for humanity. Billions of people were going to die. Less than a tenth of the human population would survive."

"Why did we want that?"

"Because we've become the plague of our planet. We are the locusts. The planet can't sustain our ravenous growth forever. This was supposed to be the correction. And now, we must try to avert the real disaster."

"And what will that be?"

"We have no idea. We haven't yet seen the vision which will explain it to us – or we would have stopped it, sooner. If it could be stopped."

Chapter Ninety-Nine

Sam asked, "What's your purpose in all of this?"

Wallis said, "To save mankind."

"Sure." Sam smiled. "But how did the Vatican get involved with Nostradamus?"

"In 1538, an offhanded remark by the then young, Michel de Nostradame, about a religious statue resulted in charges of heresy. When ordered to appear before the Church Inquisition, he wisely chose to leave Provence to travel for several years through Italy, Greece and Turkey. During his travels to the ancient mystery schools, it is believed that Nostradamus experienced a psychic awakening. During his travels in Italy, he came upon a group of Franciscan monks, identifying one as the future Pope. The monk, called Felice Peretti, was ordained Pope Sixtus V in 1585, fulfilling the prediction of Nostradamus."

"You didn't answer the question. Instead, you told me about Nostradamus being able to predict the future, something I'm rapidly learning he was very good at."

"Nostradamus didn't just predict Felice Peretti would one day be ordained as a Pope. He told him on that day, he was to start a new division from his private guard."

"The Minister for the Future?"

"Exactly."

"You see, Nostradamus wasn't the only one who could see the future. He was, unfortunately, the only one who was willing to take the time and risk to change it. The Master Builders can see future events, but not in the way you assume. You see, they don't have the vision in a lineal fashion."

"They get them randomly?"

"Yes. Imagine this. If you were to walk into a movie cinema and watch a three minute clip at any random point in the show, how much would you know about the event being viewed?"

"Not much, unless we had a point of reference. I've already had this explained to me as the way Nostradamus saw the future."

"Exactly. If you were to walk into the same movie, and see something like a newspaper the day the bomb was dropped on Hiroshima then you'd have a reference point to where the event came from. Because of this, the Master Builders require me to keep documenting when I see an event. I already have a list of all the events, but when I discover one has occurred I go to Obsidian Vault to document it. The Masters, you see, are able to reference the events through the documents stored inside the ancient almanac I've been keeping."

Sam asked, "How long have you been alive?"

"No, I think you misunderstand me. I'm fifty-two years old. I'm part of one of the longest relay races ever made. Since the inception of the Holy See, members of our party have lived as part of His Holiness's unique monitoring services."

"Why?"

"Because we're driven to believe a higher power is behind everything we do and see. That someone or something better than ourselves, has a divine plan for all of us. Inside the holy church, we've been able to witness most of the events throughout history."

"The higher powers work for you?"

"No. I work directly for His Holiness. In that position, I receive an enormous amount of information regarding events. Those events are then cross-referenced with the ancient almanac."

"Nostradamus wrote a second book?"

"No. One of my predecessors copied his down."

"Is the church behind this?"

"No."

"I think I just broke the equation," Sam said. "But I don't believe it."

"What is it?"

"The Master Builders didn't see time in a linear fashion."

"You think they saw it all as one jumbled up mess of events?"

"Yes. Nostradamus was one of them, or a child of the Master Builders – and although he could see all the events of time, he couldn't make any sense out of them because, to him, they all occurred simultaneously. The equation was used to form reference points to guide the viewer to make sense out of the events and their relative time."

"But time is linear!" Sam said, "They can't just see it from all directions: forwards, backwards, the physical universe simply doesn't work like that!"

John said, "I agree. But then, I'm not the one who recently found a book addressed to her from four hundred plus years ago, which instructed her to find an island that hadn't yet formed, to reach to find the answers." He then shrugged, as though none of it mattered anymore. "I've read your journals, Mr. Reilly. The people you call the Master Builders we call the Time Masters."

Sam asked, "When did they arrive?"

"Arrive? No we're not talking about Aliens or anything like that. They have always been here. They're here to help, to watch us and to guide us."

"And who are you? Are you a Time Master?"

"No. I am simply a witness. They need help to make sense out of the events that are going to occur. I help by documenting them. I write the major events as they are given to me. Then the Masters are able to gain a better understanding of where they're at. They have long periods throughout history where they leave us alone, followed by others where they need to intervene frequently."

"Why?"

"Because we're human. Because we're weak. And because, left to our own, we're like little children who want to fight and will eventually kill ourselves."

"They're the parents who come to intervene?"

"Kind of. All I know is if you start to see the Time Masters there's a reason. And recently, they've started to slip. They've let their presence become known to others beyond our former tight circle. There have been more than a dozen events in the past two decades where a normal person, such as yourself, might put two and two together and determine someone else, entirely different than the history books would have us believe, was adjusting the strings of time."

"So humanity is squabbling? That's what has brought them out of seclusion? Isn't that business as usual for humanity?"

"Humanity is getting close to the end."

"Can the Masters change that?"

"They intend to try. I believe they're human beings just like us, and if humanity dies out, they will pass away as well. So they need imperatively to steer us to safety. I'm not sure they know how. I believe they intentionally brought you into this game to help. I just don't know what you can do."

"But am I doing something?"

"Yes. Your presence here is affecting the timeline. They know that."

"But is it improving or worsening the event?"

"That, only time will tell."

Chapter One Hundred

Sam leaned back into the chair. It was leather, and appeared as old as some of the medieval ruins he'd explored over the years. He shook his head. A wry smile forming on his otherwise cheerful and good-humored face, he remained silent.

John asked, "What?"

"Your name's John Wallis?"

"Yes. What about it? It's a common name in society?"

Sam said, "It's not very Swiss."

"No. My father was English, my mother was Swiss."

Sam stared at him. Still unsure why he was even asking the question. "Do you know what the mathematician, John Wallis was most famous for?"

"I do. My father used to tell me as a child. In fact, I believe he coined the term infinity." Wallis shrugged. "What's so important about that?"

"Nothing." Sam stared at him, the slightest upward curve of a smile taking place. The coincidence was just too much to be irrelevant.

"Except?" Wallis persisted.

"It's just… earlier today I visited an island a friend of mine has spent her lifetime searching for. The island itself was shaped very much like the number eight laying on its side. The mathematical symbol for infinity."

"And you think it's symbolic that you were to meet me on the same day you visited an island that looked precariously similar to a name a completely different John Wallis created centuries ago? You are a very strange man, Mr. Reilly. Why did your friend wait until now to visit the island?"

"Because Infinity Island, as we decided to call it, didn't exist until twelve hours ago."

"How's that possible?"

"There was a submarine earthquake in the Mediterranean this morning. Did you hear?"

"Yes. I was told the tsunamis had the potential to do extraordinary damage, but through the grace of God, only one person was killed. Was this island damaged by it?"

"No. Instead, when the tectonic plates shifted – it forced an otherwise low lying submerged mountain nearly two hundred feet upwards. Giving birth to a new island."

All color drained from Wallis's face. "You are talking about the Infiniti Island!"

"Yes. Now I'm jogging your memory. I thought you might have heard something about it. The Master Builders built it, right?"

John nodded his head.

Sam asked, "Do you know what this means? Has Zara Delacroix changed the future?"

"Yes."

"And the birthing of the island confirms she's saved the world?"

"No."

"What then?"

"The birthing of the island confirms there is no longer anything humanity can do to save itself. The island was built as a stop gate, to provide answers when the world is in dire need. If the Infiniti Island is indeed on the surface of the Mediterranean, we need to get to it now. There's no time to waste!"

"There's something else, too."

"What now?"

"The Nostradamus Equation didn't work. It was all gibberish. Nothing explained a reference point to the events in his 58 additional quatrains."

"What did you find?"

"A looking glass. Like the others, this one showed the insides of a series of temples. One of them viewed a large stone chamber, bigger than any we've seen before. The structure was still being built. Dark skinned tribal people worked on the structure as though they had been possessed!"

"Go on, Mr. Reilly! What else?"

"I recognized one of the slaves. She wasn't tribal at all and didn't belong. Her name is Dr. Billie Swan – and I'm going to need you to show me how to find her!"

Chapter One Hundred and One

Sam watched the blood drain from John Wallis's face. He saw confusion there, wonder, bewilderment – and last of all, he saw hope.

John said, "You saw Dr. Billie Swan through the looking glass?"

"Yes! Do you know where she is?"

John stood up in his chair, as though the meeting was over. "How very fascinating."

"Where is she?" Sam persisted.

"I have no idea." John grinned broadly as he spoke. "But that's not what I find so fascinating."

"Really, what do you find fascinating?"

"The future!" John grabbed his arm and looked at him directly in the eye. "Don't you see?"

"What?"

"Don't you see? It's trying to distract you, the only way it knows how. You were close, you had the Nostradamus Equation in your grasp, and the future tempted you with another vision. We have to get back to the Infiniti Island, straight away. Before it collapses, and all is lost!"

Sam stood up. "Are you coming with me?"

"Of course. I don't see how I can trust you not to screw this up, otherwise. Good God, this has nothing to do with Dr. Zara Delacroix and everything to do with you!" He shook his head. "I should have killed you when you first dived the Obsidian Vault!"

"What are you talking about?"

"You were close! There must be a way you can change this, and everything, otherwise the future would have never tried to distract you!"

"The future tried to distract me? As if it has a will of its own?"

"Yes. There was something else inside the looking glass you were supposed to find, but instead, you spotted Billy, became irate, and came charging over here. All the while, the sands of Infiniti Island are being reclaimed, and the solution is disappearing!"

John Wallis opened the door and grabbed Zara. "We have to go."

"Where?" she asked.

"Back to Infiniti Island – to save the human race! And for goodness sake, make sure you bring the book of Nostradamus!"

Chapter One Hundred and Two

Sam entered the king's chamber with Zara and John following. Tom stood up, leaving the pedestal to meet them. He appeared somber, but focused. His face showed signs of dried tears, now replaced by vitriolic rage.

Tom lifted John by his wetsuit and held him against the sandstone wall. "Where have you taken Billie?"

Sam stepped in between, and looked at Tom. "This is John Wallis. He's going to help us calculate the Nostradamus Equation. He has no idea where Billie is."

"What about finding Billie?" Tom asked.

John held out his hand. "John Wallis. I'll try if I can, but first we need to calculate the equation."

Tom didn't accept the man's handshake and John didn't try to offer it again. Instead, John began quickly turning the dial on the pedestal, flicking through several different temples until he stopped at the temple underwater. The fish and other sea creatures all glowed with fluorescence as they were struck by the UV black light.

John said, "Flashlights off, everyone."

Each person flicked their light off until the king's chamber was dark. He waited as their eyes adjusted to the change. A moment later, John tilted his head backward, and looked up at the no longer empty dome. The ultraviolet light shined through the orb, and toward the ceiling.

The dome ceiling came alive with numbers, literally glowing. There were some words, but mostly gibberish. Nothing that made any sense whatsoever on its own. Most of the numbers were written in red, some were in blue.

"Black, Moore, Death of a Twin..." Sam started to read out the words. "None of this means anything!"

Tom stared at the ceiling. There were words there, written in English. He read them out loud.

Find the answer to the one question you must ask. Don't get greedy and search for other answers. Time is short. This was built to save humanity. Use it wisely.

John turned to Zara. "Give me the medallion!"

Zara removed it from around her neck, and handed it to him. "Why, what are you going to do?"

Sam watched, as John ignored her and placed the medallion on top of the orb. The old brass medallion fit perfectly, as though it had been purposely designed to fit – which, of course, it was. There were several holes in the medallion. Sam recalled how they were formed when Zara placed her medallion inside the pedestal of truth within the final resting chamber of the last king of the Garamantes. It had been filled with acid, and seven imperfections in the metalwork had been revealed below the dissolved plating, leaving seven holes. He remembered thinking at the time that the holes appeared too specific to have been created randomly. Now he knew. Light from the orb shined through the holes, lighting up seven individual numbers at a time. Joining them together mentally formed a calendar date.

John said, "If the words are in red, it means the future is set and nothing can be done to change it. If it's blue, it means there's still a chance to change the outcome. Zara, get your book open, we're going to need the quatrains available when we find the one we're after."

She asked, "We're going to find a specific quatrain that's relevant?"

John nodded. "Yes. And then we're going to decipher it. And we're going to do all this very soon, before the future has a chance to destroy the Nostradamus Equation."

The orb had a series of numbers, ranging from 43-100. The medallion rotated, so that each number represented a different position of the seven light apertures. John quickly began flicking through each one.

Quatrain 43 – 5/31/2020 – written in red.

Quatrain 44 – 3/5/2030 – written in red.

John looked up at the rest of them. "Tell me one of you is making notes of each of these."

Sam said, "I'm way ahead of you."

"Good." He continued working his way through each of the 58 quatrains.

Quatrain 56 – 2/14/2021 – written in blue.

Quatrain 57 – 8/2/2045 – written in red.

John continued until he reached quatrain 84. It was written in blue – meaning the future was still up for grabs and the date was tomorrow.

John looked at Sam. "What did you have planned, tomorrow?"

"Before the earthquake, we'd planned to help a man named Adebowale overthrow the rebel government of the DRC."

John asked, "How?"

Sam said, "Nearly five thousand men are being held prisoner in a mine in the north of the DRC. Next to the mine is Lake Tumba. The United Sovereign of Kongo, of which Adebowale is the leader, have been waiting to mount a mission to release them, because General Ngige would drown the slaves if they attack. We need to free them before the counter rebellion can take place."

John went quiet, as though none of it made any sense. His confidence was shattering.

Sam turned to John. "The Nostradamus Equation is telling us quatrain 84 is about the overthrow. The future's still in limbo. You said before that I might have been responsible for this catastrophe. What did Nostradamus see? What did he want me to do?"

"I have no idea," John said.

"Then what good was the equation?"

"You now know the time, and you know the quatrain that refers to the future event. I suggest Zara opens up quatrain 84 and works out what should be done."

Zara opened the book of Nostradamus to Centuries VII – Quatrain 84.

*

An ocean above and a maze below

Where the two meet over a baled woe,

The twin of a king shall die and the sun will set,

With a new ruler, and a kingdom shall grow without threat

*

Sam stared at the quatrain. "An ocean above and a maze below is obviously referring to the Lake Tumba mine. But what the hell does the rest of it mean?"

Tom leaned in toward the book, and asked, "What's a baled woe, anyway?"

"It's old English," Zara said. "Meaning a rescued person of great sorrow. Like you've saved someone from a terrible fate."

Sam shrugged. "The twin of a king. Does General Ngige have a twin?"

Zara said, "I don't know. I never even heard of the man until a few days ago, when he tried to kill me."

"John, does General Ngige have a twin?"

"Yes, I think he might. I know he was funded by someone else who first gave him the idea of rebelling. Might have possibly even financed it in the beginning. That person might have royal blood."

They bickered back and forward about the possible meaning of quatrain 84 and then stopped. A single clump of hardened sand fell directly on the pedestal, breaking apart where the orb rested. John then pressed a single pictograph on the side of the wall, which released the medallion. He looked at Zara. His blue eyes told her everything she needed to know. He'd seen the truth and it was important that no one else worked it out either.

John said, "It's time to go."

"What's going on?" Sam asked.

"The island's collapsing. The Nostradamus Equation was never built to last!"

Sam asked, "But what about the quatrain! What does it mean?"

"I'm not sure yet. I think you need to free those slaves. If you do that, I believe things will be placed back in the order that they were meant to be. We don't need the equation anymore. We have the quatrain it led us to. Now we just need to make sense of it."

Sam nodded, and felt the second clump of sand fall on his shoulder. It was small and barely noticeable, but the ramifications were deadly. Infiniti Island was breaking apart.

"Quick!" he said.

Zara placed the book of Nostradamus into its water-tight bag and pulled the zipper tight.

Sam said, "Tom, you go ahead first, and get the helicopter running!"

John had his regulator and dive mask on before he reached the water, and followed directly behind Tom. Sam made sure that Zara was right behind him, before donning his own dive mask and regulator.

They swam down the dark tunnel. As they turned to join the main tunnel's entrance, a large section of sand broke off behind Sam. He slipped through, but the tunnel to the king's chamber collapsed. It drove everyone with a sense of urgency to evacuate the pyramid, or be forever guests buried deep inside.

Sam was the last one to reach the surface. He pulled on Zara's dive belt to release it, and then ripped open the Velcro which held her dive tank. He did the same for his own weight belt, but didn't wait to remove his own dive tank.

The island around him was almost completely gone.

Thirty feet ahead, the main rotor blades of the big Sikorsky helicopter had started to rotate. The island was almost completely swallowed by the sea. The mountain behind was starting to collapse, in massive sections, like an avalanche. The obsidian spheres were starting to fall apart, and the twin islands were no longer connected. Water was already lapping at the skids of the helicopter.

Sam reached the side step of the Sikorsky as a wave rolled through under the helicopter. Tom glanced at him for a moment, and lifted the helicopter into the air. Zara and Tom helped pull him inside.

Sam slid the side door closed, and looked out the side windshield. Both sides of the island, no longer held together by the connective tissue of the obsidian spheres, now seemed to be drifting away from each other, each one collapsing in an opposite direction.

The strange obsidian spheres began rolling toward the entrance of the pyramid. A crack formed at the base of the sand mountain, and the obsidian stones rolled in through it. Every last one of them. As though they were driven by some divine power. Thirty seconds after the last stone disappeared, the mountain collapsed.

Sam watched out the windshield, as Tom turned the helicopter toward the *Maria Helena.* Infiniti Island was entirely gone, and what remained was nothing more than the calm turquoise waters of the Mediterranean Sea.

Chapter One Hundred and Three

The Sikorsky landed on the *Maria Helena* at 8 p.m. and by 10:05 p.m. a plan had been decided upon and Sam was discussing it with his entire crew, Zara, John and Adebowale. John had already given his view that it was the only possibly outcome now. More risky than had the book of Nostradamus never been discovered, but the best chance of success, now that it has. Adebowale assured Sam that he could have his men ready to start the coup by tomorrow evening.

Sam said, "Let me make it clear, our job isn't to participate in this rebellion. Our job is to free the slaves. It's then going to be up to Adebowale to bring the change of power to the DRC."

Everyone nodded. They couldn't be seen to be picking sides with two rebel leaders inside the Democratic Republic of Congo after it's democratically elected President had been killed through a ruthless coup.

"The entrance to the mine is poorly guarded. Fewer than twenty people. They have an old colonial-era Gatling gun fixed at the entrance to the mine, meaning no one can escape from the inside."

Genevieve asked, "If Adebowale has the support of so many people, why doesn't he simply raid it and release the prisoners?"

Sam said, "One of the main tunnels runs directly below Lake Tumba. The prisoners are trapped below. The lake's shallow. Only about thirty feet deep. But the mine is more than a mile deep. General Ngige has spread word that if anyone attacks the guards at the entrance to the mine, they'll blow the charge and the entire mine will be flooded, killing everyone below."

"How many people are trapped there?" she asked.

"At least five thousand. Might be as many as ten though. Apparently they provide them with the same amount of food each day. General Ngige sets the minimum quota for gold extraction. If they achieve it, they get the food if not they go hungry. Same amount of food every day."

"Lots of people would starve."

"They just replace them with more prisoners. It's a good deterrent to rebellion. Think of the Gulag in Russia. A system where you were worked to death. You build a place so much worse than anyone can imagine and they'll do their best to behave."

"So, how do you want to work this?" Genevieve asked.

"Adebowale. I'll let you explain the plan."

Elise brought up the detailed digital map of the mine. She switched on the overhead projector and the image displayed on the whiteboard in the *Maria Helena's* mission room. It showed a maze of tunnels spanning eighty-four levels. At higher levels the tunnels were scattered and sporadic as though they had kept having to change direction to avoid breaking into the lake's bed. From the tenth level and below, the tunnels became extensive. Long, deep shafts, extending miles in all directions. Three of the mines appeared open and accessible, while the fourth appeared flooded.

Adebowale stood next to the white board and pointed to the three tunnels that ran beneath the lake. "If we lay dynamite along the entrance to these three tunnels we can cause a series of cave-ins which will create a natural barrier from the lake's water when General Ngige's men trigger the release of the water. Then my men will take out the guards, and the prisoners will run free."

Sam looked at John. "Did you want to join us?"

John smiled and shook his head. "No. This mission has no place for me in it. But I wish you well with your endeavor. I truly believe this is in the best interest of the future."

Sam turned to Zara, "What about you?"

"Me?" she asked, her eyes turning to avoid his gaze. "I think you greatly overestimate my resources. I won't be useful in a jailbreak."

"Genevieve can pilot the helicopter on her own," Sam said. "But it will be a lot easier with a second set of eyes to navigate. It will also help when she returns for the pick-up rendezvous point, after we complete the mission."

She breathed in and then swallowed hard. Her cheeks flushed slightly red. "Then in that case, I'm afraid you overestimate my altruism. It sounds like a worthy cause, but it's not my fight. Nostradamus never would have predicted me to actually be involved in the operation. When it comes down to it, I'm too selfish. I really wish you luck, but I don't think I will be coming."

"That's okay, I understand. It's not your fight. Heck, it's barely ours." Sam smiled at her, reassuringly. "Then again, Mikhail may be trapped down there."

The simple comment stopped Zara in her tracks. She let the words sink in, and then met Sam's gaze directly. Her hazel-green eyes, piercing and dominating. She shook her head. Her hardened stare giving way to hope. "Damn you, Sam Reilly. I had accepted that he was already dead, and now you go ahead and do a thing like this – you better pray to whatever God you believe in that he's still alive and you haven't given me false hope."

He asked, "Shall I count you in, then?"

"Damn you. Of course, I'll join the team. But don't bother trying to return to the helicopter until you find him, or at the very least know exactly what happened to him!"

"I'll do my best." Sam turned to the rest of his team. "What do you think?"

Genevieve looked up. "Just one problem."

Adebowale asked, "What's that?"

"How do we get inside the mine?"

Adebowale said, "That's where I'm going to need Mr. Reilly's help."

Chapter One Hundred and Four

The Legacy 450 banked gently to the left and settled onto its final approach. The chartered eight-person luxury jet landed smoothly on the blacktop runway. It was the sort of landing where one had to think twice whether or not they were still in the air or on the ground. It had taken six hours to travel from Malta to Bangui on the private charter. Sam glanced out the aircraft's large side window. At the edge of the small airport, a helicopter's rotor blades began to turn.

Adebowale caught Sam's attention. "As promised, you have a Jet Ranger waiting for you. It will be fully fueled, and ready for Genevieve to take-off by the time we finish loading the equipment – no questions asked."

"Good." Sam turned to Genevieve. "How long's it been since you've flown a Jet Ranger?"

"Years." She smiled. "Nearly a decade."

He asked, "You going to be okay?"

"Definitely," she said. "It's like riding a bike."

Sam nodded. He'd been a pilot most of his life. Different helicopters had their own nuances, but once you'd learned to fly, it was in your blood. Besides, the Jet Ranger was a relatively forgiving helicopter.

The Legacy 450 stopped at a private hangar, hired for the next twelve hours only. Sam moved to the back of the aircraft. Tom had his legs resting on the empty leather chair that faced in toward him. Using the two chairs as a bed, Tom was in the sort of deep sleep of the dead. Sam kicked his feet off the chair and Tom slipped to the floor.

Tom looked up. "Hey, I was enjoying that rest. What's up?"

Sam said, "Sorry. We're on the ground. Time to go to work."

"All right, but on the way back I'm sleeping for twenty-four hours straight."

"On the return flight, sleep as long as you need. And when you wake up, we'll start our hunt for the temple where Billie's being kept prisoner."

Tom stood up. His eyes suddenly wide, as though he'd been forced back into the moment. The need for sleep was replaced by urgency. He picked up his duffle bag. "Let's get this thing done."

Ten minutes later, they had loaded the Jet Ranger with their dive equipment and three RS1 Military Grade Sea Scooters. Zara sat in the navigation seat, and Genevieve quickly inputted the coordinates into the GPS in front of her, giving Zara a brief overview of its functions. Genevieve brought out the topographical map, and showed her the main reference points.

Sam slid the back door closed and popped his head into the cockpit. "We're good to go."

Genevieve nodded. "All right."

A moment later, they were in the air. In the back of the helicopter, Sam, Tom and Adebowale quickly changed into their wet suits. Sam finished laying out his dive equipment, and turned to set up a second set for Adebowale.

Sam looked at Adebowale, "Have you ever dived before?"

"Once. I was on vacation in Hawaii. A friend from college convinced me to give it a go. I did a half hour introductory dive in about six feet of water."

Sam cringed, "That's it?"

Adebowale nodded. "That's it. But I assure you: I will be fine."

Sam attached the dive regulator to the tank and opened the air intake valve. He inflated the diving vest, known as a buoyancy control device, and handed it to Adebowale. "How do you feel about confined spaces?"

"Comfortable. I spent time in this very mine as a child. Again, rest assured, Mr. Reilly. I will get through the submerged section, if it's still possible."

Sam nodded. It was as good a chance as they were ever going to get. He carefully laid out a rectangular piece of cloth on the floor of the helicopter. Then, almost ritualistically, he placed his Heckler & Koch MP5 on it. The nine-millimeter, German designed, submachine gun was popular with military divers around the world, because its sealed chamber gave it excellent reliability even fully submerged. He removed the magazine, opened the chamber and checked that it was free from any bullets. It was clean and its parts were well oiled. He then tested the firing mechanism. It tapped forward with a firm clicking sound. He grinned. "All right."

On the opposite side of the helicopter, Tom finished setting up all three Sea Scooters. The underwater diver propulsion vehicles were small, hand-held, electric devices used by SCUBA divers and free-divers for underwater propulsion. They weighed less than twenty pounds each, and had a water bladder, designed to automatically control the diver's buoyancy.

Tom looked at Adebowale. "Have you ever seen one of these?"

Adebowale said, "No. But Sam explained what we can do with them. What do I need to know?"

Tom switched the power button forward, into the on position. It sat directly in the middle of the two handle grips. "Okay, as you can see, this button here turns the power on. You shouldn't need to touch this once we're in the water, but if you suddenly notice you're out of power, you might want to check it hasn't been bumped."

"Okay," Adebowale said.

Tom used his right thumb to depress the speed rate button, and the little propeller began to spin with a whine. "Look at this like a throttle on a motorcycle. Each time you press it you increase the speed. The RS1 Sea Scooter has three speed settings. We'll probably need the fastest setting until we reach the bottom of the mine, then we'll drop it back to the second or even first setting. Use the button under your left thumb to slow her down."

Adebowale nodded.

"Okay, these power for ninety minutes at full speed, and can maintain up to 4 knots. This one has the map of the flooded mine built into its heads-up-display screen. Think of a GPS, only this one works by correlating the image ahead, based on its sonar pings, with your initial known location. We'll set the initial location as the opening to the mine's tunnel beneath the sink-hole. Each sea scooter has its own identifying sound, which means we can keep track of each other's location throughout the tunnel, so long as we're within line of sight. That means all three of us will be able to navigate in the dark, without too much trouble."

Sam finished reassembling his Heckler & Koch MP5. He set the safety to on, and attached a full magazine of bullets. "Unless the map's wrong."

Adebowale said, "The map isn't wrong."

"It was always going to be a possibility," Tom said. "Heck, the map you gave us is nearly three years old."

Adebowale said, "No one has been down to the mine that way since the sinkhole opened up next to the Tumba River, and flooded the first ten levels of the mine."

Sam began sliding his arms into the buoyancy control device, and tightening the Velcro. He placed his fins on his feet and put his dive mask next to him. He attached his Heckler & Koch MP5 to his right arm, using a tether, and placed the sea scooter in front of him, between his fins. "Also, remember, the maximum battery power is ninety minutes. That means, it's a one way trip. Adebowale's men are going to breach the guard house at exactly 22:00. That leaves us three hours to make the dive, navigate our way through the tunnel, and blow the mines that lead to Lake Tumba."

Genevieve glanced back, "No one said anything about a one way trip before?"

Sam said, "Don't worry. Tom and I will be coming home. We'll stick to the plan as far as a pick up rendezvous point. I just want to be clear we have ninety minutes max, to navigate through the flooded section of the mine. After that, we're out of power, and we'd never be able to swim it without mechanical assistance."

Genevieve asked, "So what happens if you can't complete the mission? How do you get out?"

"We don't." Sam sat forward. "We have to complete the mission. Once the C4 is blown, and the tunnels cave-in, Adebowale's men will take the guards out of the equation. Once that's done, our job is finished. We'll make our way out of the mine, and double back to the edge of the lake, set off a green flare, and you can come get us."

Genevieve said, "I'll need to refuel."

"Not a problem. Drop us off, and return to the Bangui airport to refuel. Meet us at the designated landing zone at 2330, and Tom and I will be waiting for you." He looked at Zara. "I'll do my best to bring Mikhail home, too."

Zara nodded, but said nothing.

Genevieve asked, "What about Adebowale?"

"I'll be staying with my people," Adebowale said, emphatically.

Sam looked at Tom and Adebowale. "Let's do one final run through of the mine."

Adebowale nodded and opened the digital image on his computer tablet. "This is the last known map of the maze of underground tunnels below Lake Tumba. It was taken five years ago, and so we can expect some changes."

Tom nodded and asked, "You're sure we'll still have access?"

"Reasonably confident." Adebowale pointed to the map. "As you can see, the Lake Tumba mine is separated into four primary mines. Each one joined by a series of longitudinal tunnels at level ten. For the purpose of this mission, I've labeled each one by either, A, B, C, or D."

Sam nodded.

"A, C and D are all still fully operational mine shafts. B struck a river that runs about three hundred feet below Lake Tumba. It caused a massive sinkhole, where the water flowed into the mine shaft. The first ten levels of mine B are under water after it became too difficult and too expensive to pump out all that water. The good news for us is they left it alone. Unconcerned that anyone would be capable of getting through ten levels of flooded tunnels, they've given us the perfect route in."

Tom sat forward and studied the map. "There must be more than a hundred tunnels in mine B. Each one will be pitch dark, and silted up. It's going to be just short of impossible to reach the tenth level, let alone the top of the mine. This is anything but easy."

Adebowale grinned. The jet black and scarred skin of his face, was suddenly broken by his warm smile and his evenly spaced white teeth. It was the smile of a model or a politician, not what you expect from someone who looks like a great warrior. What's more, the smile appeared genuine. He spoke in his monotone, and deep voice. "I've seen the future, and we all get through the flooded mine to reach the surface and free my people. You and Tom will go home tonight."

Sam met his eyes. The grayish-blue looked to him like steel. There was a certainty there. Adebowale wasn't just saying that they'd make it through the tunnel. He somehow knew the future – or at least believed he did. Sam nodded but remained silent.

The last fifteen minutes of the flight was spent in silence. Each member of the team mentally prepared for the task ahead. The weapons had been checked, the C4 secured, and the dive equipment was all working.

The Jet Ranger banked to the right. Sam glanced ahead. They were flying over Lake Tumba.

Genevieve said. "Three minute check, gentlemen."

"Copy that," all three of them said in unison.

The helicopter flew low above Lake Tumba, until it reached a small river. The small river eventually met the Zaire River around five miles away. Halfway between the great African river and Lake Tumba, Genevieve took the helicopter into a steep descent, before leveling out along the river, and then hovering within a foot of the Tumba River.

Genevieve said, "GPS says this is it."

Sam opened the side door of the Jet Ranger. The water below appeared dark. On the side of the river, it appeared more like a small bay, than a river's edge. He looked at Adebowale. "You're certain this is the spot?"

"That's the sink hole," Adebowale confirmed. "That spot there ate into the river bank."

Sam looked at Tom and Adebowale. "Everyone ready?"

"Good to go," they both confirmed.

Sam said, "All right. Set watches to 19:05 in five, four, three, two, one, mark. Good luck."

Sam placed his regulator in his mouth, inflated his buoyancy control device so he would be mildly positively buoyant, and secured his dive mask. He checked that his Heckler & Koch MP5 was attached to his right arm, and his bag of C4 explosives was secure in its dry bag. He looked at Tom and Adebowale. "All right team. See you down there."

He picked up the sea scooter, and stepped onto the helicopter skids. In one quick movement Sam pressed his mask against his face and stepped out. A split second later, he dipped into the dark, murky waters of the Tumba River and disappeared.

Chapter One Hundred and Five

Two thousand four hundred and eighty miles away, in Malta's Grand Harbor, all was quiet inside the *Maria Helena*. Elise stared anxiously at four separate computer monitors. Each one feeding her different information about the mission. She had a number of background programs running. Each one aimed at providing information that might affect the mission, such as sudden changes in the movement of people, social media changes.

And despite all that information being fed to her, there was nothing that would have any effect on the mission. It made her feel frustrated and redundant, where she was usually confident and used to providing valuable digital information, or solutions throughout an operation. The clock at the base of the computer screen displayed the current time in the DRC as – 7:20 p.m.

They'll be in the helicopter by now.

The thought only confirmed her discomfort with her position. For all the information coming in, there was nothing new to help with the mission from her end. She shook her head. It was unlike her to feel redundant, and even less like her to even care. She'd built a life, a very good one, on being self-sufficient and looking after herself. Elise forced herself to smile. She didn't care whether she was needed or not, the reason she was troubled was because she was worried about Sam – and Tom and Genevieve, *too,* for that matter. She didn't care either way about Zara or Adebowale. Not that she wished them any harm, of course. They seemed like good people. They had chosen their own paths in life, and it didn't coincide with hers.

But the other three were her friends. More than that. They were part of the only family she'd ever known. Sam in particular, was like a father to her. And Genevieve and Tom might as well have been her rough and ready siblings.

They will be fine. They're all tough.

Elise needed a distraction. She knew she shouldn't. Genevieve would kill her just for having a look, but she needed to know the truth. Her curiosity had gotten the better of her, and it was a welcome distraction. On a separate tab, she opened google, and typed a single word.

Solntsevo

The search engine spat out thousands of reference pages, but her eyes never glanced past the first one.

Solntsevskaya Bratva

She clicked on the first link. It was a Wikipedia page. But it provided her as much as she needed to know. More than she should have learned and enough to make her wish she hadn't. She read the article once.

The Solntsevskaya Bratva was the biggest and most powerful crime syndicate of the Russian mafia. Founded in the late 1980s by Sergei Mikhailov, a former waiter who had served a prison term for fraud, the organization now has ties to global organized crime syndicates, ranging from drugs and weapon sales, through to internet fraud and money laundering.

The syndicate used a group of violent mercenaries and assassins to maintain its foothold in each area, while using the concept of a ten-fold response to any trespass against them as a deterrent. One such example was in 2007, when a member of a Mexican Drug Cartel killed a member of the Solntsevskaya Bratva, during a hostile takeover of the lucrative cocaine industry in Atlanta. They tracked the man down and systematically killed every person on his Facebook page. They started with the person's immediate family, his relatives, his local connections. And when all that was done, they started in on his friends list. By the time the FBI opened a special investigation into the massacre, a hundred and eighteen persons had been killed.

Elise stopped reading, as the article turned to the methods the organization used to kill people, and instead, skimmed to the end of the page.

She read the final paragraph. Re-read it, and then closed the tab completely.

Sergei Mikhailov had a daughter, Anastasiya Mikhailov, who disappeared in 2014 at the age of twenty eighty. It has been widely disputed that she was taken by one of the competing crime syndicates, in retaliation to something the Solntsevskaya Bratva had done. But no organization has come forward and claimed the kidnapping, and no one has ever seen her since.

A small beeping sound, coming from her computer, informed her that one of the background programs, searching for any changes in the frequency of news or comments on social media regarding General Ngige, had shown a sudden spike in information. She clicked on the program, and quickly scrolled through the notes.

This can't be right.

Nearly fifteen thousand comments on social media confirmed the news. It was possible it could be fake, and artificially being proliferated by those who didn't know the truth. But chances were, it was true.

Elise opened a new program. It was a DRC database for *Births, Deaths, and Marriages.* She quickly typed in the name, *Adebowale.* Followed by the string query, *Known Siblings.*

She looked at the results and swore. "What have we done?"

Next to her, the phone started to ring. It was a digitally encrypted satellite phone that used a combination of privately owned and proxy satellites to secure communications – and there was only one person who ever called it.

Elise picked up the phone. "Good evening, Madam Secretary."

She listened carefully, without interrupting until the Secretary of Defense had finished. She jotted a few notes down.

Her face hardened. "Understood, Madam Secretary. I'll do my best to let him know."

She hung up the phone and ran up the stairs onto the bridge. Matthew, who had even less to do than she did, was sitting at his desk, tapping his fingers on the old teak.

Elise didn't wait for him to greet her. "We need to abort the mission!"

Matthew's face hardened. "We can't abort the mission now. I just received confirmation from Genevieve that Sam, Tom and Adebowale have been dropped into the water, and have started their dive. There's no way to get in contact with them until the mission's complete. Why, what's happened?"

She swore three times. It was loud, profane, and unusual for her. She placed the palm of her hand on her forehead and closed her eyes. There had to be a way to get a message through to them. She opened them again. "It's Adebowale."

"What about him?"

"He's working for General Ngige."

Matthew said, "But he had the secret passwords used by the United Sovereign of Kongo, and was able to get information through their coded communications? What's happened?"

"I just spoke to the Secretary of Defense. Her people in Intelligences just informed her that General Ngige was an only child. His parents were killed in the early nineties, and as an orphan he spent time in what was then The Lake Tumba Gold Mine. You know who also spent time in that same mine, and was his best friend growing up?"

Matthew shook his head. "Adebowale!"

She nodded. "There's something else, too."
"What?"
"I'm getting a number of pings right now on social media and traditional media inside the DRC. General Ngige died this morning. Apparently his right eye had been burned with a cigarette. Horrific but unlikely to have killed him. Somehow, there was a complication in the routine operation and he died on the table."

Matthew turned to face her. "Then who was the twin who's going to die?"

She said, "His name's Dikembe and he's Adebowale's twin brother."

"Christ! Adebowale has a twin! How did we not work this out earlier?"

Elise shook her head. "We took Adebowale at his word. We had no reason to doubt him. It wasn't like it made any difference whether or not he was an only child or a twin – until the Nostradamus Equation told us a royal twin would need to die."

Chapter One Hundred and Six

Sam reached the bottom of the sinkhole. It was eighty feet deep in total. The water was discolored and murky, with a visibility of less than five feet. The heads up display showed a vague outline of the dramatic sinkhole, based on the sonar's impression. The quality was poor, but a darkened spot at the very bottom suggested it still penetrated the old Lake Tumba Gold Mine, Mine B. He waited for Tom and Adebowale to reach him, confirmed they were all right, and then opened up the throttle to the Sea Scooter and entered the mine.

The headlight positioned in front of the diver propulsion vehicle flicked light off the walls of the tunnel. It was as dark as any cave Sam had ever explored, and unlike the water in a cave which is clear, the mud and silt in the water here still blocked much of his visibility.

Sam said, "Keep close gentlemen. The vis is poor and doesn't look like it's going to get better any time soon. Keep track of the person in front of you on your sonar screen. The last thing I want is to turn this into a rescue mission for the three of us."

"Copy that," Tom said. "See your slow ass, right ahead of me."

"What about you, Adebowale? Have you got us on your sonar?"

"I can see you. Just keep going and I will follow."

Sam said, "Good man."

The navigation screen suddenly flashed green. It meant the relationship between the current outline of the mine, based on the sonar reading, had matched with a known section of the map. The two readings became superimposed, and the computer placed an asterisk, where it believed Sam was inside the mine. He grinned. It was a good start. He clicked the route button, and a red line followed a series of tunnels, like a giant maze, through to the seventy-ninth level.

Sam drove the sea scooter along the first tunnel for approximately two hundred and fifty feet, before turning to the left. He followed the directions given on the heads-up navigation display, as the tunnel opened to seven separate exploratory runs. Away from the giant sinkhole, and the disturbed water of the Tumba River, the visibility greatly improved. Sam made another turn around a corner, and the light from his sea scooter returned to him, greatly amplified.

He stopped. A large reef of quartz hung on the ceiling. Tiny specks of gold reflected the flashlight's glow mysteriously. He smiled. The shaft would have been quite profitable if they hadn't struck the river. The width of the mineshaft here increased to a total of forty feet, as the miners had once dug, following the gold-rich quartz reef.

At the end of the gold-rich section, the tunnel returned to a straight and horizontal profile for about a hundred feet, before turning to the right. On the map, the entire area looked like one giant game of snakes and ladders.

About an hour in, Sam reached the first vertical shaft. "You two still behind?"

"Sure am," Tom said. "I've got Adebowale right on my tail. What's taking you so long?"

Sam looked upwards. "I've reached the first of the vertical shafts. I'll wait until I see your lights following before I keep going."

He ascended thirty feet and stopped. It was a short shaft. There was no elevator. Only the wooden rungs of an old mining ladder. The miners must have reached a gold reef, or something which made them stop. There were two tunnels, leading in opposite directions away from the vertical shaft. Sam checked the map, and confirmed that he needed to take the one to the right.

As soon as he could see Tom and Adebowale below him in the vertical shaft, Sam followed the tunnel for a total of five hundred and thirty-eight feet. The tunnel meandered in a westerly direction, with a series of jagged dog legs and zig-zags. At that point, he stopped. Above him was the elevator shaft *Number Four*. Per the map, it ran all the way up to level ten.

406

Not only would they be well and truly out of the water by then, but at that point, they could take the horizontal tunnel to reach any of the four mines. And more importantly, they could reach the three tunnels that run below Lake Tumba, and complete their mission.

Sam waited until he saw the lights of his two companions darting along the tunnel's walls. "I'm starting on the vertical shaft, *Number Four*. I'll see you guys on dry land."

Tom said, "Good. See you at the top."

Adebowale said, "Once you see how long that shaft travels vertically, you will wish it was filled with water all the way to the top."

Sam grinned. He already knew they were going to have one hell of a climb to reach the top. Sam positioned the sea scooter so its sonar transducer pointed straight up the shaft. Thirty seconds later, the heads-up display flashed green again. The map and the sonar images matched up.

He left the sea scooter in neutral and slowly adjusted his buoyancy, until he was ascending. Once he'd begun to move in a vertical direction, Sam concentrated on bleeding air from his buoyancy control device. As he ascended, he reduced the exertion of pressure, measured in atmospheres, which in turn caused air to expand. Without letting that air bleed off, his buoyancy control device would rapidly overfill and he would shoot to the surface – most likely killing himself with an embolism in the process.

After rising nearly forty feet, Sam stopped. He swore loudly to himself.

Tom asked, "What's wrong?"

Sam said, "I don't think we're going to reach the surface tonight."

"But we must!" Adebowale's voice boomed over the underwater radio. "What's happened?"

Sam shook his head. "The elevator's permanently stopped at level twenty-nine. There's no way we can get around it, and I'm doubting there's any way we could coax it to ascend again."

Chapter One Hundred and Seven

Sam studied the electronic map in front of him until Tom and Adebowale caught up with him. There were a series of lateral tunnels with some vertical shafts all over the place, like a giant rabbit's warren, but every time he followed any of them he reached the same conclusion – he would need to return to the main elevator shaft to reach the top.

Tom slowed his ascent and came to a stop next to him. His eyes glanced at the stuck elevator and back to Sam. "That's not good."

"No, and we've already reached the point of no return," Sam agreed. "The batteries are already getting low on the sea scooters, and it would be impossible for our air supplies to last that long if we swam back the way we came."

Tom studied the elevator. "How much C4 do you think it would take to bring that thing down?"

"You've got to be kidding me. We do that and the guards above are going to be on us in a flash. The whole mission will be blown."

"If we don't do that, we'll never get out of here alive."

Adebowale slowed his ascent, just a little higher than either Sam or Tom. He fumbled with his buoyancy control device to release air, and make himself neutrally buoyant again. It wasn't enough, and he started to struggle to keep from being sent straight up.

Sam released air from his own buoyancy control device, making him neutrally buoyant and then held the back of Adebowale's tank to stabilize him.

"Thanks," Adebowale said, and then glanced up at the elevator stuck between levels. "Have you got any ideas to fix that?"

Sam said, "Tom and I were just discussing the pros and cons of using C4 to send it to the bottom of the shaft."

"You can't do it," Adebowale said, forcefully. "General Ngige's men would suspect a prison break, and if we're lucky would come down here and kill all three of us."

Sam asked, "And if we're not lucky?"

Adebowale bit on the regulator. "They'll suspect what we were going to try and do, and blow the tunnels immediately – sending the entire content of Lake Tumba into the mine, drowning everyone."

It was the first time Sam had considered the consequences of destroying the elevator. He thought the worst case scenario was that their mission would be compromised and they would have to regroup and make another attempt in a few days.

Sam expanded the computer projection of the entire B mine. "All right, forget about detonating the elevator. Do you have any other plans how we can get out of here?"

Adebowale stared at the map, and Tom moved closer so he, too, could get a better idea. Adebowale spoke with his usual level of calmness and confidence. More like a boy scout planning a walk in a park, than a man preparing a final ditch chance of avoiding the terror of running out of air hundreds of feet below ground, he pointed toward a horizontal shaft nearly all the way to the bottom. "We'll descend to this level here. From there we'll follow this tunnel until we reach a vertical shaft."

Sam mentally followed the directions given and stopped. "This map doesn't show any vertical shaft in that area, and certainly none that reach high enough to pass the immovable elevator."

"Even so, it's there," Adebowale confirmed.

Tom asked, "Why wasn't it noted on the map?"

Adebowale said, "Because there isn't a second elevator shaft in this mine."

Sam studied the markings on the map. There was nothing to even hint that a second vertical shaft would one day be built in that section of the mine. "Then what the hell is it?"

Adebowale adjusted the angle of his sea scooter so it faced downward again. "It's the ventilation shaft."

Of course, the ventilation shaft would be placed at the opposite end of the mine to the elevator shaft, allowing for a natural circulation of air. Sam saw Adebowale accelerate with his sea scooter, and descend toward the bottom of the elevator shaft.

Sam didn't wait to discuss the options with Tom. He switched the sea scooter up to its third, and fastest speed setting, and the electric machine whirred into life. No longer following the map, Sam raced to keep up with Adebowale.

Sam asked, "You still there, Tom?"

Tom said, "Right behind you."

At the bottom of the elevator shaft, Sam turned left to follow Adebowale along a horizontal tunnel. At the end of the short tunnel he watched Adebowale dip his scooter downward and descend another level.

"You certain you know where you're going Adebowale?" Sam asked.

Silence.

Sam continued to follow. "Adebowale, can you hear me? Why are you descending when we need to ascend?"

More silence.

Sam and Tom both raced to keep up. The vertical drop brought them to a depth of a hundred and thirty feet. They would run out of air quickly at that depth, not to mention what it was doing for their residual nitrogen levels. SCUBA diving 101 implores divers to plan their dive so they start at the lowest depth first and then slowly ascend. By descending to a hundred feet, then ascending to forty feet, only to now drop to a hundred and thirty feet, was comparative to shaking up a can of soda to make it fizz – only in this case it wasn't a soda drink, it was the nitrogen bubbling in their bloodstreams.

At the bottom of the shaft, Sam turned left again and then stopped. There at the end of the short tunnel rested Adebowale's sea scooter. Neutrally buoyant, it floated mysteriously in the middle of the tunnel, without a rider.

Sam glanced around the small tunnel, but Adebowale had disappeared.

Chapter One Hundred and Eight

The ventilation shaft had three massive turbo-fans. The one on the surface hundreds of feet above was the largest and most powerful, whereas the two inside the vertical tunnel were smaller. All three were used to drive fresh air to the bottom of the shaft, then out into the lowest tunnel to create a circulation of air through the tunnels and back up the elevator shaft. Adebowale recalled hearing somewhere, that the reason the ventilation shaft always reached the lowest point of any mine was because it needed to flush out any residual toxins from the air that would otherwise bundle together and form dead zone. Of course, all of that was academic. What mattered now, was how to get through the second massive turbo-fan that blocked his ascent.

He'd slipped through the first turbo-fan easily enough. It had amazed him. At ten feet in diameter, the massive blades were larger than him and were able to be feathered. This meant the blades changed their angle and pitch as they spun. It also allowed the mine operators to change the direction of the airflow if they needed to extract a poisonous or flammable gas, instead of pumping oxygen rich, fresh air into the mine. When he first looked up at it, all the blades were completely folded, and years of debris and mold made the turbo-fan look no different than the rest of the tunnel's ceilings. Of course, it was easy to get through because he could simply move the angle of the blades and slip through. There was no choice of whether or not to bring the sea scooter, so he had to abandon it.

He ascended rapidly, without any fear of an acute decompression sickness. He didn't have time to ascend slowly, taking the necessary decompression stops. Adebowale didn't even wonder what would happen to Sam and Tom. What did it concern him whether they lived or died? They had served their purpose. He felt no guilt or happiness in leaving them. He didn't have time to explain what needed to happen. Besides, what he was about to do was bigger than them, bigger than him – it was the most important single thing a human being could do for the world. He was going to categorically change the future of the human race.

He stopped after ascending approximately eighty feet. His movement was stopped again by an obstruction in the shaft – this time, by the second turbo-fan. This one was almost identical to the first, but there had been so much corrosion to the blades that they no longer feathered.

Adebowale pulled on the first blade, the same as he had done with the first, but nothing happened. He swam to the furthermost edge of the propeller, trying to use the increased leverage to move it. With his legs pressed against the metal sides, he pushed hard with his legs and pulled with his arms. The massive muscles of his arms strained, but nothing happened.

He tried each of the other blades and found none of them could be coerced to move. Adebowale removed his dive knife and used it to chip away at the rust where the fan-blade normally swiveled. He tried to move the fan again, but it was rusted solid.

Frustrated, Adebowale jammed the knife into the rusted section and then removed his dive tank. The aluminum tank moved quickly through the water. With the regulator still in his mouth he rammed the heavy dive tank into the knife. On the first attempt, the knife split just past the handle. Adebowale felt the rush of adrenalin sending him berserk. This wasn't how he was going to die – trapped in an old ventilation shaft, stuck beneath a rusty propeller blade. He pulled back on the tank and rammed it into the same section again, and again. He lost track of how many times he struck the damned blade, but eventually he rammed the dive tank into the weakened edge of the fan-blade and it simply drove right through.

Adebowale pulled himself through the small opening and continued swimming upwards. He raced toward the surface like a torpedo, breaking into the cool air high above in under a minute. He quickly removed his wetsuit, then placed the backpack carrying the C4 over his shoulders once again.

He shined his flashlight around, until he found a tunnel heading due north. He took it hoping that it would reach the elevator shaft, well above where the elevator was stuck.

He moved quickly. The height of the tunnel was too low to run, but in a bent-over stance, he moved fast. It didn't take long to reach the main elevator shaft. He shined the flashlight below. The focused beams com came to rest on the water not far below. He looked up, and saw the wooden ladder leading straight up.

Adebowale started to climb immediately. Twenty feet up the first set of ladders, and a sudden pressure gripped the joint of his right elbow. The pain was sharp and intense, but intermittent. From what little he knew about SCUBA diving, he understood there was something about the compressed nitrogen not being able to escape his blood stream fast enough if he ascended too quickly. He should have slowed his ascent, but what could he do? His men needed action, not hesitation.

Adebowale shrugged off the pain and continued climbing. He gritted his teeth, and forced himself to grin. He was getting close to the fulfilment of the prophecy and the greatest achievement of his lifetime. He'd seen the future and it wasn't the bends that was going to kill him.

Chapter One Hundred and Nine

Sam slipped through the feathered turbo-fan blade and ascended carefully. There was no sign of Adebowale's light above, but there was no doubt in his mind that this was the way he'd traveled. The question was why did Adebowale try to lose them?

He didn't wait to commence their ascent. They had a long way to go if they were to reach the top levels of the mine, and they would need to travel fast if they were to catch up with Adebowale.

Sam asked, "What could he possibly be trying to achieve?"

Tom said, "I don't know how he fooled us, but he's not on our team."

"If that's the case, why bother dragging us here, at all?"

Sam thought about that and shook his head. "I have no idea. It doesn't make sense. Maybe he has some entirely different purpose for being here. Something he obviously didn't want us to know. That doesn't mean he's against us."

"Sure. But he's definitely not with us."

Sam slowed his rate of ascent as they approached the second ventilation fan. He carefully slipped through the single opening where a fan blade had been broken off. The sharp fracture in the rusted metal appeared recent. He slipped through very carefully, and continued to ascend.

Sam said, "We might still be able to complete the mission without him."

Tom shook his head. "No we can't."

"Why not?"

"Because he took the bag with the C4."

"Christ! I thought you were carrying that?"

"I was, but just before we left the helicopter he offered to carry it. He said I already had enough to carry with all the additional diving equipment."

Sam approached thirty feet of depth and slowed his ascent to a stop. He carefully waited five minutes and then ascended to fifteen feet, before waiting another five minutes to decompress. He climbed out through the surface of the water and removed his wet suit, and discarded it next to Adebowale's abandoned suit.

A trail of water heading down the northern tunnel showed where Adebowale had gone. Sam switched his Heckler & Koch MP5 from safety to fully automatic, while Tom surfaced and skinned out of his wet suit. There was no telling how long Adebowale had taken to decompress, so they would have to be quick to catch him.

They ran to the end of the tunnel and then started to climb the rickety ladder in the main elevator shaft. It was a grueling climb, but they reached the top, where the vertical shaft joined the main tunnel on level five. From there, Sam hoped they would be able to open the locked grates for the prisoners, and still reach the main tunnel that led underneath Lake Tumba in time to block it somehow.

He and Tom made it less than five hundred feet down the tunnel, before his hopes were shattered — because the echo of a tremendous explosion echoed through the tunnel.

Sam swallowed, hard. "Oh, shit!"

Chapter One Hundred and Ten

Adebowale had no idea how much C4 would be required to bring the ceiling down onto the tunnel, so he used all of it. Better to be too much than not enough. There was no risk of bringing down too much rock. After all, his intention was to create a stone barrier between the end of the tunnel, where General Ngige had ordered dynamite to be laid and ready to open the tunnel to the bottom of the lake, and the entrance to the main tunnels of the mine.

In his nightmares he'd seen the moments directly after the explosion repeatedly since he was a small boy. But he'd never seen how he actually reached that point. So, without any concern he might not be doing it right, he'd stuck all the C4 from the back-pack onto the rock ceiling. He'd then run the ignition wires a couple hundred feet down the tunnel and pressed the detonation button.

Within the narrow confines of the tunnel, the shockwave raced toward him with an incredible force. It knocked him to the floor, and he struck his head hard. His world shook and for a moment he thought he'd already been killed. He felt the strange wet feeling on his face, and carefully touched it with his right hand. It took him a moment to realize it was his own blood. In his head, he heard the constant ringing, as his burst eardrums tried to make sense of what had happened.

There was too much dust and debris ahead to see if the cave-in had worked. Somehow, intrinsically, he knew that it hadn't. It couldn't have, could it? After all, water would soon come flowing from the other side of the cave-in and kill him.

He forced himself back on to his feet and started to run back the way he had come. A moment later the aftershock of a second explosion dropped him to the ground again. General Ngige's men, hearing the first explosion and having expected an attempt to escape, must have detonated the dynamite.

Adebowale knew he couldn't outrun it, but still he tried.

A third explosion occurred up ahead, somewhere between him and the main tunnels of the mine. In an instant he realized what always went wrong – something he'd never even considered.

Someone must have been drilling holes in the ceiling further up the tunnel, so that any large seismic activity would cause it to collapse and form a natural barrier of rock. Now he was trapped, unable to go backwards or forwards. Behind him, he felt the gust of air being blown through the tunnel, followed by the sound or raging water.

He'd been here before – a thousand times in fact.

But still he turned and ran.

Adebowale didn't have far to run, not far at all. He reached the cave-in ahead. It had formed perfectly. There was no way he could escape now. He turned to face the torrent of water that would kill him.

Despite the knowledge that he would be dead within moments, he grinned broadly – because the prophecy was complete.

Chapter One Hundred and Eleven

Sam stopped at the entrance to mine shaft A, where the prisoners were all housed. A steel grate locked them inside at night. It had a simple locking mechanism on the side of the wall, for the morning guards to use to release it, when the prisoners were to go to work. Sam pulled the lever and hundreds of men climbed out, passing them without anything more than a nod of gratitude.

When the expected torrent of water from above never came, Sam figured that somehow Adebowale had succeeded. Over the course of an hour, he watched as thousands of men, some having been prisoners for years and so withered that their skin was taut over their bones, ran to join the fight. By the time he and Tom reached the surface, the fight was over.

A man he recognized from the photos as the agent named Mikhail approached. "Sam Reilly, isn't it?"

Sam nodded and offered his hand. "This is Tom."

Mikhail shook their hands firmly, and said, "Thanks for the prison break. I guess you got the message and our government decided to send in the troops?"

"Not quite," Sam said.

Mikhail asked, "No? Well, then, really, how did you get here?"

Tom smiled. "It's a long story, but ultimately, we had some pretty convincing reasons to come here."

Mikhail frowned, disappointment across his face. "But not enough for Washington to commit?"

Sam said, "No. Putting American boots on the ground would have been an impossible sell to Congress and the American people."

Mikhail's eyes narrowed. "So then, how did you end up here?"

"A man named Adebowale ended up giving us the suggestion of accessing the mine from an old flooded section, and then from there using explosives to cause a cave-in forming a natural barricade from the tunnel below the lake where General Ngige had planned to drain the lake to drown his prisoners." Sam looked at Mikhail's confused face. "You've heard of Adebowale, I assume?"

Mikhail nodded. "I have, but I'm surprised he helped you."

"What do you mean?" Sam asked. "He's the head of the USK, isn't he?"

Mikhail's eyes darted between Sam and Tom's hardened faces. "You don't know, do you?"

"Know what?" Sam and Tom replied in unison.

A large man approached. For a second Sam thought he was Adebowale. He was a similar height, but his muscles appeared smaller and leaner. He had a warm smile and same piercing gray eyes, but below them, deep wrinkles etched a history of a difficult life, filled with pain.

Mikhail looked at the man, and then glanced back at Sam. "This is Dikembe, the leader of the USK. I think it's best he explains who Adebowale is ... or was."

Dikembe greeted Sam and Tom with heartfelt gratitude. He shook both their hands kindly, and said, "I understand you were instrumental in our rescue. My people will be forever grateful."

Sam asked, "You're Adebowale's brother?"

Dikembe nodded. "Yes. Although, my brother and I haven't seen each other for many years. I had hoped I would have the opportunity to see him one last time before he entered the tunnel, where he died."

"You're certain Adebowale perished inside the tunnel?" Sam asked.

Dikembe nodded.

Sam asked, "How?"

Mikhail stepped in to answer. "Because we weakened the entrance to the tunnel that ran underneath Lake Tumba. The hope was that any seismic rattle, caused by Ngige detonating his dynamite, would cause the roof at the entrance to collapse, and create a natural barrier of stone that would protect us from the flood."

Sam asked, "And that's why you referred to Dikembe as the leader of the USK?"

"No." Dikembe smiled at him. "It appears you misunderstand everything. Adebowale and I haven't seen each other for many years. Until tonight, he followed another leader. Someone he'd known all his life."

"Adebowale and General Ngige knew each other?" Sam said.

"I am told they were good friends until recently."

"Things must have changed. Ngige tried to kill him a week ago."

Dikembe shrugged, as though it didn't matter. "Wars change people, constantly. Alliances are formed and friendships broken. And I'm afraid it's not unknown for General Ngige to dispose of those in whom he has lost confidence."

Sam said, "But Adebowale had the codes to your underground communication system?"

Dikembe said, "So did a lot of people. It appears he infiltrated it well, but in the end he used it for its intended purpose, and rallied my troops to fight."

Tom said, "I don't understand. Why would Adebowale lie? If he was working with Ngige, why did he come through for us when we needed his men to take out the guards? What changed?"

Dikembe said, "He of all of us truly believed in the United Sovereign of Kongo. He didn't care whether I gave it to him or Ngige. He believed in the prophecy. He believed that Nostradamus had seen it all nearly four hundred years ago, when he came to the Sahara. When Nostradamus introduced a boy named Jacob Prediox to my great ancestor, he knew that we were going to go through some tough years, but one day our bloodline would return and unite the Kingdom of Kongo. I believe my brother may have just paved the way for me to do so, and that if he were alive, he would be happy."

Sam asked, "When we were preparing for this mission, your brother showed us precisely where to lay the C4 in each of the tunnels that run beneath Lake Tumba. There were three tunnels. He was very specific which tunnel he was to take. And in the end he set off the one that collapsed only one tunnel..."

"Yes?"

"His was the only tunnel that collapsed nearly a quarter of a mile back from where he laid the C4. He would have been trapped and drowned in the process."

"Yes. I know what you want to ask. So ask it."

"Did he know he was going to die?"

"Yes."

"Then why did he go through with it?"

"Because he's always known he was going to die. My brother shared the gift and curse of visions, the same as Nostradamus. Unlike the great master of prophecies, my brother only saw one vision. His death. But in it, he knew the outcome for his people."

"Why didn't he just set the damned C4 to go off after and get back behind the cave-in?" Sam raised his voice, betraying a temper he seldom released. "He killed himself for nothing! Did he want to be a martyr, is that it?"

"No. He didn't die for nothing. He died to unite his kingdom."

"That's a lie. He could have skipped the dying part and the two of you could have united the kingdom together."

Dikembe shook his head. "No. We would have fought as we always have. And in the end, our kingdom would have continued to have unrest amongst its own people."

Sam shook his head, unable to believe what he was listening to. Two brothers. Twins who loved each other. Suggesting that it was better that one of them die to protect a kingdom that hadn't existed since the Portuguese decided to colonize their kingdom.

Tom said, "One more question..."

Dikembe turned to face him. "Ask and I will answer as best I can."

Tom explained how they'd planned the entire mission, starting with entering the mine from the flooded sink-hole, through to using C4 to demolish part of the tunnel that ran underneath the lake. He finished by explaining how Adebowale had intentionally lost them both inside the flooded tunnels of the B mine.

Tom asked, "Why did Adebowale lose us in the tunnels? Wouldn't it have been better to keep to the original plan and detonate all three tunnels, just to be certain?"

Dikembe smiled, mysteriously. "Because he'd seen the future, and neither you or Sam were part of that vision. It was the one thing that must have been worrying him. If you were there, it meant the future had somehow changed." He then turned to Sam and Tom and said, "Once again, my people and I thank you for everything you have done for us, but now I have a rebellion to win, and a kingdom to rebuild."

Mikhail turned to follow Dikembe out who was about to get into an armored car.

Sam grabbed him by the shoulder. "Where are you going?"

"I've decided to offer my assistance to Dikembe. In whatever capacity I can. I don't think you really appreciate what he's about to do for the region."

"No you're not."

Mikhail asked, "Why not?"

Sam said, "You're coming with us. The future's now, and you're going to be a father."

Mikhail stared at him. "Zara's pregnant?"

Chapter One Hundred and Twelve

Sam, Tom and Mikhail boarded the Jet Ranger. Sam hadn't finished closing the side door before Genevieve took off again, over Lake Tumba. She was eager to get off the ground and far out of the reach of stray bullets. The distant sound of gunfire, reminding everyone that they were now in the middle of a dangerous warzone, and that the rebellion had started, even if it was only still in its infancy. Sam watched with pleasure as Zara's face lit up with joy as she saw Mikhail climb in.

Genevieve flew back to the Bangui International Airport. Inside the helicopter, a silence formed, as all of them quietly took in the events of the previous six hours. A lot had changed. They had all aided a rebel force to take the lead, and no-one, including Nostradamus could be certain that it had been the right choice. Sam, like any good leader, knew that many lives had been changed today as a result of his actions. Thousands would die. While he hoped he'd been instrumental in saving many more, he knew that only time would prove the wisdom of his decision.

The Jet Ranger touched the ground and Genevieve switched the engines off. At approximately the same time, the pilot on board the Legacy 450 luxury jet completed his final pre-flight checks. The small party switched aircraft, and the Legacy was once again back in the air.

The time was 0455.

Sam sat down across from Zara, who was sitting silently, holding Mikhail's hand. Sam said, "You knew about Adebowale, didn't you?"

Zara smiled. "I had my suspicions."

"But you said nothing?"

"No. I didn't know for certain until we got into the Nostradamus Equation. It was the 84th quatrain that convinced me."

She recited the quatrain from memory.

*

An ocean above and a maze below

Where the two meet over a baled woe,

The twin of a king shall die and the sun will set,

With a new ruler, and a kingdom shall grow without threat

*

Sam asked, "How?"

Zara said, "The second line in the quatrain. *Where the two meet over a baled woe*. It means somewhere between the ocean above and the maze below, the two worlds shall meet over a baled woe."

"So?"

"A baled woe is old English, meaning to help a friend in need. But it's also an anagram for, Adebowale."

"But we thought Adebowale was an only child!"

She shook her head. "That's what I thought at the time, but then I looked up his name."

Sam stared at her incredulously, and said, "His name?"

"Yes. Do you know what the Swahili name, Adebowale means?"

"No. What?"

"Second born son of royal blood."

Sam grinned. "Adebowale a twin! Of course, he was second in line to the throne."

He then got up and walked to the back of the chartered jet, to where Tom had already claimed two leather chairs for a makeshift bed. Sam opened the satellite phone secured to the side of the jet and dialed a number.

Elise answered on the first ring. Her voice was sharp, and she sounded out of breath, quite different from her normal, calm and collected self. She spoke first. "Sam, you're alive! Did you work out Adebowale wasn't on our side?"

"Adebowale's dead," Sam said, flatly. "And how the hell is it that everyone worked out that Adebowale was tricking us, before me?"

"The Secretary of Defense sent me a message after you'd left. Adebowale and Ngige had spent time in the mines as children. Their lives took vastly different directions, but Adebowale had always maintained loyalty to the man. Last night, after you'd left, I received information that General Ngige had died."

"He's dead?" Sam asked. "How did that happen, before the coup?"

Elise said, "Infection. He had an operation after his eye was burned, and he got an infection. It traveled to his brain, and killed him before the doctors knew what was going on."

Sam shook his head in silence, staring at the darkness outside the aircraft's window, and becoming lost in thought as he wondered what Nostradamus would think about any of this.

Elise reminded him that he called for a reason. "What do you need, boss?"

Sam paused for a moment. The sound of the Legacy 450's twin Rolls Royce engines humming in perfect harmony filled his world. He took in a deep breath and said, "I need you to patch me through on a secure link to John Wallis."

"Understood," Elise said, returning to her natural composure. "By the way Sam. Congratulations. I'm glad you and Tom are all right."

"Thanks, Elise," he said. "I just hope we all made the right decision and chose the right side for humanity."

"You did. We all saw the signs. It needed to be done."

Sam waited until the sat phone started making new sounds, as it was redirected through a series of proxy servers and privately owned satellites.

Sam recognized John Wallis's voice on the other end of the line. "What news do you have for me?"

Sam said, "It's been done, John."

"Very good, Mr. Reilly," John said, refusing to address him informally. "I suppose you're calling, because you want to know?"

"Yes. Did I just risk my team's life for a reason?"

John said, "It worked, didn't it?"

"But did I change the future?"

Sam heard the sound of old pages being carefully turned, read and then turned over again.

John said, "Yes and no."

"Yes and no?" Sam repeated the words, shaking his head. "What the hell does that mean?"

"Nostradamus saw things the others did not. The timeline has been changed. The extinction of mankind will no longer happen this year."

"But it will still happen?"

"That we don't know for certain." John spoke slowly and tentatively, as though he was unsure of himself, and more importantly, that he was unsure how much to reveal to Sam Reilly. "I've studied the new event lines. The one attached to you is the only one that shows any sign of the human race surviving."

"What does that mean?" Sam said. "Am I supposed to do something?"

"I don't know. The future's a very determined thing. It took a mastermind like Nostradamus to outmaneuver it. All I know so far is that at some stage in the future, somewhere along the strings of events that are connected with you, one of them will have two separate outcomes. The first will be that you fail, and humanity becomes extinct. The second, you succeed, and humanity gets to continue on its current course."

Sam asked, "How long?"

John said, "Until this event occurs?"

"Yeah."

"It could be a day, a week, or a year. It might happen on your deathbed. I'll keep monitoring the events as they come in. If I see a sign that the event is nearing, I'll let you know."

"Like a code to extinction?"

"Something like that. Most likely very subtle. Thanks again, Mr. Reilly. I hope it's truly a very long time until we speak again."

John Wallis disconnected the phone.

Sam replaced the satellite phone into its socket on the aircraft's wall.

Tom shuffled in the two seats and opened his eyes. "Now what?"

Sam looked at Tom, his face hard and determined. "Now we go find the last temple of the Master Builders – and bring Billie back."

Tom asked, "Any ideas where?"

Sam shook his head. "Not a clue. But I know someone at the Vatican who's going to help us. Whether he wants to or not."

The End